FOLLY'S END

The Peverill Family Saga
Book One

Doris Leslie

SAPERE
BOOKS

FOLLY'S END

Published by Sapere Books.

24 Trafalgar Road, Ilkley, LS29 8HH

saperebooks.com

ISBN: 978-0-85495-623-4

In loving memory of Constance, Lady Boyle

FOREWORD

The chief characters in this story are fictitious; the minor characters and incidents are not. Lord Folliett's adventures after the Battle of Worcester are founded, in part, on the Boscobel Tracts. The band of Royalist conspirators known as the 'Sealed Knot' did actually exist, and under that very name. Wynford Eagle, the home of Doctor Sydenham, the great seventeenth-century physician, can be seen to this day, much as it was when he lived there. The prototype of Folly's End can still be found somewhere in Dorset.

If there are those who care to read in this reconstruction of a period both violent and transitional, a parallel of our own confusions and antagonisms and ideals, they may do so, but I did not write this book with that intent. It is first and last a romance, with the England of civil war, the Commonwealth, and Restoration for its background, and Prudence Folliett as the mouthpiece of her age.

Among many other authoritative sources consulted in my compilation of the contemporary picture, I am most gratefully indebted to Osmund Airey's *Charles II;* to Sir Walter Besant's *London in the Time of the Stuarts;* Gardiner's *History of the Civil War; the Memoirs of the Verney Family*; Clarendon's *Great Rebellion* and his *Life*; and above all to those time-honoured diarists, Pepys and Evelyn.

DORIS LESLIE.

CHAPTER ONE

It was when my grandson Robin came to visit me last Eastertide that he let fall the chance remark to set me pondering: *Why not? And why not I, indeed?* For if not I, there's none other of our stock now left to tell it; and it would be, I thought, a good thing told to give my son's dear son, and his son too, this tale of their grandparents to cherish. Yet never did I think at my age to be taking up my pen to tell a tale and recapture youth, fresh-blooming, green, for all the world as though spring danced again in a dead orchard.

'Gran'marm,' — for thus always he addresses me save when I have chastised him, then 'tis 'Madam', sulky-mouthed and snow-cold with politeness — 'Gran'marm, you that have lived so long and seen so much should make a book of it to give me, for there have been great happenings in your lifetime.' And with no pause for my answer which was on my tongue to tell him: 'Sixty odd is not accounted a great age, my lad, and I look less than that by fifteen years,' and, 'I to write a book? Sure, you are crazy!' Before, I say, these words were out the boy was off upon another tack, of how he had been reading a mighty proper work by one Defoe which gives a true and horrid picture of the Great Plague that smote our London City and half England, come to that, and swept away ten thousand or ten hundred thousand, he disremembered the full toll. 'But you,' he said, 'Gran'marm, lived through that time, and the Great Fire too.'

'And worser still than fire or plague,' said I. 'War — between a brother and a brother, than which no deadlier, more

relentless fight can ever be, for I who speak have known —
yes, and have seen the devastation wrought upon our lands,
our homes, our people, by those crabbed, accursed, crop-eared,
canting hypocrites who murdered, ravaged, and laid waste to
God's own sanctuaries, to violate His laws in His Almighty
Name, their eyes to heaven — may they rot!'

'Why, Gran'marm,' cried Robin in his cracking voice, which I
noted since last he came to visit me, had changed from its
childish treble to a harsh distressing croak to break your heart,
'I'll wager you could tell as bold a history of the Rebellion as
my tutor who swears he fought at Worcester and followed
Charles II to France *aetat* fourteen. But none of us believes
him. He can lie as glib as any old wife of Windsor when he
figures as the speaker in an apologue, and to have followed
Charles at that age, he'd be near seventy now, which he is not,
though I'll allow he's old and yellow as a carp.'

'There's some who did,' I murmured with but half an ear for
this and thinking back. 'There's one whose seed is planted deep
in you who followed him — aged not much more — along the
self-same way from here to Charmouth, riding hell for leather
through the dust the grey mare kicked up behind her, as if she,
like her master, spurned from her heels the sight and image of
that other, who stood outside this very door to watch him go.'

Robin nodded, quiet. 'Yes, Gran'marm,' his hand came out
to touch mine, patting it, 'I know.'

'You'll know more one day, my dear,' I said, and stroked his
hair that is the colour of rusty iron, and as fierce and wiry as
though there were some metal in its compound; so was that
other Robin's after whom we named this one; and his eyes set
wide beneath dark tilted brows have a gold light behind them,
in colour hazel brown. He has a freckled nose, a square blunt-
cornered mouth, and that same cleft chin — dear God! — as

like as peas; so that I have only now to look at him where he is sitting in the window — being here again for his midsummer holiday, bent over some obscure chess problem he has set upon the board — I have, I say, only to look at him to ask myself, *Is Time then what we make it? Can they that live and die within the past come back, or is there for us who tread the downward years no life but memory?* Yes, there he sits, as so often I have sat, one leg tucked under, not, however, musing on chess problems; no. My face was stuck against the lattice watching the long stark dreary drive, planted today symmetrical with trees dividing spacious lawns and terraced gardens, but fifty years ago no road better than a cart-track led to Folly's End.

For so our house is called.

The name derives through local dialect from Folliett, and marks the western boundary of the estate that edges the chalky grazen spurs of Dorset, before they sweep down to the rich verdured red earth and wooded vales of Devon.

There have been Follietts in these parts since our forbears came here from Normandy with the first William, and overlorded all of Wessex, where the powers and holdings of Godwin then were concentrated. It was a Piers Folliett, who having pillaged and plundered his way thereto, leaving a trail of fire and blood behind him, halted at Wynmonath, murdered its abbot, drove out the quaking brotherhood, and set his standard on the tower, his arms upon the gate-house, and himself within the abbey walls. The hamlet that sprang up around them grew in time to be a village, is now a market town, and is still called Wynmon Abbas to this day.

Our line is long, too long to my mind, for a sturdy breed and no loss to be bred out, notwithstanding that you'd need seek far to find a braver, a more gallant gentleman than my dear father, who fought to the last though worsted, and dragged himself, sore maimed and bleeding, in his disguise of peasant rags, back to this outpost of his ruined acreage, all that those murderous vandals had left to him of Wynmonath and its tradition.

I was born in the year 1639, and my young girl-mother died of me almost before I drew breath. She was a Folliett too, a cousin of my father's. They were no more than a brace of children when they mated and then wed. I have heard all from my nurse Thirza of the child she nursed before me, who, while pledged by her parents to another, loved my father, and he her, in secret madness, until it was discovered she was big with me. Then they hustled her to church to make her honest, turned away the tenant farmer who leased this house at Folly's End, and proceeded to transform it into a habitation fit to receive the bridal pair; and while my grandfather was handing out a soothing dole to the disgruntled swain, my grandmother and Great-aunt Rossiter hotch-potched a fairy tale up and down the county that the marriage had been accomplished unknown to them six months before, to hide the shame of my precipitate appearance. Though where the shame in love is I have yet to know.

Less than three years after I was born came civil war, and the close family of Follietts was divided. My grandfather, a fierce Royalist, with my father and my uncle Piers, followed Rupert to Edgehill. Neither my grandfather nor his elder son survived that fight. Of the two Folliett cousins, next of male kin to my father, one turned traitor while in attendance on the King at Oxford during His Majesty's occupation of that city. So corrupt and rank did work the poison of the parliamentary fever that even there in the very seat and centre of the Royalists, some, perforce, were tainted by the vile infection. Thus did our renegade Folliett forswear his blood and birth and, effecting his escape at night over Magdalen Bridge in the guise of a lackey, ranged himself alongside the russet-coated Roundheads, and set out to kill his brother according to the word of Cromwell's god.

He died, a mouthing Puritan at Marston, and left a son, aged eight. 'Percy', we dubbed him, though a Piers again. The name runs through the family.

That greatest, bloodiest battle exterminated all male Follietts in the direct line of descent save my father, fifteenth Baron Folliett of Wynmonath, and young Percy.

His mother was a Fairfax, kinswoman to Thomas of that name in command of the Yorkshire Puritans. I have heard from Thirza, who had our family's part in these concerns as pat as she had her Bible, that this Mistress Folliett was a bouncing tomrig of a girl, riding her horse like a man, cross-saddle. She paid full penance for her mettlesome foolhardiness, though in that I do not blame her. I might have done the same in such a case, for it seems despite that she was six months gone in pregnancy and against the warnings of her doctor, she rode out to meet her husband from whom word had come that he was homeward bound from Marston, wounded. She did not know that he had died upon the field. The shock of hearing it, and doubtless her hard riding, brought her to bed of a still-born son and killed her out of hand.

During the lull occasioned by the twenty days' conference at Uxbridge between the rebels and the King, my father caused his orphaned young cousin and heir to be brought to Folly's End, along with his tutor, Mr Moon, a kinsman of Piers Folliett's, though not, thank God, of mine ... I, for my sins and sorrows, was schooled by him till I had grown beyond what his dead languages could teach me.

There was yet another orphaned boy to come to Folly's End: young Robert Peverill.

Thirza used to tell, but I do not know how much to take for truth nor how much for truth's embellishment, since in all of her recountings Thirza's fancy was wont to trespass far beyond the boundaries of fact; yet she did tell as gospel that my father and the mother of this lad had long been lovers — of the spirit, not the flesh, she being a Lucrezia of virtue, and my young wifeless father a Saint Anthony, to resist all bodily temptation. As my father's daughter I may doubt it. This, though, is surety: I had it from that pillar of discretion, my Great-aunt Rossiter, that when the excellent — and elderly — Sir Robert met his death in the cause of His Majesty the King, his widow mourned him with due reverence, but she did not mourn him long. One should in lovers' reasoning forgive her, and remember that in those convulsive times of enmity and bloodshed, love was worth much and life little.

She and my father had planned to wed before he rejoined the King at Oxford where His Majesty's forces were mustered, prior to their campaign in the north. It seems that this prospective marriage was none too graciously received by my father's few existing relatives, in especial by my Great-aunt Rossiter, who drove over in her rickety old coach from Colyton in Devon, where with her mild-mannered husband she resided, to express her views in no mean terms upon the match.

There may have been some warrant for this interference since Lady Peverill was a Roman Catholic. Her husband, however, had been a member of the Established Church although their son was reared, according to the Papal ruling, in his mother's faith.

My father had not much of worldly assets to offer his betrothed, yet I do not doubt she would have come to him if he had been possessed of even less than a few neglected acres and a farmhouse. The cataclysm that had engulfed all creeds and classes had shattered the hide-bound feudalism of our forefathers, deep-rooted in the holdings of the squirearchy. Impoverished, their lands invaded, bereft of all that they had lived by, the Cavaliers, in their unselfish loyalty and reckless valour, had come to realise that the collapse of their material existence was as nought compared to the disembodiment of an ideal.

Folly's End, then, was in readiness to receive a second bride, and my father here at home again recovering from a leg wound got from the pike of a Parliament man in a skirmish. My Great-aunt Rossiter was also here installed as mistress of the ceremonies, and in the hope, perchance, that even at this eleventh hour she might wean my father from his rash romantic venture, by bringing to bear upon her argument the prophecy of dire consequence to come as a result of his marriage with a Papist.

Certain it seems that fate — or, as my Great-aunt Rossiter insisted, the hand of God — had intervened in answer to her prayers, thus saving the house of Folliett from Papistical corruption and black magic; she would have it that my father was bewitched.

That is as may be, but this I know: were it God's decree or Fate's, or the mere daily accident of war that caused the parting of yet another pair of lovers, that marriage was doomed never in this life to be solemnised.

My Aunt Rossiter has oft repeated, and with much satisfaction, how that one night a horseman came a-gallop to our door and was closeted some hours with my father. They rode away together in the dawn. She heard them go. And whence or from whom that messenger was sent unless from God, she could not tell nor never knew. This occurred in April '45, and in June Robin's mother was dead.

She died on the day of the Battle of Naseby, where my father in one of his headlong charges drove the left wing of the Roundheads into instant confusion and flight, and captured Colonel Ireton. Thus according to my Aunt Rossiter, though there are some that say Prince Rupert claimed this same distinction. As my father never spoke to me of his part in these brave doings, I leave the question open and let history decide.

It must have been soon after this that Robin came to us. His father's seat in Warwickshire having been seized by the insurgents, he and his mother — she no doubt still waiting for news of her errant lover — were lodged in a farmhouse on the Peverill estate when she was taken with the smallpox from which her son escaped. He, to avoid infection, had been removed to a forester's cottage, and there in the charge of the good man and his wife, Robin was cared for until the time when Mr Moon, at my father's bidding, went to fetch him and bring him here.

So here we were, the three of us, Percy, Robin, and myself aged six: being two years junior to Robin, and Percy a year older than he. And here we stayed throughout that fevered time, while my father fought a losing fight in the cause of his martyred King; and we fought with one another, we three at Folly's End.

I thought of them as brothers. I knew no different. How should I, who at the time of the Battle of Worcester was no more than twelve? I can scarce remember my first few years without them; nor can I remember Wynmonath save as a blackened ruin. The Roundheads, having passed along that way in '42, first looted bare the abbey and then fired it.

Thirza told me how that when they came, a good two hundred horse and foot, there was but a handful of our people left to tackle them. My grandfather and his sons were with the King, and we could not muster more than fifty to put up a fight, since our tenants, servants, almost all had gone with Folliett. 'If my lord,' said Thirza — I can hear her now — 'If my lord, God bless him, had been with us, I do not doubt but we'd have saved the abbey, for with such a one to lead them as that dare-devil, your father, they'd not have lacked heart, though they lacked weapons. Yes, they fought those blackguardy curs with their bare fists, empty-handed, and were overcome, first one and then another, cast down and done to death.'

And she told too how my poor grandmother was taken there before her captive servants — Unfailingly did Thirza pause at this point, while I, agog for more, would urge her on, never tiring of a tale, recounted a dozen dozen times, to lose nothing of its garniture by repetition. I have often thought that Thirza's true vocation should have been the playhouse, for never, save upon the stage, have I seen such broad dramatics, such wealth of gesture and expression, such winks and nods and smiles to endow the simplest sentence or remark with subtle flavour.

'Well, Thirza, and what then?'

'Why then, my dear, those meal-mouthed maggots, that filth and offal clothed as men, they took her, the greatest lady in the land, your grandmother, before the eyes of her pop-eyed lackeys, where they, poor sots, were lying trussed like capons on a spit — though most o' them were bleeding corpses by this time — and having taken her they proceeded forthwith to strip her mother naked. A rare fine figure of a woman was my lady, a very Venus of perfection — well-covered in her flesh but still young enough, not being past the age for man's enjoyment, to bear my lord another brace of sons. Yes, there she stood, in her ripe womanhood, noble and defiant —'

And Thirza would stand too, head high, full bosom swelling, till she looked to burst her laces while her recitative rolled out as rich as cream.

'"You drunken snites," my lady called them, "violators of a woman's grace, you stinking laystalls, witches' spawn, and devil's dung of vice and black iniquity —"'

'Thirza,' for I was ever one to have each item understandable and proven, 'did you *hear* her say these words?'

'As good as heard. I was not there upon the scene, being here with you, and my hands full to mind you in your toddling, but I had it all brought to me by those present, word for word. May I be drawn and quartered if I'm lying. And now you've put me out. Where was I?'

'Of vice and black iniquity,' I prompted.

'Ah, so! And saying which her ladyship did seize upon a dagger —'

'A dagger?' echoed I, a doubting Thomas. 'Last time 'twas poison, Thirza.'

'A dagger, child. Where should she find poison on her person? She had nought upon her body but her shift.'

'You said,' I argued, 'she was naked.'

'Hell's torment! Who's to tell this tale — you or I?'

And by the end of it I was not much the wiser, nor was never certain to what extent my poor grandmother suffered at the hands of the ruffianly Roundheads, before she died of a fit in her chair in this room. She came here when the abbey was taken.

I have no recollection of her. Thirza's was the only woman's love vouchsafed to me, and the only mother's care I ever knew. Thirza, as I later learned, had come to mischief with my father's valet, and having lost her babe near the same time as I lost my little mother, she being full of milk and lusty, took me to nurse and fostered me. From her indiscretion she escaped uncensured, since so opportune for me was the result of it.

I flourished and was healthy, running wild in the pastures and ragged as a gipsy for all that Thirza was for ever spinning, patching, mending, to keep me trim. Percy fared better than Robin or I, because it seems that Mr Moon, who came of Fairfax stock, had not been utterly pauperised by the Rebellion, and favoured his young kinsman as he would never favour us.

Thirza declared that despite his vowed allegiance to the King, and his voiced disapproval of the atrocities performed and sanctioned by the Parliament, Mr Moon was a Roundhead to his marrowbones.

There may have been some point in this, for while the abbey and the lands of Wynmonath had all been seized by the marauders, our cattle stolen and our woods stripped of their timber, this house and its small holding stayed secure. But you must remember that Folly's End lies in a fold of the hills some distance from the main road between Dorchester and Bridport, and moreover there is not much arable or pasture land attached to these few acres which the Parliament men may have deemed scarce worth their plunder. Yet, upon consideration, it does seem strange that while fierce skirmishes were fought again and yet again in this vicinity between the rebels and the loyal men of Dorset, Folly's End went ever unmolested. And Mr Moon was here through all that time — not at the first attack on Wynmonath, but later: and no harm befell us. Maybe God heard his prayers on our behalf, for Mr

Moon did spend much time upon his prayers, and kept us praying too, and would read chapter and verse aloud to us and sermonise for hours, till I was aching stiff with sitting still, and a mountain of hate for my teacher. A worthy man, I'm sure: and I was sinful.

Nor could all his catechising save me. I knew that he believed me past redemption: for my quick temper, for the way I quizzed poor Percy, for my sloth and detestation of the classics, for the trick, regrettably, I'd learned from Thirza, of covering a misdemeanour with a glib veneer that hid the baldest truth, and was not quite a lie — though Mr Moon did never hesitate to label me *A Liar* — writing the words in capitals on parchment to make into a fool's cap, that I must wear as penance day in, day out, till I was chastened, yet unsaved. Mr Moon had long made clear to me that I had lost all hope of heaven, and would burn.

The Reverend Mr Moon, having been a member of the Yorkshire Follietts' household since before Percy was born, had schooled his young charge from his earliest years, and I think loved him, in so far as one so contumelious could love. Oliver, his name was: an ill-omened ugly name, and he an ugly man, narrow-eyed and lantern-jawed, with a perpetual blue shadow on his chin, being swart and hairy, and never cleanly shaved. A pious man, according to his principles, and according to the same, God-fearing, devout. I'll grant him a shrewd intelligence and a scholastic pedantry above the common run, but of kindliness and sympathy, of quick perception for the mind of any other save his own, he was devoid.

So through veils of distance does he appear to me, and maybe I do him wrong to thus present him, since my sight is jaundiced with unforgotten miseries endured. Birchings were the least of them. His icy sarcasm and Latin doggerel, his rigid discipline and his fount of knowledge instilled without one shred of mercy for the agonised perplexities that it aroused, and which I, for one, dared never have explained or clarified — all this, and all his thundered judgments and his threats of hell, distort my memory of the dark figure that shadowed my childhood's days. Only for Percy did he allow himself the least indulgence; and during our time of penury, while Robin and I were a couple of slubberdegullions, Percy went fine as a prince. No patched and threadbare rags and tags for him. Percy had the best of what remained of decency in our out-at-elbows world.

Regularly twice a year, Mr Moon rode forth on a mysterious excursion, to return with a laden pack-horse behind him; and while Percy strutted and postured, trying first this gewgaw and then that for our envious approval, we learned what the packages contained: new suits, bales of cloth and rolls of satin, bands and laces, combs for the hair, plumes for the hat, pomanders for the nose — to ward off bad smells and fevers — and such-like titivations and devices which Robin and I had never seen nor dreamed of.

Unmercifully then did Thirza, green-eyed for my sake, twit our Percy: 'Hey, forsooth! Someone's been trading with the devil. Here's a change from psalm-singing and piety — well, well! And His Reverence the first to forswear the Whitsun-ales and the maypole dance and the Jack-in-the-Green, and all like innocent philander as ungodly. Yet here we are decked out like a Jemmy-Jessamy with lace on our boots, and a doublet of silk, and musk-scented gloves — a-tricksy! Come, give 'em here! I'll warrant I could put 'em to some better use than to cover your lily-white hands!' And Thirza would snatch at his fine embroidered gauntlets and make much indecent play with

them, while Robin and I laughed to cry at her droll gestures —
and I blush now to think of them. But Thirza was a product of
her times which were coarser far than ours, and she as curst
and unseemly in her manners as any God-damning trooper, for
which I love her none the less. If her tongue was foul her heart
was fair — for me. So may she rest.

Then Percy, pale with rage, would let fly at her. He fought
like a girl, clawing, screaming, blubbering — no, I misjudge my
sex and myself, for I never blubbered nor screamed, though I'd
not hesitate to use my nails — and — 'I'll have you pilloried,'
yelled Percy, 'I'll have you hanged and quartered. I'll throw
your gizzard to the Roundheads! Only wait. You wait until I'm
master here — I'll turn you out! You stinking mound of fat,
you hell-hound bitch!'

Then Thirza would clout him hard and set him howling
more, to bring His Reverence from the room above — (my
father's chamber, be it noted, of which Mr Moon did not
scruple to possess himself during my father's absence) — and
he would proceed to pour Jehovah's wrath upon our heads:
while Percy, subdued, ashamed of his lack of dignity and
unbecoming temper, would smooth his hair and right his laces,
and put away his gloves and sit mim and prim as a spinster, his
lids cast down, and his lips pursed up in their quirking smile.

'What is this brawling?' would demand His Holiness with
thunder. 'What fresh abominations —' and on me Mr Moon
would fix his narrow glinting eye to make me quake — 'have
you committed, Mistress Prudence? Get you to your tasks, and
you, woman,' to Thirza, 'to your kitchen. Your tongue
contaminates and your voice is like a screech-owl's … Sir
Robert!' Robin, stifling his giggles, stood. 'Since it appears that
you have ample time to spare from more profitable labours —
I heard your loud guffawing above all others in the din — you

will write out five hundred times this dictum: *Hoc scio pro certo quod si cum stercore certo, vinco seu vincor, semper ego maculor.* And you, Piers,' he turned to Percy, 'you, sirrah, will construe it, if you please.'

Then Percy, who always had his nose in a book, would stand likewise to declaim in his neat, precise voice, his brows puckered to think it out and have it right: '"This I know for certain —"' pause — '"that when I strive with —"' pause — '"with filth —"'

And Mr Moon would nod approval.

'"Whether" — hem,' quoth Percy, 'hum — "whether I vanquish — or am vanquished, I am" — *semper ego maculor* — that is to say, sir, "I am for ever stained thereby."'

'Correct. Take it to heart, Sir Robert, and avoid corruption. Mistress Prudence —' for I was ever the chief culprit in any misbehaviour and to Mr Moon's discrimination, 'you will apply your imbecile intelligence to Deuteronomy, chapter twenty-eight, verses twenty-seven to forty-five, beginning *The Lord will smite thee with the botch of Egypt, and with the emerods and with the scab and with the itch whereof thou canst not be healed.* Note well, Mistress Prudence, the vengeance of the Lord who in His righteous indignation *will smite thee with madness and blindness and astonishment of the heart,* because that *thou hearken not unto the voice of the Lord thy God to keep His commandments* — and because you are a sluggard and a slattern, and pert, Mistress Prudence, and bone idle, and idleness is the womb of evil, so beware! Therefore read, committing to memory by tomorrow morning, without one single fault in the recital thereof, these verses, Deuteronomy twenty-eight. Piers, do you come with me.'

And Piers would go in his new finery, docile at the heels of his kinsman and toady and tutor, that estimable scholar, Mr Moon. But not before our Thirza, as brazen as you please, with arms akimbo, her head a-nod, and her teeth bared like a vixen's, had put in her word. 'How now, your Reverence, if you could be as sure, when your time comes, as this innocent here —' and she'd point her red finger at me — 'of the peace of the Lord hereafter, you'd not be so ready with your cursing, nor would you lie wakeful every night with the cramp — as you call it — in your belly. Easy sleep, an easy conscience, so they say. And if, when you ride out on your errands, you would bring Master Folliett a warm homespun suit and a hamper of good vittles instead of fine silks and satins and gloves which he can't wear nor eat neither in this benighted spot — where we're scraping the rind off cheeses for a meal — he'd not be the whey-faced, peaky, unaccountable, undergrown child that he is. No, sir, you hearken now to me — I'll have my say though I may swing for saying it — boys like whelps should be well fed, and this frippery won't feed his stomach, nor will the Scriptures. No, nor Greek nor Latin, nor all the tongue-twisting poetics and versifying and such-like, nor all the wisdom of the Lord Himself. And my young mistress, sir, I'll have you know, has learned all the lessons she need learn for today. I want her to help me in the buttery.'

And before Mr Moon could get his breath, I was whisked away under cover of Thirza's apron. Her tongue would stand for no man, not even for my father — least of all for Mr Moon. Poor gentleman! He must have been most sadly put about by her flaunting high-handedness, but what was he to do? He could not dismiss Thirza for her impudence, since my father was the master of this house and she my father's servant. Nor could he depart in dudgeon with young Folliett for this reason: he had nowhere else to go. The seat and lands in the north, that had been Percy's heritage from his renegade father, had in their turn been seized by the Cavaliers under the

Earl of Newcastle, and the house near Ripon used as a billet for their troops. So hirdie-girdie and distorted was our world become that warred to its destruction, kith against kin, father against son, and God against the devil over all.

I cannot think that Mr Moon's was an enviable vocation as tutor to three young children, two of whom were wild as Goths, with no woman but our Thirza to act as mistress of the household, and devoid of contact and companionship with any man of his own rank and calling. Yet I am sure he was devout and conscientious, and while he swallowed Thirza's insolence and bullied me and Robin, he may have acted only in our interests. Thirza used to tell me, for I was too young to have remembered this, that when Robin first came to live with us, Mr Moon applied himself — and with what patient diligence! — to the salvation of young Robin's Papistical soul: and that the child, accepting the word of God howsoever it was given (Thirza likened him to a starved fledgling, receiving in his open maw each titbit of Established Faith Mr Moon popped into it) was soon weaned from the pitfalls and snares of Popery, and his own Mother Church.

But in spite of Mr Moon and our penurious existence, we were no worse off than were a million other children of our time. We had our pleasures, simple pleasures doubtless, and not much of gaiety save the spontaneous joy of extreme youth; but we were care-free and well cared for — Thirza saw to that — and happy in ourselves and in each other. The boys, indeed, were bosom friends; devoted. Strange that these two, so opposite in physique and character, should have been so drawn together. Piers would have shared all his finery with Robin if Robin would have wished it; but he did not. He was a hulking, coltish lad, long-legged, long-armed, with eyes full of light and a face full of health, and his hair a rusty flame upon his shoulders.

Percy was gentle, and pale as a primrose; his hair like flax, and curling, long. I have seen him stand for twenty minutes, unaware that he was watched, combing his silken tresses until my held giggles spluttered over, and he'd wheel round, shell-pink with anger at my jeers: 'Hey, fol-de-rol! Here's a lily-lady gallant! Shall I lend you my high-day holiday gown o' lavender silk, my pretty? 'Twas the one my mother wore to her wedding and you shall wear it to yours, believe me, my carpet-knight o' curls.'

Then he'd answer gently back, looking as pure and big-eyed as a saint in a church window. 'Why, now! Surely 'twere better to dress my hair and comb it and have it neat and cleanly than a-crawl with lice like yours, my little snotty-nozzle scarecrow. Cleanliness is next to godliness, remember, and I've never known *you* clean! You stink of the stable and cow-dung and mice, and you look like —'

But he was not allowed to tell me what I looked like, for I was up and at him with my nails to his face, till Robin was called to come and pinion me, while I kicked out with my heels at both of them. Then they would bind me with a rope and carry me — yelling to split my lungs — to our great barn where they would throw me on the hay and sit on me, talking unconcernedly together, and as unheedful of my cries and plaints as though I were a maggot. And there they'd stay, with myself squirming underneath them like a basketful of eels, near to suffocation and sneezing the hay out of my nostrils to scream mercy, until I was released at last to crawl out abject and beg Percy's pardon for the bleeding scratch I'd put upon his face. Then he would have to beg my pardon too, and swear, crossing his heart, that never a louse had feasted on my head; nor was I a snotty-nozzle scarecrow, but as comely as the Queen o' the May. And then we'd kiss and go a-hawking.

That sport, of all our country pastimes, was our favourite. We each owned a horse, raw-boned clumsy nags to be sure, but we rode them well and fearlessly. I was always to the fore, lest the boys should think me girlish. To give Mr Moon his due he did not interfere with our out-of-door pursuits. Once clear of the house, the woods and fields and downland were our playground, untrammelled, free as air.

We went hunting too: not that there was much to hunt, since the Roundheads had taken the best of our buck, and left us the badgers and foxes. These we chased and killed with the crossbow — that is to say the boys did the killing, for I was never skilful with the arrow, and moreover, I abhorred to think that I had slaughtered a wild woodland creature. Yet, these principles forsook me when we went hawking. That was a sport I loved, and I would ease my pricking conscience at the sight of a feathered corpse, by telling myself that my falcon was the slaughterer, not I.

The boys tended and tamed our hawks, and though I would, if occasion warranted, be called in as assistant, it was understood the mews was their own province, and woe betide me should I trespass there without permission.

Many a time, however, have I watched the taming of a passage-hawk, which on being snared was hooded, and set down on a block of turf with the jesses fastened to her legs. She would be fed on the gloved hand, and gradually learned to step upon it from her perch, increasing the distance daily until she was obliged to fly to reach the fist. Then began the training. The falcon would be called off to the lure, when if none other were available, I would be requisitioned to tie a long line to the end of the jess and hold her, hooded, on my hand, until Robin or Percy, both expert falconers, would stand at a distance of some five and twenty yards to swing the lure. I would then, at the given signal, remove the hood, and the hawk would fly to the lure, and in this wise was she exercised daily until she became sufficiently tractable to be trusted without the line. We must be careful not to feed her until she was flown, and always to reward her for coming to the lure, with a morsel of the meat with which it was garnished. She would then be entered at the quarry — partridge or rook or whatever — at which she was intended to be flown, by first giving her a live bird at the end of a long line and allowing her to go off the fist and kill it. Eventually the line would be done away with and she would be flown at wild quarry.

I had my own two favourites, a jerfalcon and a peregrine: long-winged, dark-eyed and proud as queens. I named them Martha and Mary. We used these for taking feathered game of all kinds, wildfowl, crows, magpies, even herons. For taking hares and rabbits we used the goshawk. This latter was a demon. I never flew her, for I did hate to hear the scream of the doomed prey as she stooped, wings closed, to bind and seize. Yet how I loved to ride out to the chase with my falcon belled and hooded on my wrist, and our dogs behind us, riding free of my lessons and Mr Moon over the dewy pastures in those damp sun-lost mornings, when the trees were ablaze with autumn gold and in my nose the sweet bitter tang of dead wet leaves and wood-smoke... And suddenly, our dogs would halt and stiffen, and we would stay our horses, while with a chattering rush and whir of startled wings up flashed a covey, and away, our falcons after them.

Then would the chase begin: we a-gallop through stubble field, through copse and undergrowth and out again on to the clear downland; while our hawks, fierce soaring, hover, stoop, and bind, and the next moment, so it seems, my peregrine is back on my wrist again, preening her feathers, bloody-beaked and quivering with pride, and we know that we'll have partridge pie for supper.

Besides our field sports we had our games: club-kayles — which you call ninepins — and pale-maille, now gone out of fashion. We played it in this wise: by striking the ball with a wooden mallet to drive it through a hanging hoop, and so score points. I have often seen King Charles II play this game in St James's Park, and in that very walk which is known as Pall Mall to this day.

I had my especial occupations too. I helped Thirza in the bake-house and the buttery and learned from her all housewifely pursuits, though I confess I was never much of a needlewoman, and cobbled my sewing disgracefully. From Thirza I learned too the value of herbs and how to distil them, and which were good for this ailment or that. Our domestic staff being reduced since the war to two aged stablemen and a half-wit scullion, Percy and Robin and I would be commandeered by Thirza for all and sundry duties. The boys were put to groom their horses and mine, tend the falcons, help the herdsmen with the cows, besides having willy-nilly to go off for a day's fishing if Thirza were short of food for us — not that they need be bidden to that sport, for both were keen anglers and seldom failed to bring back a well-lined basket of trout, bream, chub, or whichever fish in season they'd been after.

So time slipped by and the war dragged on, but we in our rural retreat knew little, save from hearsay, of the grievous battles that were raging through our land. I seldom saw my father. His rare visits when he came and went, staying at most a couple of nights, grew still more rare after those murderers had committed their most foul and blackest crime.

I heard it first from Mr Moon.

I remember this so clearly...

It was a raw February morning, full of a white crawling mist that had crept in from the sea and hung about our hills and woods, corpse-cold.

We sat, the three of us, at the long table in the hall awaiting Mr Moon's appearance; I, wearing my dunce's cap, with *Sluggard* — not *Liar* for once — writ large upon it; Robin muttering and frowning over a verse of Cicero, left unscanned until this last five minutes, and Percy with his books neatly placed before him, carefully trimming a quill to have all in readiness for his lesson, which you may be sure he had by heart. He was far more studious and cleverer than Robin, and as for me, he had forgotten more than I could ever learn.

The clock struck eight, and before the last chime had died down, Mr Moon — punctual to the minute, having breakfasted alone as was his custom — appeared. I thought that he looked more than ever dreary in his clerical black suiting, and certainly his fiddle-face was longer and more gloomy than its wont.

We stood; he sat, in my father's big chair, and cast his eye upon us all in turn. On my dunce's cap it lingered for a second, and the hairy nostrils of his sharp nose quivered, as though at a smell. He motioned us to take our places. I slid into my seat and prayed within me, *Let him not bark nor sneer, dear Father God. Let me recite my theorem of Euclid correctly. Let me not fall at the* Pons Asinorum, *and let me escape a birching for this week...* For I often spoke to God in this wise within myself, which was not as I'd been taught by Mr Moon. I could never, despite my tutor's scriptural dogmatism, regard the Almighty as the stern avenger His Reverence depicted. To me, He is, and always was, my friend; and I misdoubted Mr Moon's dark warnings of hell-fire, for Thirza did assure me our Heavenly Father was most loving kind and would never let me suffer torment for my sins — if I repented. So comforted, I sat, and opened my book of Euclid at the page, and waited, trusting.

Mr Moon then stroked his chin and hemmed, drew down his lips, and gazed, not at us, but at the ceiling, with his eyes rolled up until nothing of them showed except their dingy whites, and 'A dire calamity has befallen us and the whole nation,' in dismal accents he pronounced.

I saw Robin start and the colour drain from his face. He opened his mouth to speak, but our tutor raised his hand for silence. Percy's eyes widened; he began picking at his thumbnail, a trick of his when he was nervous. My heart beat sick and heavy in my ribs. *Befallen us...* No dire calamity could befall us worse than the fear that ever stalked beside me that I should some day hear my father had been ... no! Mr Moon had said 'the nation'. My father's death, brave Cavalier and King's man though he was, could not affect the nation, only me.

'On the afternoon of Tuesday, January the thirtieth,' Mr Moon said, weightily, 'His Majesty, King Charles the First, was brought to the scaffold and there executed.'

I heard Robin take a hissing breath; I dared not look at him. A sound like a puppy's whimper came from Percy, and I sat still as stone.

Mr Moon proceeded. 'I wish no comments from any one of you,' he said, and saying it, his eyes returned from their contemplation of the ceiling and were lowered, 'that which has been done is done — by the order of the Government; and only God Himself can see the right of it.'

'Sir!' Robin was on his feet, and his face that had been pale was now a surging red. 'No God could see the right of such a deed. God save the King!'

'There is no King, Sir Robert.' Mr Moon's thin lips were tight against his teeth. 'The King is dead.'

'Long live the King!' Robin cried, with a catch in his throat.

I echoed it: 'Long live the King — his son, King Charles!' piped I.

'Silence!' thundered Mr Moon. 'I say again there is no King. This is the end of monarchy in Britain.'

Percy, his gaze fixed on his master, picked his thumb; his tongue came out to wet his lips; he swallowed. 'Sir, why have they killed him? Of what was he accused?'

'Of High Treason and other Crimes and Misdemeanours in the name of the Commons of England,' Mr Moon said awfully.

There came a pause, then, 'If he were a traitor,' burst forth Robin, 'he was traitor only to himself and His own Majesty.'

I dug my nails in my hands that were tight-clenched at my sides while I awaited the deluge of Mr Moon's reaction to this mutiny; but no! Enveloped in a god-like calm, His Reverence replied, 'I have said I wish no comments. It is not for me — or even you,' his thin lips sneered, 'to judge. *Minimus ad majorem in judicium vocat.*'

Which was all we ever heard from Mr Moon upon the subject of that dreadful murder at Whitehall. Nor, during the time that followed, did I know on what missions my father had been occupied, though I might hazard a guess that his journeyings up and down the country, broken by intermittent hurried visits paid to us, were not disconnected with the cause of a certain tall and dark young man who stood for everything we Royalists had lost.

Not until after the Worcester fight did my father cease to be a figure, remote and unsubstantial, constantly recurring and dissolving in the background of my life. Not till that day which changed the trend of my existence and turned my dream of him to warm reality. And from that day, though I was still a child, did my destiny begin to shape its course.

CHAPTER TWO

We three were in the winter parlour on that October afternoon. It had been a dreary day of rain and wind; not a laughing, mischievous impish wind that plays a jig in the tossing tree branches and sets the dead leaves capering with a hop, a skip and a jump. No: this was one of your snivelling days, and one of those maundering winds that goes moaning and whimpering on the heels of the hag-ridden clouds like a sick brat at the skirts of its mother.

My lessons being over, I, with one leg tucked under, sat in the window seat, and for want of better to do, counted the trickling raindrops on the lattice and stared out between whiles down the drive, hoping against hope that I perchance would see, at last, him for whom I daily watched, come riding to our door. But the drive was full of nothing save a skulking mist that had drifted in from the coast, bringing with it the cry of unseen gulls to join a mournful chorus to the cawing of the black-coated congregation up there in the rookery.

These solemn personages seemed to be engaged on some tremendous issue, bowing and nodding and conferring one with the other, and flying up to circle round their ragged village in the swaying elms, to return and bow again. One among them all was certainly the leader; a paunchy parson of a fellow, delivering a prodigious long prolation to make me yawn, though I could hear no word of it, and would not have understood it if I had. Yet, to be sure, as a child I did come to learn the language of some birds — those that speak pert and pretty, with a song to set you dancing the coranto; the throstle and the lark, the linnet — very dainty and precise is his tune, and he a gallant for the ladies — and then, the blackbird. He of them all is the gayest of gay cavaliers when he goes a-wooing, and shouts his serenade to burst his heart. But this meeting of the rooks, now — there is nothing gay in that. Of all cantankerous, Puritanical, raw-throated sermonising Roundheads I ever did see and hear, give me a parcel of rooks — and I'd bake them in a pie without compunction.

Well, so there I was, counting raindrops and scowling at the rookery, and turning sulky as the day itself with this idle mood upon me; though withal I did have the strangest unconformable sensation, alert and eager, ready to start at my shadow, with a curious great pricking in my thumbs: and what this token could portend, whether for good or evil, there was no knowing.

Behind me at the table Percy and Robin played at chess: Percy worrying his thumbnail, with his mouth pursed like a button and a frown above his nose, and Robin with his chin in his hand, brows bent upon the board and not a word from either for the space of half an hour. *There's a dullard's game for you,* thought I. *A greybeard's game, no game for boys — or me.* I'd never learn it. Kings and queens and knights were well enough — but bishops! The Lord preserve us! No game that had a bishop in it could be merry. These meditations may, however, have not been entirely unsoured, since neither Percy's patience — and he had, I'll grant him, more patience than Robin in the exploiting of his knowledge for my puny understanding — nor all his laboured explanations had succeeded in teaching me anything of chess more than how to move the pieces, only to find my poor king hunted to a fool's mate every time.

By the great open chimney, where the crackling logs lit the room with cheer and lent to the oaken beams a burnished glow in welcome contrast to the ugly day outside, sat my Great-aunt Rossiter. She had been staying with us for the better part of a week, on one of her gratuitous bi-annual visits, when she would descend upon our house unheralded, save for the sound of her hoppety-croppety coach in the drive, to appear of a sudden like a witch, lacking nothing of dark magic but her besom. For in truth did this good lady resemble to my childish fancy all I had been told by Thirza of such hags. And God forgive me that I wronged her, since never, I vow, did tread a more excellent, more worthy soul than my Aunt Rossiter.

Very tall, very thin was she; so thin that she appeared to have been carven from one solid piece of bone; and the skin tightly stretched upon it seemed to grow there as lichen grows upon a wall. She was lichen-coloured, too; even her hair, drawn painfully back from a high dome-shaped forehead, had a grey-greenish tinge. She carried proudly the Folliett nose — a jutting fortress of a nose that recurs in some degree or other in all our Folliett men, and often in our women. I, thankfully, escaped it. My Aunt Rossiter did not; and on a woman, believe me, 'tis a beak.

She had a quick bright eye, as quick a wit, and a voice as raucous as a parrot's. She dressed outlandishly, favouring the ruff and farthingale of the old Queen's time, and this gave to her lower parts a monstrous wide circumference, and made her body look as narrow as a pin. Her husband did not often attend her when she came to visit us, staying behind at her bidding to superintend the ordering of her household — or not, as she decreed. Poor Great-uncle Rossiter! A chirping little bird of a man was he, bearing, as it were, a perpetual apologia for his own shortcomings as the mate of such a paragon. I have heard from Thirza that my Aunt Rossiter did not marry until her parents had lost hope she ever would. Her harsh voice and downright manner scared away all suitors, notwithstanding that a handsome dowry went with her. Having, however, in her thirty-fifth year chanced upon Timothy Rossiter, Esquire, of Colyton in the county of Devon, a gentleman of means and property and some ten years her junior, she determined to secure him — and herself. Her parents were not, it seems, consulted. Nor was Mr Rossiter, who before that merciless pursuit fell as helpless as a sparrow to Mary, my peregrine hawk.

The firelight played on Aunt Rossiter's face; and I watched her, where upright in the great carved chair she sat, her eyes fixed on the fire as intently as were mine upon herself. Her petticoats were drawn back over her bony knees, the while she warmed them: and on those same knees, very comfortable and purring, dozed our kitchen cat, a terror for the mice and a favourite of mine — and of Aunt Rossiter's. This partiality of our tom-cat for one so old and grey and sharp, and strongly bearded, filled me with trepidation, so that if with a screech Aunt Rossiter, along with Tom, had vanished up the chimney I would have been alarmed but not surprised.

While turning from my contemplation of the rookery and the rain-swept drive, I ruminated on these things, the door opened with a rush to admit Thirza.

'Madam! Madam!' Thirza was in a rare state, her hair escaping in disorder from her coif and her arms covered to the elbow with the flour she had forgotten in her hurry to wipe off, before coming from the bake-house. 'Praise be to highest heaven!' declared Thirza, not, I think, unmindful of her entrance as she stood, her powdery arms flung wide. 'Here is great news, madam, of the King!'

At which announcement Robin reared his head, Percy's thumb went to his lip, and Great-aunt Rossiter jerked her knee to send the shocked cat flying with his tail up. 'What news, woman? Brush that mess from your arms and curb your tongue. Speak slowly.'

'Madam,' Thirza filled her bosom with a breath to hold her words without a break, 'Ham — one of our stablemen riding into Bridport this morning to fetch a sack of meal and it being market day to buy a cockerel we having killed our last fine gentleman for —'

'Yes, yes, yes!' croaked my aunt, 'keep to your point, girl. Well?'

'Well, madam — and God bless us! Well indeed it is as it transpires — Ham being at the inn for a glass of ale heard there a buzz of His Majesty who had come to that very house — The George, madam — a sennight since. And the King, they say, was disguised as a servant with his hair cropped short, and his face as brown as a walnut and with him rode a lady and a gentleman thought to be —'

'Wilmot, I'll wager!' Aunt Rossiter interrupted.

'The very same, ma'am. So it was. My Lord Wilmot. And, madam — what think you of this? The King groomed the horses out there in the stable yard like any hostler, and none knew him for His Majesty!'

'God bless him!' said Aunt Rossiter, a-grin.

'They say, ma'am, however, he was followed, and my Lord Wilmot — and the lady, whose name is Mistress Coningsby —'

'Juliana,' said my aunt, a-nod. 'I am acquainted with her family. And so?'

'So, madam, they advised the King begone without delay. And away they went.'

'Why was the lady with the King?' enquired Percy.

'To further His Majesty's disguise,' snapped my aunt. 'Hold your mouth and listen. So, Thirza, what then?'

'Why, then, ma'am, they were gone in a trice full-tilt up the London road, until a mile out of Bridport they found themselves pursued by Massey's troopers.'

'The vermin!' quoth my aunt.

'But the King, madam,' cried Thirza, 'the King, God save his precious life, turned down a side lane — you know it, my poppet —' to me — 'the one that skirts the barley-field where you came to grief jumping your nag at a fence out a-hawking last —'

'What matters *which* lane?' said my aunt, through her teeth. 'Get on with your tale, you gaby!'

'Yes, madam, if you'll let me tell it in my own way and by your leave,' reported Thirza, giving back as good as she was given. 'So then — hell take me, now I've lost the thread of it. Where was I?'

'Down the lane by the barley-field,' I muttered, with my hands fisted, and hard put not to use them to pound her story out of her.

'Ah, yes! Well, down that lane, then, madam, went our King with Massey's Roundheads after him, and by a miracle or God's good providence, the villains over-rode their mark and galloped on, helter-skelter, into Dorchester!'

Robin, who during this recital had sat, his mouth compressed, his eyes hard on Thirza's face, unblinking, let out a long-held sigh. Percy turned pink and bit his thumb; Aunt Rossiter smiled grimly. 'And so he still goes with the price of a thousand pounds upon his head — uncaptured.'

'But madam — so near — so near to us! Conceive it!' gabbled Thirza. 'He might have come to this house.'

'Oh, if only he had,' I cried. 'Perhaps he will!'

'Perhaps he won't,' said my aunt. 'I trust by now he has found a ship to take him over the water.'

'There's still another morsel, ma'am,' which Thirza evidently and with true dramatic instinct had kept to the last to bring the curtain down. 'His Majesty has been in hiding at Broadwindsor!'

'Nearer yet!' I squealed. 'Oh, Thirza, is it true? That's not five miles distant.'

'*Will* you let the woman speak?' commanded my Aunt Rossiter in a voice to dry your tongue.

'Yes, madam,' I answered, as small as could be; and stood tying my fingers in knots.

'And, madam,' Thirza was in highest fettle now, 'they say His blessed Majesty lay for the night at a humble rat-begotten hovel of an inn on the top o' the downs, where the good landlord, being a true Royalist, made him welcome thinking him in his disguise to be another fugitive cavalier, but never dreaming on the truth of it, however. And while they fed the King in an upper room, some more of Cromwell's whoreson troops arrives with one o' their doxies —' Here Thirza paused to give the fullest weight to this pronouncement, and with such a display of eye-winking and brow-raising and smiles that I could have screamed to bring the roof down in my impatience, while my Aunt Rossiter favoured this exhibition with a look to freeze your marrow — but not Thirza's. Medusa herself could not, I think, have petrified our Thirza, or stayed her tongue when it was well away.

'And would you believe it, madam?' unblushingly submitted Thirza to my Great-aunt Rossiter's stare, 'this camp-following mopsy was in labour and brought to bed that very night upon the kitchen table! Which occasioned, madam, so much stir among the rabble who each in turn were taxed by the slut to be the bastard's father, that none on 'em had a thought for their errand to that place, which was to hunt the King! And off they were again next morning nor never knew the room above the kitchen had sheltered His Majesty's Grace!' And Thirza flung her head back, laughing to kill herself, till my aunt, in tones as steely as an axe, bid her have done and begone, adding that if she discovered Thirza had been lying she would see to have her whipped.

So here was smoke enough to start a fire: and you may be sure we three made a great blaze of it with our conjectures and surmises, and Robin's views upon the case that His Majesty would most likely be making for the coast, that he would give his hope of heaven to be with him — and that who could tell but what he mightn't yet?

Percy said, 'But how? You cannot follow him. You do not know which way he'll take — or have taken, by this time.'

'*I'll* follow him!' I boasted. 'I'll saddle Ebony and go find him now!'

'You?' Percy jeered, and twisted his nose.

'Yes, me!' I bristled. 'And why not? I can ride ahead of you any day in the week, my sickly little lollipop o' marchpane.'

'Ah! I am that — am I?' quoth Percy, with a movement like a snake's to take and turn my wrist while I shrieked, '*Pax!*'

'Call me that again and you'll carry your arm in a sling for a month,' said Percy, smooth as silk.

But no sooner had he let me go than I was at him, claw and hoof, he standing curved to be clear of my kicks while he held me in a vice. He had strength enough to hurt though he was little.

Then Robin, slouching up to bestow a sudden lunge with his foot at Percy's backside, caused him to drop me and receive a buffet in his face to lay him flat. Whereupon, ungratefully, I turned upon Robin, my saviour, thanking him to hold his peace and mind his business: to which no reply came but a teasing laugh and the devil's own tweak to my hair. At that, Percy, not to be outdone, sat up, rubbed his jaw and sprang at Robin's throat, and I at Percy's tail, praying him, 'Take guard! He'll pummel your nose to a jelly!' For when they started fighting there was no knowing where they'd end.

Aunt Rossiter, behind whose back these antics were performed, and who doubtless had been musing on more profitable concerns than us or our calf-play, now rose to send us packing: Percy to his Mr Moon — 'Who may, sirrah, have taught you Greek but has not taught you manners'; Robin to the stable yard — 'A more fitting place for an uncurbed colt than a lady's parlour'; and me to my seat in the window, with Mr Burton's *Anatomy of Melancholy* open on my knee, which she bade me read for the good of my soul.

For never, vowed Aunt Rossiter, had she witnessed such hoydenish, wanton, ill-bred misbehaviour in a young gentlewoman, who disgraced her sex, her status and her dignity by rampageous racketing that would put a trull to shame; and moreover, quoth my aunt, she well knew who was responsible for my immodesty and lack of decorum: That Woman, who had fostered me from my beginnings and from whom I had learned my harridan's tricks. She must see to it, said my aunt — to sink my heart into my stocking — that she carry me away with her to live under her roof and supervision, where she would strive to instil into my addlepate the ways and discourse of a lady.

Which threat sufficed to keep me close-mouthed and as still as an oyster. With one eye on Mr Burton and the other on Aunt Rossiter — who, I was encouraged to perceive, had returned to her meditations by the chimney-piece, and had seemingly dismissed me from her ken — I sat and led my thoughts astray.

Here was spice enough our Thirza had unloosed on us! Yet not by any means the first tale of its kind that had flown by word of mouth to Land's End from John o' Groats, since the day in that year, 1651, when our young King was crowned in Scotland.

Thereafter came news, known to all of us by this time, that the son of our martyred sovereign had taken action to march against the regicides with a loyal force of Royalists and Presbyters behind him.

Hollow alliance though this proved to be, in that the bitterest blood still flowed between Presbyterian and Cavalier, the motive that impelled both parties sprang from a mutual, fierce determination to restore the heir of England to his throne.

How that plan miscarried, first at Dunbar and finally at Worcester, where the grim last fight was fought in open meadows, and on Severn's banks, and hand to hand within the city's walls, we who waited with our prayers for Britain's future, had already learned. We had learned too to know the courage of our young King Charles, whose own men gave out before he did, and, flinging down their weapons in surrender, left him with but a handful of supporters to stand alone against all Cromwell's army.

Three thousand of our Royalists were slain, and six or seven thousand taken prisoner. It was an overthrow complete and deadly, astonishing to conquered and conqueror alike. Only with the utmost difficulty was Charles persuaded to save himself, and the story of his daring escapade went blazing through the country.

Our men brought news of it each time they went to market. We had heard tell of adventures to fill a volume of romance, nor did we query one tittle of the truth, since every tale told the same: how that His Majesty had hid in the boughs of an oak while the soldiers hunted him below in the thicket of the wood, passing beneath the very tree where their fugitive sat perched. How a proclamation had been issued threatening death to any that should aid 'One Charles Stuart, a long dark man above two yards high'; and how he had travelled four days and three nights on foot, up to his knees in dirt, and wearing ' a steeple-crowned hat and country-fellow's habit, threadbare cloth coat with a sweaty leathern doublet over a coarse noggin shirt', and how that he had stained his face with walnut juice and cropped his hair to his ears; that his shoes were 'slashed for the ease of his feet and full of little rolls of paper placed between the toes to save them from galling'.

Much of this had come to us in open secret from our men, who had heard it from this one and that in Bridport and in Dorchester. But even these most loyal subjects of His Majesty may have clacked too often and too long of the King's incognito, for we heard how that he had changed his guise again and yet again, affecting that of a lackey to ride before young Mistress Lane, who journeyed pillion thus with him to Bristol. There he stayed at Abbot's Leigh, the home of the Royalist Nortons.

We heard too that he had hid himself in a barn, in a marl-pit, and in the priest-holes of the houses of his Roman Catholic hosts: how that he had changed his dress on one occasion into that of an aged market-crone with her basket on her arm, and went hobbling, bent double, through the village of Lyme, muttering and snickering below her breath — till he was all but chased for a witch. This, Thirza's telling, and I for one swallowed it whole, though His Majesty did omit that episode in his own version of the story when he dictated it in after years to Mr Pepys.

One thing is certain: that his escape so far had been a miracle, for wheresoever he hid he went pursued, with half England on his track thirsting to have his blood on the block where his father's was spilled before him.

It is known now that his preservation was largely due to the good services of the Papists, who without thought for their own safety and the dire risk they ran of the rack, the hurdle, and that reeking death at the end of the rope, without any thought but to save their King, they took and hid him in their secret chambers, and sent him forth again in fresh disguise, and the care of their own young daughters.

And now it was Mistress Coningsby who shared with Mistress Lane the honours of this royal charge; she who had brought His Majesty to Dorset, and to the borderland of Wynmonath itself.

Can you wonder that I had no head for Mr Burton, nor were my thoughts attuned to melancholy now? No, they were buzzing like a swarm of bees around the honey-pot of romance and adventure... The King! 'A long dark man above two yards high,' thus ran the proclamation... If only, I dreamed, if only I could be the lucky one to chance upon His Majesty and lead him here to safety in *our* house! We had a priest-hole too. Folly's End, built in the time of Henry VIII, had harboured a Catholic family during the reign of Queen Bess, and it was then that the Jesuit Nicholas Owen, who devoted the greater part of his life to constructing such secret places in Roman Catholic houses throughout the country, had built our hiding-hole which is still here to this day.

The entrance can be found behind the wainscot on the right-hand side of the hall as you come in at the screens. Concealed in a panel that slides open by pressing a knot in the woodwork lies a recess, not high enough to hold a man upright but a grand place for children to play at hide-and-seek; for by lifting a trap in the oaken floor you can lower yourself into a narrow passage ending in a spiral flight of stairs that leads upwards to the roof. There, if you run along a narrow ridge — a precarious journey this — you come to a false chimney that has a most ingenious arrangement of bricks to hide the door to yet another stairway, leading down; and thence by its exit giving out at last upon the stable yard, you could make a clear escape.

A favourite game of ours was that of pursuivant and recusant, which part Robin did invariably take, having, so he insisted, prior claim to it, being born a Catholic. I have often wondered why I, for one, did not go crashing to my death when Percy and I followed Robin out on to the roof, I clinging like a cat to its sloping sides and with a sickly turning of my stomach. But Percy never flinched, though he had not yet succeeded in a capture. Robin was a will-o'-the-wisp at evasion, and knew each twist and turn of the way as he knew the palm of his hand.

So, thought I, remembering our priest-hole, *if I could bring the King here I would hide him, and how proud I'd be to have the honour!* Who knew but what he might not even now be on his way to us, ours being the only house in miles of any size and fitness for a king…

And thinking thus, the book of Melancholy fell to the floor with a slap, and its face in the rushes. I gave a scared look at Aunt Rossiter, and saw she was a-nod, though she still sat very upright with her head a little sideways and her jaw a little dropped, and a rattling, whistling snoring in her nose. Praise be that Mr Burton's fall had not aroused her!

The day was closing in with shadows; the rain had ceased, and a pale westering light spread scarves of gold across the hooded clouds. I fumbled at the window latch and opened wide the casement. I heard a bird cheep sleepily, and then another, louder, in the rain-soaked privet where a starling preened himself and shook his wings and hopped down as saucy as you please, as though he were readier for breakfast than for bed.

And then...

I think there comes to all of us at some time in our lives a moment of significance; a beacon point that marks, as from a centre radiating outwards, the vital essence of our being; a moment when in one lightning flash of pure reality the Past, the Present and the Future are merged in the Eternal Now and Fate's pathway shines revealed. In some such moment, when the human spirit, startled from its earthy binding, soars towards the mountains, it hovers near to magic; and while all else dissolves and fades away the sense of super-consciousness remains, as the sun's afterglow stays in a darkening sky.

So, looking back upon my childhood's self as I knelt in the window sniffing at the bitter-sweet scent of that drowned autumn day, my mind still busy with gallant tales told to set imagination flaming — in that moment's charged expectancy, half-dismayed and wholly tranced, I waited, ears pricked for something that was not a sound yet heard; a step not yet a footfall; for words unspoken that must set the seal upon my whole life's future... Then all was veiled, and through the gathering dusk, as though called from my dream of him, a man came, walking.

'A long dark man', well above 'two yards high'!

I had no eyes nor ears now for Aunt Rossiter, whose snores increased in volume as my heart increased in size, swelling, beating, like a drum, unbearably.

I did not pause; I did not hesitate. I scrambled up and out of the open casement to drop, noiseless as the starling from the privet, on to the grass below.

I had no instant's doubt but that he who now advanced with a slow, halting gait along the rutted cart-track was none other than that same 'Charles Stuart' whom Cromwell's men had harried from Worcester city, through the midshires of England, by wood, and field and river; by twists and turns and byways; and over Salisbury's great plain, to drive him here to our own Dorset hills to bide with us... And that I, Prue Folliett, should be the first to watch and wait for him! Even as I watched and waited for my father — who in truth, had been a trifle ousted from my most fervent thoughts, since Thirza's latest tale had brought the King so near to Folly's End.

To my exhilarated fancy he seemed, though he walked lame, to walk in light, for light was all about him: in the paling sunset sky that reflected pools of gold in the road puddles; in the light that shone on the fallen rain-washed leaves that lay heaped in the mud like drifts of golden pennies; and in the light that lingered in the tracks and limned his shape as before him went his shadow in the grass.

There he came, 'The Black Boy', as they called him: black for his hair, cut short to show his ears under a steeple-crowned hat! That alone sufficed to verify my recognition.

Hands to my skirts, swinging them outwards for the curtsy, head up to fill my lungs and hold my breath, I was away and down the drive as fast as my legs could take me.

But when I looked for him again, my King had vanished.

I stared, mouth open... Nothing. No man, no King, no sight of one, only the jeering of the rooks to fill the emptiness, and my heart a leaden weight under my russet bodice. Well! I had led my fancy on to let me down. Yet my thumbs had pricked all day: that was a sign of something, a possible abodement of no good. Sure enough I was bewitched. I crossed my fingers, with half a glance around my shoulder, fearing to find my Great-aunt Rossiter come riding on the stable broom behind me, to catch me up for punishment and take me back to Colyton, if not to some more ill-conditioned place.

I rubbed my eyes; I looked again. Surely now, there could not be *two* kings that walked abroad in steeple-crowned hats and ragged jerkins! Yet it seemed there were.

Out of the road's elbow I saw him come again, limping a little slower, to halt and stand not half a furlong's distance, peering forwards, raising up a hand, calling out my name, his name for me: 'Holla there, my Imp!'

I knew him then, as my heart, were it not contorted with bold tales, should have known him though he walked down from the sky.

I ran towards him, laughing, crying, my petticoats soaked at their hems in a muss about my ankle. I lost a shoe in the mud and ran on without it, feeling the ooze and squelch of the waterlogged clay like ice between my toes, and my breath a noisy sobbing in my throat. 'Father! My Father! I have been mistook ... I thought ... I thought ... I thought you were the King!'

He caught me up to him and held me very tight. I saw his face, a boy's face still — he was but eighteen years older than I — haggard, worn, and stained with walnut juice; and his hair, a rich brown, long and curling, as I'd known it, was as black as the wings of a crow. He went in rags in a grease-befouled high steeple hat, and he looked and smelled like a beggar.

'Are you disappointed, my Imprudence?' His voice was a whispering laugh in my ear.

I made no answer but to put my arms around his neck and hug him close, with kisses. Then his hold upon me slackened. I slid down and stood beside him, gazing.

'Are you hurt, my soul?' I asked, on tiptoe to reach and stroke his cheek that was sprouting a fine rough growth of bristle.

'Just a small hurt, my darling.' His teeth showed in the flash of a smile, marvellous white in his dark stranger's face. 'I've been chased for a hundred miles and have walked near fifty on 'em.'

'Chased!' I echoed, dry-lipped.

'Hunted, if you will, then, like a badger. But the hounds are not after me now. Don't fret yourself, my pretty. They're after bigger game than I...' His smoke-grey eyes, deep in, and faintly slanting at the corners as mine do, stared round about as he were in a daze. ''Tis good to be here,' said my father. 'And good it is to see my Imp —' his eyes came back to me with a twinkle of laughter behind them — 'grown from a demon to a beauty — were she washed! Come give me your shoulder, sweet, I'm mortal weary.'

Proud was I to have him lean on me to bring him home.

CHAPTER THREE

He lay in his great four-post bed, and I sat at the foot of it, adoring. Six months had passed since his return to us, a God-sent safe return as we soon learned, for no hand but God's could have upheld and led him through the perilous adventures he had faced; adventures that matched the King's in daring and audacity, and not a pin to choose between the courage of them both.

My father had stayed with His Majesty to the last clash of steel at Worcester, and with Lords Derby, Wilmot, Leviston, Talbot, the Duke of Buckingham, Colonel Blague, Mr Darcy, Mr May and other gallant gentlemen, he followed the King from the field and thence divided.

Some were overtaken by disaster, some, as did His Majesty, had miraculous escapes. Derby, the first to suffer, was captured and brought to the scaffold at Bolton. Buckingham took refuge in a cottage and lay in a bread-oven hid by the good wife, who scattered flour over him and kept him there when a party of soldiers came to search. Her entreaties not to spoil her batch of bread in its baking entirely deceived the pursuers. They poked and probed in every hole and corner, but not in the oven that held His Grace, who got away with nothing worse than too hot a seat to his breeches.

Talbot took the road to his father's house at Longford; Wilmot hid in a malt-house, clapped into the kiln, almost as warm a spot as Buckingham's bread-oven. Darcy, May, and Colonel Blague, doubled across country in various disguises, and as far as my father knew were yet at large. My father said that when he last saw Buckingham, he had assumed the role of a mountebank, wearing 'a jack-pudding's coat and a little hat with a fox's tail in it adorned by a cock's feather'. His face was daubed with flour like a clown's and he carried a fiddle, to go prancing through the villages singing lovelorn ballads under the very noses of Cromwell's men, who joined in the chorus of 'Corin Was Her Only Joy' and stood him a tankard of sack for his pains — if that's to be believed.

Because my father dwelled more on the exploits of his fellows than his own, I had to dig his tale out of him in a series of disjointed incidents before I could piece it together as a whole.

I gathered that he rode with the King to 'White Ladys', a house some twenty miles beyond Wolverhampton, that once had been a monastery and was now the habitation of a Catholic family of wood-cutters named Pendavel or Penderel — he could not quite remember. These honest folk received His Majesty, and proceeded at the King's direction forthwith to strip him of his clothes and dress him in his grey cloth breeches, green jerkin, noggin shirt, and the high steeple-crowned hat. They cut the King's hair short to his ears, and 'Believe me,' said my father, 'he looked as scurvy a rogue when they'd done with him, as you'd meet in a day's march.' My father then took his farewell of His Majesty, whom he left in the care of the five loyal Penderel brothers, and went his own way.

He was wounded. His leg, never healed from the first slicing it had got, now suffered a hole from a musketeer's ball that had glanced off his knee-cap to chip it. He still had his horse and rode him westwards, hoping to overtake his brother officers — Darcy, May, Tom Blague and Lord Leviston — who at the King's command had dispersed with their men, His Majesty judging that too great a troop of horse might arouse suspicion. But finding no trace of his friends, my father turned in his tracks and rode through the Forest of Arden.

Dusk came down and the moon swung up. His horse was almost spent, and my father not much better, with the blood he had lost and such an aching in his knee-joint that he could scarce keep his grip on the saddle. Twice he was thrown when his poor beast stumbled at a tree-root. At this second fall he lay in a sweat from his pain, cursing to bring the devil on his shoulders, and thought he had when a brawny fellow, over six feet high with a great horn on his head, rose up beside him.

'Then,' said my father, and I will tell his tale in his words as I recall them, 'then my horse that had been drooping, head down to nuzzle at my knees, showed sign of fret. I soothed him with a word and got upon my feet. Remember, I had no disguise, my dress was that of a king's man; and whether or no this fellow were a Roundhead or Satan's own servant, or Satan himself, 'twas all one for I knew I was damned.

'However, thinking to give the lie to the devil, I bowed him good evening as pleasant as you please. I'll say he was the dirtiest, most sinistrous rascal I ever beheld, with a foul black beard upon him, black greasy elf-locks framing a face like Goliath's, a leathern jerkin that stank to high heaven, and a grease-sodden steeple-crowned hat. That hat I'd mistook for the devil's own horn. I think I must have been running a fever — I shivered and was hot, burned and was cold, and so I had been for twelve hours. We'd had some rain, and I'd lain out in it and slept and caught a rheum with a knife's stab in my side each time I breathed; so maybe I was in that state to see no man in his true colours.

'This one proved to be nothing worse than a Romany gip out for a night's poaching. He had a brace of pheasants slung from his belt and three plump rabbits from his shoulder. He had a great fist upon him too, which he brandished in my face while I stepped back and laughed at him. "Look you! I don't want your plunder. You're welcome to it. These preserves are not mine." He growled out something and produced a pipe and filled it with tobacco, as evil-smelling as himself, and lit it with his tinder-box, his eyes never budging from me; and if ever I were naked in man's sight I was in his. He had taken full count of my riggery, and he knew me for what I was. I had yet to know him.'

Then my father said that although half mazed he had a spark of insight. 'I stood the same height as the King, and while in colouring we differed, we each carried a hugeous nose...' And this bearded apparition, by some amazing chance, coincidence, or what you will, was wearing a similar apparel to that in which my father had last seen His Majesty. He guessed the King's incognito would soon enough leak out, and a hue and cry be raised for him throughout those parts. Meanwhile he could serve two purposes — his master's as well as his own. For 'I was not unmindful of my case which was to get out of my Cavalier's dress and into another for safety. So, "Hearken to me, my man," said I, "if you be not as deaf as you're dumb, what say you to striking a bargain? I like your hat: I like your shirt. I like your suit — it suits me. I am ready, if you are, to effect an exchange. I'll take your gear for mine."

'His villainous eye rolled over me then, while the stink of his pipe almost choked me. I saw his bared yellow fangs in the thicket of his beard, and a voice like a corncrake came out of him. "I'll be taking more than your gear," said he; and he snickered, very evilly, I thought. My hand went to my sword-hilt. He grinned wider. "Your life is worth less than your horse's to me, but I'm not fightin' you for neither. No, sir. You

be one o' the men o' the King, and 'e be our King fer we."
Then he thrust out his hairy paw to wring mine and crack my
knuckles.

'I'll grant you,' said my father, 'I was touched. We made our
exchange in the darkening wood; then I mounted my horse,
and Blackbeard took the rein and led me away to his people.'

One can picture that scene: the gipsy camp in a clearing on
the edge of the forest; the dark threatening faces crowding
near, lit by the ruddy glow of their charcoal fires; the first
suspicion waning under the Romany gibberish growled in an
undertone by my father's fantastical host. They made him
welcome after their fashion, a churlish sullen fashion, surely,
but none the less honest for that — perhaps more so than your
graceful lip service in a mansion. They gave him to eat of roast
pheasant and savoury stew, cooked excellent well by their
chattering women — 'and not a few beauties among them,'
related my father, who had ever an eye for such. And when
they had fed him they put him to rest on a pallet of straw in
one of their painted wagons. They brought to him there an
aged crone with a face as brown and wrinkled as a medlar. She
washed and dressed his wound with healing balm, and bound it
with linen, 'approximately clean,' said my father. And she
offered him drink from a hunting horn, something bitter and
strong and winey. He slept for fifteen hours and woke to find
the sun slanting through the bottle-panes of one crazy little
window in his rickety bedroom on wheels. He had 'a rare stink
of roast pig in his nose, and a damned infernal headache.'

The rough wooden walls of his caravan swayed towards him
and receded, whirled and dipped through the mist before his
eyes. When this cleared from his sight he peered through the
slit of a window and saw he was on the move, bumping along
with a jolting, grinding, scraping sound of wheels and the clip-

clop of a horse's hooves. The road was rough; he saw little of the country, which appeared to be placid meadowland with the gleam of a river winding through and no sign of habitation. Turning again to his dingy chamber, he perceived what he took for a bundle of rags at the foot of his straw couch. A face reared itself out of the shadows and gave him a toothless grin. His haggish nurse of the night before, was, it seemed, still in attendance, to offer him food on a platter, at the stench and sight of which he all but vomited. He asked for drink. The old beldame brought him his horn cup filled to the brim with a draught of pure spring water. Then she began to croon and mutter over him, and stroked his burning temples with a touch, to turn him sleepy. He knew no more until he woke again some several hours later.

His fever had now passed from him, his stomach steadied, and his knee, although still sore, had ceased to throb.

Once more the cavalcade had halted, and under the light of the moon the Romanies were busy with the occupation of their latest site. This appeared to have been pitched in the cup of a desolate heath, ringed round with craggy hills, and shelving forests. The night was full of the scurry and plash of running water that dulled the stir of the gipsy folk, and this, and the rolling vastness of the distance, and the glimpse of rock and tor backed by that strong ridge of highland, suggested to my father that he had been brought to the border of Devon.

After a while his bearded friend returned wearing my father's feathered hat and war-stained finery, the tunic of which had, he noted, been slashed here and there for ease, since this dark gentleman was too broad in the chest and too stout in the arm to carry my father's dress in comfort. From him my father learned that a troop of horse had passed by an hour since, riding westwards. My father was advised to quit the camp and go his way on foot. Nor did his host scruple to tell him that his presence in their midst was a menace to their own security. They had no wish to bring suspicion on themselves and have their camp searched for a Cavalier. If such a one were found harboured among them, they would be shown no quarter. Hitherto, it was explained, they had escaped the law and its abhorrent penalties. They lived their own lives and they made their own laws unto themselves, bowing to no man, not even the King whom they acknowledged. Their welcome to a hunted fugitive would not extend to danger for their community.

They had brought my father, so Goliath told him, to the hinterland of Exmoor. There was a plenty hiding places to be found among these tors and crags. He had best be off without delay, and with thanks for a whole skin. They had done their share to save it.

During his deep sleep — which my father swore had been induced by a drugged potion brewed from poppy seed — his face had been stained brown. This he discovered when his old witch of an attendant returned him his pocket mirror that had been stolen from his suit — a gold-framed jewelled trinket not large enough to see two eyes at once, but large enough for him to see that his long curling hair fadged ill with his barbarous habit. He bade his gipsy host to cut it, which was done with a pair of shears under a pewter basin. 'And if 'twere black,' said my father, 'you would not know me for the King.'

These Romanies, he said, have every kind of medicinal craft at their command: unguents, potions, dyes, herbal drugs and physic to do justice to great Sydenham himself. At this hint from my father the old crone brought a phial and dabbed the contents on his hair with a dirty rag. When they gave him his glass again, his hair was black as pitch. He was for putting his mirror in his pocket — it had been a gift from his mother that he cherished — but like lightning the hag's hand shot after it, and 'the old vixen would have been at my throat if I'd insisted that the property was mine. Much good may it do her! She had been good to me.'

So my father took farewell of his uncouth hosts, grateful enough to them for their aid, but sad to lose his horse, to say nothing of his sword. He had lost more than that, too. His purse that had held ten gold unites had been replaced by one sewn from a rat's skin, containing a silver crown piece. 'But if I lacked cash, I lacked no company,' my father said, 'for every inch of my flesh was a-crawl with lice, and I itched from my head to my toes.'

He walked ten miles through the moonlight, taking his course from the north star to bear south. The night, though fair, was cold and sharp with an early frost, and at the first breath of dawn his sinking stomach told him he had fasted long enough and was content to fast no longer. It had been rough going, lamed as he was, over that wild wasteland, through bog and loam and heather, with no path but the moon's and the track of strayed sheep to guide him. At sunrise he found himself on the edge of a village, not more than a handful of cottages huddled together on the brink of a stream at the mouth of a wide green valley. Here he espied the sign of an inn, and with some misgiving as to the welcome he would receive in his vagabond dress, he presented himself for a meal. That he, however, could produce the wherewithal to pay for it concerned the landlord more than the filth my father brought with him. Having refreshed himself with a hearty breakfast of mutton collops and ale, and taken his bearings — which he discovered would lead him, were he permitted to follow a direct course — to his Aunt Rossiter's house at Colyton, he made off again. He walked another ten miles that day, and seeing no sign of rebel troops, he halted once more at an inn for the night, for which comfort he paid his last penny.

He was now reduced to begging for his bread, to gain little, he said, in charity. It seems he played his part too well. The good cottage women took him for a gipsy — or worse — in his dirt and his steeple-crowned hat. One honest soul damned him to his face for a warlock, and vowed he'd cursed her cow to lose its calf, and raised a buzz in the village that would have got him in the duck-pond but that he took, timely, to his heels.

My father's disguise did, however, on divers occasions serve the King's cause with the success that he had hoped for. The rebels misled by the hat, the height and swart face of its wearer, followed the track of my father, to be led from the track of the King. And how he escaped from pursuit of those bloodhounds was as great a miracle as any in these perilous undertakings. Twice over Exmoor they passed him riding full gallop where he lay hid in a bog. They picked him up at a ramshackle inn at Tiverton where my father had applied for the post of hostler, and despite his rags, was accepted by the landlord in exchange for a week's food and keep. He had not been there a day when the soldiers arrived to menace the scared host with accusations of harbouring 'Charles Stuart' — and extorting confession at the pistol-point that such a one as they described was in the stable yard.

My father, hearing the din and much of its purport, was in two minds whether or no to take his host's horse and bolt for it, but he decided he would not stand a fox's chance as one against so many with better mounts than a spavined old beast, short in the wind and knock-kneed. He therefore made bold to face them and give himself up for the King, affecting to be a simpleton, witless and half dumb. The ruse succeeded beyond his expectations for no sooner was he surrounded, than his captors, seeing foam on his lips and his vacant eye and his gibbering gestures, kicked him to one side with curses for time wasted on the village zany.

He stayed no longer in that place than to see them gone from it before he was away. He missed the road to Colyton and made off upon another, letting his instinct guide him, and the stars. He went bare-headed, carrying his hat, which he now deemed too conspicuous. He would use it only as a cover in the rain.

And how it rained! To wash his hair in streaks and chill him to the bone when he lay out all night, and night after night, eating berries for his food, and stealing garbage from the pigs' troughs, so starved was he.

One lucky meeting stood him in good stead. A miller, pitying his plight, and thinking him a beggar, as in truth he was, brought him to his house and let him sleep in the mill on the flour sacks. The miller's daughter gave him meat and drink — a pretty young maid, my father said, and had he been in better case he would have rendered her more than verbal thanks. However...

He struck Cromwell's troopers once again a few miles beyond Lyme, and again he drew them after him and away from the trail of the King. This time they almost got him. He saved himself by hiding in a stream where he lay prone with his face in the bank and his body in the rushes. They did not think to look for him there and rode their horses past him where my father was stuck in the mud under the osiers, and one of their nags slipped its hoof and all but trod on his neck. That last adventure put him in an ague and brought on a recurrence of his fever. Next day it rained without ceasing, but he had only twelve miles to go...

So, after weeks of peril, he came to his home, and me.

And here in his great bed he lay, his long hands idle on the coverlid, his eyes fever-bright and large in his wasted face. His hair had lengthened and was turning streakily from crow's black to a warm brown as the dye faded.

'Twill soon be long as ever,' I said. I think he scarcely heard me, for his gaze was in the distance watching what I could never see.

Thus had he been for all these months since his return, resting in a pale languor, his once sturdy body stretched beneath the covers, so frail and light that even I in my ignorance of sickness wondered, and wondering, feared.

Although I had seen him so rarely I had always seen him young and gay, and full of laughter; even now with his fever upon him, he still had a laugh on his lips to tease me and call me his 'Imp of Imprudence', and jog Thirza's arm to send her physic flying and demand stronger waters than hers.

There had been a tussle for supremacy between my Great-aunt Rossiter and Thirza, in respect of whose right it should be to nurse him when he first came back to us. My aunt, extending her visit for another month, refused to acknowledge any prior claim to these attentions but her own; while Thirza, seemingly blind and deaf to Aunt Rossiter's presence at the bedside, bustled back and forth between her master's chamber and the still room with every conceivable concoction, plasters for his chest, and delicacies from the kitchen for his appetite. She even went so far as to send into Bridport for leeches. At which my father had his way with such a volley of oaths and plain-speaking to effect that he'd be pox'd before he'd be bled; and let that whoremonger the devil disparage his parts but he would *not* be bled; that Thirza was a bow-legged, hopper-hipped, superannuated punk to think to bleed him, and did she take him for a Jemmy or wish to make him one? And more, to such violent purpose that his outraged aunt stalked from the room and left Thirza in command — to have her way and clap the leeches on him despite his protestations.

Such a hurly-burly as his arrival roused had not been known in these parts since the Conqueror. From Aunt Rossiter to Jack, the half-wit scullion, our small household was astir with an agitation that affected every one of us, not excepting Mr Moon who had us all upon our knees giving thanks for my father's safe deliverance before the master had been home a half-an-hour.

That my father did not participate in these ceremonies nor attend the peroration of our chaplain, delivered in sepulchral tones more suited to an interment than to so joyful an occasion, did, I think, displeasure Mr Moon. I remember how His Reverence gathered us together in the winter parlour: my Aunt Rossiter having graciously rendered the best chair to my father, had taken her seat in the window; we three were at the table, and Mr Moon at the head of it. The men, including my aunt's coachman, who exuded a powerful odour of rum, were lined up by the door. Thirza, taking no more heed of Mr Moon than if he were a spider on the wall, was at my father's feet with a basin of warm water and balm to bathe his wound, which she said was maggoty and festered.

My father had a bottle at his elbow and an empty platter on his knee, and was mopping up the last of the gravy with a hunk of bread. He had not yet changed his clothes, and I saw Mr Moon's nose quiver at the stench of them before he turned to open his address. 'Dearly Beloved, here assembled —'

"Ods blood!' roared my father, clawing at his groin. 'I'd liefer face a regiment of Roundheads than of lice.'

'I'll have your lordship's breeches off in half a minute,' Thirza soothed him. 'Do you stay still, my lord, until you're cleaned.'

Mr Moon lowered his chin, turned up his eyes, hemmed, and began again. 'Dearly Beloved —'

'One moment, Mr Moon,' said our Aunt Rossiter sitting straight as a ramrod in her seat, 'there is nothing, to my mind, to equal witch-hazel for the cleansing of a wound.'

'I beg leave to differ, madam,' replied Thirza, sharp as knives, 'witch-hazel is good for certain inflammations but not for those that are stinking to mortify like this.'

'What then,' my aunt rasped, high-nosed, 'do *you* propose to use?'

'A brew o' my own,' Thirza said, honey-sweet; and closed her mouth on that.

'Hell take me!' exploded my father. 'It burns like the devil and all! Let it be, wench, and get me out of these louse-sodden rags before I am eaten alive.'

'Sure I will, my lord, I promise you,' purred Thirza. 'Have patience. I am just about to bind it.'

'Witch-hazel,' repeated Aunt Rossiter, a danger spark in her eye and an edge to her voice, 'is the best — the *only* application for flesh wounds.'

'Hem!' uttered Mr Moon, chin down and eyes up. 'Dearly —'

'Goddam!' yelled my father, as, with a plunge of his foot he over-set Thirza's basin and sent the contents cascading to bespatter the table, us, Thirza's apron, and, disastrously, Mr Moon.

'A thousand apologies, sir,' grinned my father in the chaplain's discomfited face. 'This good woman's attentions, though well-meant, are confoundedly painful. I am never one to bear my pain in silence. So, sir, if you will forgive these interruptions —' my father drained the last of his bottle before he got out of his chair — 'I will relieve you and your ministrations of my company.'

Mr Moon, wiping the drops from his chin and his collar-band, bowed, looking sickly. I heard a splutter from Robin, and glancing sideways saw he was red as a turkey in the effort to hold himself in. That set me off to sit shaking with the giggles, and Mr Moon's eye upon me to bore holes; and the more he stared the more I shook, swelling to burst myself, until Percy kicked my ankle-bone under the table, which caused hurt enough to sober me before I aimed to kick him in return and missed my target, while he sat pure and pretty as a seraph. Then Thirza, her face one broad smile, mopped up the mess, retrieved her pewter basin, and followed my limping father from the room.

A bad beginning; and one that Mr Moon, I was convinced, would be unlikely to forget or to forgive.

My father was a sick man; no doubt at all of that. The weeks of exposure to which he had been subjected, coupled with lack of nourishment and the inflammation of his wound, had put him in a low recurrent fever. The first excitement of his homecoming lent him a false energy that deceived us all for a week or so — all save Great-aunt Rossiter. Even Thirza with her knowledge of herbal brews did not see what that shrewd eye of our aunt's had seen. When my father had been with us nigh upon a month, Aunt Rossiter without a word to him or anyone of us, departed in her coach and was gone for a day and a night.

My father would have it she was mortally displeased with him for preferring Thirza's attentions to her own. ' For much as I revere our excellent aunt, my Imp,' he said to me with one of his droll looks, 'and am well aware of the sincerity and kindliness that underlies a certain harshness of exterior, I cannot,' my father dropped his voice, 'I cannot abide her beard!'

And what a beard she had, good soul! As well I knew to my cost when she kissed me: as prickly as a hedgehog and formidable rough.

'Our Thirza,' said my father, 'is, I'll own, a bawd, but none the less, she's comely and has the shape and body of a woman — not a pike-staff. Beauty they say is only skin-deep, but ugliness goes to the bottom.'

So here was further trouble: Thirza crowing of her triumph like Chanticleer upon his dung heap after he has trodden his hen-wife, and Aunt Rossiter turning truculent and needle-sharp, and bonier than ever. I tell you, what with Mr Moon as wry as curds, writing *Sloven* (but not *Liar* now my father was come home — just let him dare!) upon my fool's cap, and what with Thirza in a scold when she was not in the still room busy with her phials and her herbs; and what with Robin coming to blows with Percy for gloomily declaring that the King had *not* escaped to France and was like to lose his head as his father had before him: and what with me beside myself for love of my father and pity for his plight, we were all and every one of us, down to our scullion Jack, poor soul, as crazed as he.

We were, therefore, less astonished than relieved when one morning Thirza came to give us news that Mistress Rossiter had been up betimes before the household was astir, to summon her man from his bed in the loft above the stable. Madam, Thirza said, had been found in the kitchen drinking warm ale from a tankard and eating the chicken pasty prepared for my father's breakfast. To Thirza's query as to the meaning of this untoward procedure, and where Mistress Rossiter might be journeying, and on what business bound, 'No business of yours, you demirep,' Madam had offensively replied. Which retort did nothing to sweeten the relations between Thirza and my aunt, who had departed in high choler, if Thirza's recording can be credited.

My father said that he for one did not regret this exodus, since Aunt Rossiter's coachman had drunk himself prone every night on my father's choicest metheglin. It is to be hoped the fellow was restored when his mistress came to rouse him to drive her away. We thought never to see her return: but she did, the next day, with another.

I heard the unmistakable sound of her monstrous old coach bumping and grinding its way along our cart-track, that owing to recent frosts was rendered as hard and slippery as onyx, and how it and its owner, coachman, horses and all, escaped overturning or any worse harm is a wonder, since each held equal parity in decrepitude and age, I do believe. And besides these too-familiar sounds to scrape your teeth and sink your heart, I heard the trot of hooves betokening a rider.

I went to the door. Percy followed. We saw our Aunt Rossiter descend from her conveyance. In her ruff and farthingale, with her stiff peaked bodice, her high hat and her rapier nose, I do declare she looked the very shade of the old Queen in whose reign she was born.

But my eyes were less for my aunt than her companion. My ears had not deceived me; she had not returned alone. While Percy — who when he chose, could play the courtier very gracefully, and did so choose when his aunt was about — hurried to give her his hand and escort her within, I took startled note of a stocky, sturdy gentleman who leisurely dismounted.

My manners were certainly wanting. I should, by every code of courtesy, have summoned one of our men to lead his horse away; instead, I stood agape and staring while he stood, too, holding his mount, unattended. Strangers were rarities in these parts, and this one was a novelty to me. Very trim and point-device did he appear in his sad-coloured habit, his band and cuffs without lace, his plain hat without a feather. His hair, uncurled, but equally uncropped and falling to his shoulders, was of a nondescript shade, light as dust, and framing a round, pinkish face like a porker's.

I darted back to my father, who was sitting in the inglenook playing chess with Robin. 'Aunt Rossiter is here again,' I whispered. 'She has brought with her a gentleman.'

'Ah,' said my father, not moving an eyelid, while Robin, deep in his game, might have been carved from wood for all he heard, 'I thought as much. That would be the Prince of Darkness she's been after.'

'No, Father,' I told him, ''tis a fair man, this one, dressed in grey. He has a pig's face and a pig's snout.'

'The devil takes all manner of shapes,' said my father, with his eyes on the board. 'He is still our common enemy, I'm thinking.'

Nor was he far wrong in that, since this gentleman, as we learned later, had served with the Parliament's army. Yet to give him all justice, and no matter what his politics, he was no enemy to man, but mankind's friend: none other than young Doctor Thomas Sydenham.

And young indeed he was at this time, no more than seven-and-twenty, yet he had already commanded the attention of the medical world. A Dorset man, born at Wynford Eagle, a manor house not fifteen miles distance from our own, he had graduated at Magdalen College, Oxford, taken a Fellowship in physics at All Souls, and done his share of fighting with the Roundheads.

It was bold of my aunt to go after him into the enemy's camp, with the purpose of enlisting his service in the cause of a sick Cavalier. She judged, however, rightly, that no sacrifice is too great for your true physician, who acknowledges no ruling but his own when he is called upon to give his skill, whether it be for friend or foe. And besides all, the war was over, the Royalist party broken, our King in exile, and the Commonwealth established, to reign supreme in governance for near upon ten years. Nor is it the way of an honest man to bear grudge against or gloat upon another's downfall, least of all the way of an honest physician. This one at his worst was that; at his best, let the history of medicine speak for him.

Upon arrival at Wynford Eagle, where Doctor Sydenham resided with his parents, my aunt found him she sought from home. Although on vacation, the doctor, she was informed, had been called to a suspected case of plague in Dorchester.

My aunt, who had that way with her whom none could dare gainsay, then declared her intention of awaiting his return, and, refusing the hospitable advances of Mistress Sydenham, the doctor's mother, she betook herself back to her coach.

There, for some hours and in a downpour of rain, she sat behind her disgruntled coachman, who perched on his seat without cloak or cover, was very soon soaked to his skin. My Aunt Rossiter fared not much better, since her primitive equipage lacked any kind of protection, all parts being open to the elements, save for a rough wooden roof sadly in need of repair. When at length the physician returned, my aunt was almost as wet as her driver. Her spirit, however, remaining undamped, she hailed Doctor Sydenham as he dismounted.

Briefly she gave him to understand the purport of her visit, and exacted from him a promise to attend her nephew the following day. Resolutely refusing the invitation of Mistress

Sydenham to be their guest for the night, my Aunt Rossiter drove on to Maiden Newton, a village some three miles beyond Wynford. There at the inn she lay, vowing she would sooner sleep in a ditch than in the house of a Parliamentarian. This seems to me a quibbling contradiction, since she was nothing loath to make use of the knowledge and skill of one who had fought against the Cause.

Next day she was back at Wynford Eagle to find her man waiting and ready to depart.

Doctor Sydenham, riding at her coach-wheels, was, not unnaturally, interested to know how my aunt had heard tell of his prowess. He was a modest young man, seemingly unaware that his name and fame, even in those early days, had spread beyond the narrow confines of the then-limited medical world. My aunt answered tritely that she too had been born in Dorset, and had watched his career from the cradle; that time was when she and old Mistress Sydenham, his grandmother, had been children together; that his granddam would have turned in her grave to know a descendant of hers had joined arms with the regicide rabble; and that he, unfortunately, being the only man between Dorchester and London who had any more knowledge of medicine than how to treat the pox, she had been left with no other choice but to command his attention to Lord Folliett.

Whereupon Doctor Sydenham assured my aunt he would render what service he could; and thereafter, one takes it, the conversation halted. For the remainder of the drive my aunt was dumb.

Thus came Doctor Sydenham, later known as the 'English Hippocrates', to undertake the treatment of my father; yet not even his knowledge and skill could withhold the onslaught of a hidden enemy as ruthless and pernicious as any to be met in open fight. Having made his first examination of my father's case, Doctor Sydenham ordered him to bed, and, deaf to his patient's objections, proceeded there to bleed him.

More than ever now did Thirza crow. 'Was not I the first to bring him leeches?' she demanded of my aunt, who returned that the method employed by Doctor Sydenham was not to draw the blood by leeches but to cup it of two pints, thus ridding the body of its evil humours.

'Whatever way the blood be drawn,' was Thirza's reply to that, 'who but I, madam, insisted a month back that his lordship should be bled, and who but I took upon myself to bleed him?'

'The physician clearly states,' retorted my Aunt Rossiter, 'that his lordship be cupped and *not* leeched.'

'So, since we split hairs upon it,' answered Thirza, 'where, may one ask, lies one spot o' difference between cupping and leeching, so long as the blood be let?'

This argument might have proceeded *ad infinitum* had not the entrance of Doctor Sydenham, at that moment, put an end to it. My aunt pointing to the door ordered Thirza to the buttery. 'And go you, Prudence, with her. I wish to speak with Doctor Sydenham alone.'

This was all against my inclination, for who in that household had more right to hear the doctor's verdict on my father's case than I? Yet while I hesitated my aunt repeated the commandment: 'Go!' And though indignation swelled my heart I went, on Thirza's heels. Nor did she go willingly. The set of her back, her squared shoulders, proclaimed her own opinion of this high-handedness; and no sooner had the door closed behind us, than 'Quick, my poppet,' Thirza whispered, reprehensibly, 'stick your ear to it and listen. Glean all you can and then repeat to me.'

She flounced off muttering something to effect that she would tear the gizzard out of that curmudgeonly old cockatrice one of these fine days, and that Job's patience would not stand for such vexatious, unwarrantable, contrary interference — no! Not from the Queen of Sheba, much less from a faggot of gristle and bone with its witch's nose in everybody's pie.

I did not need any more prompting from Thirza to put my ear to the keyhole, where I eavesdropped without shame, and with the reminder to my conscience that I was but obeying Thirza's orders.

And this, as near as I remember it, I heard.

'You have now made a full report upon his lordship's case?'

'Yes, madam.'

'Well?' barked my aunt.

'Madam, it is not well, I fear.' I fancied Doctor Sydenham reluctant to go farther, but that my aunt was not disposed to leave him with his knowledge to himself.

'Say what you have to say, sirrah, and don't quibble.'

'Certainly, madam. No. By all means.'

With that hawk's eye glance upon him I could well believe that even a learned physician would find himself a little at a loss.

'His lordship's case,' said Doctor Sydenham, 'is grave.'

My knees turned weak and my hands icy.

'Yes, yes!' rapped out my aunt, 'so much one knows already. But from what disorder is he suffering, and what the actual cause of his condition — if you have found a cause?' Her intonation gave the doubt to that.

'I have found symptoms,' came the answer, guarded.

'Such as?' queried my aunt.

There followed, then, an exposition couched in terms that to my anxious ear might have been in Greek for all I understood of it: yet, those lost words striking some unforgotten note, now echo through the corridors of memory where in some innermost recess they have lain silent till this moment, when in the light of long experience their meaning lies revealed.

'Lord Folliett appears, madam, to be suffering from an ulceration of the lungs which causes a general wasting away of the entire body, and other symptoms peculiar to the nature of the disease which I have no hesitation in declaring to be phthisis, one of the most ancient of all distempers known to medicine, *vide* Hippocrates, Book One of the Epidemics. Fever, accompanied by rigors, constant sweats, sputum small, dense and concocted —'

'Come to your point, man,' my aunt tersely intervened. 'Do you infer that my nephew is in a consumption?'

'That is my inference, madam.'

'Not more than I suspected,' my aunt muttered. 'What do you suppose to be the cause of this condition?'

'In the first place, madam, I would say that Lord Folliett contracted a pleuritis due to long exposure to damp and chill during his — ahem —' The doctor paused. 'During his lordship's courageous evasion of those damned barbarians who hunted him and the Sacred Person of His Majesty from Worcester to the county of Dorset. But,' said my aunt, her voice thick in her throat, 'they were foiled. They have not run their quarry — yet — to earth. The King goes free in Flanders.'

'Undue exposure to the elements, madam, I would say,' pronounced the doctor, clearly, ' has occasioned a suppuration in the cavity of the chest forming an empyema from whose acrid humour is ejected, by a dry recurrent cough, a secretion of pus pointing to an ulcer containing certain tubercles —'

'Cut this puffery,' growled my aunt. 'How can I follow your jargon? Are you certain of your diagnosis?'

'As certain as I can be, madam, from the evidence deduced.'

'Then you must set about to cure him,' said my aunt.

'Madam, the prognosis is as grave as the condition, which is, I fear, incurable.'

'In the name of the Prophet — figs to that!' My aunt, I gathered, was now pacing the room: the boards squeaked to her tread as she followed this ejaculation with another. 'There should be no such word as incurable in medicine!'

'Madam, all physicians through the ages have worked and studied with that one goal in view. But we are not, alas, endowed with more than mortal powers.'

'Why not?' my aunt demanded. 'Such powers of healing as you doctors possess have been bestowed by a benevolent Almighty. Use them — use all the knowledge that lies at your command. You are young but I have reason to believe you gifted. Consult your elder colleagues. Call all and everyone in consultation. Spare no expense. He must — he *shall* be cured. Do you realise what it would mean to our line if —' for an instant my aunt's voice faltered — 'if your prognosis prove to be correct? He has but one heir — a weakling. No breed worth the breeding could spring from his loins. So! Lord Folliett of Wynmonath must be saved to remarry and re-establish the descent. I am a Folliett, sirrah, and proud of it. You young folk of today, and in especial those of your rebel party, have uprooted and reversed the very core of life and living as we older generation understand it. You have no pride of race, no inherent love for this great England and for those who moulded her to what she is — what she *was!*' declared my aunt with bitterness. 'For she is now so crippled, so stained and mauled and so disfigured with corruptible deformities that her face would seem to wear a loathsome mask. One day, young gentleman, that mask, I warrant, will be lifted, and England in the light of her lost glory will shine again as the sun of the world. Pray God I live to see to it!'

A silence, for some seconds, fell. Then: 'Madam, with all my heart I do uphold your sentiments. The recent happenings that have tormented our brave land were sprung from a misguidance on both sides. Yet each and all of us involved are bound by one common tie in mutual service, howsoever that service be mistaken, for England's spiritual grace and her salvation.'

'H'm!' said my aunt, 'as represented by a Commonwealth? By hypocritical fanatics who befoul the name of God and desecrate the churches raised in His Established Faith?'

'As represented, madam, by the souls of the people of England.'

'By regicides. By murder. By black death!'

'From death, madam, we are promised resurrection.'

'As it will come, mark ye, and not, perchance, as those *you* follow do intend it… But we wander from our point. Your politics condemn you, sir, and have no interest for me. You are summoned here upon a worthier cause. See to it. Lord Folliett must have every aid and treatment known to medical science. It speaks well for what I have heard of you, that despite your odious doctrines I retain your service to his lordship. I adjure you to bring every atom of your skill to bear upon his case. You shall be paid your fee in full. If put to it I will sell my husband's house and what your Commonwealth has left us of his land to meet the —'

'Madam,' swiftly, a trifle sharply, came the interruption, 'a physician asks no greater fee than to effect a cure. All that is humanly possible will, I assure you, be —'

At this juncture the door was flung wide by my aunt, the rustling approach of whose petticoats my ears had not observed, so intent were they upon this dialogue. There, stooped to my eavesdropping, was I discovered. I scrambled up and murmured I was searching for a mouse-hole. To which palpable lie my aunt did not demean herself to answer; gazing through me as though I were a pane of glass, she passed on and up the staircase to my father's room.

Doctor Sydenham was about to follow her. I stayed him.

'Sir!'

He halted, and with his face cleared of all expression save astonishment, he stared at me who stared back at him through a smarting mist.

'I ... I listened, sir ... I heard...'

Well might he stare, indeed. I was small for my years and looked smaller in my shame of this guilty confession; that I looked, besides, the veriest urchin, I have no doubt at all. My gown was patched and mended, and so discoloured from rough wear and tear that it more resembled Joseph's coat than its own russet hue. My hair, unconfined by coif or riband, hung in a mat of uncombed curls upon my shoulders. There was possibly dirt on my cheek from the engrimed oaken door where I had glued my ear, and the tears that I could no longer keep in check were brimming over to leave grubby runnels in their traces.

'I heard...' Again I faltered.

'And what did you hear?' enquired Doctor Sydenham. His small greenish eyes overswept me from my disordered head to a hole in my slipper where one of my toes peeped through. I wriggled and glanced all ways at once and back at him to find his eyes a-twinkle.

Now there is that in the look of some men to draw a child or a dog, as a magnet draws a needle: such a man this Doctor Sydenham, for all he lacked presence and was puffy-cheeked, inclined to be too fat, too pink, with nothing of distinction in his person save his honest spirit that transfigured his homely face, as the jewel which the toad in the fable carried in its head did beautify that humblest of God's creatures.

So, encouraged by what I saw in that clear direct gaze, I essayed to be bold with him: 'Sir, more than I could understand, but I did hear you say my father's case is grave. Pray, sir, how grave? Does it mean that he...?' And there I stuck with a stone in my throat and words in my mouth that I durst not speak.

Nor did the doctor immediately reply: then he answered my question with another. 'How old are you, my child, or — how young?'

I made rapid calculation. 'Twelve years and seven months, sir, come next sennight.'

He had that trick of smiling with those little eyes of his while his face remained composed and very serious.

'Did you believe me younger?' I asked, a trifle piqued. ' I know I am small, but I have grown a whole half-inch since I turned twelve, and am now as tall as Percy was a year ago. I do not think if a person be well-meaning, even if that person be pert and a sluggard, and more sinful still than that...' And now I was pleating my petticoat between my fingers while my tongue twisted itself into tangles; yet stop its mumbling I could not, spurred by some obscure desire to stand well in this gentleman's regard, for who could know but what our Mr Moon might not poison him against me? To be found with the imprint of the keyhole on my face was a bad enough indictment. If, therefore, I be punished let me be fairly judged.

' An eavesdropper, sir,' I hurried on, having dared thus far to dare farther, 'and a sloven and damned to everlasting for a liar, yet I do not think, as I began to say, sir, that the age of a person counts so much as goodwill in the sight of the Lord. Do you?'

'I do not,' emphatically responded Doctor Sydenham; all his face now was a-twinkle and not his eyes alone. 'Sin is a matter of degree — and circumstance. To rob a bird's nest, for example, were a greater sin to my mind than any you have named, save the sin of lying.'

I hung my head. ''Twas only white lies, sir; not black ones.'

'Prevarication is a stumbling way to truth,' said Doctor Sydenham. 'And truth's way is the only way of life.'

I nodded, near to tears again. 'As for birds' nests, sir,' I blurted, 'one would never touch a thrush's nest, nor any songster's, nor a robin's, but one might take a hawk's eggs to hatch them in the mews, and not be thought the worst kind of thief?'

'One might,' said Doctor Sydenham, twinkling more than ever. 'I have done the same myself a score of times.'

I brightened.

'As for the first point in your argument,' continued Doctor Sydenham, as if he were addressing an assembly of his fellows, instead of only me, 'youth is considered by some to be the most enviable of life's possessions.'

'Is it?' I pondered on this; and determined to quote it as a weapon of defence in my next clash of arms with the boys, both of whom were disposed to treat me as a grossly inferior being, as much for my tender years as my tenderer sex. 'In which case, sir,' said I, having arrived at this conclusion, 'I am not too young to hear the truth about my father.' And I returned him as straight a look as his.

'If we who seek the truth could always find it, there would be no sickness or no sorrow here on earth. But how can I answer you who have overheard so much — and yet so little? Your father is ill and I am here to cure him, or at least to render him every advice and aid that lies within my power. You, in your turn, Mistress —' he paused and glanced at me enquiringly.

'Prudence, sir.'

He bowed to that as gallant as though I were a lady. 'You, Mistress Prudence, can aid me?'

'You!' I squeezed my hands together. 'How can ... oh, I will indeed! But can I?'

'Certainly you can. By offering your father a daily draught of good cheer diluted in equal parts with patience, and of courage — an overdose. For I think you have courage enough and to spare, Mistress Prudence, to meet and carry the weight of whatsoever burden lies ahead of you and him you love. Such is my prescription, which if carefully followed will prove more beneficial than any of my drugs. I look to you for that much help. I know you will not fail me.'

'Oh, sir!' I tried to speak but no words could pass the ache in my throat; and from his touch on my heaving shoulder, from the pity in his face, I turned away, and fled to my chamber under the eaves. There on my bed I fought and struggled with this first blinding shock of revelation.

I will have courage, I vowed within myself, *God helping me, I will!*

Spring came early that year; a joyous gay unfolding surcharged with flower scents and a rare wealth of blossom, following so swiftly on the wings of winter, one could scarce believe the foam and fall of petal in our orchard was not a shroud of snow upon the green.

In the first week of May, my Great-aunt Rossiter, whose visits to us since my father's illness had been more frequent, returned again, and this time with her husband. The meekest and the mildest of his sex, short of stature, rosy and rotund was he, and so completely overshadowed by his partner, that he seemed to be enveloped in apologetic fog. He spoke but seldom and almost never in the presence of his wife unless called upon by her to do so in support of her argumentations, when he would invariably voice a stammering echo of her words with his head a little on one side and looking like a pouter-chested sparrow.

Yet between this timid gentleman and myself existed a curious affinity, tenuous and unsubstantial but none the less persistent. Nor, I think, to none but me did Uncle Rossiter divulge such mind as he possessed and which had not been devoured by his lady.

My great-aunt and uncle, then, were staying with us when my father, whose health for some weeks past had shown marked signs of improvement, called to a confabulation these remnants of his family, together with his heir and kinsman, Percy, and his chaplain, Mr Moon.

This meeting, from which Robin and I were excluded, was held in the winter parlour, my father having been advised by Doctor Sydenham to leave his bed and take advantage of the sun and the glad spring weather. How I rejoiced to see my father now sufficiently recovered to resume his normal life, dressed again in his gay clothes — though to be sure they hung upon him as upon a broom-pole, so thin had he become — and taking an interest in his starved herds, his ravaged lands. Seated once more at the head of his table he would make plans for another winter when he would have this field ploughed for barley, and that for rye, and build a new mill in place of the old one demolished by the Roundheads, on the mill-stream which runs through Wynmon Abbas — and he would be a farmer. 'For what better life, my lads, I ask, can man desire?'

'None better indeed, my lord,' answered Robin, 'I am with you there. When shall we start to sow?' While Percy sat and smiled, and Mr Moon gloomily said grace.

I was thinking how my father had spoken of farming his wasted land again, when I walked in the orchard with Robin on the day which proved for me so fatally significant: the day my father called that meeting in the parlour.

'He must be better of his illness, Rob,' I said, 'to be already planning for the future. It is an omen of good ... I am happy!' I was, with the sun so bright, the blossom so full, the grass a shouting green, criss-crossed with a pattern of leaves in a game of dappled shadow-play, and all the birds returned from foreign parts singing very sweet and wild. My heart was singing too — a song of thankfulness.

'Even a great physician like Doctor Sydenham might sometimes be mistaken. My father is himself again, I am sure of it,' said I; and when Robin made me no reply, but held his lips pursed in a whistle, and his eyes screwed up in the sun, and sauntered on as though he had not heard, I nipped his arm and asked him, sharp, 'Are *you* not sure of it?'

'I am not a physician,' returned Robin in that lazy absent way of his, as though half his thoughts were on the march ahead, and the other half lagging behind him: and he pursed his lips again to sound his tuneless tune, and stooped to watch an ant-hill in the grass. 'Fantastical,' he murmured.

'What is?' I demanded.

'The ways of ants. Come you here.' He pulled me by the hand. 'Now watch. You see this fellow?' He pointed to a struggling atom that was bearing along with it an infinitesimal load, the merest fraction of a straw, yet twice its size. 'See how he labours with what to him is heavier than the Stone of Sisyphus. But he will not give up. He is bound on some important mission which he is pledged to fulfil, and nothing will hinder him from his purpose.'

'And if you were to take his load from him,' I ventured, 'what then would he do?'

'We will see.' Robin stooped lower, and very gently removed the tiny burden to place it some inches behind its bearer.

'Cruel!' I muttered.

'Wait,' he said, 'and watch... Now see him turn. He is bewildered. Some mighty malevolent giant has bereft him of, and apparently destroyed, his immediate life's work. Very well! Does he moan or wail? Does he wring his hands?'

'Stupid! He has no hands.'

'Does he wring his legs, then? Does he despair? Does he call upon his comrades to condole with and witness his discomfiture? Does he dramatise his loss and make great noise of it and ask for pity? No, for if he did there is not one of this industrious community would listen. Each is concerned with his own business, and cares nought for any other's.'

'I call that selfish,' I declared.

'Egotistical, perhaps,' said Robin. 'There is a vast difference between love of self and love of Ego.'

'But how,' I argued, 'can an ant possess an ego? *Ego* means "I" in Latin, and an ant is not a person.'

'Are you so sure of that?' Robin was kneeling now beside the ant-heap to watch his little victim. A sunbeam caught his hair and made a glory of it. Such hair he had! Which many a court lady might have been inclined to envy, and to wish, as I did, that my hair, too, could catch the light and blaze as full of fire as our copper warming-pan when the red coals are in it: a more seemly shade of colour for a girl than for a boy, although I could but own there was nothing of the girl in Robin. He had outgrown Percy by a head in this last year, and broadened, too, beyond his shabby suit which I observed was splitting at the seams, and had shortened that his freckled wrists were a good three inches longer than his cuff-bands. The seat of his breeches was threadbare where it was not patched, his leathern jerkin sadly frayed, his shirt in tatters. Well! I sighed, forgetting insects and their habits in a sudden longing for I knew not what. Fine clothes, maybe; a yellow satin petticoat, a kerchief of silver gauze, a cherry-red plume for my hat, and a prince to come and marry me and call me his lovely dear. But who, and least of all a prince, would woo a scrubby pig-widgeon like myself whose face was always dirty?

Surreptitiously I hitched up the hem of my dress and spat on it and rubbed my cheeks while Robin went on talking. And I'll wager that neither of us was aware, any more than the ants, of strong forces at work between us: he less than I, in whom blind instinct prompted this first unconscious overture to the eternal cause...

'My particular ant,' continued Robin, 'is, I think, very much of a person. Look how carefully he retraces his steps, going back the way he has come to recover his burden, and if not to find another, even heavier, to carry. He is in two minds now whether or no he will take up this little round globule which I believe is an ant's egg, and which I'll dare say weighs to him the equal of a ton to me. Yes! He will ... See! He attacks it. He rolls it forwards with his head — his head, mark you! — bent forward to the task like a battering ram's. There's a lesson to be learned in how to tackle life. A brave knight this! His motto should be *Nil Desperandum*.'

'Your sermonising is all very fine,' said I, 'but it does not compensate this poor ant for the property he has lost and which you have seized as the Roundheads seized ours. You are no better than a whoreson Oliver yourself to do such wrong to a little weak insect.'

'I have not seized his property,' said Robin, 'I have merely roused in him the urge to greater effort by placing difficulties in his path. If all achievement were easy to come by there would be nothing to gain in success.'

'Lord bless us, you talk as smug as our Reverend Maw-worm!' was my retort to this. 'And I still do not know why you bring me to ants when I was speaking of my father — God save him!'

'Amen to that,' returned Robin, but he said it absently, his attention far from me or my preoccupations. And so I left him, and betook myself to Thirza for more comfort.

I found her in the kitchen, trussing a capon. Another was already on the spit, where Jack, our scullion, tended it, and chattered to himself in his poor foolish way, while the flow of good rich fat dropped into the shallow tray beneath. 'See how it runs — like milk from the breast — the beautiful fat. A prime tasty fat it be, I'll warrant! I'll lick the dregs of it, I will an' all. Yes, an' wipe the pan clean with my tongue...'

'That you will not!' Thirza rounded on him, shrill. 'Keep your filthy tongue to yourself, you stinking addlepate, and mind that bird don't brown too fast or I'll have your ears off with my carving knife... Ho! So now *you've* come —' and Thirza flashed her eyes very tigerish on me — 'to worrit the soul out of a body with guests in the house making work for twenty hands to do and only one pair of 'em —' she flung wide her arms — 'to do it.'

Her face was red, her hair in wisps escaping from her coif, as was its wont if she were put about. She had a trick of shoving her cap to the back of her head when in a perturbation, and I noted now that it was halfway to her neck. On her cheek I observed a mark, not unfamiliar to me, a circular smear of dust with a trace of oak grain in it. I nodded to myself and smiled at her.

'Thirza, have you been at the parlour keyhole?'

'May I be slit if ever I did hear the like of this one,' stated Thirza, her cheek a deeper red, and her eye a fury, 'it never was the babe I suckled — no! I'll be bound that old witch has been up to ill-mischief to bring us a changeling in the image of my dear. So denaturalised and sagittary does it grow that I would never know it for my own!'

'So, you *have* heard something, Thirza.' I went to her and put my arms around her ample waist to hug and coax: 'Come, tell me. You have learned what all the talk's about in there, and I know nothing. 'Twas you taught me to listen —'

'So did I! May the devil burn you for a lying, froward, falsifying Judas if I ever in this world did so demean myself!'

'No, Thirza, then you did not. Only say —'

'And what in heaven — or hell — *is* there to say, my precious heart?' cried Thirza, catching me close to squeeze me breathless. 'What should *I* know that my good lord withholds from his own child?'

'Last night I saw a white owl,' mumbled Jack, 'that means a death for sure, and yester morn came a magpie to my window... *One for sorrow...*'

'Quiet!' roared Thirza, releasing me to snatch a knife and lunge at him. 'Stop your croaking, dizzard, or you'll have a taste of this to silence you for ever!'

Accustomed though I was to Thirza's tantrums, I could not but feel that this irascibility was due to more than extra work entailed by the reappearance in our household of Aunt Rossiter and her mild-mannered husband, while poor Jack, threatened thus, sat down on his heels, dropped his jaw, and dribbled into tears.

'Never heed her, Jack,' I murmured. 'You shall have a bright new penny. Good boy, Jack. Don't cry!'

He rolled his fish-eyes at me, muttering, 'Mum — mum — mistress my lady... You shall walk in slippers o' gold and the king o' the fairies shall carry you...'

He was the oddest creature with his shaggy elf-locks and pointed ears sticking up like a pixie's either side his wizened face: for although I called him boy he was not one. None of us knew his age. He had been at Folly's End since ever I remembered, and Thirza said he was old as the hills. Sometimes I felt afraid of him, yet there was nothing to fear from that poor twisted mind which had nought of evil in it and much good; he being full of fantasies of fairies, elves, and the wild woodland things that came to his whistle like friends. He could tell you the name of a bird by its song, and was a skilled hand with the beasts on the farm, but he went in mortal terror of our falcons.

'Let him be, let him be!' cried Thirza. 'I'd drown him myself for two ha'pence, which is a deal more than he is worth.' And with a break in her voice, she added, 'That I should live to see this day of misery!' With which, sitting down on a stool, she caught up her apron, flung it over her head, and rocked herself to and fro, bewailing, 'Oh, oh! Such monstrous sacrifice! The lamb to the slaughter indeed. Woe, woe is me! And woe to you, my darling ... oh!' and so forth.

Now taking in consideration Thirza's love of the dramatic, this display of grief did not at once alarm me. It might have been occasioned by some minor disturbance in the culinary arrangements, or the failure of the poultry-man to produce two ganders in lieu of the capons now preparing for our dinner; or by the refusal of my father to permit Thirza to escort me into Dorchester to buy me a new gown, for which ever since he had left his bed she had been pestering him, to be told that none but he should choose me a gown, when, at such time as his coffers were replenished he would buy me such an one as had not been seen in Wynmonath since the old Queen visited the abbey. So while Thirza rocked and wailed, I helped myself to a slice of fresh-baked cake with a good sugar coating upon it, and with my mouth full, enquired, 'Say — what *is* all this to-do?'

'Oh, me!' moaned Thirza. 'That listeners never hear good of themselves, 'tis true, but I did not think to hear bad of another, and that one my own sweet poppet!' Then, whisking her apron off her head, she sprang to her feet and shouted, 'Keep your mischievous fingers off my sugar cake, you little glutton! Did I not bake it ready for his lordship's dinner, him having ordered it particular? "A sugar-icing cake, Thirza, stuffed with almond cream, would be an appetising change from syllabubs and egg-slops..." Alackaday! That my lord should be the one to plunge a dagger in the heart of his ewe lamb!'

'Of what,' I asked, impatient, 'are you speaking? Of this smallest possible piece of cake I've eaten or —'

'Small?' snorted Thirza, interrupting. 'If you call that small then your stomach's bigger than your body, and now you've ruined the sight of it to put before his lordship, picking and digging at it with your grimy paws.'

'If they be grimy more shame to you, then!' I retorted. 'You are my nurse and you should tend me better.'

Thirza groaned. 'D'ye hear it?' She apostrophised the rafters. 'D'ye hear it turn upon the hand that fed it and the breast that gave it suck? — if indeed 'twere this same infant that I reared and not a hobgoblin in human shape. Your nurse, am I? You should be shamed to ask for nursing now — at an age when your womanhood would be upon you were you natural, which you're not. Well, well I The time will be, I dare swear, when it'll go squawking and crying for its Thirza to come soothe it.'

'Ah!' Light dawned upon me, and with it the darkness of death. 'I see! I see what your trouble is. Aunt Rossiter and Mr Moon have worked upon my father to have you sent away.'

'Me? Away?' Thirza's face was now so red she looked to have an apoplexy. 'Ho! If that were all — indeed! Just let them try. They would easier move mountains. Me? Ha! Though I'll warrant there be some and not the least of them His Reverence — that griffin — which would give what hairs are left on its slimy head to have me the other side of nowhere. Not but what your Great-aunt Madam put her foot down, I will say, *and* His Reverence, too, against his lordship's abnormalous decree. The first time in all my dealings with my lord that I have contraried his wisdom. Methinks his ailments have affected his good judgment, nor would I have believed — no, not though the angel of the Lord Himself announced it — had I not heard what I *did* hear, namely and to boot —' And Thirza paused.

'Oh, what?' cried I, now greatly agitated; and while relieved to know my fears of losing Thirza were not yet to be realised, I could no longer doubt but that an event of some grave import had been decided in which I was involved.

'Hear then as much of it as I dare give you!' exclaimed Thirza. 'Your marriage, this day, my dear, has been arranged.'

I heard, and yet I did not hear: my ears were numb before reverberation came with a crash as if a star had fallen; then: 'I?... My marriage?... *Me*?' I squeaked, falsetto. 'Am I to be married?'

'Mumble-mumble... White owls and a magpie for sorrow,' slobbered Jack.

'Shut your mouth!' I screamed at him, my mind a-jangle, and in a fair way to be as mazed as his at Thirza's tidings. 'But how, Thirza? To whom? There's no one here to marry. *Who* am I to marry?'

'The white owl ... it cried and sighed with a mortal great sobbing,' droned Jack. 'But I dreamed of dogs for friendship.'

'For mercy's sake!' I stamped at him. 'Stop blabbering. Thirza, is this true?'

'Am I a liar?' demanded Thirza. 'Go to your father, then. Ask him — and ask your future bridegroom. Go to the devil, for his hand I see in this. And God send you do not breed. Cousins should not mate — 'tis nature's warning. That his lordship who himself did wed his cousin once removed should run my poppet to that risk to keep a roof above its head, and at its young age, too, before 'tis flowered. Eh, dear! The pity of it ... oh!' And Thirza was back again at her bemoanings. 'I'd sooner see you beggared than the wife of such a one.'

'But *who*?' I repeated, beside myself with suspense and bewilderment. 'What one, Thirza? What cousin have I...?' My words stayed on my lips. 'I have only one cousin,' I faltered, 'and he...' Then in a flash I was illumined. 'Why,' I shrieked between splutters of excited, incredulous laughter, ''tis Percy, then, whom I'm to marry! Percy... my cousin! So I'm to be married to *him*!'

And thrusting aside Thirza's hand that would have held me, I ran out of the kitchen like one crazed and with one thought only uppermost: That I, Prudence Folliett, was chosen for marriage, no matter how, or by whom. A wife, me! A matron. No longer the ragged, betattered, betousled scapegoat of a dunce in a fool's cap, mute receiver of Mr Moon's scorn… but *persona grata*. A lady. A wife … in my mother's best lavender gown.

CHAPTER FOUR

Thus, at the age of thirteen, was I plighted to my kinsman, Piers Folliett. That my father had been urged to this decision from no other motive than to secure me the birthright of which I would have been deprived by his decease, I do not doubt. The only habitable house now owned by my father would, according to the laws of entail, revert to his heir. His tenants, from whose leased holdings much of the Folliett wealth had formerly been drawn, were scattered far and wide. Some had met their death in the Royalist cause, some had been imprisoned, to languish in foetid dens, chained, and perchance tortured, to their end. Those that escaped death and did return, found their homes a shambles, their wives and families reduced to beggary, their cattle and possessions stolen.

Nor had my father the wherewithal to aid them, so devastated was his land, so crippled he in health and substance, drained of all material resources, and with nought but the roof of a ramshackle farmhouse and a few barren acres to call his own; yet better placed than his young sovereign king, who had fled, an exile, to France, and lived on such poor charity as could be smuggled to him by his stripped following in England.

In that year 1652 events were moving with a rapidity and violence precedented only by the war itself. The establishment of a Commonwealth was but a first step on the way to the supreme dictatorship of him who had been the first to resist and avenge by the foul crime of regicide, the 'violation of the privilege of Parliament', so-called by the enemies of Charles I.

Now Cromwell, holding reins of governance with a victorious army at his back, was to prove himself a greater despot than he, who condemned as a tyrant, had laid his gentle, misguided head on the block to live in death, a martyr.

If Worcester was an end, it was also a beginning: the end of civil strife, the beginning of an era still more deadly and destructive.

It had been a war of political and religious ideals, of sieges and blockades, repeated again and again around the strongholds of a castle, the walls of country homes, in fair fields and orchards, in meadowland, on moor; it had struck at the very heart of every home, enflamed by an impassioned fervour on both sides: for the King; for the determined abolition of exceptional powers conferred upon sovereignty since the days of the Tudors; for God, or for the right of man to rule, according to his principles, in God's image. Who can select from the accumulation of dissents, of hatred and fanatical intolerance, the ultimate first cause of that most bitter contest? We, of a younger generation, saw only the result. Old quarrels resurrected between the Parliament and army; a pack of wolves that rounded on each other, Cromwell and his Ironsides protesting against Government's control; Parliament demanding the supremacy of rulership as represented only by its satellites, not by the nation as a whole. For as such, we as a nation had ceased to exist. The last remnant of constitutional life had fallen with a monarch's head. We stood, a kingdom brought to desolation: a broken house, divided.

In this aftermath of turmoil, in the ruins of life as my father had known and lived it, stricken with a malady — 'incurable' — and with his responsibility to me for ever pressing on him, weightier for the certainty that he must leave me homeless, pauperised and unprotected, one can understand how, apprehensive for his little daughter's future, he sought the only means that lay within his power to ensure it. Whether or no he judged rightly in thus disposing of me to his heir, and at so young an age, I do not question. It was my father's will: enough for me.

That he encountered opposition from his aunt and Mr Moon, I am convinced. But my father was of that cast which once decided on a course of action will not be deterred by any argument, nor had those that queried his decision any claim to do so. He and he only could decide my fate, since Percy was a minor and my father his sole guardian.

My aunt, having emphatically expressed her disapproval of my father's choice of a mate for me, and receiving no quarter from him, gathered together her bandboxes, her bags, her coach and her husband, and left Folly's End in a dudgeon.

The evening before she departed she sent for me to her chamber. Seated in a high-backed chair, her faded purple gown in silken folds about her, and her chin in her ruff, she received me regally. My Great-uncle Rossiter, who had effaced himself as far as possible from this interview, stood by the bedpost, his head a little on one side, and looking like a meditative sparrow in his sober suit of brown. A frail prop indeed, yet ready and waiting to be called upon in support of his dominant lady should need arise.

Hands folded on her stomacher, her eyes ensnaring mine with a stony, fixed regard, my aunt proceeded to inform me how she had endeavoured to dissuade my father from his 'unnatural' — as she called it — 'proposition'. She told me too how, years before, she had intervened at the proposed marriage of my father to Lady Peverill, Robin's mother, and how God's hand did at that time prevail against so dire a calamity. 'And though his choice of a husband for you,' my aunt said, 'is less preposterous than that choice of a wife for himself, since Lady Peverill was a Papist and Piers Folliett, thankfully, is not, yet he is your cousin, twice removed, and a pauper: and moreover you have for seven years dwelled in this house together as sister and brother, so that such a union savours to my mind of incest, and is a sin against nature and God... Am I not justified in my judgment, Mr Rossiter? Give an ear and stop your fidgeting. Do you agree that this marriage proposed on the part of nephew Folliett between these two children is incestuous — or not?'

My uncle — who during this address had been indeterminedly tracing with his forefinger the carven pattern of fruit and flowers on the bedpost — thus commanded to attention, jerked his head a little more to one side, smiled nervously at me, cleared his throat and opened his lips to stammer, 'In — in so far as the — the relationship is not in actuality that of a — of a brother and a sister —'

'Foh!' exclaimed my aunt in great disgust.

'I was about to — to suggest, my love,' deprecatingly pursued her spouse, 'since that our g-great-niece Prudence is not in — in actuality the — the sister of our — of your — great-nephew Piers, your particular objection to the — the m-marriage cannot in actuality be — ahem —'

'If that is your only comment, keep your mouth shut,' his wife adjured him.

'I was about to say,' my uncle with unwonted temerity continued, 'that there is nothing —' his glance fluttered apologetically from his lady's uncompromising countenance to mine — 'nothing so bad but it might not be worse — eh, Prudence, my dear? Marriage is the aim and — and p-purpose—' here he nodded and smiled, very encouragingly at me, who, at pains to follow his argument in conjunction with a word I had seen only in the Bible and which conveyed no meaning whatsoever, was put in some perplexity — 'and purpose,' repeated Uncle Rossiter, his greying head more than ever on one side — 'of every — ahem — of every well-deserving little maid.'

'Ass!' was my aunt's rejoinder to this non-committal summary. 'So! We will leave your uncle out of the discussion, since he dares to contradict me.'

'I did not, my love, in actuality,' began my uncle, 'contradict—'

'Am I or am I not to understand,' my aunt demanded, 'that you are in favour of this unseemly, deplorable, and entirely impecunious match nephew Folliett desires for his daughter?'

'It is not for me to — to dispute or to — to depose,' my uncle ventured.

'Very well, then,' said my aunt, 'hold your peace. Prudence, come here.' She held out her long, brittle, white hand, on the forefinger of which was a handsome ruby ring presented to my great-grandmother by King Henry VIII — or so I always had been given to understand.

I stepped forward and my aunt took and clasped my hand in hers that felt as dry to the touch as the skin of a lizard. Gazing searchingly into my face, 'Although you know it not, my child,' Aunt Rossiter said in her deep rasping voice, 'you have the makings of a beauty. While you lack the finest feature of the Follietts — our Norman nose, unmistakable sign of intelligence — you have eyes, hair and a good enough complexion to bring you better fortune than to wed with one who can add nothing to the ancient name that you already bear. Your father is and always was an impetuous, hot-headed fool. And while you inherit his handsome looks, I fear you inherit his folly.'

At that I raised my chin and stared her full in her stone-bright eye and told her, clear, 'Whatever be my father's will, madam, that must I obey.'

I felt rather than saw my uncle nod approval, and though my aunt's stern gaze upon me never faltered, I fancied she was not displeased with this reply.

'Obedience is a virtue only when prompted by reason, my child; but this I wish to say in the presence of a witness —' and perfunctorily Aunt Rossiter pointed her nose in her husband's direction — 'that if at any time, before it be too late, you should decide, young though you are, to alter your decision and refuse to act upon your father's ill-advised decree, which disposes of your person, soul and body, to Piers Folliett, my house — which though in point of fact your uncle's house — is now and ever will be, while I live, at your disposal. If it in its turn were not the entailed property of your uncle's next of male kin, that same house and all within it would be yours hereafter. Husband, do you bear me out in this?'

'With all my heart!' responded Uncle Rossiter, more fervently than I had ever heard him speak.

'So now you know.' My aunt released my hand to lay hers upon my head. 'And may God be with you, Prudence Folliett, in all your undertakings. You have in me a friend and kinswoman of your blood — in your Great-uncle Rossiter a more material support. I will see to it, that, in the event of my decease, which in nature's course and seniority of years should take place before his —'

'God forbid,' interpolated Uncle Rossiter, somewhat less fervently than he had previously spoken.

'— before his own,' my aunt dispassionately continued, 'and should you at such time remain unmarried, you will be provided with an adequate dependency.' My aunt paused to add grimly, 'Always presuming that Oliver Cromwell has not by then deprived us of all right to an existence beyond that of the beasts of the field. So! I have done my part, have delivered myself of my opinions, and have no more to say or to do with this most lamentable affair. Tomorrow I leave this house, never, I hope, to return to it. Niece, you may kiss me.'

I offered my cheek to be pricked. I curtsied to my aunt, and to my Uncle Rossiter, who smiled and nodded, and astonishingly, if my sight did not deceive, lowered his left eyelid — the one farthest from his wife — in a conspiratorial, and almost roguish, wink.

Which display of untoward audacity caused me greatly to fear that long endurance of marital subjection had produced in that meekest, most mild of men, some form of distressing derangement.

Spring blossomed into summer, and the disturbance in our household occasioned by my betrothal to Piers Folliett came to be accepted by our Mr Moon as one accepts a climate; that is to say, since no outcry against the elements can one whit alter or determine the course of the winds or stay the storm or the tides, or the sun's journey from its rising to its setting, so neither could His Reverence wean my father from his purpose.

This being so, and all disputes, expostulations and embranglements proving of no avail with his patron, our chaplain turned his dialectics upon Percy, but found in him a neophyte of flimsiest adherence; one who could, in fact, support his own and his tutor's opinions for no longer than it takes a dandelion clock to tell the time of day. Indeed, so far as Percy did attempt to voice his views upon the subject in which he was, undoubtedly, the chief person concerned, he expressed himself agreeable to my father's choice of me, his cousin, as a bride.

True, he had been offered no alternative; moreover my father lacked the power to disinherit his young heir, even had Percy made bold to refuse me, although such measure of defiance was, I am convinced, never contemplated by my cousin. He, despite his affectations, vacillations, and much else of superficial liabilities, was possessed of a strong asset inherent in the Follietts — loyalty: or as our motto gives it, *Fidelitas in domino*. With the one exception of our renegade, Percy's father, that motto through the ages has been upheld.

How far Percy's loyalty extended beyond his family pride, one can, however, only judge by subsequent events, which — viewed in the unbiased light of retrospect — did, I think, arise less from the will to injure those he loved than from a cankerous grudge against his manhood's deprivation. But however that may be, of this much I am certain: Percy held a staunch affection for my father. Moreover, he was of an age to realise that, impoverished though our holding of Wynmonath had become, he — as the future representative of all we once had been — must, in duty bound, marry and produce an heir to his name. And since he, Piers Folliett, had been bereft of all near kin save my father, and was unacquainted with any young gentlewoman of his generation other than myself — and since, beyond all reasoning, my father as his guardian had the right to dispose of his heir in marriage while that said heir remained a minor — what other course had he but to accept?

That he did so with ill grace, I well remember; and that he and I together suffered no little ridicule from Robin and were unmercifully quizzed for a pair of love-birds, and teased and scoffed beyond endurance, I remember too. I fancy I returned such mockery with interest, and with plaints and pleas to my betrothed to show himself a gallant to his lady. Failing satisfactory response from him — who, most unloverlike, took sides with Robin to discomfit me, calling all heaven to witness that he, i'faith, was cruelly cursed and must have greatly sinned to be for ever coupled with this waspish, unsavoury, tinder-box of a termagant Prue — I fell upon my sweetheart to claw his face and leave my mark upon it.

'So, if I be waspish you can taste my sting! And if you think that I desire *you* as husband you are woefully mistook. If I was cast upon a desert isle,' I repudiated loudly, 'with only you for company, I vow I'd sooner couple with a purple-nosed baboon than a finical, simpering jackanapes puppy decked out like a—'

'Robin!' cried Percy, interrupting my flow of abuse to seize my hand and crush it within his. 'Do you pity me? Is this a wife for any man, think you?'

'Man, do you name yourself? Monkey!' I shrieked. 'Let go my hand, or I'll bite yours!' I made attempt to do it.

'Sweet soul,' murmured Percy unmoved, while Robin, greatly entertained, joined his chuckles to my yells. 'Harken to her, Robin, how she utters *such dulcet and harmonious breath — that the rude sea — grows civil at her tone — and certain — stars — shoot madly from their spheres — to hear —*'

'Let be! Let be!' I was near weeping now, from pain, for betwixt each pause in this misquotation, Percy had bestowed upon my fingers a mighty hurtful squeeze. 'Do you think to win me by slow torture? You are like Nero of old — a torturer!' I kicked his shins. 'A beast in human shape — no! Not human, neither, for I have ne'er set eyes upon so mincing, ladyish and dainty a rare morsel that durst call itself... *A-ah*! S'death! Would you turn the screw upon me?' I shrieked again as his grip tightened. It was wonderful what iron strength lay in that delicate thin hand of his. 'Ruffian!' I sobbed. 'You Noll-poll bantam-cock! May you burn for this — I'll brand you!' And inexcusably I ducked my head, to fasten my teeth in the back of his hand.

'Damnation!' Percy flung me from him, snatching the offended member to his mouth. 'You have fetched blood, you harpy! Rob, an you love me, do you take this female gorilla, this boggart, this noisome wild-cat — and strangle it — or marry it — for I will not. No! Though I be drawn with it to the altar on a hurdle!'

Was ever woman in such fashion wooed? But I was not yet a woman; scarce grown beyond a child, and late in growing, too.

Such scenes as these were frequent, and save that they now were prompted by more personal attack, differed in no other way from those former tussles to which we three were long inured.

Throughout that summer, my life, unchanged by this first surprise of circumstance, resumed its normal course along youth's leisured, sweetly nonchalant highway: for to me, glancing back across the distance, I see how Time goes halting for the young, how that the days, the hours stretch farther; how that a sennight seems as seven months, a month as seven years, and a year eternity to impatient, restless, questing, eager youth: yet how untenable its passing, how irretrievable its loss. Strange that in youth's impulsive race and hurry, only Time stands still. But, at the declining crossroads on life's journey, Time's pace quickens and takes wings to turn the flight of years to months, to speed the clock from dawn until sundown when all life's span is but a yesterday, and death is a tomorrow...

To me those summer months of my betrothal were set at snail's speed. Handfasted to Percy I accepted him as he — and Mr Moon — accepted me, upon compulsion. Even Thirza thought better than to offer more than a back-handed resistance to my father's resolution. Obstinate, his aunt had called him, yet I would sooner say tenacious, and unyielding to any principles or dogma but his own, if he believed his way the one and only right way. And in that, throughout my life have I followed him.

Towards the end of August the marked improvement in my father's health showed signs of waning. His cough recurred, dry, incessant, worse at night, according to Thirza's report. She, good creature, would bring her straw pallet and place it outside the door of my father's bedroom, that she might be within call should he need her.

'Yes, he is ailing,' she replied to my anxious query, 'but you've no cause to fash yourself. That Doctor Sydenham may be full of learning and wise saws, but my potions ease the tightness of the chest to bring the pus from it better than all the doctor's physic. Keep a brave heart, my lollipop, and you'll go hawking with his lordship in October, never fear.'

But I did fear, and with unchildlike perception watched from day to day the very shrinking of his flesh from off his bones; yet he still laughed, and cracked quips with the boys, and enjoyed his flagon, sitting at the head of our long table, and holding forth against our Mr Moon in argument. For he did love to rile that worthy on the subject of ecclesiastical dissent, which at that time conveyed to me no meaning, and I confess, has never yet entirely explained itself. This, though, I do believe: so that we have ears to hear the Word of God, howsoever that Word be given, then what matters where or how we worship Him if He be understood? This may be heretical and had I voiced such apostasy in my day I would have likely been racked for it. Happily with the dawn of this new century the bigoted beliefs of an older generation are decreasing, and one can prophesy a future not far distant, when all religious disputes will be settled in a new freedom of thought.

In my childhood, however, and for the better part of all my life there was and has been nought but wrangling and violence, torture, expulsion, or death, wrought upon those who, true to their beliefs, upheld them: and although I firmly adhere to the Established Faith, I do not agree with the doctrine of intolerance, no, not though it be directed to a poor untutored heathen, much less to a minister of God.

Such I fancy, from the little that I gathered from his talks with Mr Moon, was my father's attitude to the religious controversy, which beyond all other, was the burning problem of that time. While in these discussions I and the boys sat mum, Mr Moon expressed himself with thunder. Whatever my father's own belief, he would, I think, have denied it, for the satisfaction of rousing Mr Moon, poor man, who like a well-played trout to the fly, jumped at the bait my father so cunningly dangled before him.

I distinctly remember how on one occasion my father gave utterance to a remark which brought Mr Moon to his feet in such vehement protest that one feared to see flame issue from his lips. My father had certainly taken a full share of metheglin, and may have been somewhat more than ordinarily loquacious; yet that, in justice to Mr Moon, does not excuse him, for 'When all is said,' proclaimed my father, 'what *is* religious doctrine but a superstition?'

'My lord!' His Reverence started up. 'I cannot, in duty to my calling, hear —'

'Nay,' my father smoothly interposed, 'you have not heard. I was about to add — a superstition founded on a truth, as in fact is every superstition.'

'Heterodoxy!' spluttered Mr Moon.

'Or worse,' my father answered, leaning his head against his chair back. His hair, long and silken again now, fell either side of his narrow cheeks, down to his shoulders. He raised his pewter tankard, smiled over its brim, and then drank deep. 'But hear me out, good sir, before you burn me! As all truth becomes a lie when bandied from mouth to mouth, so has the fundamental truth of Christianity become distorted since God's Son first spake these words, "'He that entereth not by the door into the sheep fold but climbeth up some other way, is the same as a thief and a robber.'"

'My lord, I do protest —'

My father waved aside the interruption. 'How say you, sir? That war, bloodshed, or the gibbet, is the way to the door of the fold? Is it Christ's way, think you? Did He preach that man should rise against his brother in order that the word of the Lord shall be revealed according to man's feeble misconception and not according to the word of Him, Our Saviour, whom God sent to deliver it? Did Jesus die for men to live in enmity and hate, because of that they preach with — or without — white sleeves? What follower of any creed or doctrine, whether it be Anglican or Anabaptist, Nonconformist, Presbyterian or Papist, can stand before the Lord at Judgment Day and tell Him, "I have loved my brother as myself"?'

Mr Moon's dry lips unclosed; he licked them; his chin quivered. 'Your lordship speaks — if I may so presume — in ignorance,' his eye glinted at the flagon of wine, the last of which my father had now emptied, 'if not under a more potent persuasion.' And glancing round at us who sat all ears and silent, his voice rose from a murmur to a roar that might have been heard from here to Wynmon Abbas. 'As a minister of God, I feel it my bounden duty before these innocents —' I saw Robin's mouth quirk at the corners, and Percy pick his thumb — 'these innocents,' vociferated Mr Moon, 'whose souls are in my keeping, to declaim against such iconoclastic theory. Do you not realise, my lord, that all our present evils are due to this same stiff-necked defiance of pure doctrine, which you so lamentably decry? Is it not said, "He that hath an ear let him hear what the Spirit saith unto the Churches"? But you, my lord — you *have* no ear to hear, for,' Mr Moon raised a threatening finger, 'your ear has been possessed!'

It was at this point that, taking my cup to drink, I swallowed too hastily and fell into a choke. Whereupon my betrothed, seated beside me, sought to alleviate my distress by pummelling my back, the while I coughed and whooped and all but vomited my dinner, and was in so sad a case, and the worse for Mr Moon's disgusted glare, that I, still whooping, must be led by Percy from the room: so I never knew the end of that discussion.

Summer passed; the last of the Michaelmas daisies withered to seed in our garden. Great gales tore the leaves from the elms to send them spinning in showers of gold. Once more the rooks held sermons in the tossing tree-branches where their tattered nests swayed and swung to the dance of the winds. The flame of scarlet creeper on our walls rusted and fell. Robin and Percy went hawking, but my father and I did not. Seated at the foot of his bed, for the autumn mists had laid him low with a distressing rheum, I kept my watch beside him. Sometimes I read from the Bible, but more often from a book of verse which most of all he loved, the fanciful, lyrical, limpid rhymes of Robert Herrick, who sang:

'...*Of Brooks, of Blossoms, Birds and Bowers,*
Of April, May, of June and July Flowers,

Of May-poles, Hock-carts, Wassails, Wakes.
Of Bride-grooms, Brides, and of their Bridall-cakes.
...Of Groves, of Twilights, and I sing
The Court of Mab, and of the Fairie-King.
I write of Hell; and sing (and ever shall)
Of Heaven, and hope to have it after all.

When the heavy rains, that for near upon a month had deluged the countryside, ceased, and October's sun shone out again with the fierce embracing heat of August as if to atone for the days when eclipsed by sorrowing clouds, then did my father obstinately 'refuse to lie a-bed' as he put it, 'like an ageing spinster who has nought but her pillow for her comfort.'

His rebellious spirit would not admit the havoc wrought upon his body. Unheedful of Thirza's warnings and Doctor Sydenham's advice, he walked with me in our neglected garden to gather a late bloom of roses, to trim with his shears the straggling box hedge, to talk of this and that and with such hopeful vigour of how he would shape the garden into terraces, and cut the spreading yews, and buy a peacock, for 'there is no fowl of earth or air so arrogant and glorious, a very king of birds,' and on the lower lawn, 'which i'faith,' he said, 'is grown so lank 'tis but a meadow now,' he would make a fish-pond, and edging all would be a parterre set about with rosemary and lavender and lilies, and come next primrose-tide 'a new planting of tall tulips dressed in coats of red and gold like soldiers, and great ox-eye daisies, Prue, a row of winsome lights-o'-love to set them all a-courting,' that I rejoiced to hear him, and thought, thankfully, to see him well and strong again before next blossom-time.

Once only did he speak of my future, and in that droll way of his which seemed to turn most solemn talk to jest: 'For it thus transpires, Imp, that I have nothing in this world to leave you, save our Piers. God knows if I have done right or wrong — time alone will tell, though I may not be here to see —'

'You will, my soul, you will!' I clasped and kissed his hand to silence him. 'Why should you not be here?'

'Why should the swallows leave for foreign parts in autumn's fall?' returned my father. 'Beldame Nature is a wise old hag who weaves the woof and warp at life's loom in her own way, and after her own pattern.'

'No, no!' I murmured, for though he spoke in riddles, yet I glimpsed some hidden meaning in his words.

'Harken to me, my child — for child you still are, and a hoydenish wanton too, at times, but you have a good headpiece on your shoulders, so I can talk to you beyond your years. I have this to say…' And very soberly my father said it, while we walked together in the sunset. 'It is my wish that you and yours reign here at Wynmonath —' My father paused, and shading his eyes gazed under his hand at the battered towers of the abbey rising gaunt above the tree-tops. Caught in the red glow of the dying sun, those smoke-begrimed grey ruins were as if washed in blood. 'The time will come,' my father said, 'when Wynmonath will be restored and to its rightful owners — to the sons of my kin, if not of my name.' He shivered then as though a chill had struck him, and, turning, took my face between his hands to look deep into my eyes. 'This I know,' he all but whispered it, 'your issue shall inherit this earth of ours that we have had and held for more than six hundred years, and which shall be held again — *fidelitas in domino* — when the King shall come into his own.'

And stooping, he laid his lips to my forehead, straightened himself and laughed; put his arm around my shoulders and sauntered on humming a drinking song:

'Here's a health to all those that we love,
Here's a health to all those that love us,
Here's a health to all those that love them that love those
That love them that love those that love us...'

His face was a boy's face still, for all it was hollowed, ravaged, worn, the skin so frail and so tightly stretched that the bone structure beneath showed like the bones of a skull; but, though stricken to death's door he yet could sing, his ear so tuned to laughter it was as if he hid a chuckle in his shroud.

The months crawled on and still he lingered, weathering the heavy rains, the snows and frosts of winter with indomitable determination to conquer the enemy that hunted him by day and night, while visibly he weakened.

Spring came round again and we who watched and loved him grew more hopeful, until in the last week of April he was seized with an attack to bring him once more to his bed with the doctor in constant attendance.

Thirza told me how that she had heard him taken with a fit of coughing 'to tear the heart out of his body.' Going to his room she saw him lying in a puddle of blood, and thinking that a robber must have got in through the window or God knows how, to stab him, she shrieked, 'Murder!' At which my father, even in his weakness, grinned to quiz her: 'Pity 'tis to disappoint you of a melodrama, wench, but 'tis nothing worse than a red vomit. And I'm cold.'

She flew to fetch the warming-pan and rouse Ham from the stable, bidding him take horse and ride with all possible speed for Doctor Sydenham at Wynford. All this took place while I slept, but Robin, whose chamber backed on to the stable yard, was wakened by the noise below his window. When he got himself out of bed to look, he saw Ham saddling Caesar, a Roman-nosed short-winded bay, better used to carting than to racing. 'What's to do?' called Robin: and Ham told him how his lordship was took badly, and that he was bidden to go fetch the doctor with all speed. 'You'll make no speed with Caesar,' Robin said. 'Best take my mare.'

Ham confessed he was afeared to ride her, she being vicious.

'Dolt!' cried Robin, 'then I will. Do you saddle her quick. I'm coming.'

Percy and I slept on; nor did I wake till long past breakfast time, Thirza having forgot, in her disturbance, to call me at the accustomed hour. When I came downstairs I heard how Doctor Sydenham had arrived with Robin, and was closeted with my father. Mr Moon had likewise been called to the sick room, and Percy too. And presently my father summoned Thirza to fetch me, 'And see to it,' he said, 'that she be clothed in her best, and cleanly.'

His seizure, Thirza told me, had passed; nor, save for weakness, did he seem the worse for his blood-letting, which she declared was nature's way of ridding the body of its humours. The doctor had assured her such emissions were to be expected in the course of so grave a malady, and that there need be no immediate cause for alarm.

Yet alarmed I was, and trembled while Thirza dressed me in my mother's best lavender gown. She brushed my hair till it shone, and twisted it in curls around her fingers, and bound it with lavender ribbons sewn with pearls as my mother had worn it.

'Why so, Thirza?' I asked, bewildered, and with a sick fear at my stomach of I knew not what. 'This is not a Holy Day, nor is it yet my birthday: nor any anniversary or feast-day that I know. And my father, being sadly, would keep no company today, even were there company to keep in these parts, Thirza … Would he? Or maybe he expects a visit from his companions-in-arms who fought with him at… Ow!' I let out a shriek as Thirza, currying my tangled curls with a none too gentle touch, tugged at a refractory lock to tear its roots. 'Boggart! Would you pull my hair out by the handful? That hurts, believe me!'

'Then you should stand quiet and not toss your head,' returned Thirza. 'And as for whys and wherefores I obey my orders though there be more afoot this day than I nor you wot of; and if my lord be not deranged with this letting forth of his life's blood, then all I can say is may God help us all, for none else can, nor will.' Which mysterious communication did little to lessen my misgivings.

'Now there's my little lady!' Thirza cried with falsest cheer, when her titivations of my person were completed. 'See yourself, my lovely!' She gave me a push towards a mirror on the wall — the one treasure my room contained. Mirrors were a rarity in those days, and this had been my mother's, brought from Venice. In it I gazed at my reflection.

I saw, framed in dusky, curling hair, an elfish face, colourless save for the lips that in contrast to its pallor appeared crimson; and thin childish shoulders rising from the shadowy folds of lavender silk which in the dimmed glass looked grey; grey, too, were my eyes, the darker for their lashes — ('long as spiders' legs,' Robin used to say) — set wide apart under faint surprised eyebrows.

I heard Thirza mutter behind me, "'Tis the very ghost of my own dear … Never was mother and daughter such twins as this … but she was of a larger build, and this one is a fairy.' Then, gathering me in her arms, Thirza knelt to hug me close and kiss me; and with her cheek to mine she whispered, 'If I could give you all the joy in all the world, my darling, you should have it. But I misdoubt me that such joy is yours this day. I commend thee now and hereafter to thy Heavenly Father's grace, and I pray Him that no wrong shall come of what I fear me is mistaken right. God bless you…' And rising, she bid me on a sharper note, 'Hurry yourself. They're waiting.'

More mystified than ever, I followed at her heels till she reached the door of my father's chamber. There she halted, sighed, and shook her head, adjusted a straying curl upon my forehead, kissed me again and left me there.

I entered.

It was evident my arrival had interrupted a heated discussion. Mr Moon, seemingly more than ever crabbed, his lips compressed as though the words he would have spoken had been forcibly withheld by my appearance, turned a sour eye upon me. Doctor Sydenham, grave-faced and sober-suited, was at my father's side checking with his great silver watch my father's pulse. Percy, in his best finery — rose cloth breeches, buff-coloured tunic braided in gold, and cuffed and banded with lace — stood at the foot of the bed.

My father, propped on his pillows looking very white and wasted, greeted me with his most loving smile. I curtsied to the gentlemen, and kissed that frail hand outstretched on the coverlid; then, the bed being so high, I clambered up to kiss my father's cheek.

'How goes it with you now, my dear?' I whispered. 'Are you better? Say you're better!'

The smile deepened in his eyes. He returned my kiss, and with a comical sly glance at our chaplain's disapproving countenance, gestured me to get down off the bed. 'For,' he whispered back, 'we are observed. We must be circumspect. Sirs,' he raised himself on his elbow, 'we are now properly assembled and may proceed with the ceremony. Why, my little Prue!' Again his eyes overswept me, appraising. 'You sure are translated! This is no draggle-tail mudlark I see before me, but a princess ... so fine... If ever I saw her mother,' his breath caught in his throat, 'so do I see...' Another spasm choked him. Stifling the cough that racked his frame he sank back upon his pillows.

I turned in alarm to the doctor, who told me hastily, ''Tis no more than a normal weakness subsequent to all such seizures. It will pass.'

Mr Moon, whose face expressed nothing but the most profound dejection, sighed deep, hemmed, and uttered, 'Is it your wish, my lord, that I acquaint Mistress Prudence of your intention?'

My father answered, 'Thank you. No. I will.'

Percy stepped forward to take his place beside me. He was, I noticed, more than usually pale; his flax-gold hair, neatly combed, fell in soft shining ringlets on his shoulders. He smelled of flowers. I gazed at him in wonder. His eyes were on me, too, and in them I saw for the first time a look that brought the blood to my cheeks and sent a startled tremor through my body — and, I think, through his, for I felt his touch on my bare arm slide down till his hand found my fingers, and his were trembling.

'What...?' I faltered, filled with vague tumultuous emotions in which anxiety and fear struggled for mastery with something shy and strange and inexplicable, something never before experienced, sprung from some source undreamed, unsavoured. Nor did I know that in a moment's unfolding, a child died, a girl was born: that instinct, tremulous, expectant, was ripening to youth's unconscious, irresistible demand.

I knew only that Percy and I together shared a secret to make him tremble and me burn; and that I, his mischievous, teasing, graceless Prue, had found favour in his sight. Yet my sense did not entirely desert me. *'Tis my mother's best gown, not myself that makes him kindly,* I conjectured, remembering how often I had suffered his taunts, his jeers, his cruelty; and how Robin and he both avowed that a bogle, no matter how ugly, was never so ugly as Prue. And I found myself envying his flaxen curls, his elegance, his grace, his dainty manners, and his smell: most sweetly was he scented.

'What,' I stammered, 'is afoot? Or what's amiss?'

And still with his gaze upon me, half-bold and half-caressing, and with his touch surprising mine to turn me hot, Percy answered, 'Nothing, dear, to fright you.'

Dear! My heart fluttered. Such endearments had never come my way from him before. I felt myself blush, and to hide it I giggled, saw Mr Moon's face and composed my own... *Dear!*

My father raised himself to speak again. Briefly, with painful pauses in between his words, carefully chosen for my understanding, he revealed to me the wish that the marriage ceremony between me and my cousin be performed without delay. 'It is,' he said, 'a ceremony only. That is agreed since you are still too young for marriage. Piers,' my father smiled at him, 'must wait for his wooing until the bud's a flower.'

I felt Percy's hand tighten on mine, and glancing from my father's face to his, I saw it suddenly suffused with pink.

It was at this point that the doctor intervened. 'My lord, I must remind you that the religious ceremony — as I was about to explain when Mistress Prudence entered — does not bind according to the law.'

If a cannonball had fallen at the feet of Mr Moon, his face could not have expressed a greater horror. His whole body looked to have been petrified; even his eyes were frozen, as with commendable restraint he enquired on what authority Doctor Sydenham based his assumption. 'For,' said His Reverence, seeming to grow some several inches taller where he stood, 'the Church recognises no marriage save that performed and sanctified by Holy Writ.'

'My lord, according to the decree of the Commonwealth —' said Doctor Sydenham.

'I do not, sir,' my father haughtily interposed, 'conform to any decree of the Commonwealth.'

'Nevertheless, I feel it my bounden duty,' Doctor Sydenham doggedly persisted, 'to submit to your lordship that unless you *do* conform to this present decree of the State, the marriage you desire between your daughter and your heir will be proven null and void.'

'My lord!' Mr Moon's hairy nostrils quivered. The fumes of righteous indignation burst forth beyond control. 'My lord! As a priest of God I do protest against this unwarrantable interference of a layman in that which concerns the Church alone.'

'Layman or not, sir,' said my father, waxing cold as Mr Moon waxed hot, 'I wish to hear the argument of my learned physician and friend. If what he says be true, our case is at once obstructed. Nay, hear me!' My father's feeble voice gained strength to silence him. 'Since when, doctor, may I ask, has the State declared its power to control our most intimate and sacred rites? When was this preposterous decree made absolute in law? For I have never heard of it.'

'I cannot give you the precise date, my lord, but I can assure you there has been a recent revision by the Government of all previous legislation, including that appertaining to the rites of matrimony, which renders compulsory the presence of a magistrate at a marriage in order that the union be valid.'

'I protest and declare,' again expostulated Mr Moon, 'that a marriage conducted by secular ministration remains unrecognised and unaccepted by the Church.'

'Which being so, my lord,' the doctor collectedly continued, seemingly oblivious to our chaplain's words or presence, 'I am fully prepared to procure the services of a magistrate at Bridport with whom I am acquainted, and who will make all necessary arrangements that the civil marriage be conducted duly and in order, and with the least possible delay.'

'How long will that be?' asked my father, with the fretful peevishness of a sick man. 'I am not prepared for a postponement. I object to a delay.'

Doctor Sydenham hastened to assure him that there was no necessity for a postponement of the ceremony; that the service could be performed according to my father's faith and by his chaplain, when or wheresoever he might choose, providing always that the union be legalised before a magistrate.

'This, my lord,' exclaimed Mr Moon, 'is insufferable! A deliberate insult to, and defiance of my calling. Have I not, at your lordship's request and by reason of your failing health, petitioned for and received the gracious dispensation of the Archbishop himself that the marriage shall take place, if need be, at your bedside? I maintain that neither this — nor any other man — has the right to gainsay the grant and decree of the Church.'

'That is so,' my father dubiously assented, glancing from the greatly perturbed priest to the imperturbable physician. 'You have every cause for complaint, good sir, and so have I. But keep your wrath for Cromwell's dupes, not for our friend here, who whatever his politics — may they be confounded! — has served me well in giving me a statement of these facts of which I do confess an ignorance... 'Ods blood! Is there to be no end to the tyranny of those that ride us?' cried my father, hoisting himself to a sitting posture, while with a mighty effort he shook off the demons of his malady that strove to stay the torrent of his words. 'Have I not already suffered enough from their execrable demands that have drained me of my lands, and my resources? Have I not been forced to relinquish the last of the depleted revenue left over from my wracked estates and the home that has been held by my forbears through centuries? Have I not seen the sacred chapel of my abbey befouled by those accursed ruffians who made of God's temple a stew? I, yes, I, Folliett of Wynmonath, have been forced to sign my very soul away for the protection of her — my daughter — that this one remaining roof of mine be not sequestrated — Cromwell's word, gentlemen, for loot — and that I, a delinquent who fought in the cause of my King, might be spared my few remaining years, or months — or days — in freedom with my child and not in a prison in chains! And am I not by these atrocities become a beggared tenant of the State and not the master of my house? Yes, sir — you, doctor! I pay rent, I lease my own few remaining acres, my own homestead from the State! Is *this* not enough?'

Too much for his body's enfeeblement. He fell back with a gush of blood to his mouth. I screamed and started forward to his aid, but the doctor forestalled me and, motioning me aside, gently supported my father and wiped the scarlet dribble from his lips.

'Thank you, thank you, 'twill pass,' gasped my father; and he smiled reassuringly at me. 'No need to be scared, my darling ... I am in good hands here. Go, my friend —' regaining command of himself, he rejected the doctor's assistance — 'Go you and seek your worthy gentleman. God send him not *un*worthy — eh, Moon?' A gleam lit up those smoke-grey sunken eyes that even in this extremity held some hint of laughter. 'Take that cloud from off your brow, sir! This is a wedding, not a funeral ... yet. So, doctor, do you stay to see these children married, and then go you for your sheriff or your bailiff or your constable, or whatever knavish Jack is put over its in office by order of the republicans — and your dictator.'

To this outburst Doctor Sydenham made no acknowledgement beyond a formal bow; and having satisfied himself that the seizure had subsided, he turned from my father to me and spoke very simply and kindly.

'Mistress Prudence, permit me to wish you all the happiness that you deserve this day. May the sun ever shine upon your path in life.' And to Percy he said, 'Young sir, I offer you my heartfelt felicitations and the earnest hope that you two may walk in peace and joy on earth, as in heaven, handfasted.'

'I thank you, sir,' said Percy, cool.

And I, who truth to tell in my bewilderment had only just begun to realise the purport of the foregoing argument, said nothing, but took my hand from Percy's and placed it in the doctor's. He bowed over it and kissed it ... I had no words to say.

'Mr Moon,' my father bade him, 'pray proceed.'

Together we knelt at my father's bedside. Together we vowed our vows to God before God's minister in that room, with death's shadow our guest and my father's physician our witness.

'I, Prudence, take thee, Piers...' I repeated the words as Mr Moon gave them.

Percy drew a ring from his finger and placed it on mine. '...With my body I thee worship...' His hand was hot and trembling still; but mine was cold and I was frightened.

My father's white face on the pillow; His Reverence in his white surplice reading aloud from his book, bound in ivory, white; the doctor so silent behind us, and Percy, my bridegroom, all of a shake. This was a dream. I must waken.

'For better, for worse, for richer, for poorer...'

We knelt for the blessing. We rose from our knees, a boy and girl wedded ... till death do us part. Too young to be husband and wife.

Not until long afterwards did I learn, or understand, to what extent my father had been penalised by the disruptive powers that ruled us in those unhappy days.

In order to meet the great financial difficulties with which the Government was faced during the interim between the end of the first civil war, and the execution of Charles I, Parliament had sought to alleviate its difficulties by seizing the property of the defeated Royalists, or 'Malignants' as they were so basely termed. Thus, those who had fought for their King were forced to render to their triumphant victors the remainder of their lands and the moneys therefrom in exorbitant fines: and thus was my father deprived of his last small holding here at Folly's End, and was in truth a 'tenant of the State'.

How we managed to live in comparative ease I know not, but from Thirza's hints I gathered that although my father discharged his full account, he retained in his coffers sufficient for our moderate needs. I have reason also to suspect that Aunt Rossiter, or more correctly her good husband, may have aided my father's disbursement. Mr Rossiter, not having taken an active part in the fight against the rebels, was let off at less cost than the Cavaliers who had been more directly involved; and despite that he had paid a heavy fine for his avowed loyalty to the King's cause, Great-uncle Rossiter contrived to contribute a stipend towards the exigencies of my father's illness.

That he, whose material resources had already been so sadly depleted did act on Doctor Sydenham's advice that our marriage be conducted in accordance with parliamentary arbitration, was less a gesture of compliance than convenience.

'Better concede an inch than lose an ell,' he told his aunt, who having heard from Doctor Sydenham of her nephew's seizure, drove over at once to learn the worst — that Percy and I were married: twice married it seemed to me, when he and I were brought before a portly gentleman in snuff-coloured doublet and breeches, with a wart on his nose and a cast in his eye, at sight of which I crossed my fingers, for I knew from Thirza that any person thus affected had at some time or the other been in discourse with the devil.

This worthy received us in the winter parlour, with a blustering familiarity and a leer upon his face that I was hard put not to poke my tongue at him. The ceremony, if such it could be called, was of the briefest. We were given a paper to sign in the presence of Doctor Sydenham and my father, who had risen from his sick-bed for that purpose, since he determinedly refused to have his bedchamber, wherein a sacred service had already been performed, defiled — as he put it — by such pharisaical proceedings.

In his great carved chair he sat, looking less like a man than the shade of one there at the table, while Cromwell's nuncio declared us man and wife, and read us a short homily on the responsibilities and duties of our married state. And when all was done and he, fee in pocket, departed, my father returned to his bed again, declaring that the 'rats' were now appeased. 'For,' said he, 'should they have scent of any contumacy or resistance on my part to their abominations, they will gnaw holes in what is left of my last remnant of a homestead, and that my girl must — and *shall* have — while I live and when I die.'

Of the weeks that followed I have but a hazy recollection. The first strangeness of knowing I was Percy's wife soon passed, and save that my youthful husband now treated me with some slightly more respect, no marked change in our relationship existed.

True, we suffered some increase of ridicule from Robin who let pass no opportunity to snigger at and mock us, calling me 'Madam Mopsey' and Percy 'Benedick', and in loud asides to plague me, would condole with his good friend Percy on the misfortune that had befallen him that he, the better horse, should be yoked to the grey mare, and that he must look to it he did not find his head endowed with a pair of horns: which, far from riling Percy, seemed to have a reverse effect, for he would titter and blush, and glance around at me and whisper to Robin, who would guffaw in his turn to make me mighty scornful, while inwardly beside myself with fury. Percy, indeed, took Robin's jeers and jibes in excellent good humour, and oft-times joined with Robin against me, declaring I was now his 'goods and chattel', and reminding me that I had vowed to honour and obey him and he would see to it I did.

Their taunts and merry-making at my expense, which I did not doubt were ribald, only enraged me further. I was, as well they knew, the veriest simpleton, unaware of and unschooled in nature's mysteries: that such mysteries occurred from birth to death, and more than all in marriage, I suspected. I knew enough of farm life and the mating of bird and beast, to rouse my curiosity, and I was of an age when curiosity is rife.

Yet a shy reticence, in particular since my marriage, refrained me from questioning Thirza, my father, and most of all my spouse, on matters that I dimly felt concerned none now but he. I remember how on one occasion when teased beyond endurance, I sought vengeance on my husband for making game of me, his 'lesser half'. Whereupon, in my accustomed manner, I attacked him, to be held, squealing, in his arms, and kissed, when before I would have had my wrist wrenched, or a clout on the ear for my pains. But, 'I do not know which is the worser,' I retorted, when my husband thus did manifest his rights, 'your squeezings and bussings and such-like disgustful advances, or your cruelty and pinches and twists. I vow and declare I would as lief be mauled by a pig as by you — with your airs and graces. Yes, you may laugh — to split yourself! And Robin, too —' I wriggled free of Percy to turn on him — 'you whoreson blotch-faced mis-created carrot!'

And, 'Heed him not, my gentle duck,' crooned Percy, 'can you not see he envies me my prize? My sweet lady, my darling, my dove, who no matter that she be a snub-nosed dwarf with a face like a lump of dough and eyes like oysters, is the rarest, loveliest, most gracious —'

Then, red-hot, I fell on him again to be tumbled in the rushes with Percy a-top of me. I remember too, how seeing his shining eyes, his flushed face, his parted lips, not an inch above my own, I was seized of a sudden with delicious, queerly frightening sensations, till Robin's boisterous laughter and his words, 'Nay, lad! You'll never manage her although you mount her!' brought Percy to his feet, looking sheepish and me in a flurry to mine.

So save for these and similar occurrences, my married state did not very much disturb me. I slept in my chamber under the eaves, as I had always slept, alone. I knew that it was customary for man and wife to share a bed, but Percy was not yet a man, nor I a wife, except in name, and even that remained unaltered. Prue Folliett was I still.

One concession only had been granted. No longer did our Mr Moon chastise me. His tutorship done with, I was free to devote all of my time to my father.

As the days lengthened and summer blazed again in its full glory, so did he seem to fade beneath the sun. Yet resolutely, he refused to lie abed. We brought his chair out to the garden. I sat on a buffet at his feet.

I never left him now, and in the night I often woke to go to his door where Thirza, ever watchful, lay on her straw pallet, to ask her if — and reassure myself — that all was well with him; for child though I was, I knew and would not know, what all must see: the slow wasting away of that young precious life.

The end when it came was merciful and swift.

I had bidden him good night at his bedside, for he had retired earlier than usual, at that hour when twilight spreads a bridge of dusk across the day between sundown and the rising moon.

It was a wonderful still evening with a sky of rose and gold, and the light that poured from it seemed to spend itself in one last brightening ray across my father's bed, touching his pale brow with warmth and beauty. So young he seemed even to my years then; so young he was, and is, and ever will be.

'Sleep well,' I whispered, 'may your dreams be sweet.'

'My dreams,' he said, 'are always sweet, sweetheart, but' he smiled, and took a curl of my hair to his lips, 'but they'd be sweeter still if they came true.'

'Some dreams come true,' I told him. 'Perhaps yours will tonight...'

I left him lying there, his head turned sideways on the pillow, his eyes watching me, and on his lips, that smile, half-sad, half-gay and tinged with mischief; wholly his.

That night, for once I did not wake to steal to his door for my fears' comfort. That night I slept, and strangely dreamed: that my father and I were walking in our garden, but we walked divided, for between us flowed a narrow stream that surely had never been there before.

Such light was on his face and in his eyes that my own were dazzled and I could not see him clearly: and when I ran towards him and felt that shining water so chill, so icy at my feet I shuddered and drew back. He laughed upon a breath; I heard him say, 'Not now, not yet ... in all good time... And I shall still be with you.'

I called to him, and calling, woke, to find Thirza at my bedside. She was weeping: and I knew that she wept for him who had passed, but who was not far away.

CHAPTER FIVE

I have heard it said that children are incapable of suffering; that they may grieve at the death of one beloved but are not agonised; and that though their sorrow may cut deep it is not lasting, is soon healed, and soon forgotten.

That may be so; but I did not forget, and can still poignantly remember the ache, the loss, the loneliness of my young desolation. Yet, dazed and stricken as I was, I gave no sign; I sought no comfort. I have never made of tragedy a monument and did not then. Only my pillow knew my tears and the stifled paroxysms of a child's heartbreak, while to my small world I held myself aloof, guarding my despair beneath an armour of frigidity, that even Thirza believed me less indifferent than insensible. Indeed in my hearing she let fall to Robin the remark that I was fortunate to be so made for lightness and the sun of life that grief could cast no shadow. And Robin answered after his slow fashion, for he was ever one to weigh a word before he spoke it, 'Do you think that? Then I could tell...'

But what he could have told I never knew.

Doctor Sydenham, who had been sent for, stayed with us until after the funeral, which I, at his advice, did not attend. He ordered me to bed and kept me there with a draught that put me to sleep till the last rites were done.

Aunt Rossiter and her husband, our few remaining tenants, the servants, Thirza, Robin, with Percy and Mr Moon to lead the cortège, followed my father's bier to the vaults of his ruined abbey.

Both Robin and Percy were marvellous kind to me in those first bitter days. Each vied with the other, not now to quiz and plague me, but to offer their unspoken sympathy in careful speech and studied courtesies, while even dour Mr Moon was hush-voiced and dismally respectful; all of which served only to increase my conviction that life as I had known it was now ended and a strange new life begun.

Aunt Rossiter and her husband returned to Devon the day after the funeral. Two weeks later Mr Moon rode off on one of his excursions. He departed at sunrise, and we three rose betimes, dutifully, to take our breakfast with him.

We must have looked a dreary company seated there in our mourning clothes at the long table in the hall; Percy at the head of it in my father's chair; I at the foot, Mr Moon and Robin either side of us.

Very grand, very pale, very conscious of his dignity was Percy in his black of richest satin, laced with silver; and where in that benighted spot and in this emergency he managed to procure himself such elegance I did not enquire, though I have since suspected Mr Moon may have held in readiness these trappings of woe for a twelvemonth. Robin, in comparison, seemed more than ever shabby in Mr Moon's moth-eaten cast-offs, hastily converted to his increasing size by the Bridport tailor; while I, in a black taffety belonging to Aunt Rossiter and cut down to fit me by Thirza, was so overpowered and conscious of its owner whose very smell seemed to cling to its folds, that I feared to look at myself in the glass lest I see my aunt's head on my shoulders.

Robin and I sat in silence. Percy, ever polite, cared for his tutor's comfort, replenished his tankard and trencher, and, all the time, eating little himself, he chattered of this and that: of the fine weather, of the hay that should be cut, and the lack of labour on the farm to do it; of how the woods were overrun with foxes; and of some gossip gleaned from the stable-men that the Dutch Fleet was in the Channel and that the sound of cannon-fire had been heard along the coast.

'If the Dutch should sink Parliament's ships,' Robin loosened his tongue to say, 'I'll be the first to salute them.'

'That,' Mr Moon ponderously retorted, 'is a foolish shortsighted policy. Would you have a hostile power blocking the seas against the life-giving produce that brings England her wealth?'

'What wealth can England have, sir, when all is Common Wealth?' demanded Robin, hotly.

'The Navigation Act,' stated Mr Moon, not deigning a reply to this question, 'passed by English Parliament in the reign of Richard II, enforced a limit to the admission of foreign shipping in English ports. Therefore any defiance by foreign agents of our laws, whether monarchical or governmental, must be severely dealt with. My lord,' turning to Percy Mr Moon put a conclusive stop to that argument, '*Tempus fugit* — and I too must fly. My horse is waiting.'

He rose; we stood.

'Lady Folliett —' I started; my ears were not easily accustomed to this new manner of address — 'my duty, madam.' Mr Moon, punctilious and sombre, gravely bowed. I, as gravely, curtsied. His Reverence gathered up his gauntlets, his hat and his cloak from the settle. 'Sir Robert, I hope to see on my return that you have construed the whole of the last act of the Hippolytus of Euripides. This same applies to you, my lord, in respect of the Medea. I do not ask you to construe from the same work, since it is evident that neither your lordship nor Sir Robert can resist the temptation to render and obtain mutual assistance to and from the other. Your annotations show a suspicious similarity. Your handwriting, Sir Robert, and your spelling are execrable. See to it you do not blot your pages or I shall be enforced to compel you to rewrite the script, not once, but one hundred times.'

With his hat in his hand and Percy in attendance Mr Moon stalked out. From the window-seat I watched him mount his horse and ride away.

'There goes an ass in a lion's skin,' remarked Robin at my side. 'He roars, but his noise is no more than the bray of a donkey. His mind is a library of knowledge which he has not the means to impart. And I cannot —' Robin screwed his eyes against a sunbeam that was sliding through the window to his hair — 'I cannot and never have been able to determine whether he be knave or fool; honest I *do* believe him — to his principles. And yet — what *are* his principles? Is he *for* Cromwell or against him? Is he Puritan, Republican, or one of those fanatical Fifth-monarchy men one reads of in the diurnals? All are equally...'

Thirza entering to clear the dishes from the table at that moment put an end to Robin's cogitations, which although addressed to me, were, as well I knew, merely the voicing of his thoughts aloud: this was very much his habit when alone in a room with me, because maybe he realised that I would not and could not dispute them.

As she went out at the door with her tray Thirza halted. 'Have you wrote to Mistress Rossiter yet to thank her and her good gentleman for their kind attention and condolence?'

'What must I say?' I asked, very much taken aback, for I had never penned a letter in my life.

'Dear to goodness! You with your book-learning not to know what to say? Would you have a poor ignoramus like me put you wise? Express your gratitude mannerly, enquire how she does, say how much you appreciate her visits, and thank her for the gown, for without it and with all respect — and respect I give where it is due — I doubt not but you'd have mourned our dear departed in the tattered old black petticoat I wear to milk the cows.'

'But I don't thank her for the gown,' I demurred, while Robin grinned. 'It smells.'

'Do as you are bid, my lady,' Thirza said, 'and remember that you *are* a lady now and not a codlin.' Saying which, she left us.

Robin brought his books, his pens and papers from the cupboard, and sat down to his studies at the table. Percy passed the window walking slow and dragging his feet on the cobbles of the court. His chin was down, and his eyes too, with a frown between them. He was picking at his thumb, a sure sign that he was vexed or in a pother. I wondered what he'd heard from Mr Moon to put him out. He turned the corner of the house and passed from view.

I sighed; and Robin, looking up from his book said coaxingly — and he had a very coaxing way with him to melt you, even at a moment when you hated all the world — 'Please, an you love me, Prue, trim me a pen.'

'I don't please and I don't love you,' I answered, glum; for I was full of emptiness, and such a longing for my father that the pain of it was like a gaping wound.

'Come here... S-stt!' Robin put out his hand, snapping his fingers as if he were calling a dog.

I hitched up a shoulder and turned my back, with a pricking in my eyes to make them smart. So used my father to call me. He had caught that trick from him.

'Prue,' Robin said, soft, 'if you trim me a pen — and none trims a pen better than you — I'll write a letter to Mistress Rossiter for you to copy. It will be spelled and worded so fine she'll be amazed. And if you trim me *two* pens, I'll write it myself in your name and my best calligraphy.'

'I will write my own letter,' I told him, 'and I'll trim no pens for you. When I gave you my fine grey goose-quill for a present you let Peg's puppy take it. But you can tell me what to say to my great-aunt that will please her.'

And I went to fetch my own quill from the cupboard and a fair page to write on, and then, because he looked so woebegone, although I knew he was only play-acting, and because perhaps of his threadbare black, his broad shoulders and his freckled nose, and his teeth, white as almonds showing beneath his upper lip; because of nothing I could lay a name to, save a sudden great surge of affection — 'You can have my pen,' I said; and handing it to him went back to my seat. 'Now you can give me yours.'

'That's my *kind* Prue!' exclaimed Robin, as with a flick of his nail he sent his pen flying across the polished oak to me. 'Take your quill to your paper and I'll dictate. Set it down as I say: *Dear Madam, I am indeed beholden —*'

'*...beholden,*' I murmured, and stuck my tongue between my teeth and laboured to write as neat and ornamental as ever I could with a fine flourishing *B*.

'*...to you and my Great-uncle Rossiter for your —* no! I have forgot! 'Tis you and Percy now. Begin again. Take a fresh sheet and say *My —*' Robin paused; and glancing up I saw his face turn red. '*My husband and I,*' he corrected.

'Be damned!' I cried, shockingly. 'I'll not waste a fresh sheet of good parchment. I'll insert it.'

'And spoil your copy,' said Robin.

'That's true,' I admitted; and I brought from the cupboard more parchment and took up my quill again.

And then a strange thing happened.

As I sat there at the table, Robin leaned forward. 'Prue,' he said, weighing each word, his eyes lit and burning on mine, ''tis a pity you're married to Percy. I have just come to wish that you weren't.'

I stared back at him, while the startled blood leapt to my face. 'Why...' I faltered, 'why should you wish...?'

'Because,' Robin answered, as cool as you please, 'I think I would have married you myself.'

I was in great trouble now. The emotions of the past few weeks seemed on a sudden to have dissolved in one clamorous urge to hold this moment in its passing, to gather all that I was and all that I might yet be, into the desperate effort to grasp at and retain this dazzling glimpse of a lifted, new horizon which even the dark clouds of recent sorrow could not entirely obliterate ... a moment only, and it died like a breath on glass, as swiftly fading. And I, who between a second and a second had glimpsed the woman in the girl, the man within the boy, knew only a profound regret as of something precious, lost.

Those words of Robin's so lightly spoken, yet so pregnant with the sense of deeper things to come, and of which not he nor I were consciously aware, had shattered the careless innocence of our relationship: between us now had risen the shade of an uneasiness that was akin to guilt.

'It needs consent of two to make a marriage,' I said, shrill, 'and if I were asked to choose I'd name Percy the lesser of two evils.' Then, hurriedly, for there was that in Robin's eyes to shake my hand so I could scarce hold the pen, 'will you tell me, please, what next I am to say?'

Robin rose from his seat and stood over me. 'What,' he asked in whispers, 'do you want to say?'

'*I* don't want to say at all,' I stammered. ''Twas Thirza made me write the letter... Please, no, Robin! No!'

What hidden fears quickset with exaltation had wrenched that protest from me? Was it the instinctive recoil of youth from the first breath of youth's fire? Was it a foreboding of future storm, of fatal forces stirring, to take and break and then remould us to their pattern? I could not guess at miracles; I knew only that my young unripened blood spoke and answered with sweet urgency all that my words denied.

Robin leaned lower till his drooping hair, so russet-red, was mixed with the curls of mine.

'Write as I tell you,' he said, with the breath of his words on my cheek. 'Write this: *Robin loves Prue and will love her for ever ... and ever.*'

I turned to look at him in wonder and saw him changed; or maybe I had changed or was enchanted. For now it seemed I could see through him deep down into his heart, and that was aflame as were his eyes with a red eager light: and I knew he shared with me the same ache and longing to be closer, to see deeper, to see more, to grasp at unimagined secrets, not yet to be revealed. Then, while we gazed and trembled on the brink of startling new adventure, a faint sound like a puppy's whine splintered the silence, and our scared moment fled.

Percy stood in the doorway. His eyebrows were up, his lids were down; through his lashes he glanced from Robin to me, and smiled with tight-closed lips. He held in his arms two whelps of Peg, his spaniel: the one black, the other golden red.

Robin strolled over to the window; I dipped my pen in the ink, wrote on my parchment *Dear Madam*, and made a great spluttering blot.

Percy set the puppies on the floor and watched them tumble over one another, and laughed at their play. I laughed too, on a high breathless note, and cried, 'The darlings! One black and one red!'

'One for you,' said Percy, narrowing his eyes while the laughter died on his lips, 'and one for Rob. Each to your own colour.'

'I am not black,' I said.

'Your hair is ... as near black as hair can be.' From behind his high Folliett nose he looked me full in the face.

'I like the red one best,' I murmured, foolishly, ''tis prettier.'

'The black's the better of the two,' Percy answered with the smile returned to his lips but not to his eyes; they were like stones, hard and cold, seen through bluest water. 'The red's a dog and the black's a bitch; and bitches are always more faithful.'

Robin at the window, with his back to the room and us, swung round on his heel to say, scowling, 'Peg was let out in her last heat, and got herself served by Ham's greyhound. Her whelps are mongrel curs.'

'A mongrel cur,' said Percy, gentle-voiced, 'is considered more intelligent and cunning than one of purer breed, although I'll grant his nose is not so keen as that of his better bred brother who knows a false scent at the stir of a wing no matter how far away. Instinct,' Percy spoke as if to himself, his eyes on the tumbling puppies, 'is nature's most wonderful gift to beast — as to man — alike.'

He took from the folds of his sleeve a cambric kerchief edged with lace, shook it out and inhaled its perfume, then patted his lips as though to pat his smile from them; but it stayed, and the room was full of a smell of musk and roses.

Robin's face was now as fiery as his hair, but I could see nothing in this talk to make it so; yet I was aware of trouble brewing all about us, and it seemed we three, divided, groped alone in the dark on the edge of an abyss; though withal there was excitement in the danger.

Then as smooth as Rob was rough, Percy said, 'If you can spare a moment from your Euripides —' he paused — 'and from my Prue,' his eyelids flickered, 'I would be glad to have your hearing and advice.'

'Advice on what?' Robin asked, wry-mouthed.

Percy did not immediately reply; he sat himself on the table, and taking his kerchief to his nose, sneezed daintily, complaining, 'I have caught a plaguey cold.'

'You may keep it!' I told him, thankful for this return to norm, 'and I beg you won't give it to me.'

'I am not likely to give it to you, my dear,' Percy said, swinging his foot, ' since although I have your company, I am not yet permitted your bed. Rob,' this he flung carelessly over his shoulder with the hint of a laugh in his voice, but his eyes held no laughter in them, 'was ever husband in so sad a case? I am half sick of waiting for my bud to burst its sheath.'

'If you seek my advice on the forcing of a flower that grows in open field,' Robin retorted harshly, 'then let me tell you — I'm no horticulturist; but I would say first come, first served, and let the best man pluck it.'

I looked from one to the other; Percy's face had blanched; his foot stopped swinging, and for all his careless nonchalance he seemed to be iron-clad; while Robin stood rigid as though on guard, his hand to his swordless hip.

There was now no mistaking the submerged hostility that flowed between these two: but from what unfathomed depths it had arisen, for how long it had lain dormant, or from what hot secret fount it seethed and boiled to flood with poison the easy current of our lives, I could not know, and could but dimly guess.

'I do not seek advice on how to grow my garden,' Percy said, close-lipped, 'for that is mine to do with as I will, and I'll admit no lurking sneak-thief trespassers upon my property.'

'Say that again,' Robin said in his throat, 'and I'll knock the teeth out of your head.' He took a step forwards as though to do it — and would have, I think, but that Percy asked, wide-eyed and mocking gentle, 'Say what? Why so tetchy? Prue heard me, did you not, my lady-wife? You heard me say I'll have no thieves upon my precincts. They are mine now — all mine.'

He smelled at his handkerchief again, while Robin, awkward, glowering, and still ready to spring, fell back a pace or two.

'No,' said Percy thoughtfully,' I do not seek advice on what concerns none but myself and,' he pointed a look at me, 'mine; but I *am* anxious for advice on certain other and less intimate affairs that will prove, I think, of equal interest to you.' Percy's speech, ever clear-cut and precise was even more so now, as if each word were chiselled by his tongue in utterance. 'My problem, Robin, is one that concerns you and every one of us who has been connected directly or indirectly with the cause of His Majesty the King.'

And at that name, as when the tight-drawn bow-string pulled back to the bowman's hand, relaxes to speed the arrow on its way, so did the held tension of these charged moments wane and slacken. Robin's fist fell to his side; Percy put away his handkerchief and carried his thumb to his lip. I released a long breath and took up my pen to write, *My dear Great-aunt and Uncle Rossiter*, for *Madam* was surely too tart…

It was over, the strangeness; and these strangers, these two I loved most in the world, were strangers no longer. I was still Prue; still myself, not a bone between quarrelling dogs.

All was as before and as it ever had been; and, as I knew with fateful certainty, could never be again.

'The fact of the matter,' said Percy, 'is this...'

I paid little heed to their talk but went on with my letter till a word here and there caught my attention, and finding my ears astray I abandoned my writing to listen.

Percy was frowning, Robin saying, 'The devil knows his own business best.'

'Or worst, but he is no devil; you mistake him. The devil has less Latin and more sense. Well now, this is as I see it...' And would you have believed these two, not five minutes since, could have be en in a lust of hate one for the other? No sign, no shadow remained of that menacing cloud above us.

'As I see it,' said Percy, 'I, and you too, Rob, can claim redress for sequestration of our property.'

'I have no property,' Robin stooped from his seat in the window to grab at the red-gold pup; 'my father's house was sacked, his estates plundered.'

'As were mine — by the Royalists,' said Percy.

Robin, pulling at the puppy's ears, glanced up. 'Which means the Commonwealth will give them back to you — in part?'

'Yes,' Percy nodded, 'so I believe, if I insist upon it. And that is what Moon is after — unless I'm much mistaken. He threw a hint before he left as to the nature of his journey north. He goes to confer with my Fairfax kin to nose out the lie of the land — or how much of it reverts to me on demand. 'Twould be, I think, worth having.' And at Robin's stare, Percy flushed to his flaxen eyebrows.

'Am I answerable for my father's misguidance or misdeeds?' he asked pettishly. 'Whatever he did was done in good faith. It is fortunate for me that my Yorkshire property has not suffered a similar wreckage as here, where I am left with no more than a rat-hole.'

Robin said nothing.

'Why,' persisted Percy, hunching his thin shoulders, 'why must I forgo what is my right because my father's principles did not agree with mine?'

'Why indeed?' Robin raised an eyebrow. 'Take what you can *while* you can.'

'I hope,' Percy fidgeted and looked sidelong at me, 'I hope to have an heir.'

'What you have or may have,' Robin answered, without moving, 'you must hold.'

Percy bit his thumb. 'I am not liable to pay a fine. My father was not a delinquent. And the fine here has been paid already. I believe one can "compound" — as it is called — for an estate.'

'Compound?' The word was new to Robin as to me.

'Yes, my Cousin Folliett compounded for this property — I do not understand their arbitrations — 'tis only one more nail in our coffins when all's told — and Moon will tell me nothing or as near to nothing as a mole can see the light. But if the debt here is fully rendered to the State, then I could sell some part of my Yorkshire holdings, and live well upon the proceeds.'

'You mean,' said Robin, still staring, 'you will hunt with the hounds in Yorkshire and run with the hare at home.'

Percy returned him a grin. 'I'll not dissemble. I'll have my last pound of flesh, my last acre of land from those hell-hounds. Wouldn't you?'

'That depends what it be worth to my conscience,' said Robin, dry.

'A king's ransom!' cried Percy. 'That's what it's worth.'

Robin's face warmed. 'Then if so —'

'If so, believe me, I can vindicate my father's honour — and rebuild Wynmonath.'

'With a crown piece?'

'For Crown property. What is his is his own, and what is mine is his also. God save him!'

Percy had flung this out, I thought with a flash of bravado, not unaware of the figure he cut in his new-found dignity and his black-and-silver suit: he made a pretty peer and saw himself, I'll swear, as well-nigh peerless.

Robin gleamed again. 'And Moon?'

'Moon will act,' Percy answered, chin high, 'as I instruct him.'

Robin's gleam turned to a smile. 'Are you so sure of that?'

'As sure as I am of myself.'

'Which is not so sure, my friend. First catch your hare — then jug it. As for me —'

'Yes, as for you,' Percy broke in eagerly, 'you should compound for your estate as I shall, although you are unlikely to recover so much return as I, in that your father fought for the King — and mine — alas! did not. But since you were too young to take up arms against the rebels you cannot be dubbed 'Malignant', and it is they who are called upon to pay the heaviest indemnity — as my poor Cousin Folliett who was bled white. That much I gleaned from Moon.'

'But how,' demanded Robin, 'can I compound? Surely to do so would cost money? I have none. And who would represent me? I must have an agent or some trusty counsel. My father's bailiff at home was murdered. God knows what's become of my house, my poor tenants —'

'Moon would act in your interests,' said Percy.

'Not he — on my life!' returned Robin. 'He has no interests beyond his own — and yours, which march together, and that only while it suits him. He'd not scruple to lead you blindfold to the Pit.'

Percy twitched a nostril. 'Two can play at blind-man's-bluff — or even three. Why do you not enlist his aid in your affairs? He has, besides his classics and theology, a mighty shrewd perception of the law.'

'There is no law today. A pack of wolves sit and howl among themselves and the bones of the men they have destroyed. Can those bloody-jowled beasts understand or dictate the laws of this heritage of kings, and those who have made her great under such kings — this England?'

'Bad laws or good laws, and no matter what laws,' said Percy equably, 'Moon is your man. He'll advise you. You should use him.'

'I'd sooner use a carrion crow,' said Robin, showing his teeth.

'You misjudge him.'

'I mislike him.'

'Your Papist blood mislikes him.'

A long minute passed.

'Maybe.'

'You need some new clothes,' Percy said, eyeing him over.

Robin crimsoned. 'Yes, I have forgot; I owe him for these... And there is something more I have forgot.' The puppy he was holding gave a sudden yelp. Robin set it aside and stood, with jaw and shoulders squared, 'I am grateful,' said he, clear,' for the reminder. I owe *you* for more than a suit of clothes. I owe you for my lodging, for my board, my —'

'Rob!' cried Percy sharply, and caught him by the arm. 'You complete fool! Have you run mad to talk so — to dare to say? Damnation! Do you suppose —'

'I don't *suppose*,' Robin's eyes were as hard as his voice. 'I face a fact. The late Lord Folliett was my guardian. The present Lord Folliett is not.'

'I am more,' Percy said, with rare sweetness. 'I am your friend as you are mine. My only friend … my brother. Nothing is changed.'

'Everything,' said Robin, low, 'is changed.' And his glance slid over Percy's head to me.

Thus came to me the knowledge: these two were almost men: the one long-legged, long-armed, and growing daily in height and breadth and muscle, while his beardless cheek sprouted a golden down like the bloom on a sun-tanned peach; the other fine and frail as a goblet of rare blown glass. But I knew and all knew, and he knew, none better, that his silken white skin encased steel. Yet, though their years belied their manhood, Nature did not.

Why do the poets name her Mother? She is not my notion of a mother; no, indeed. There is neither tenderness, nor tolerance, nor pity in her dealings with mankind. She is ruthless, tiger-cruel and serpent-cunning. She takes her sucklings to her bosom and throws them off before they are half-weaned, to grope and flounder in a wilderness of fancies, touched by secret fires that leave an itch and ache for comfort that none but she can give. Yet she gives nothing. She is without mercy or discrimination. Having cast her babes adrift she leaves them to find their bearings unguided and alone. She instils into young blood a thirst, into young bodies a hunger that turns to torment in unexplained desires: and as the bee carries the pollen, so does she scatter the seeds of jealousy, hatred and lust, the ugly half-sisters of Love; for withal her mischief and abominations, Love was born from her blind-eyed soul.

And if I, ungiven, green, ungrown, and late — too late in growing — was scorched by her dark witchery to savour in my lonely dreams her tempting, provocative fruit, with what eager healthy young appetites must those two fledgling Adams have watched for the coming of Eve?

During the short interim between the day that Mr Moon set out upon his journey and the day of his return, events were moving swiftly to a crisis.

Nature, that crafty old procuress, once bent upon her purpose, cares not a tinker's curse for the proprieties. Why should she, who couples birds, beasts, and butterflies, man and woman, boy and girl with a like impartiality, and let the devil take the consequence?

He must surely have been with us in our house, and in our hearts to twist and turn them while we children played with fire we had not learned to dread...

Mr Moon had been gone a week and the boys were out fishing, when one afternoon I came upon Thirza in my father's chamber. That room had not been used since his death, and at my earnest wish all was as he had left it. I was therefore not a little angered, though more hurt, to see Thirza shaking up the bed with a rolling of it this way and a tumbling of it that way, and such a pounding of her fists to make the feathers fly, you would have thought she held a spite against the thing.

'Well, now, Thirza!' I cried. 'Could you not have waited? 'Tis not yet four weeks since he —'

'The bed must be aired and the room fumigated,' Thirza said with a last shake, a last punch. 'Those be his lordship's orders.'

'Oh,' I said, glum, 'so Percy is now giving orders.'

''Tis to be your room in future, my dear.' Thirza pushed her coif to the back of her head and wiped her red face on her apron. 'Body o' me! This is warm work. I'm all of a sweat.'

'*My* room?'

I was not happy to know it. A fine room, certainly, the best in the house, oak-beamed and oaken-walled with some good carving over the fireplace framing the Folliett arms. Built in the reign of King Henry VIII, Folly's End had originally been designed as a small dower house. Later, converted to a farmhouse, and again re-converted for my father's use, it still retained much of its former dignity. The furnishings were both elegant and solid, and here instead of rushes, the floor was spread with rugs from Persia, at that time only just coming into fashion: carpets, being virtually unknown until the Restoration, were more commonly used as coverings for tables. The bed, a gift from my grandfather, was itself as large as a small room, the bedposts heavily carved, the curtains of purple velvet, the valance and counterpane of silk, lavishly embroidered in a design of birds and flowers. An oaken press containing my father's clothes stood over against one wall, and beside it a great chest wherein was stored all that remained of my father's wealth in gold.

The mullioned windows did not allow of much light, and the sombre curtains, the dark panelling, the great bed, the shadowy corners, attached an added gloom to the memory of death. Both my parents had died in this chamber, and who knew but that their spirits, drawn hither by love for their child, might not return at night to visit me? The thought sent a shudder down my spine, for while with all my might I worshipped him, I could not contemplate my father's ghost; nor come to that, my mother's. I saw her in my mind, a gentle shade in her lavender gown, with a tender pity in her eyes, a light about her head and the oaken wall seen through her; at her side my father — not as I had known him in his everyday dress, his gilt-braided tunic, his wide lace-edged band, and his hair grown down to his shoulders — but a spectre cold in his shroud, jaw wrapped, eye-sockets empty, and his skull's face a-grin. Horror seized me.

'No!' I flung myself at Thirza. 'I won't sleep here! I'd be afeared. The room is haunted.'

'How now! What's this? What's this?' Thirza loosed my clinging arms. 'Fie! You should be ashamed to show yourself so simple — and you in your fifteenth year!'

'Fourteen last birthday. I am not so old.' I wished then I were younger. 'If I must sleep here, Thirza, I'll not sleep here alone.'

Said Thirza, looking sly at me, 'You'll not be asked to sleep alone, my lady.'

'You'll sleep here too?' I tugged at her hand. 'You'll bring your bed and sleep here with me ... won't you?'

'I?' A huge laugh broke from her lips: I hushed her, thinking it unseemly to laugh by my father's death-bed. 'What would my lord say to that?'

I stared at her, stupefied.

'Percy? Is he to ... no! Not Percy!' Fear again, and something more: a tingling in my palms, a twinge and burning in the centre of my body, a rush of blood from my heart to my cheek. 'I'll not have him here in my room, nor ... nor in my bed,' I faltered. 'I will not!'

'Then you'd best tell him so,' said Thirza, tittering, 'and make him all the hotter, I don't doubt. Will the drake leave his duck, or the young bull his heifer, or young Jack his Jill when she squeals?' Her eyes raked my face, swept over me with so sharp and so knowing a look, it was as if she uncovered my nakedness under Aunt Rossiter's gown. 'Well, well!' She pursed her lips and sunk an eyelid. 'You'll soon be ripe to sing another tune.'

From my head to my toes I blushed; and unable to endure Thirza's scrutiny, her rogue's smile, her winks and her nods that gave me more clue to her meaning than all of her riddlesome words, I turned and ran from the room, out to the garden, through the wicket-gate into the orchard. I wanted to fly from myself...

Under an apple tree heavy with fruit still green on the bough I lay, with my burning face in the cool long grass and my ears in a buzz; but whether it were the ferment of my thoughts I heard or the bees at their work in the foxgloves, I could not tell, for my mind was in a tangle and my blood was in a heat.

Then while I lay there throbbing, with the sun on my back, tremors in my body, and the scent of warm hay in my nose, I became aware of voices. The boys were returned from their fishing.

I lifted my head but could see no more than the sunshine like gold powder on the leaves, the wind's fingers in the grasses, the swoop and flight of swallows, the blue above, the green below, and a bumble bee in the cup of a harebell. With amorous clumsy legs he clung quivering, probing; the tiny flower swayed and seemed to die beneath his weight; I watched, detached, ears cocked for words that floated by and fastened to my senses; somewhere near a thrush trilled, and Robin's voice rang out. They must have halted behind the hedge and stood not a man's length from me.

'I tell you the situation becomes intolerable! Can you not realise — are you so blind?'

'Are *you* so foolish?' Percy's words were soft, yet penetrating. I could almost see how they were said, his lips against his teeth, and closed in his thread of a smile.

'There is none can keep me here against my will.'

'You do mistake. You have no will as yet to call your own. You, like myself, are under age. We are both infants in law.'

'I know nothing of the law.'

Robin's voice was sullen; Percy's a caress.

'But the law cares for you.'

'There is no law today I choose to recognise. "I am that I am" — my own master.'

'Then, prithee, good master,' Percy fell a-laughing to sugar the acid of his words, 'for my enlightenment as your —' a pause — 'your host, tell me when you plan to take your leave and by *my* leave.'

That left a sting in its tail: I heard a breath, quick-drawn.

'Your leave! Who gave you leave, my lord, to order me?'

My lord! Never yet had I known Robin formal. What new note was this to ring alarm? What latest strife had come between these two who left the house at sunrise — I watched them go — in amity, together; their baskets slung across their shoulders, Percy's arm in Robin's, his face to his in laughter, and Robin's loud guffaw to answer him. As merry as grigs, the pair of them, and now … what now? What next?

But I had missed what next. They had passed on, their voices raised and dwindling as they went to a low duet like the mutter of thunderous storm streaked with the crack of Percy's high-pitched cry: 'Sneak-thief! You think to threaten?'

My strained ears returned from Robin no retort. Percy repeated his challenge: 'Thief! Who sneaks behind me in the dark — my friend who eats my bread and then turns coolly to my face to name himself whoremonger. Yes, you did! Are you not stinking hot, on your own confession, to push me out and yourself in?'

The sound of a flat-handed clout upon flesh splintered that volley of abuse. I sprang to my feet, and unheedful of Aunt Rossiter's silk, scrambled through a gap in the hedge and ran. As I guessed they were at it, bare-fisted and stripped to the waist. No half-measures here. Their coats and shirts were on the ground as were their rods and baskets, these overturned and disgorging. But I'd no thought for fish.

I had seen them fight before, though not with such ugly purpose, such grim thud and interchange of blows. Percy, despite his disadvantage as the smaller, fought lithe and swift with a ripple of sinewy muscle under his skin, as when a greyhound is poised for the race; yet his attack was no more than the patter of hail on cobble-stones. Robin, heavier, taller, stronger, stood to take and return as he chose, keeping Percy on the hop, with a dodge and a skip and a ducking this way and that to avoid the well-aimed punch as it came with the weight of Rob's arm behind it.

'Stop! For pity —!'

The wind turned my scream to a whisper, played tricks with Percy's hair, grabbed impishly at Robin's, spread all ways like a lion's mane.

To the left, to the right ... Robin's arm shot out; his muscles were as big as my two fists. Right, left, a sickly thwack and Percy was down, Robin over him.

'Shame on you both!' I scolded, 'to fight like swine-herds — you should be ashamed. Oh, Percy! Robin! Look... O God, he's gone! You've killed him!'

Percy's fine Folliett nose was pouring blood, his white body agleam with sweat. I knelt to raise him up. His head lolled on my arm; his closed lids fluttered open.

'He's not gone yet, nor will he go so easy,' muttered Robin.

I rounded on him, blazing. 'Murderer! Or near as bad. Will you stand there and see him bleed to death nor lift a finger to his aid — you filth!'

Said Robin, stooping for his shirt and coat, 'He's only winded.'

'Only winded! Beast! His nose is broke and half astride his face. If you've not killed him you've disfigured him for life. Let that rest on your conscience, Robert Peverill. What in heaven's name,' I cried, 'brought you to blows?'

Robin gave no answer beyond a sheepish grin, and passed his shirt over his head to hide it. From Percy came a sudden snort; the red from his nose bubbled horridly, then, his eyes in a daze, he sat up saying, 'You.'

'Me?' I repeated, agape. ''Ods sakes, why me? Percy!' I shook him, forgetting his hurt.

His lips sneered through the blood on them. 'Yes, *you* — mooncalf. You mischievous, ogling, gabble-mouthed numps — you and all women — a curse on 'em!'

I still gaped, amazed at this unwarranted attack on one who had so staunchly defended him. Then, recovering my wits, 'Much *you* know of women, you devil's kin!' I bawled. 'And I'll thank you to speak more civil of your wife.'

'Wife?' Percy struggled to his feet, where he stood swaying and tenderly nursing his nose. 'A fine species of wife this, i' faith! A witless, piping, drivelling dolt, that is neither maid nor girl nor woman, but a cross between a child and an ape.'

At that I flew at him, claws ready; then, seeing him so pale and his nose so sore, I refrained from using them and poked my tongue for my relief instead.

'Well, sirrah,' my injured spouse turned, sour as pickles to Robin, 'it seems you have won this round. I'll not forget it.'

Robin, awkward, held out his hand; Percy put his own behind his back.

'No, the fight is not yet ended. 'Tis only just begun... Prue, give me my shirt and coat. If I bend for them my nose'll flood.'

I gave him his garments, helped him into his shirt.

'I'll not wear my coat,' said he, 'you can carry it.' And seizing me roughly by the arm, he pulled me to him. For the life of me I could not hold my giggles, for with his nose twice its size and like a squashed plum he resembled a clown at a fair.

'So you find me laughable!' His poor swollen eyes flashed and narrowed. 'No doubt I am — I am! But he laughs best that laughs last...' His grip upon me tightened. 'You, my little maggot, come with me.'

I went with him, scared. I did not like the turn of this affray. At other times they fought and then were friendly; nor was it always Percy who went down. I have seen Rob winded before now, and his eye blacked for a week, and have seen them shake hands on it afterwards, but I had never seen a hand refused.

Unwillingly, with Percy's grasp like thin iron on my wrist, I dragged my feet along, and glancing back across my shoulder saw Robin standing with the sun on his hair, and his shadow pointed like a sword behind us.

At table in the hall an hour later, Percy and I sat alone. Thirza, who had tended his nose which was now turning blue, declared the bone was cracked. While she waited on us at the meal, she treated Percy to a diatribe on the behaviour of two young gentlemen who could demean themselves to a vulgar brawl, bare-handed.

'Swordplay is the only way a nobleman should fight — so I was always told when I was young,' said Thirza. 'Would my precious lord, think you, have lowered his dignity to use his fists? That is the way of a small-trash town-bull, not a —'

'Stop your braying, she-ass!' shouted Percy. 'May you be struck dumb.'

'And may you be forgiven for those words,' Thirza's eyes rolled heavenwards. 'Reflect, my lord, before you utter curses lest they return to you like dogs to their foul vomit... They say the hard breasts of a nurse make children short-nosed, by which showing your lordship's mother must have had teats as soft as cream, for your nose, poor soul, never little at its best, is twice its size and purple as a beetroot that has lain too long in the dung.'

'You filthy drab, get out! I abominate the sight of you!' snarled my husband through his teeth.

'Fie, my lord! Such language. As I was saying, 'tis high time His Reverence returned to keep your lordship at more profitable labours than *be*-labouring.' Thirza chuckled at this heavy pun which only she enjoyed. 'Satan finds much idle work for idle hands —'

'And idle tongues,' groaned Percy, whom long custom had inured to Thirza's jibes. 'Open your muzzle again and I'll have you sent from here to the cart's tail and whipped till you're dead for your insolence.'

'Insolence, say you? Ingratitude, my lord, is sharper than the serpent's tooth. Have I not given you a mother's love since you were so high? Thirza bent before him with one hand low to the rushes, 'And now 'tis insolence that I'm accused of — me, who cares for nought but your well-being, who has mended, spun, and slaved to have you fine, who has washed and pressed your laces that you shall be cock o' the walk —! Yes, yes, I'm going. I have more to do than wait on you, my lord.'

And Thirza winked at me and mouthed below her breath, and gestured to the ceiling behind Percy's chair, and then at him, and bore the trenchers out and left me mystified, until I was reminded of her words that morning concerning my father's bedroom and my use of it. Thirza's miming, therefore, must be a hint I should enquire of my husband his intentions.

But Percy, nibbling his thumb, his face sullen and staring past me through the window, gave no encouragement to venture on so intimate a path. To gain time and find my bearings, I scrabbled like a mouse before it takes the cheese-rind laid to trap it.

'Where,' I asked, 'is Rob?'

No answer.

'Maybe he's gone to snare that vixen with her cubs up in the woods. Ham says she has killed eleven hens these last two nights.'

Percy filled his pewter mug with ale, but did not drink.

'May I have some ale, Percy, please?'

Glowering, he pushed the jug across the table. I rose to fetch it, stood beside him. 'Percy.'

He jerked his head round. 'What now? Don't pip at me. Sit down.'

'I won't!' His rudeness stung. 'I have to speak with you.'

He closed his eyes and felt his nose. 'Hell's misery! Must I be pestered?'

'Yes!' I snapped at him. 'I'll pester you until I have this clear. Have you been giving orders in my house?'

'*Your* house!' His eyes opened, his lips quirked. 'You poor loobie! You have no house. 'Tis my house now and I'm the master of it.'

'Ho!' Hands to my hips, I nodded, brazen as Thirza. 'So you'll be denying me my rights. If you're the master, I'm the mistress here, and the mistress rules the roost in households as all the world knows — and the Bible says *A good wife is priced above rubies*. Am I not your wife?'

'That you are indeed,' he returned, mocking. 'God help me!'

'The devil will if God will not, but we won't quibble as to which of us has first claim to this house where *I* was born.' I pointed this, yet speaking smooth-tongued for peace's sake, not feeling ready for a further scene and apprehensive of him in this ugly mood with his face so changed, his eyes so small and his nose so sad — poor Percy. 'We will agree to share and share alike even though you have sworn to me endow with all thy worldly goods — so it seems already you prepare to break your marriage oath. However, thanks be, I am not greedy. All I ask is that my own room remains my own. I do not,' I said, trembling at the thought of it, 'like to lie in my father's great bed along with his and my mother's ghost.'

Percy darted me a look; then his lips quirked again, and he asked, honey-mouthed, 'Why this sudden surprising decision from my little pretty wife?' His tone, for all it was sugared, had an acidulous taste, to bring a sour answer to my tongue.

'Yes, I am your wife — for my undoing — and I'm little, but I am not pretty, and I know it, Master Milksop.'

'You have not enough conceit of yourself.' His eyes slid over me and narrowed. 'I find you disturbingly pretty.'

'Be damned!' I cried. 'What's come to you both? First Rob says, and now —' I paused, mouth open to swallow my words. For if ever a fool asked for trouble I did; and would get it.

'And what does Rob say?' asked my husband with ice in his voice and a glint in his eye.

'Nought but what you've said just now to plague me,' I gabbled. 'Can I help it if I'm dwarfish and unhandsome? I'll be a beauty when I'm grown, as Great-aunt Rossiter told me, and then you can jeer till you're blue in the face — I'll have a dozen gentlemen come courting.'

'A dozen?' Percy laughed under his breath. 'I'll have my work cut out to fight 'em all. As for your natural reluctance in taking a ghost to your bed — that I can well understand. You might even prefer — were you given the choice — to take me.'

And though his tone was jesting, his words I think were not, and his eyes, warm on mine with that same look I had once seen in Robin's, first confused, and then scared me to panic. I backed in a flurry and turned to go out as Robin came in from behind the screens, booted and cloaked for riding.

'I have come to bid you goodbye, Prue,' said he, standing as still as a statue.

My knees went weak and my sight went blurred. The room spun and then rocked like a galleon afloat; my lips moved and a whisper came out of them: 'Where ... where are you going?'

'Away.'

No word, not the stir of a finger from Percy who sat in a huddle, chin dropped.

'I am leaving here,' said Robin, speaking louder. 'There is no place in this house for three.'

'Rob!' I could feel the whiteness in my face and the pinch of fear in my throat. 'No, Rob, you can't... You must not go! You have often fought before. This is no more than a passing tiff...'

Robin spoke, looking over my shoulder. 'I shall take Silver, my mare. She *is* my mare, you know. Your father gave her to me. I shall ride her to Charmouth.'

'Great heavens! What nonsense is this?' I grabbed his hand. 'What are you saying? Why Charmouth?'

'It is the way the King took. I shall follow him.'

'Percy!' Would he never come out of his trance? Would he sit for ever bunched in his chair, staring before him at nothing from behind his swollen nose? 'Percy!' I cried again. 'Do you hear? He is going! Rob's leaving us. Why? 'Tis a trick. He can't mean it. Rob, say you don't mean it!'

Percy sat with eyes fixed like an image; the room ceased to spin and was still.

Robin stooped for his hat, and fastened his cloak. There came the sound of a snuffling whimper, a whine at his feet: Peg's red spaniel puppy had followed him. He lifted it and cuddled it up to his face, and touched with his lips the round satiny head. 'I can't take you,' he whispered. Then, setting it down, and without another word or backward look, he went.

I ran after him into the courtyard. Ham was there holding his horse.

'Rob!' I flung myself into his arms. He held me close, his cheek to mine. 'You must not leave us so!' I sobbed. 'You will come back — say you'll come back!'

'Some time — some day I will come back — to you.'

For an instant I felt the leap of his heart against my own. Then his arms released me and he turned to Ham, whose eyes were round as pebbles at these doings. 'God be with you, Ham,' said Robin, 'you have served me well and I shall not forget you.'

'Nay, now, young master,' Ham protested, 'what new mischief be you plotting? Be careful o' the mare, sir, she be blown wi' corn and has not been ridden these two days past.'

'I'll take the stuffing out of her,' said Robin, 'never fear.' And he sprang into the saddle, clapped spurs against the grey mare's sides and was away.

'No!' I found breath then to scream at him. 'No, Rob — Robin! Stay!'

'Tis better,' said Percy's voice at my side, 'much better he should go.'

'He will come back,' I whispered, but my mouth was dry as ashes and I shook. 'He will come back — he told me so. This is a prank to fright us...'

Percy's lips were closed and smiling; he spoke no word, he gave no sign; he stood with me and watched him whom he called 'Brother' riding to outstrip the wind along the Charmouth road. We glimpsed him through the feathering tree branches leaning forwards in the saddle to urge the grey mare on, with the dust from her heels in a cloud behind him, and his hair aflame in the last of the sun. Then a blindness came and hid him from my sight, and when I looked again the road was empty.

And, 'I shall hate you for this, Prue,' I heard Percy say, 'though I'll love you all my life.'

Strange that while he smiled still I saw his tears.

CHAPTER SIX

How my Aunt Rossiter learned of this upheaval in our household can only be conjectured, and my surmise she was possessed of magic, either black or white, but surely not vouchsafed to ordinary mortals, became a certainty when she returned to us once more to take command, as a genie called from the blue. Yet in the light of older reason, I prefer to think Thirza herself not guiltless of a hand in those events that followed swiftly on the exodus of Robin.

I remember how on the morning after his departure having cried myself to sleep the night before, I woke to the sound of a horse's hooves on the road, and leapt from my bed in joy, as I thought, for our truant's return; but it was only Ham off on some errand.

All that day and the next, and throughout that week I waited, hoping against hope long after hope had gone. The house was like a tomb with the sorrow of death and this more recent loss upon it. As for Percy, since his startling declaration at the door, he had scarce addressed me. We sat at table and exchanged no word. He seemed to brood, shut in himself, white-faced and mumpish. His nose had ceased to swell, he nursed his injury and took it to his soul to leave a scar.

That he mourned for Robin I have no smallest doubt; that he loved him with a deeper love than his distorted love for me, I doubt not, too; but that insatiable torment which like a fruitless flower was grafted on my life to bud and blossom there, fed by its own bitter passion, that was a love to crucify the heart as none save I and his God may know...

I know this also: that after Robin left us, he went haunted. From my window I would see him skulking in the garden, head bent and thumb to lip: and sometimes I would follow him, in pity for his grief, which was a deeper thing than mine for all I knew he blamed me for what had come about. Blamed me! But why? I may have shrunk instinctively from knowledge, or the answer to that riddle. What had I done, I asked him once, that he should hate me for Rob's going? They had fought, and Rob broke Percy's nose, but had not, it seemed disfigured it, since no sign save a little bump on the bridge remained to mark the blow, and Rob had offered his hand to be refused. If they had fought with swords, I said, a worser hurt or even death, might have been done…

Thus I, at supper, while Percy sat and gave me nothing, neither word nor look. Only when my voice faltered and died did he say, after five frozen minutes and staring at the table, 'You have no need to lock your door at night.'

I confess I was staggered, for how did he know that? I still slept in my attic room under the eaves, while Percy slept in his, although my father's chamber was prepared and waiting for me — or for us; yet no more on that subject had been said. So what obscure and purblind apprehension had prompted me to bolt my door? The fear of ghosts or of this stranger in the house who sat at the head of my father's table in my father's chair, dressed in his mourning black; this boy who was almost a man, my cousin, and now my husband, who looked on me with loathing if he ever looked at all?

One day he rode out at sunrise to return at sundown, his horse dark with sweat, his clothes grey with dust; and when I asked him where he had been he told me curtly, 'Charmouth.'

That same evening our Great-aunt Rossiter came to Folly's End.

I see her now descending from her decrepit old coach in her tall hat and her cumbrous red gown, her bony face encircled by her ruff, her sharp eyes peering over it at me who peeped behind the lattice. Yes, she saw me and nodded, and lifted a finger to beckon, and wrinkled her lips in a smile to show her yellow teeth.

'May the Lord have mercy!' I muttered.

Percy looked up from his book. Conscientious was he in his studies. I'll swear he had faultlessly construed the Medea Mr Moon set for his holiday task.

''Tis Aunt Rossiter,' said I aghast, 'she's at the door.'

Percy rose at once, set down his book, and hurried out to greet her. I lagged behind, reluctant and slow as if there were lead in my shoes.

'So, nephew!' Thus my aunt bending from her height to peck at Percy's cheek; I saw him surreptitiously rub it. 'When the cat's away, the mice — Has Moon returned?'

'No, madam,' answered Percy, standing stiff.

'He is a long time gone to poke his finger in the Fairfax pie. Take care that he don't cook *your* goose, my lad, although God knows when the golden eggs are like to drop from it.'

'It is always a pleasure to see you, madam,' said Percy, ignoring this sally, 'but may I ask the reason of this — this very — welcome visit? I trust you bring us no ill news. Is Great-uncle Rossiter well?'

'He is always well,' returned my aunt with a sniff, as though she thought that an offence, 'a healthier man than he never stepped. And why in the name of fortune should I bring ill news to you?'

'Why indeed, madam — no, certainly — I —' Percy picked at his thumb as he floundered — 'we have had some trouble here of late to add to our sad bereavement. You perchance may not have heard —'

'I *have* heard,' said Aunt Rossiter grimly, and rustling past him with a gesture to her man to bring her baggage, 'Carry it to the guest-chamber,' she ordered. 'Prudence!'

I came forward to curtsy. With her finger under my chin she jerked up my face to receive her kiss. 'You are looking peaked,' said she, severely. 'Where is your woman Thirza?'

I murmured she was doubtless making ready the guest room, and would my aunt take supper or had she supped?

No, she had not supped and was, she stated, hungry as a wolf. And, on my word, she looked it, with her fangs bared to the molars in a smile, that, though meant to be propitious, had such an opposite effect as to appear to my alarm as if she might be persuaded in her hunger to eat me. Whereupon I was about to hasten to the kitchen to give orders, when my aunt taking me by the hand, said sternly, 'No. Leave the servants to their own work. Your place is the parlour.' She made a swift survey of my small person. 'Methinks you've grown. And high time, too. You may shoot up as I did when once you are — hem! Piers!'

'Madam?'

'How long is it since that young scapegrace left the house?'

'He has been gone five days,' I piped, before Percy could answer.

'And no trace of him yet?' My aunt, still holding my hand, had now entered the room.

'There is a trace, madam,' Percy said, with some heightened colour in his cheeks. 'I have this day rode into Charmouth where I learned —'

'Why to Charmouth?' my aunt interrupted, while I felt my heart beat faster.

'Because, madam,' and Percy paused before he blurted in one breath, 'Robin told us before he left that he would go the way of the King.'

My aunt nodded approval. 'He could choose no better way. Yes, the King, as we know, went to Charmouth, hoping to take ship there, but the plan ran amok and he finally embarked from the fishing village of Brighthelmstone in Sussex. So young Peverill followed His Majesty's route and you have now traced him to Charmouth. Carry on with your story, sirrah.'

But thus commanded Percy did not carry on with his story to very much effect. The gist of his preamble, delivered under his aunt's piercing eye, gave only one outstanding clue to Robin's whereabouts. He had sold his mare at Charmouth, in order, Percy ventured to presume, that he be provided with sufficient means to undertake his journey. He had lain at the inn for a night and boarded a ship the next morning, bound for the coast of France.

'Ay, France!' Aunt Rossiter nodded again, till her witch's hat slid sideways. She dragged it off and cast it down upon the settle, and seated herself in the chair. 'I must write at once to Chancellor Hyde that he keep watch for our young gentleman, though I suspect he'll not be over-welcome. 'Tis one more mouth to feed when the King and his court are starving. I hear the King himself owes for all and more than he has eaten since last April. But that's no reason why *I* should starve. Where is that slut with my supper?'

'Here, madam.' Thirza bearing a tray came in, very red in the face. 'Being possessed of but one pair of hands is, I'll own, a *handy*-cap.' She darted venom at my aunt as she mouthed this sorry pun, and placed her tray upon the table and her hands upon her hips. 'Your supper is ready, madam, the best the house provides, which is better I don't doubt than what the

King, God bless him, has in exile, being nothing worse than cold pig's trotters, cooked, madam, these two days against your coming, since I expected your arrival sooner in answer to my — well, so there it is.' And Thirza glanced aside at Percy, sucked her teeth, and started off again. 'And had you taken up the notion to honour us earlier with your appearance, madam — and my thumbs and big toes pricking all that day and the night through as always when you are on your way to us, I am forewarned —'

Which was as great a lie as I have heard our Thirza utter; and why she stood so more than ever garrulous with her words so glib and oiled, when I guessed her spoiling to bandy them, was unaccountable; yet trust her to know her business best, and so: 'Such neat's tongues, madam, as were waiting here, juicy and plump, delicious — that we had to eat them lest they taint. 'Tis a sin to waste good food.'

Neat's tongues! This the first I'd heard of that.

Percy was frowning, I staring, my aunt rising majestically to say, 'Pity 'tis *your* tongue, woman, be not cut out and cooked, though I misdoubt it would make rotten eating to purge the body and poison the blood.'

'Will you take cowslip wine, ma'am?' asked Thirza, twisting her mouth.

'I will not. I'll take metheglin, sack or —'

'His lordship holds the key of the wine-cellar, madam,' said Thirza, syrup-sweet.

'His —?' My aunt started, then glanced at Percy. 'Oh, you! Go, boy, and fetch me a bottle.'

'Yes, Aunt,' said Percy, hurrying off.

'And see you don't shake it in bringing it up,' called out Aunt Rossiter after him. She then filled her trencher, took up her fork, and ate with a great appetite. 'The longer that I live,' observed my aunt between mouthfuls. 'the more I see the hand of God in the ordering of human lives.'

'That is so, madam,' agreed Thirza, and quoting from the only book she ever read, which she had conned by heart, having learned herself to spell when I was taught my alphabet, '*He putteth forth His Hand upon the rock, He overturneth mountains by the roots; His eyes seeth every precious thing and the thing that is hid He bringeth forth to light. But where shall wisdom —*'

'As I was about to say,' interposed my aunt raising her voice to drown Thirza's, 'that which might appear misfortune or even a calamity may prove to be a blessing in disguise.'

'How more than true, ma'am,' Thirza said, eyes up.

'Take the case,' my aunt proceeded, 'of Sir Robert's truancy—'

'Ah, the sweet young gentleman,' sighed Thirza in a rapture. 'I loved him as my own!'

'Then you might,' I interrupted with some heat, 'have shown yourself less of a scold to him, Thirza. I'll not forget how you would pull his ears and come at him like all the Furies when he mussed the kitchen flags with his muddy boots.'

'— of Sir Robert's truancy —' pursued my aunt with chill determination. 'If he should reach the coast of France alive —'

'Mercy on us! Oh, I hope he will!' I gasped.

'He,' said my aunt with a look to shrivel, 'will do better in attendance on the King than loitering here, the guest of charity.'

But this I would not pass though I be turned into a toad for it. 'Was Rob to blame,' I cried, 'if he and his lands were beggared by those swinish swag-wagging whoreson suites?'

'Silence! Shame on you, girl!' My aunt pounded the table till the pewter jumped. ''Tis high time you learned civility and gentle speaking. You are foul-mouthed as any rake-hell, you have the manners of a bawd. You defile the room and my presence. Leave it.'

Thankfully I left it, colliding with Percy as I slunk out.

'You've been a mighty long time in the cellar,' I snapped, for having been bitten I was sore to bite back. 'Your hair is full of cobwebs and your hands are as black as your heart.' And I ran from him before he could clout me with the bottle, as I could see he had a mind to do.

I undressed in the dark and crept into my bed, and lay there, straining my ears for the boom of Aunt Rossiter's voice rising up from the open window below to drone in at my casement like the hum of an angry cockchafer. I heard Percy's, too, answering, in a plaintive minor key, and although I could not distinguish the words, the tone of them told me some lengthy discussion was taking place, and I heard my own name mentioned once or twice. But I could hear nothing of Thirza and soon I heard nothing at all, for I fell sound asleep and dreamed of Robin.

We were walking on a seashore gathering shells, and his arm was round my shoulders and his face was close to mine. We had found a great shell which he gave me to hold to my ear. 'Now listen,' he said, 'to the voice of all those that you love, and the voices of those that love you, and the voices of those that love those that love those —'

'That will be my father,' said I, 'and you and Percy and Thirza and myself.'

'You do not love me, nor yourself,' said Robin, 'else you would have followed after me on Ebony when I rode away on Silver to join His Majesty the King.'

'So you *have* gone to the King!' I cried. 'Aunt Rossiter spoke aright. She knows everything even to the smallest sparrow that falls to the ground, for from her nothing is hid, not even the manners of a bawd. God save the King and you, Rob!' At which I clapped my hands, so happy was I for his safety, and let drop the shell I was holding. As he stooped to recover it I perceived it had grown as long as a stag's antler.

'Lend your ear to this,' Rob said again, 'and you will hear the heartbeat of the world and all the angels singing; and the King himself shall marry you and call you his lovely dear.'

'Good morrow and thanks be to Your most gracious Majesty,' I answered, curtsying low and very humble, for now I saw that Robin wore a crown. 'Do they call you the Black Boy in France, sir?' A foolish question that, since Rob's hair was the colour of red iron. Whereupon he kissed me very kind and offered me a comfit which proved to be no nicer than a pig's trotter served cold. So then I fell to crying and woke myself with sobs, to hear a great commotion in the yard.

I sprung from my bed to look.

It was moonshine and a night for fairies, the sky a burning blue ringed round with darkness and bestrewn with stars; but I'd no thought to gaze at them. My eyes were on the earth. Nor did it need much vision to persuade me that the horse Ham led away was Mr Moon's.

He had returned a few days earlier than was expected, opportunely as it chanced, to meet my aunt and to confer with her upon the case of Percy and myself. For once, in this, Aunt Rossiter and Mr Moon were in complete agreement, and Percy and I no more than pawns upon the checker-board in this game of our joined lives, to be moved by the guiding players as they willed.

'And remember,' said Thirza next morning — she having, I suspected, made good use of the parlour keyhole the night before — 'remember, my dear, that though it tears your

Thirza's heart out of her body, it were best you follow madam's inclination. All birds must leave the nest — that is the law of Nature — yet it be not always Nature's way to mate them first and then divide them — no! Yet so abortive is life become for us since our fair land was first dismembered by those jackals who have set Beelzebub to reign as Lord Protector of Misrule, that nothing is as it was in the beginning nor as it ever will be — while I live.'

Which oblique allusion to yet more disturbance imbued me with fresh qualms. 'Nay now, Thirza,' I pleaded, 'if you have anything to tell me, tell it, pray, in open words and not so double-tongued. What is afoot within the house and why is Aunt Rossiter come? And why —'

'And why and wherefore!' Thirza caught me in her arms and kissed me heartily. 'Never cross a bridge until you come to it, my darling, and believe me when I say I know no more than the cat what lies ahead, for the secret things belong unto the Lord thy God, to be revealed in His own way and His own time. But this much I can say, that changes be afoot for you and his young lordship — which is only right and proper since he approaches manhood and you are still as green as a spring onion, for all that I have dosed you daily these three months past with penny-royal...' So she had, and telling me the noxious brew would give me a complexion like a rose, and sweep me clear of pimples, though I'll swear I never had a spot in all my life.

'And,' continued Thirza, 'would it not be asking too much of any male cub to withstand the call of flesh when temptation trots beside him, to which being gentle-bred and gentle-minded and not a lecherous coarse-grained rip he dare not yield?'

'Oh, deary me,' I sighed, for accustomed though I was to Thirza's overcharged multiloquence this left me more than ever in a puzzle. 'Drawing water from a dry well would be easier than drawing sense from you.'

And straightway I betook myself to Percy hoping he might be disposed to give me a clue to this conundrum; for though he seemed to shun me like the plague and look upon me as upon a cockroach, I would have sooner braved his jaundiced eye than my Great-aunt Rossiter's.

I found him in the orchard prone upon his stomach, under the very tree where I had lain on the day of that unhappy fight. He was, or appeared to be, conning a book. His hands supported his face and covered his ears, which may have been the reason that he did not hear my footfall, nor stir to my approach. Gingerly I touched his backside with my toe, whereupon his head jerked round, and seeing me he glowered.

'Well, what now?' he demanded crossly. 'Am I to be allowed no minute's peace but you must come mewling after me?'

Little enough encouragement this to set me probing for whatsoever he might know that I did not, and which concerned myself no less than him; but since my curiosity had been already piqued I was not content to go unsatisfied. Seating myself beside him in the grass, I nursed my knees and treated him to my most winning smile.

'Is it always to be thus between us, honey-bird?' I asked. 'Why should I pester you? Can you not speak gentle to me sometimes? Am I so loathly in your sight?'

At that he stared astonishment, as well he might, it not being my way to take rebuffs and snubs so silken-voiced and ladyish.

'And who,' my husband asked, his eyes upon me, narrowed, and a reluctant smile pulling one corner of his mouth to answer mine, 'who has said I find you loathly?'

'Every look you gave since Rob went says the same,' I told him with a pursing of my lips.

'And is it loathing — are you sure of that?' enquired Percy, rolling over on his side to gaze up at me while I gazed down at him; and when I gave him no reply he snatched at my hand and opened my fingers one by one and spread them out upon his palm, and blushed to the roots of his white-gold hair. 'Or is it ... is it...?' And on a breath, his eyes a-shine, 'God knows,' he said, 'what spell or mischief you have put upon me, Prue, but I find you as vexatious as a tick.'

'Well, now,' I answered mincingly, 'if that in truth be so, you had best show me how to mend my ways, for I have no wish to gall you, and am willing to be dutiful and kind.'

Which brought from him a response unexpected. Kneeling beside me in the grasses and in a cracking whisper Percy asked, 'Are you such a babe as not to know what you are saying? Oh, Prue! If I could think you knew what you were saying I'd send Aunt Rossiter and Mr Moon to hell and take ourselves ... to heaven.'

Now what was I to make of that? Surely witchcraft, of which I still surmised our aunt not guiltless, must be about the place and in the air to bring Percy to his knees so flushed and stammering, 'None but I has any right to you, and yet they want to part us, Prue, because they say you are too young for... But I'd wait ... I'd wait till you were ready for our mating if you will bear me out in this and stand with me to defy them. Will you? Will you? I am not of age, I know, and Mr Moon is yet my guardian, curse his guts! But I'd forgo all they may offer me as bribe — Paris, the Hague, the King's Court, the Grand Tour — and a course of study at the University of Heidelberg, which I own I'd give my soul to have, yet would I whole-heartedly renounce it if I could hear you say that you will live with me ... and be my love. That's how the poets sing it, Prue. Could anything be sweeter?'

Nothing indeed to my ears at that moment, and we all eyes in wonder, each for each; I the more flustered to see him thus so changed, so burning pink, so shaking white in this first flood of his boyish passion. And confusedly, my voice a-quiver with the stirring and rebirth of those incomprehensible emotions which every so often did of late possess me, I whispered, of a sudden shy, '*Am* I your love then, Percy?'

And what would have come of this under that apple tree with the birds shouting a jubilant chorus to the surge and song of our hearts there is no telling; for even while he leaned to me, eyes closing, hands touching, lips greedy, a shadow fell, and we were disenchanted.

Mr Moon stood over us, black as a raven in the dazzle of the sun, his mouth pulled down and his nose drawn up. 'My lord, you are late for your lesson.'

In a scramble I came to my feet. Percy, pale as I was red, came to his senses.

'I crave your pardon, sir,' said he, looking daggers and standing straight, 'but I was not aware my studies were to be resumed today.'

'And why should you suppose that your enforced vacation be interminably continued?' queried Mr Moon, with ponderous irony. He glanced aside at me and coldly bowed. 'Good morning, Lady Folliett.'

'Good morning, sir.' And this being my first sight of him since his return, I felt it incumbent upon me to enquire, 'I trust you had a comfortable journey?'

'A not *un*comfortable one, I thank your ladyship. I have never felt that travel, no matter though it be on horseback or by coach, is an embarrassment. Fortunately.'

There he paused, his eyes askew at both of us to make me cross my fingers; yet it may have been the sun caused him to squint.

'Why fortunately, sir?' asked Percy sharp.

'Because,' His Reverence answered blandly, 'I — and you, my lord, in the near future — will travel much together. The continent is wide.'

'England,' Percy said, tight-lipped, 'is wide enough for me.'

'No doubt; but yet not wide enough to provide you with the necessary and final adjuncts to your education. Do you return with me to the house, my lord, I wish to speak to you —' he glanced at me again to add — 'alone.'

'Yes, sir,' said Percy, unwontedly bold, 'but before I go I wish to make it clear in the presence of,' he took my hand and held it to his side, 'of my wife, that this separation which you and Mistress Rossiter do insist upon, is made without my sanction or desire.' He flung this out with a defiance that I inwardly applauded and let him know it by a squeezing of his fingers.

'My lord forgets he is a minor,' answered Mr Moon, stretching his lips to a smile.

'I do not forget,' retorted Percy, with his chin up, 'that I am master here and that this child —' his hand upon mine tightened — 'is my lawful wife and that none, nor man nor woman, has any right to put asunder us whom God hath joined. My place is now and evermore beside her. And,' continued Percy, waxing warm and bolder still in his vernal if belated self-assertion, 'should it be essential that I go abroad to complete my education, I demand that my wife shall come with me. Where I go, shall she go. That would have been her father's wish — as it is mine.'

Such daring from one hitherto so tractable was not the least of this accumulation of surprises; and while I gaped, admiring, and squeezed my husband's fingers yet again to urge him on, Mr Moon capped all with the announcement, serpent-smooth: 'A laudable and very natural desire, which, alas, in view of her ladyship's excessive youth —' and I felt my youth indeed a slur upon me — 'cannot for the meantime be achieved. It is thought best by those in charge of her, and has now been arranged, that Lady Folliett leaves this house — today.'

This then was the outcome of Aunt Rossiter's appearance and Mr Moon's return. All had been discussed and planned and brought to a conclusion overnight. What mattered though we mutinied — and you may be sure we did — our voices were less than the hum of a gnat to the sound of the trumpeter's horn. Nor did Aunt Rossiter hesitate to give us her views full blast, finding a ready echo from her erstwhile antagonist, Mr Moon; while even Thirza gave support in tune to the conspiracy to form the third in this triad against us, who save for each other, now did stand alone.

Today… Thus ran the edict, and wisely, no doubt, since delay at this stage of proceedings might have resulted in open rebellion. Those in authority saw to it we should not be allowed sufficient time to consider their verdict. They had the last word and that was the end of the matter. Nor were we permitted to offer a petition in our own defence. Percy, after his one attempt to stand upon the order of his going, had made no further effort to stay mine. Go I must, and with all speed from my home to my great-aunt's at Colyton.

That which for so long I had dreaded had now come to pass.

In vain did I question Thirza while she packed my small possessions; but she could tell me no more than that Mistress

Rossiter had decided my manners and deportment were such to claim instant correction. 'And,' said Thirza, 'though it irks me sore and ravages my bosom to tear the babe I suckled from my arms, I must give that old curmudgeon right and myself wrong if I debar you from so much advantage. Here is your opportunity, my darling, to be guided in the ways best suited to your high station of life. When you are a woman grown, these scurvy knaves that rule us will be feeding the fires of hell, please God! Then my lamb will thank her Thirza for this sacrifice upon the altar of propriety. Madam Rossiter, for all she be a stern task-mistress, is better placed to teach you how to be a lady than this poor ignorant jobbernowl that knows no more than how to love you.' And Thirza, kneeling by the coffer that was to take my clothes, fell to weeping with loud sobs to bring me to her side in tears myself.

'No, Thirza, I'll not go! I'll never, never leave you. I do not wish to be a woman grown. I want only to stay here with you and Percy. This is my home, I'll not be taken from it. No ... and oh...!' And so on, till our joint bewailings brought Aunt Rossiter from below to bid Thirza hasten with her preparations for my exit, and me to cease these cat-cries. Whereupon I dried my tears and stopped my noise, and asked with desperate courage: 'Aunt! Have I no voice in this disposal of me? Must I indeed be forced to come and live with you? Do not think I am ungrateful of your interest, but surely it is given in the Word of God that a wife shall cleave unto her husband, and above all, madam, am I so attached to my home for the sake of my dear father — and he so lately gone. It does seem to me unfeeling, Aunt, that I should leave this house, where every nook and cranny speaks of ... of...' And here I went no further, but broke in tears again.

'This,' my aunt said, not unkindly, 'is one excellent reason why you should be removed from these surroundings. Believe me, child, your father would have never wished that you should brood upon your sorrow. Grief is natural but the nursing of it is destructive to young life, and turns in time to fungicide like mistletoe upon a sapling oak. As to your husband, though I grant you wedded, you are not a wife. When you are ripe for marriage then will you return to your home and your lawful mate. Meanwhile he will travel with his tutor to complete his education in wider fields than these few poor acres of his heritage. During which time you will abide with me — and your Great-uncle Rossiter — at Templecombe.'

I swallowed a sob to enquire for how long that would be. To this my aunt vouchsafed me no reply, but bade Thirza pack only the barest necessities, since clothes and equipment would be provided for me at her house. 'And look to it, woman, you put all in some portable baggage. My coach will not carry a coffer.'

'May I take my dogs and falcons, Aunt?' I asked, while Thirza, cross as crabs at this latest behest, flounced from the room to obey it.

'Dogs?' repeated Aunt Rossiter in a tone to bode ill for my pets. 'We are dog-ridden at the Hall already. I will have no more.' Then seeing my woebegone face, my aunt relented. 'One dog then, child, I'll allow you, but see it be house-trained. I'll have no piddling nor messing in my corners.'

'Yes, Aunt, our dogs are marvellous cleanly in their habits,' I lied with haste. 'And I pray you, madam, may I bring Martha and Mary?'

'Bless and save us!' my aunt exclaimed, 'who in the world are they? I'll have no females about the house. One is enough, I'll warrant.'

'Yes, Aunt, certainly,' I answered, trembling, 'but these be no females, madam. Indeed I think that they be neuter for they never lay an egg.'

'Eh?' cried my aunt in a voice of the greatest amazement.

'If you please, they are my hawks, ma'am,' I besought her, 'and I love them dearly.'

Over my aunt's grim lips a spasm passed: sternly she suppressed it and with a lofty air conceded, 'One hawk then, also, child, but not two. Our own mews is well enough supplied. And now, no further argument. We shall leave here this forenoon and I have no time to waste.'

It was evident my aunt would give no loophole for escape from her firm clutches: in which I grant her shrewd enough perception, for I vow that had she spared me one more night at Folly's End I would have found some means to free myself from my predicament, maybe to follow Robin on his way: and I do not doubt but I would have incited Percy to come with me.

Some such wild scheme was in my mind when I ran to the stables to bid farewell to Ebony; but Ham was in the stable yard, and my aunt's aged coachman, and the coach itself standing ready to receive the horses in its shafts. No hope here with all these eyes about, and Jack, the scullion, slouching from the bake-house to tell me, 'God be wi' ye, lady. Joy is sorrow's daughter an' you'll not bend your neck to any man alive... No, not for the King himself. I'll not forget ye in me prayers … and here's a four-leafed clover.' He unfolded his grimy fist to show his findings, which he begged me take — ''twill bring your ladyship good fortune if you brew it in the first dew o' the morning, and drink it fasting... Beware of rooftops and cry pardon... They know not what they do.'

'Why should I beware of rooftops?' I asked him, startled. But he only slobbered and looked sideways, blinking his silly eyes, and mumbled he was mortal feared of roofs and all high places — 'though you be bound for the highest place, good mistress, in God's time.'

Then Ham came at him with a pitchfork to prod poor Jack's behind and tell him, 'Stop your yauping, zany, and go fetch her ladyship's jerfalcon.'

But that Jack refused to do. 'They be birds o' prey, and sinful in the eyes of the Lord, so be as they catch and torture mouses and such-like gentle creatures besides the singing birds o' the air... No, lady, I'll not touch 'un.'

'Then I will,' I said, and betook myself to the mews, glad to be quit of poor Jack and his outlandish talk.

As I passed into the courtyard from the stables, I heard my name called softly, and there was Percy throwing glances round his shoulder as if the devil were behind him.

'Prue!' he whispered coming up alongside, and I thought how he had changed from the proud young gallant who had made bold to claim me in the orchard; now he looked shrunken and walked as sadly as a cur after a beating: and beaten he was, surely, being in no mind for further fight. 'Prue,' said he, as one repeats a lesson, and sucking at the thumb he had picked raw, 'though they take you from me now, 'tis not for ever. I'll return when you are ready. Meantime you will be taught —'

'Oh, taught!' I cried. 'I am sick of being told that I'll be taught... Taught what, pray? What can that sharp-nosed old flint, our great-aunt, teach me of the things I wish to know?'

'And what,' Percy took a step nearer, 'is it you wish to know?'

'Everything,' I answered, 'that is hidden. And why the poets make a song of love, and what love is ... and why there are a dozen kinds of love. For I have loved my father and I love you and Rob and Thirza and the dogs and —'

'If you love me,' said Percy, interrupting, pink-flushed, with a glance this way and that, and up at the windows overlooking the courtyard where we stood, 'if you love me that's all *I* wish to know.' And having satisfied himself we were unseen he put his arms with a shy awkwardness around me, and kissed me warm and full upon the mouth.

'This, for a start,' he murmured. 'You have much to learn that only I may teach... Say you will love me always, for I swear I shall love you. Say after me, "You, Piers, are my faithful husband as I am your true wife."'

I repeated the words and returned him his kisses, nothing so shy as he; and I marvelled at the softness of his lips that played with mine till I was burning and he breathless.

'How can I leave you?' he panted. 'How cruel it is to part us now. My sweet ... how sweet you are! Like honey... And to think that I have lived beside you for so long and never... Prue,' he stopped to kiss again, and said in broken whispers, 'promise me, when we are parted, to take your Bible to yourself and read that loveliest of all the poet's songs ... the Song of Solomon. You know how it goes? *By night on my bed I sought him whom my soul loveth.* Will you read a chapter every night? And I will read the same.'

I nodded, speechless.

'If,' whispered Percy, caressing, 'if absence makes the heart grow fond, I'll be all heart for you when I return. Is it not wonderful, Prue, to know that we are bound to each other heart to heart? But the greatest wonder of all,' said he, his eyes catching the sun, 'is to see you now as my Rose of Sharon and not as a malapert slut!'

At which I found voice to ask him, 'Must you tease me to the last?'

'Sweet, I tease because I love you.' And how sweet that was indeed. Never in my life had I been sugared, and the taste of it was luscious to make me thirst for more. Then, 'Swear by this ring I have put on your finger,' he urged, 'to be true to me whom your soul loveth.'

'I have said —'

'I'll have you swear.'

Solemnly I swore and kissed his wedding ring and told him, 'Now you must swear to me.'

'With all my soul I swear —'

'No, wait.' I took his hand that had gone straying to surprise me. 'Swear as I tell you — not to bite your thumbs! And I'll pray God to help you cure the habit.'

Whereupon he laughed, bright-eyed. 'I see that you'll be teaching me as much as I'll ever teach you. Yes, my dear darling, I swear.'

And so we parted.

I sat beside Great-aunt Rossiter in her ramshackle old coach with Martha, my jerfalcon, on my wrist and Rob's red spaniel puppy on my knee, for since I was bidden, 'Take only one dog,' I took him, not his little black sister. But when I waved my farewells to those at the door and despite love's first vows in my heart, love's first kiss on my lips, and the tears I shed into my handkercher, I confess that my grief was divided, for I sorrowed as much at this parting from Thirza my nurse, as from Percy, my pretty young husband — and Mary, my peregrine hawk.

CHAPTER SEVEN

When I left Folly's End I had thought and had lived as a child; yet I learned in a month at Aunt Rossiter's house to put away childish things.

Such an utter and complete subversion was wrought upon my mind and mode of life by this departure, not only from my home but from all previous standards of existence, that more than ever now did I believe myself transformed by my aunt's witchcraft. She, good soul, nothing if not thorough in her undertakings, allowed no vestige of my former self to hamper her instruction. Metaphorically and in the literal sense was I stripped bare to be refashioned.

Templecombe Hall in the county of Devon, seat of the Rossiter family, is a far grander habitation than the converted farmhouse which had been my home since birth. Rebuilt in the reign of Elizabeth on the site of the original and smaller timber-framed house, it had remained unchanged through the vicissitudes of civil war, notwithstanding Mr Rossiter's avowed adherence to the cause of the King and his father.

True, part of the property was sequestrated, for although he had never taken arms against the rebels, my great-uncle had been marked a suspect, and brought before the commissioners as a delinquent. One can only suppose his artlessness and lack of guile saved him from imprisonment — or worse; and I often wondered if that mildest of men were as foolish as his wife would have him be. Certain it is that in this grave crisis his timidity and diffidence stood him in good stead; for, as my aunt gave me to understand, he was eventually dismissed as a harmless half-wit, with the reserve of a fine upon him to the tune of five thousand pounds plus one-third of his estate. By such foul means did Parliament's bloodhounds secure the wherewithal to meet the war's demands. And thus was my Uncle Rossiter left with three parts of his land and his home intact, but with little enough for its upkeep.

A fine example of a Tudor residence is Templecombe: it stands in a dip of the hills a few miles inland from Sidmouth. There is something unusually striking in this mansion, which, when I went to live there, though scarcely a century old in reconstruction, bore even at that time a venerable, dignified appearance. Indeed, to my fancy, its grey walls, lichened roof, and mossy pavings, reflected the very spirit of my aunt, while even her domestics, grown old in long service, were grey and as hoary as she.

Entering through the archway on the south side you pass into the courtyard and thence by a broad passage to the lofty rectangular hall, with the staircase to the left of it and the parlour to the right. The screens, more massive than at Folly's End and exquisitely moulded, are pierced by twin arches leading eastwards to the buttery and kitchens, and westwards to the court. Above is the Great Chamber, and the sleeping and guest rooms, one of which was allotted to me. A splendid apartment this, the walls hung with tapestry, the curtains of embroidered satin threaded through with gold and silver. The furniture consisted of an immense oaken press, a high-backed chair, and stools covered in velvet embossed with the arms of the Follietts and Rossiters entwined; these were repeated above the fine carved chimney-piece and on the bed that towered to the Gothic beams, and was to my eyes large enough to hold a coach and horses. I should rightly have been awed by such magnificence; nor was my aunt unmindful of her grace in thus bestowing so regal a bedchamber upon one so insignificant, for not without pride did she inform me that in this bed Queen Elizabeth slept for two nights and on it was my great-uncle born. Despite of which honours I would have given all hope of salvation if, at that moment, I could have found wings to fly to my attic at home.

I had not been at Templecombe more than a week before my aunt, true to her word, equipped me with an entirely new wardrobe: from my head to my feet, over and under, was I re-clothed in silks and rich satins, black for my mourning, but of a daintiness to equal if not to surpass Percy's most elegant suit.

Much did I wish that he could see me so fine, with petticoats of taffety that rustled as I walked in my silver-buckled shoes. My hair was bound with silver ribands, my gown exposed my shoulders — and mighty cold I found that style too. I had a dozen silken handkerchers, and some of cambric edged with lace; I had lace bands, and tippets of lace and silver gauze. I had an overmantle of black velvet lined with purple and a snug black velvet hood; and a little fur muff for my hands against the winter.

But with all these bounties and delights upon me I still lamented: for what use to go in silks and satins when there was none to admire? How Percy would have eyed and envied me, and how Robin would have teased, and how much more respect would I have earned from both had I been thus beautified before them; yet to be sure Percy had named me his Rose of Sharon when I wore my aunt's ugly old gown. Yes! But could he have known me now I would have been his Lily of the Valleys, and, 'How beautiful are thy feet with shoes,' he would have said; for according to my promise I had read the Song, one chapter for each night since I left home, and found it lovelier than I had dreamed; and though I asked forgiveness for such a sinful thought, I do confess I felt that so much adoration was never written for the Church, as Mr Moon insisted and as the Book did say, but by a lover for his beautiful beloved. And more than ever did I yearn for my young spouse to see me, or failing him, a looking-glass that I might see myself, which pleasure was consistently denied me. The only mirror that the house contained was in Aunt Rossiter's chamber, where I dared not go without permission, nor never on so trivial a pretext.

And there were more restrictions. I had been accorded a waiting-maid named Deborah, as grey and gaunt as her mistress. She kept the strictest guard upon me, by order of my aunt I have no doubt, so that however much and often I may have schemed and plotted — as I most surely did — to escape from this prison life of luxury, even though it meant surrender of all my fine new clothes, the chance of such contingency was circumvented. When I walked in the garden Deborah kept her respectful distance in the rear. She slept in a closet that opened from my room, nor could I be permitted to perform a natural act but that Deborah forestalled my need with a receptacle. She never spoke unless I spoke to her; and then always with due deference. She was in fact the perfect maid, and I abhorred her. No gaoler could have been more unappealing. The sight of her stern visage at my bedside set my heart aching to burst itself for my dear Thirza and her bawdy talk, her scolding tongue, her kisses.

I do not know for how long I endured this homesick misery, nor for how many nights I drenched my pillow with my wretched tears, and vowed and sobbed into the darkness that I would not submit to be thus dragged away from Percy, turned so loving at the last; from Thirza who had been my second mother, and from Folly's End and all I cherished there. Nor had I yet forgotten Robin, and never failed to pray God he would return as he had promised, and was for ever questioning my aunt for any news that she might hear, to be told she had written to Chancellor Hyde concerning Robert Peverill and now awaited his reply.

Soon, however, so readily does youth adapt itself to circumstance, I ceased to chafe against these unfamiliar customs and conditions, which were, I knew, incontrovertible. Therefore did I accept my present lot with resignation, striving to make the best of it and count my blessings.

Great-uncle Rossiter was one of them. He, the merest cipher in his house and the estimation of his lady, had learned to some extent to live within himself a separate life in which he moved and had his being undiscovered and alone, and happily for me, uninterrupted.

To the secluded cloisters that this gentle gentleman had raised around his wife's dominion, I found myself admitted; so gradual was my approach, so tentative his invitation, I was scarce aware his door had opened to receive me before I found myself a welcome visitor to a terrain filled with rare delights and novelties, and not the least of these my uncle's herb garden.

Now I had learned something of distillery from Thirza, but her knowledge of herbalism was as a pin's head to the mountain of my uncle's. And what a new-found pleasure did this prove for me: for him also, I think, thus to act as Mentor to my Telemachus.

I know of nothing more charged with delights than a herb garden; not even a garden of flowers, which at Templecombe is still a thing to wonder at. Enclosed within high box hedges, its smooth-razed, terraced lawns flaunt a gay parterre decked out in every conceivable hue, with a fish-pond and a fountain in the middle, and yews carved in fantastic shape of bird and beast; yet with all this motley grace it maintained an air of spinsterish severity which was absent in my Uncle Rossiter's herb garden. Nor do I quarrel with any such deficit, for in that fragrant pleasaunce of cheerful odours and comforting smells, where all kinds of plants are ranged informally together, some modest, some brightly garbed and bare-faced as town-women, some virtuous as nuns, some retiring as hermits, some proud and many humble — each one is a doctor's disciple: and to each one is attached a history more enthralling than a fairy tale, when recounted in his hesitant way by my uncle.

From him I learned the quality and nature of a great many of these herbs whose names were hitherto unknown to me, and so-called from the things they resemble. As, for example, Hippuris, because it has the likeness of a horse's tail; Alopecuris, because, similarly, it resembles the tail of a fox; Pysllion, the flea-wort, shaped like a flea, and Myosata like a mouse's ear, and Coronopus like a crow's foot. And some herbs, my uncle told me, are named for certain features of the gods; such as Jupiter's Beard, and Mars' Blood, and the Hermodactyl or Mercury's Fingers. And I learned too that in ancient times the names of certain plants were bestowed upon him or her who first discovered them: such as Panacea, the pain-killer, from Panace, the daughter of Aesculapius; Armois or Artemisia, from Artemis, the goddess of the chase, the juice of which herb, so my uncle said, makes sickly blood flow strong and is excellent for females' complaints. Mercuriale, named after the celestial messenger, is a speedy cure for boils, pimples, warts and other blemishes, and is much prescribed by doctors for the small — and the great — pox.

My uncle told me also that in divers plants there are two sexes, even as in human life; the Laurel, the Mandrake, the

Birthwort, the Turpentine — of an offensive odour this, but of such virtue that it will destroy all parasites that feed upon the body, and keep heads cleansed of vermin: the Penny-royal, that is much loved by women, and the Rose of the Mount by men: all of these contain in each the qualities of male seed and feminine *ovum* — 'which as you have learned in Latin, means an egg,' said Uncle Rossiter, 'from which all life is sprung in some form or another.'

And he went on to say that among the Ancients, to whom we are primarily beholden for the medicinal advantages of herbs, did oftentimes arise some controversy in the naming of a plant. Thus, Lynceus, King of Scythia, would have slain young Triptolemus sent by Ceres to instruct mankind in the use of the bountiful Corn: for so greatly did Lynceus desire the credit of being the first to discover the precious grain by which man lives, that he planned to murder Ceres' messenger, Triptolemus, and take immortal honour to himself. But his evil intention having been revealed by the goddess, he was thwarted and transformed by her into that most treacherous of all felines — the Lynx.

And all this is but a fraction of Great-uncle Rossiter's herb-lore, which, so he told me as a secret not to be divulged, he had thought to compile in a book. Whether he did or not I never knew.

But above everything he taught me, am I indebted for the introduction to one of the greatest pleasures of my life, and one that has stayed with me through all these years of it: the joy of music.

My father, unlike most young men of his generation, was not musically inclined, nor used he to play on the guitar or the viol or any such popular instrument. We did at Folly's End possess a lute which once had been my mother's, but it had been sadly damaged by rougher usage than that for which it was intended. On more than one occasion had I snatched it from its hook upon the wall to wield as a weapon of attack — or of defence: and sometimes my father, who had a tuneful voice, would take it down to pluck from its frayed strings a halting accompaniment to one of his drinking songs, but neither I nor Rob, nor Percy, had ourselves been moved to play upon it.

So not until I came to Templecombe did I hear real music. My great-uncle played the guitar; his wife, amazingly, the viol, and an old-fashioned instrument called the clavicytherium, shaped like a harp or upright dulcimer, forerunner of the present-day spinet. And more amazing still was it to hear my great-aunt sing, in a cracked falsetto, words she had set to a tune of her own. There was one song that I remember as a very mournful dirge:

'She sighed in her singing and after each groan
Come willow, willow, willow.
I'm dead to all pleasure, my true love is gone
Sing willow, willow,
The salt tears ran by her and murmured her moans...'

until I was in tears myself, so sad it was. Then my uncle would give us 'Greensleeves', I joining in the chorus, and Aunt Rossiter declaring I had a pretty treble and must be taught my notes. This my uncle offered to do, to which suggestion his lady expressed herself agreeable.

I proved an apt pupil, and soon could play 'Shepherd be advised by me' on the clavicytherium and 'Greensleeves' on the guitar. Among other songs and ballads taught me by uncle, this, as I recall it, was his favourite:

'The pleasures of youth are but flowers of May,
Our Life's but a vapour, our body's but clay,
O let me love well though I love for one day.'

Which my uncle said was an old man's wish and not for young maidens, and I had best not sing it to my husband.

So by degrees I settled to this unfamiliar life and came at last to find in it some compensation for the loss of all that I had lived by, and much, that but for this change in my environment, I would likely not have known. And over and above these explorations there were letters to be written and received.

Percy proved a prolific writer of letters. Indeed during the time I lived at Templecombe he wrote me a budget of no less than thirty-six in all, giving me a complete and careful record of his travels; while from Robin I only had but three.

The first of these I quote in its entirety.

Palais Royal.
Paris.
October 17th 1653.

My deare Prue,

Thinginge you would be wishfull of some news of me since I left home I herewith take my pen to give you an accounte of my Adventures to this date. I managed to secure my transport in a fishing Vessell from Charmouth by selling my old Mare for Ten Pistoles to a Farmer who prommis'd he would use her well. With this monney I pay'd for my Voyage and did arrive in France without Mishap.

I cannot tell you of all the Adventures that did befall me before I came to Paris for it would tak toe long allso there are other reasons for my Retisence since God knowes if these Wordes will ever be reade by you all our Movementes being close watched by Rats and Ferretts.

My little knowledge of the langwidge did serve me ill not beinge Proficiente therein since Moon did teach me a plenty Dead Tongues but none that are alive or of good use. Howevere I had the Happy Fortune to fall in with a French Gentleman whose Ackwaintence I did make during a night's sojourne at an Inn. His owne man haveinge fell sicke of the Small Pox and dye'd I boldly offer'd my Service and was accepted. This Gentleman who spoke good English question'd me of myself saying that he recogniz'd I was not born to be a Servant. Whereupon I told him as much as I deem'd necessarie he shuld know and did give him allso my name. By a curious Co-incidence tho' I cannot but believe some Greater Good than Chance did guide me to him, this Gentleman it seem'd had knowne my Father when he visited the Court of Charles I at the time when my Father was a Gentleman-in-Waiting. Takinge me at my Face value and the Ring upon my finger which bears our Creste and Mottoe thereby giving further proof of my Identie, My Benefactor whose name is the Vicomte d'Auteuil, express'd himself well satisfy'd and beinge bound for his Country Residence near Blois did invite me thither as his Guest.

To him and his Great Goodnesse I owe my Preservation for I was destitute of Means when I met with him and in Truth I wonder at his Perspicacitie in judgeing me as anything other than a Vagabonde for my bootes were worne to ribands, my cloathes verminus I haveing slepte in Ditches and under Trees for nigh upon a month earninge a Sou here and there or even reduc'd to beg until I had means enough to buy this one night's lodgeing. He did, howevere, tell me that my Resemblance to my Father in Colouring and Feature is remarkable.

At his Chateau I was treated by the Vicomte and his Lady with the utmoste Courtesie. The French are sympathetick to our Cause and depplore the Abominations we have suffere'd. My Hoste's Daughters are of my Age being twinnes but they do appear to be much older. One of them is the wife of the Duc de… (illegible) *the other betrothed to the Count de Fontenelle, a Page at the Court of Louis Quatorze. Their marriage will be solemnized next month. I think that you and I and Percy* were much younger for our yeares than others of our Age, certain than our Contemporaries here in France. I have learn'd more since I left Folly's End than Moon hath ever taught me. The Manner of Life is of a gaietie and Ease which we under the misrule of Puritannical Hypocrits have never knowne and cannot have imagin'd notwithstanding that France has also had her own Misfortunes during the recent Wars of the Fronde that drove the King's Cousin Louis from his Throne in Paris. But the French King's exile was of short Duration for he was return'd in Triomphe to St Germain within a few monthes. How long it will be before our owne King's Restoration is the ever Burning Question here. More of this howevere I may not wrighte.

After staying a sennight at the Chateau d'Auteuil I proceeded to Paris with letters of Introduction from my kind Hoste to Her Majestie Queen Henrietta Maria and Chancellor Hyde. I do not know how I shall ever repay the Vicomte d'Auteuil for his Generosity and his Trust in me. Not only did he equip me with a well-filled Purse and a complete outfit of cloathes but with a horse and servant.

In due course and without any Mishaps since I traveled as a Gentleman and not as a vagrant and how you would have open'd eyes to see me thus attired in Buckskin Bootes, embroider'd Tunick, my Breeches tyed with Ribbands, a plum'd hat on my Head and a sword at my side tho' I had not learn'd at that time how to use it which Deficiencie I have now overcome and am accounted a Faire Experte at Sword Play.

So to the Palais Royal where our Queen receiv'd me with a welcome so kinde and graciouse that I was overcome and had no speeche but stammering that Her Majestie must sure have Thoughte me witless.

Here againe did my Parentage stand me well since it appear'd Her Majestie had been ackwainted with my deare Mother's Family and had knowne my Mother as a childe and I being borne tho' not rear'd in Her Majestie's Faith the Queen did graciously appoint me her Page which office I do now hold and am learning to speake in French that I find myself forgetting my English.

The Povverty of our exiled Court doth beggar Description. All here are Poore as Mice and all are cheerefull. And now for the Crowning Moment of my journey, my Presentation to His Majestie the King.

This the greatest Honneur of my Life which all my Life I have look'd forwarde to and Dream'd on feelinge within me that some day some Time it wuld most surely come to pass, for I do know that an we wish a Thing enough shuld the wish be worthie we can bring it to us by the Power of Will.

But not untill I had been under the Queen's Protection for nigh upon three weekes did this great Event take place. The Presentation was perform'd by Chancellor Hyde who is an agreeable pleasant-faced gentleman and very Fat with all he says he hath not eat more than one meal a Day for a Twelvemonth.

Well now my deare Prue my meetinge with the Kinge being as it were my Ultima Thule I find I cannot wrighte of it or him for I am loathe to express my most sacred Thoughtes on Paper to be Reviled by Knaves and Tygers should this fall into their Paws. Sufficient that more than ever now am I pledg'd to his Service for, saveing your Father, he is the most gallant Gentleman that I ever have known. He sets all here an example of Courage and Fortitude in our Adversitie. Of a dark Countenance His face in Repose is melancholick but when he laughs his whole expression changeth. He has a Humerus Twist to his Lips as if he jested with himself — and Life. He is whimsickal and quickly roused to anger, but more quickly to the laughter that is as much a part of him as his swarte Complexion and his fine black hair.

His Majestie spoke to me very kind of my Father and yours. You will be glad to know that the King hath not forgot Lord Folliett's faithfull Duty to him and said to me these words: 'I learn'd how Folliett of Wynmonath contriv'd to borrow my cloathes and how that he was near to lose his head in exchange for mine when we were both upon our Travels.' His Majestie express'd a deep concerne at hearinge of our Loss and express'd the Hope that in a not far Future he would have the Plesure of making the Ackwaintance of Lord Folliett's Daughter. I also told His Majestie of your marriage to Piers Folliett of which the King was pleas'd to approve.

I have heard from Chancellor Hyde that Mistress Rossiter has made enquiries of me. When you see her Pray tell her this News I give you and tell her allso that I am deeply gratefull for her interest in my Behalf.

So no more now This being the Longest Lettere I have ever wrote and Moon would say my spelling is 'Execrable'. That word I can spell haveing wrote it a manny hundred times as Penance. Faith, Prue, I wrighte French with fewer errors than I wrighte English. I trust this will retch you safe and not be open'd by any scurvey Spys who if they read it will read no good of Theirselves but only my earnest Hope that Soon or Late they will be brough't to Justice and that I may be one privileged to have a share in the slitting of their Gutts.

Your most Affec'ate
Humbel servant
ROBERT PEVERILL.

Postcript
You may if you wish shew this Lettere to your Husband and tell him I am still and evermore his Freind.

By which I could only assume that when Robin wrote this, which took a month to arrive, he had not heard of my removal. In the meanwhile I received much news of Percy. The first of his letters to me was dated on the eve of his departure from Folly's End.

August 15th 1653.

MY OWN DEAR WIFE
For such you are strange tho' it is and wonderful. I miss you every hour of the Day. Tomorrow Moon and I go forth from here Whither I know

not and care less. I am broken in Heart and Spirit. I did not think I would have loved you so but, Amor animi arbitrio sumitur, non ponitur *which is to say, since certain it is you cannot construe it, 'Love begins at the Mind's bidding but is not thus to be cast off.' I am distracted with Longing to see you and with Hatred for these Vypers who part us.*

I have spent these few days since you went, in reading the Poets in English, Latin, Greek, and writing Verse. I always knew I had an Aptitude for such and could I but have chosen my own Destinie I would elect to be a Troubadour and go up and down the World stringing words upon my Tongue like Beads upon a Necklace.

However, as the Powers that Be rule otherwise I must bow pro tem *to their Authority and accept the Burden of our Millstone Moon around my neck in lieu of Sonnets and my Dear Sweet Heart. Perchance I shall find solace for my Sicknesse in new surroundings. In the mean Time I salute thee, sweetest Prue, with a thousand and one Kisses, this one over being for the tilted tip of your most adorable Nose. Have you read the Song of Songs as you have promised?*

Here is a Song composed for you
By your devoted
Miserable
 and always Loving
Husband
FOLLIETT.

To Prudence
What tho' some say she be not fair
I say she's fair for me
What tho' she be no Beauty grown
I love her since she is my Own,
What tho' she be unform'd, unkind
She is most comely to my Mind.
Hungry my Dreams and empty my Heart

Languishing, sorrowing, thus do we part
That I go famish'd while I tarry
Until my Wife and I may marry
For ne'er was Love more mock'd than this
To feed, and starve, upon a kiss!
God pity me and keep her true
My lovely, laughing Lady Prue.

Other letters followed in rapid succession, couched in similar vein and all containing rhymed couplets of Hearts and Darts, Kisses and Blisses, and such-like catfish vapourings which I treasured as pearls and hid in my clothes-press tied with a rose-coloured ribbon.

But this phase of adoration was soon dispersed in the light of other interests, these so varied and highly flavoured as to make me *Green-sick with envy,* so I answered him, *and do not doubt but you will have forgot your Prue who for all your vows and verses is nought but a Country Mouse tho' I have Gowns to make you stare as fine as any Lady in the land and am grown taller...*

And was growing up.

I became dimly conscious of another self who dwelled within me, bore my name and wore my clothes, spoke in my voice, and yet remained a stranger in my house. Who was she, this double — or familiar — whose face in secret I had glimpsed in the glass in Aunt Rossiter's room to make me marvel at my own reflection: white-skinned, dark-haired, large-eyed, with lips as red as though they had been painted?

I went perplexed and restless in my new perception, while smallest things assumed a multiple significance as I became aware of beauty in and all about me: surely never had I seen on some spring morning such a miracle of loveliness as the first frail-spun blossom out-flung like silver lace against the April sky; nor never had I watched, and with what wistful musing, the unfolded sweet deliverance of bud and leaf and bloom. Each moment was replenished with perpetual motion, a change and interweaving of new thoughts and new perplexities, so swift and so bewildering I could scarce keep pace with the ebb and tide of my emotions that alternated between ecstatic moods of happiness and the depths of indefinable despair.

I reacted with incongruous extravagance to trivialities; while a scolding from my aunt would make me melancholic to the verge of idiocy, so conversely would I be raised to heights of rapture at some promised treat, or a drive into Sidmouth with my uncle, or the present of a pair of perfumed gloves; and I, who had never wept unless for sorrow, would now dissolve in tears at a sad song or a lingering sunset, or the aching flower-scented warmth of summer nights, when at my window I stood and dreamed, star-gazing, filled with a yearning for what I could not tell.

Aunt Rossiter, had she been asked, might have enlightened me as to the cause of the pulsations and upheavals that stirred the swell and budding of young breasts under my tight-laced bodice. But not to her, nor in my letters to my husband, nor to this stranger Prue who so disturbed me, could I confess to these unnameable confusions, that were, when all is said, no more than growing pains...

Thus passed two years at Templecombe, and I was still no nearer to my married state than when I parted from my husband. His letters, no longer couched in lovers' terms, maintained a faithful record of his continental tour, and greatly did he benefit therefrom, or so I gathered, he having met with many notabilities of the French and English courts.

He had travelled far, through Flanders, Holland, Spain and Germany; he had spent some months at Heidelberg; he had spoke with small Electors and great Prussians. He had been presented to our King and gave some guarded gossip of His Majesty, whose name, it seemed, was coupled with a galaxy of ladies, beginning with:

A certain Lucy Walters who hath bore the King a son in Holland as they say. And there is also Mademoiselle Montpensier, "Mademoiselle" so-called (albeit I swear she is no 'Miss'), and being a kinswoman of His Majesty she takes first place among all Beauties at the Court.

In another letter Percy wrote from Paris:

I have recently made acquaintance here with the young Comte de Fontenelle, husband to Germaine, daughter of the Vicomte d'Auteuil. The Comte is a good friend of mine. We are inseparable. He is waiting on King Louis, to whom I have not yet been presented but am promised by my friend that I shall be.

The Comtesse de Fontenelle is a bold, flashing belle, with the finest eyes in France, and much admired by the Gentlemen, saving your Husband, since I do find her manner overpow'ring and care not for fleshly charms and ample Bosoms, rememb'ring the dainty Boyish Angles of my little Prue whom I can swear would put to shame the most ravishing of these French Madams. This one pleaseth me not — nor dare I hint — her Spouse, for they are at it Cat and Dog, the Marriage being one of Convenance and not of mutual Desire. Talk is that they will soon be parted…

This information was of more interest than any other, Robin too having wrote me of this lady, daughter of his good benefactor. And in his next letter Percy gave me the best news of all, an account of his meeting and reunion with Robin.

This happened on a day when he had been permitted to attend the royal hunt in the woods on the outskirts of Paris, which was also the occasion of Percy's first presentation to our exiled King Charles:

…who is here on a short visit to the Queen Mother from Cologne where he has been for these last few months. The King address'd me with a gracious warmth and buoyancie of Manner, and told me how that he holds my name in High Esteem by virtue of the service render'd by my Kinsmen to his Cause. I trust His Majesty hath forgot my own Father did serve the rebel Army, which, however, is no fault of mine. And who should be in attendance on the King that day but our Robin! Ah! My dear Prue, ce n'est pas possible de me t'exprimer ce moment profond et exalté… *Do you understand French? This Language trips so easy from my pen that I forget I am writing in English.*

I do not question you will be impatient to hear how our Robin appear'd to me after a two years' Absence. On my word I was amazed at the Transformation which Courtly circles hath wrought upon our Bumpkin who when I saw him last stank of nothing sweeter than the Stable, whose speech was ever slow and weighty, whose wit was never sharp, and whose hands were red as the undercooked rump of an ox; who was in short as dull a Clown as ever was reared in the Country. I tell thee, Prue, I would not have recogniz'd him but for his freckles and his splendid hair which is the envy of all the young 'Mounseers', who look to tint their own dark locks comme le Peverill! *Believe me or believe me not, our Robin is a Charmer. I swear he has already half a dozen conquests to his name. I am told that Madame de Fontenelle is sick with love for him. He has too, incredibly, a taste for Dress which he cannot indulge to suit his fancy since he, like the King and all of us, is beggar'd. 'All of us' I mention inadvisedly, for by God's good grace I am better endowed than many less fortunate, having now regained some return from my Yorkshire property, and shall, I trust, make a more proper use of my means than in personal* adornment. I hope in all good time to restore Wynmonath. Meanwhile I have other and still more honourable usage for the moneys that Moon's careful solicitation has recover'd, but of this it were best I write nothing, since the Devil knows who may or may not read these words. There is much talk here of the Major-Generals that are established now in England to wrest further Taxation from the 'Delinquents'. Let me know if you have heard of this latest arbitration, and if you are able to give me some résumé of this same. Do not overburden your little head, however, with what you do not understand, but ask particulars of our good Aunt, if you will, that I may know how I am placed should my estates in the South be molested.

Now to Rob again, for I am sure you will be glad to hear of him. He enquired after you and much we laugh'd together at the Remembrance of our Quarrel, for which I do bear him no Malice, and before all those assemble'd there, and the King himself, we did shake hands upon it, I making the first Gesture since 'twas I who once refus'd acceptance of l'amende honorable. And then we rode off to the Chase shoulder to shoulder as oft-times we have ridden, for in truth I love him as the Brother he has ever been to me. Since when, we come together almost daily.

Moon, Thanks be, has return'd to England to preside over my affairs in Yorkshire, so for these last few weeks I am free of him to follow my own Concerns. Dancing is not the least of these, being also His Majesty's favourite Pastime. Next week I go to Frankfort where is to be held a Great Fair which the King is anxious to attend: so, since he sets the Fashion, all of us who can scrape two sous together go to follow him.

Robin, let me tell you is in Highest Favour with His Majesty and also with the Queen Mother, who has converted him to her Catholicism, or to use Rob's own words to me: 'I have made my Peace with God and with my Church, the one and only True Church which in my Heart and Soul I never left.' Like all such converts, and in especial those born to Popery, who have by better guidance been led away from their Heretical persuasions, he is now deeply zealous, attends Mass, and is in consequence *much esteem'd by the French nobility no less than by the young King Louis. It is said also that Charles, our King, is inclined to Papistry, his own Brother, the Duke of York being an avowed... However this is Scandal to benefit Nobody and t'were best I stay my pen which runs too free...*

Which news I read with more misgivings than delight. Robin turned Papist! Here was something, truly, to brood upon in secret fear for his damnation and prayers for his deliverance from the omnipotent rule of the Romish priests, who according to Mr Moon's instruction were a perpetual menace to the Established Church, and the root of all our evils.

But how or why this was had never been explained, nor could I well imagine that any priest of God, no matter what his faith, could lean to evil, since God's Word in whichsoever way it shall be taught, must surely overcome all evil thinking. Nevertheless, so beset was I with fears and memories of Mr Moon's denunciation of Roman Catholics, that I straightway took myself and Percy's letter to my uncle, not daring to submit this to my aunt, she having an Elizabethan horror of all Popery.

My uncle, seeing how I was overcome, sought in his stuttering way to calm me: 'If our good King Charles the First did marry with a P-Papist, then Papist blood is — is mixed with the Blood Royal. Therefore to condemn or fear it is to mistrust the — the Divine Right of Kings. I have known — yes, I have known good Papists and — and b-bad Papists, and I have met with monsters in the shape of — of God's own ministers, as for example —' and here my uncle paused and blinked his eyes and looked sly at me as though he would have more to say on this point if he dared — 'for example,' continued Uncle Rossiter, 'they that p-preach today in the pulpits of our desecrated churches are more evil to my mind than any man who does … who does attend the Mass.' And I wondered if that were all he had upon his tongue to tell me or if he had lost the thread of his own discourse, for he went on in his timid fashion, with a glance at me, and at the rafters, and at his riding boots, which he had not changed since he had come in from hawking: 'There is no sin in loving God, my child … and here I forgot to leave my b-boots for cleaning. There was little catch today however, and that reminds me I must see to it they repair the b-broken bridge over the waterfall, for my mare all but — all but slipped me and herself into the t-torrent, it being rotted with the heavy rains — and — and —'

'You were saying, Uncle, "there is no sin,"' I interrupted.

'In loving God,' returned my uncle promptly, with his head aslant. 'That is so, and l-let none refute it. But the greatest sin of all mankind is — is ignorance. When man has learned to know the God within himself, then will he know *him*self and — and — and all good things. And now go call my man to take my boots and bring my shoes — and say nothing to your aunt of this or of my v-views upon religion.'

Which I most willingly did promise and was comforted.

If my uncle at this time was more than ever vague, and my aunt the more contentious, they had cause enough to warrant some dismay. The Major-Generals, to whom Percy had alluded in his letter, were now by Cromwell's order placed in high command, further to persecute the King's supporters.

This intolerable tyranny was Parliament's device wherewith to draw the last drop of blood from the squires, landowners, and all loyal men of the King who already had been drained to their uttermost and were only just beginning to recover from the fierce strife of civil war and their earlier taxations.

While the industrial and commercial classes, apprentices, merchants and shop-keepers were on the whole prosperous and well contented, and since almost all of these accepted without question the Puritanical autocracy of their dictator and all his lies and promises and cryings unto the Lord and speech-making of Liberty: 'Liberty of conscience and Liberty of subject, two as glorious things as any God hath given us,' (he to talk of Liberty and God!) while his dupes, then, listened to such-like thunderings and saw the living Spirit of the Lord Himself in him, their 'Lord Protector,' we, his opposers and unhappy victims, were suddenly involved in fresh exactions.

The reason or excuse for these envenomed measures was due to the inception of a plot perpetrated by the faithful. In this endeavour to restore our King to his rightful heritage, Chancellor Hyde, the chief instigator, financed by the French Government, had been moved to raise a rebellion in various quarters of England, thinking by co-ordination in the time of the attack to take Cromwell by surprise. The plot, however, having been uncovered, this abortive plague of Major-Generals was the result. These gentlemen — ' Cromwell's Mastiffs ' as they were called by those who suffered from their brutal fangs — had been chosen by the 'Protector' of the State from his own army officers, and kennelled in every district all over the country, to maul and ravage and uproot us from our homes, and to rob us once again of any means we had possessed.

It must have been somewhere in the month of February, 1655, when the first breath of an attempted rising reached us. I remember well that day for I had just received a letter from Robin, the second in two years, to tell me of what I had already heard — his first meeting with Percy in France, and how that *Your husband has growne beyond all knowledge, and is become a prettie*

Swordsman and can speake the French and German langwidge like any Native and is much though't of for his Wit and Grace of Mannere...

And little else besides did Robin tell me, and nothing of himself save that he hoped to journey in due course to Rome, but on what mission he did not say; and signed himself *Your Ladyship's oblige'd and Humbel Servant.*

This epistle scrawled in the space of one page and as short as his first was long, I read and read again, hoping to find between the lines some more personal allusion; but nothing there to tell if he did think of me as kindly and as loving as I still thought of him: and, since so contrary and foolish is the mind of a maid, I was a trifle dashed to see so formal and polite an ending, which might have been addressed to my Aunt Rossiter rather than myself.

It had been the hardest winter known for many years, and that day in February cold as any, on account of the icy winds that came blustering at doors and windows and shrieking down the chimneys with eerie howls like hordes of witches at their revels. A day too bleak for snow, too boisterous for cloud, with the trees tossing their bare arms in a frenzied dance, and creaking while they jigged, as though each bough were a gibbet hanging a dead man's bones.

A dreadful day, indeed, and one on which the poor starved birds dropped frozen as they pecked in vain at the ice-bound earth. I had rescued a few of these small famished creatures, too weak to fly from me, and had carried them into the house and placed them warm and cosy in the kitchen, in nests contrived from lamb's wool, twigs, shavings, or any oddments that our men could bring, to the unvoiced disapproval of my woman, Deborah. She, I knew, considered it unseemly that I should be out in such weather in thin slippers with no cover but a hood on my head and a fur tippet on my shoulders to save me from the fate of the poor birds. But when I had seen my waifs revived, and grateful, I will say, for my attention, as their faint cheeps and chirpings told me, I was glad enough to return to the comfort of our fire in the hall.

There, on the chimney-settle, with Rob's letter in the bosom of my gown, I sat and hugged myself for warmth. On the other side of the wide hearth sat Uncle Rossiter, a-nod; and upright at the table with a list of household matters in a sheaf before her, and her forehead puckered in long lines while she added sums upon her fingers, sat my aunt. At my feet, his head on my shoes, Rob's dog, a pup no longer, snored and twitched and whimpered in his dreams; and I dreamed too, though not asleep, seeing bright pictures in the dancing flames: Rob and Percy at the hunt, riding 'shoulder to shoulder', friends once more united, and a handsome pair of blades did they appear to my mind's eye. And how much longer for a nearer view of one or other must I wait, I sighed; and asked myself, *If you were given the choice to see either which of the two would you wish to see most?* Nor with honesty could I make a decision, and thought Robin surely, first, since the change in him is greater; and then Percy for the memory of his boy's love — if love it were — that revived his kisses in imagination; and then Rob again, who once had said he would love me for ever and ever, and now himself was loved by those French minxes, and this Madame la Comtesse de Thingumbob who should make better use of her eyes — the finest in France, forsooth! — than to ogle our Robin with them for his folly. And thinking thus I fell into a torment to see Robin turned rake-hell and woman-hunter, and if he wished to be so — let him stew! As for Percy, he on his own showing cared nothing for the ladies, which thought was soothing, and I a fool to put myself in such a flutter with these fancies, for was I not Percy's wedded wife, although unmated?

And I felt it very shaming that everyone should know, as sure they did, that I was a virgin still, untouched by any man, with a husband in no haste, it seemed, to alter me.

I was thinking on these things, half in and half out of a doze, when Rufus, as I had named him for his colour, stirred and sat up on his haunches, pricked his ears, and barked at sounds approaching.

'What is it, lad?' I whispered, with my heart in a jerk. I was ever on the watch these days for some arrival: it might be Percy come at last to claim me, or Rob returned, having forsworn that pair of eyes — and *Oh, dear me,* thought I, *if it should indeed be so, and myself bound heart and soul to his best friend ... and what nonsense are you saying, for 'tis only Colonel Ashton come to call.* I had recognised his voice above his coach-wheels: no bull's roar could be louder.

'Is Squire Rossiter within?'

My aunt reared her head, set down the quill with which she had been making her sum total, and issued her commands: 'Take the ink-horn, child, and these papers. Put them in the cupboard. Sweep the hearth and place the stools around it. Mr Rossiter! Here are visitors. Stop snoring.'

My uncle, starting up as though he had been shot, rubbed his eyes and blinked them, smiled vaguely at his wife and asked her, 'Did you speak, my love?'

Deigning no reply to this enquiry, my aunt smoothed her purple silk, settled her farthingale on her hips and herself in her great chair, and taking from the table at her elbow a tambour frame, she set to work upon it as though no thought of housewifery had ever come her way.

'Now what,' she queried, her needle poised mid-air, 'can Colonel Ashton want of us that he comes visiting on such a day and with his wife and daughter?'

True enough; Aunt Rossiter's hearing, almost as keen as my spaniel's, had observed what my ears had missed: that our nearest neighbour, Colonel Ashton, had not come alone.

This gentleman owned a small property a mile or so beyond the fishing village of Beer. He had fought bravely as a Royalist in all our fiercest battles, and was so, rumour gave it, fighting still, being a member of the Sealed Knot, a society of Cavalier conspirators, pledged to the service of the King.

They worked in secret, but such secrets have a way of leaking out, and I had learned much that I kept to myself when Colonel Ashton came visiting at Templecombe. True, Aunt Rossiter did not allow of much discussion in which she had no part, and would peremptorily hush her husband's timid contributions to the talk from which I was debarred more often than I wished; and having learned discretion as I grew, I had given up the ugly trick of eavesdropping at keyholes. Thus was I unable to make good the loss of any discourse I had missed upon this subject. Yet I had gleaned enough to know that year in, year out, and day by day, Colonel Ashton went in danger of his life.

You could not have conceived a man less conspiratorial in bearing than the colonel. Very massive, red of face, and almost half as broad as he was long, his hair and beard prematurely silvered, for he was no great age, he had been a champion wrestler in his youth and had strength enough in his right arm to fell an ox.

His lady, on the contrary, was small as he was big, gentle as he was rough, and as great a fool as he was not, despite his size: for in general, as I have noted, your great bull of a man is sometimes lacking in full power of the brain, as if nature having put a mighty head upon his shoulders, leaves it empty of the stuff wherewith to fill it.

In this case, however, for all he was a giant, rude and noisy and nothing to my liking, Colonel Ashton's shrewd blue eyes and wide expanse of forehead denoted strength beyond his bulging brawn.

Their daughter, Anastasia — Tansy as they called her — was an only child much beloved and spoiled by her parents. And because at that time she was the only young gentlewoman of my age and acquaintance, and despite that we had not a single taste in common, there existed between myself and her, an intimacy which I accepted failing any other, for Mistress Tansy was not one I would have chosen as a friend. Nevertheless, when two young maidens come together, living isolate as we did in the country, it must follow that some confidences are exchanged, or in my case, having none to give, invented.

She was a plump little partridge, favouring her mother, with a fall of golden curls to frame a face as empty as a clam's, and giving the impression it had been fashioned from a ball. Her cheeks were round, her eyes were round and blue as periwinkles; her rounded chin had a round dimple in it; her lips were perpetually rounded as though ever ready to kiss, and even her eyebrows and eyelashes — with which she made great play — were curved like gilded crescent moons... And this is how I see her still, though she and I are grandmothers today.

'Well, Squire!' Thus roared Colonel Ashton, entering with his womenfolk behind him, hooded, wrapped in furs and shivering, their teeth clicking like dice in a box, the while they gave and returned greetings with little cries of, 'Oh, the cold! The bitter day! So unseasonable for the time of year,' and 'How do you, Mistress Rossiter?' and 'Oh, the comfort of the fire! I declare I am an icicle!'

'Then come, madam, and thaw yourself,' my aunt invited in a tone as frosty as the weather, and with one eye on me and one upon my uncle, who, his hair in some disorder and his collar-band awry, stood in the chimney corner looking foolish.

I came forward to curtsy and to be chucked under the chin by Colonel Ashton — a familiarity that I detested — and kissed upon both cheeks by his lady who declared me a feast for the eyes, or some such flummery. Then said Tansy — for always she made the most of her smallness and the least of my height, which never was great — 'Oh, Prue, how you *grow* and you *growl*' rounding her lips to say it, and rounding her eyes to look me over, taking good note of my gown. Whereupon at a signal from my aunt I relieved her and Mistress Ashton of their trappings, and went to order some refreshment and hand the ladies' cloaks to Deborah.

When I returned, the visitors were seated at the hearth. With Tansy I retired to the window to sip mulled wine and nibble caraway cakes and comfits; as I stooped to give Rufus a titbit, Rob's letter fell to the ground.

'Oh!' said Tansy, her eyes and lips in circles. 'Oh! A letter! A letter from your husband? Only think now, to receive a letter all the way from France! I have never had a letter from so far in my life. Does Lord Folliett write to you three times a day? I had an admirer who —' and here she giggled and looked coy and glanced at her mother and lowered her voice to a whisper — 'who sent me a love-note by his servant every hour.'

'If my husband,' I retorted, recovering Rob's letter and quickly hiding it again in my bodice, 'were to send me love-notes every hour I would suspect him.'

'Oh, Prue! *Suspect* him? Of what would you suspect him?'

'Of —' I hesitated; for in truth I had no notion, but having read the poets, and the dramatic works of Masters Beaumont and Fletcher, I hurried to amend my ignorance with romance. 'Of faithlessness,' I told her, 'since it is certain that such attention from a husband to his wife must result from an uneasiness of conscience.'

'Oh, Prue!' said Tansy, giggling, 'you talk just like a book. Why should your husband's conscience be uneasy?'

Now I regretted I had started her on a false scent; to stop her mouth I stuffed it full of marchpane. 'Eat this, my dear. 'Tis fresh made and delicious.'

'Oh, Prue!' mumbled Tansy, her cheeks bulging while she munched, 'so 'tis! Most delicate and tasty. But do tell,' and she gulped down the last morsel, 'is Lord Folliett perchance *not* so utterly adoring as you ... as a wife should expect?'

Why must I be forced to suffer this intolerable fool? I enquired inly; and to her I said, 'So utterly adoring, I assure you, that he has wrote me a whole volume of verse, each one addressed to Prudence, my Beloved Soulful Wife, which when he returns to England he has promised to have published in a book, bound in white calf and blue velvet, exquisitely printed and illumined.' Which was, I'll own, a most tremendous lie, and for which, below my breath, I begged God's pardon.

'Oh, Prue!' began Tansy, visibly impressed, and reaching for another piece of marchpane.

'And if, my dear,' I told her gently, 'you say "Oh, Prue!" again, I hope and pray that piece of marchpane chokes you.'

'Oh, P — Well! What a thing to... Gracious goodness,' spluttered Tansy, 'how droll you are! Why, quite a wit, indeed. I vow your tongue is as sharp as a spinster's. But oh! I have forgot. You *are* a spinster. Fancy! And you a married woman too and still a maid. Of all odd situations!'

'I have known odder,' I replied and held my hands for fear lest they should jump. My temper, for all Aunt Rossiter's curb, was prone as ever to rise boiling at provocation, and Tansy's rounded lips and pointed words brought an itch into my finger-ends — a danger signal. 'Oddest of all and greatly to be pitied is the plight of a maiden', said I, 'who has on her own telling a score of likely suitors at her feet and not one on whom she can decide — that is very odd indeed, and very vexing, in especial when in these parts suitors are not so plentiful as blackberries and who must come from Jericho if they come courting, for never a one 'twixt here and Exeter have I seen that has the means or tongue to make an offer to a female be she girl or goose, all being clods of farmers, or simpletons — or beetle-headed curates.'

'Oh, you think? So let me tell you then, my sweetest Prue, you are mistook. There are gentlemen enough in Devon to pick and choose from, but I dare say that most of them are hard to please and will not be content with all or any, but will choose the most sought-after —'

'Being Mistress Tansy, I've no doubt,' said I, popping a sugared almond between her pouting lips.

'Oh, if that were true!' purred Tansy, while she scrunched, 'but you know, my love, 'tis not. Who should seek me when Lady Folliett is about, un-mated, though she *does* wear the ring upon her finger? I have heard it said you are the prettiest girl in Devon — or would be if you were not so thin.'

'A fault that can be remedied by lapping cream,' I told her, full of smiles, 'which is the reason why some kittens grow so fat.'

'You are so sarcastical, dear Prudence,' returned Tansy, her face a deeper pink, 'and I am told that gentlemen mislike more than anything a serpentine, sarcastical sly manner. Which might account for Lord Folliett's tardiness in —'

'Cease babbling for one moment, Tansy, pray,' I whispered. 'I want to listen to what is being said.'

'You are not supposed to listen to the talk between our elders,' answered Tansy, her lips pursed, and sitting prim; but I had no eyes nor ears for her; a sentence drifting from the hearth had claimed my attention.

'Is it possible?' my Aunt Rossiter was saying, and by her face so sternly set I knew her to be put out though not put down by Colonel Ashton's words that had been spoken *sotto voce,* but were now loud enough for me to mark them well.

'More than possible, good madam. What I have told you is a fact.'

'But this man Allen is a low republican. Do you infer that he is with us?' cried my aunt.

'He is in prison, madam, as I tell you — if that be with us — having been arrested in his father-in-law's house in this very shire on a charge of raising disturbances at Bristol and in his own county of Devon.'

'Which has, by this endeavour,' rasped my aunt, 'become a hot-bed for the rabble broken loose to serve *their* ends and not ours.'

'All ends that serve in mutual accord lead to one goal, Mistress Rossiter,' replied the colonel, subduing his voice to glance over his shoulder at me; whereupon I began to giggle like a nonny and said high-pitched to his daughter, 'Now tell me, love, have you thought yet what you will choose for your new spring taffety?'

'Oh, yes!' replied Tansy, on sure ground again, while her father, satisfied that I had interest in nothing but such fiddle-faddle, returned to his discussion. 'Oh, yes, indeed, Prue, I have thought, and am settled in my mind upon sky-blue — there is the sweetest thing at Madame Partlet's shop in Exeter but not in taffety, I think, for I had taffety last year and this year I shall —'

'For heaven's sake!' I hissed to her astonishment, 'cease cackling!'

'In which case,' boomed Colonel Ashton, 'we should be prepared for all emergency. The hounds are after us full-cry.'

'Oh, Prue! The hounds? What hounds? Are we in danger?' chittered Tansy, clutching me.

'*You* are not, at all events,' I told her, 'so you keep your mouth shut that I may hear...'

And this much I collected from stray scraps of talk, that the rumours of a rising had materialised.

So swift and sudden was this first attempt at agitation on the part of the loyalists here in the south-west, that even those involved scarce knew it had been planned before it burst like a dam, to flood them.

The man Allen to whom Colonel Ashton had alluded, and who had been arrested in the neighbourhood, was none other than Cromwell's Adjutant-General and a zealous Anabaptist. He and another of his fanatical colleagues, Colonel Wildman, who had been ejected from Parliament for refusing to sign the Recognition, were taken at his lodgings at Exton in Wiltshire, in the very act of dictating to his clerk a declaration from the *free and well-affected people of England now in arms against the Tyrant Oliver Cromwell*. Thus it seemed the parliamentary party were deciding to split among themselves in a war of discontent.

Wildman, with his confederates, having been secured, was thrown in the Tower; but in spite of prompt and merciless reprisals, the undercurrent of a general revolt against the Government persisted among Cromwell's own supporters, to spur the Royalists to fresh endeavours.

Colonel Ashton had himself been involved in a recent attack on Salisbury under the command of Sir Joseph Wagstaff, when with near upon two hundred chosen followers they entered the city at dawn, surprised the High Sheriff and two judges in their beds, and ordered them the alternative of hanging, to the public proclamation of Charles Stuart as their King.

The alarmed Sheriff and the justices, vehemently protesting, put up a fight for it and would likely have been strung upon the gallows or had their necks broke in Colonel Ashton's hands, had not Cromwell's troopers arrived, full-armed, upon the scene to overcome the loyal rebels by superiority of force.

Colonel Ashton with his leader, Sir Joseph Wagstaff, escaped after some strong fighting, but others of that gallant band were taken at South Molton, to be axed at Exeter. Some fifteen others suffered a similar fate at Salisbury; and those who were not executed, hanged and disembowelled, were sold as slaves to the Barbado Islands.

But of these evil doings and their consequences we at Templecombe knew nothing, since news at its best was slow. Colonel Ashton, the first to bring us tidings of the revolt at Salisbury, had not at that time heard how his comrades fared; nor did we learn of the horrific penalties they paid until long afterwards. All that concerned our friend the colonel on that day of his visit to my uncle, was to warn him to be prepared for the Government's vengeance on all known or suspected Royalists. There would be, he prophesied, a severe tightening of the noose around our necks and an increase of persecutions. Cromwell had already marshalled a formidable constabulary in the south, dividing each county into military districts, with an officer of his own breed in command. The 'Protector' of the Commonwealth was not likely to let the grass grow while he kicked his heels to wait for further risings.

Colonel Ashton, as a marked man, with Cromwell's 'Mastiffs' on his track, had made plans for his own removal from the neighbourhood. His property having been almost entirely depleted, he had little to lose by leaving his house to be sacked. He could not, however, endanger the lives of his wife and daughter, nor abandon them to the mercy of his pursuers. Therefore he had come, beyond all other reason, to solicit my uncle's aid on their behalf, and find a haven for them there at Templecombe.

'For,' I heard the colonel say, 'if they catch me, they'll have my head upon a pike.'

'Oh, Prue! Oh, gracious heaven!' gasped Tansy in a pretty fright, this being all she had understood of such grave talk.

'Your father is too big a man to catch or kill, my dear,' I reassured her.

'Oh, Prue!' And then she fell to crying the smallest tears I ever saw, round as pearls upon her rosy cheeks. Poor Tansy, she had no mind to grasp at issues greater than lollipops or lovers' vows and kisses; or a new sky-blue spring taffety — and why should she indeed? She had not been reared, as I was, on a farm along with boys, and none to teach me manners or the lighter things of life.

Her father, seeing that I had taken in much more than I was meant to do and that his little daughter no less than his good lady — from whom one gathered he kept all weighty matters — were both on the verge of the vapours, soothed and comforted his wife with a cannonade of bussings like miniature musket shots. Then, seeing her recovered, he beckoned Tansy to him and engulfed her in his arms.

'Now, now, my petling, there's no cause for fears and tears. You're to abide here at Templecombe on a visit with your mother. Mistress Rossiter invites you — could anything be nicer?'

'Oh, No! Oh, dear!' sobbed Tansy. 'And are you really going to leave us, Father, and will we all be catched and hanged? Oh, don't let them put me in prison!'

'Prison! Fiddle-de-dee!' pronounced my aunt, having little patience with these flippertigib amenities.

'Oh, Mistress Rossiter!' Tansy turned upon my aunt, in tears again. 'Oh, madam! Dearest Mother! Oh, I know we'll all be murdered in our beds.'

Said my aunt with a snort, 'Better we die — if we must — in our beds than out of them, murder or nothing.'

Yet what could one do with such a ninny but to comfort her? Which her giant of father did to her heart's content, placing her on his great knee and cuddling her head against his chest with elephantine pattings and strokings and kissings, that I who had never ceased to ache for my own dead darling, hitched my shoulder at the pair of them and turned my back to stare up at the sky and keep the shake out of my chin and say, 'The Lord be praised! 'Tis snowing. That will be the end of this long frost.'

'Prudence,' said my aunt, 'go tell the maids to make ready two guest-chambers. Colonel Ashton, my husband and I are happy to place this house at the disposal of you and yours —' and my aunt eyed the sobbing Tansy with a most withering look — 'for as long as you like to stay.'

CHAPTER EIGHT

They stayed all through that summer and well into the fall of the year. My sixteenth birthday came and passed, and it wanted scarce a month to Christmastide, when Colonel Ashton returned to take his wife and Tansy home to Widders Cross, his ransacked house at Beer. That his activities during this interim had been fulfilled without further reprisals against himself or his estate was reassuring, but on what mission or to what end the colonel had been bound, we were not then enlightened. Much, however, had occurred since his departure to affect not only individuals but the nation as a whole.

From all over the country came news of attempted insurrection; nor were the Royalists, driven to desperation by increasing despotism, the sole instigators of these risings. The Anabaptists and the Levellers had joined forces with the contending parties in revolt. These Levellers — self-styled — were a formidable body of agitators who having translated the Scriptures into terms of Republicanism to suit their purpose, declared that they had found in the election of Saul by Israel, a clear denunciation of monarchy, and that they would have, and did insist upon free government and free religion for all. Nor would they submit to the rule of King or overlord, but to a leader selected from among themselves: and they demanded, according to their interpretation of the Word, an established and positive equality, with the final abolishment of class and creed distinction.

But when under Cromwell's dictatorship, these pietistic reformers found themselves submitted to a far greater tyrannical subjection than they had suffered under the man whose kingship had brought him to the scaffold, they threw in their lot with the opposing forces to restore the Throne they had denied. Thus Cromwell, despite his careful vigilance, was faced on all sides with angry swarms of hornets rising from their nests to defy him, his 'Mastiffs', and his latest ruthless measures of suppression. Yet those who paid the penalty of imprisonment or the reeking death upon the gallows for their brave resistance, suffered and died with the light of hope in their souls. The misery which for years they had endured, the levying of incalculable fines, the robbing of their homes, the prolonged torture of the prison cell — the penultimate doom of all those who refused the stranglehold of their oppressors — were but the labour-pangs of a rebirth; the first faint gleam of dawn in our darkest hours.

For those days were dark indeed. Words passed from mouth to mouth, new and dismal words, coined to meet inexorable laws: Composition, Compurgation, Decimation, and that omnipresent horror, Sequestration. Weightier than ever fell the burden of these fresh demands in taxes — save the mark to call them so! Robbery, virulent and savage, replaced the ancient rights of justice and dissevered from a last resource of tolerance or pity all those who still prayed for their King.

My Uncle Rossiter was among those to be further affected. That he had already paid a heavy fine carried little in his favour with Cromwell's latest body of Commissioners. These, directed by the Major-General of the shire, were ordered to deal with the utmost cruelty and severity against any persons who had not only borne arms for but were declared members of the royal party. Thus my poor uncle found himself 'decimated' which, notwithstanding the disbursement of his former penalty, drained his estate to the extent of another one-tenth part of it.

That was a grievous time for us, and for those similarly victimised. From all sides one heard the same distressing story, how that no mercy or reprieve was ever granted; how that the said 'Tax' must be paid in full within fourteen days, or, in the case of those proven powerless to raise the extortionate sum demanded at such short notice, they must give a signed undertaking — as alternative to jail — to remit a monthly payment until the total be discharged.

Among certain family documents that have been preserved, is the assessment of my great-uncle's property at Templecombe. My Aunt Rossiter, rising to this sad occasion with her customary spirit, did herself prepare a paper to be submitted to the local Committee. Whether this were a full return of her husband's goods and chattels, his rents, his land and all that appertained thereto, was not for me to question: my part in this melancholy overture was to make three fair copies of the script, one to be rendered to the commissioners, another to be retained and guarded by my aunt, and a third as further evidence, in the event of the destruction of her house, that she might prove in writing the particulars of its contents should enquiry ensue. This last copy my aunt relinquished to my charge. I sewed it to the lining of my petticoat, slept with it under my pillow, and having written it three times I can almost quote it now, by heart.

My aunt returned the Templecombe estate as worth something under £1500, which sum even I knew to be greatly minimised. The remainder of the property — unscheduled — my aunt claimed to be part of the marriage jointure settled on her by her husband. As for rents, my Uncle Rossiter signed a declaration to the effect that since the greater part of his

209

property had not been leased since the wars, he declared himself unable to set down the exact total of the yearly income accruing from his tenants, but that he judged it to amount to something near upon £200 per annum. He admitted to possession of *seven Cows*, which I knew to be a deliberate understatement, since the home farm at Templecombe harboured a herd of fifty. However, it was none of my affair, only that in making out the inventory I prayed that neither I nor my poor uncle would find ourselves in jail or the pillory on our own village green, for conspiring to and signing a false declaration. When I ventured to remind my aunt — my uncle having no say in the matter — that she might perhaps be well-advised to keep within a certain limit of the facts, I was ordered peremptorily to attend to my own business which was to write as she dictated and as follows:

'"Twelve (12) draught bullocks —"'

'Twenty-four,' I murmured, daringly.

'"One coach and two coach horses (spavined),"' said my aunt, 'and put in brackets that last word.'

Which after some deliberation for the spelling I achieved.

'"One saddle-horse,"' my aunt dictated, '"the four other horses in the stables being the property of Mistress Rossiter's great-nephew, Lord Folliett of Wynmonath —"'

'But —' said I.

'Take it down, girl, as I bid you. "His lordship being now in France, his three saddle-horses and one mare are temporarily loaned unto his lordship's wife — now resident at Templecombe. I have besides,"' my aunt proceeded, quelling with her eye my hesitation to declare this bold-faced perjury, '"four young steers, one yearling calf, and one bull — in a consumption!"'

'What if they should send an officer to prove that my uncle owns at least four bulls, and all in best of health?' I faltered, for in truth I could see only one end to these prevarications, and my own head in a collar for my share in them.

'"The hay and timber,"' my aunt went on, taking no more heed of my remonstrance than as if a gnat had buzzed, '"is assessed at £250, my household goods and servants at £500 — " no, we'll say £300. "My beds and bedding and one carpet — "'

'Oh, Aunt, six!' I blurted. 'And what of the fine Moorish, rugs in my bedchamber?'

'They will be removed,' replied my aunt — 'and buried in the garden in oak coffins, if need be...'

Which fantastic document, quoted here in smallest part and meekly signed in due course by my uncle, resulted in a visit from a hectoring official attended by two underlings, and a more cut-throat, crop-eared three I never had beheld. Armed with swords and muskets they exuded a smell of stronger waters than the tankard each of ale, that my aunt to my amazement offered them with smiles. In truth, I had seldom seen her in such gracious mood: but for her eye as chill as any iceberg's, you would have thought she had an understanding with the beasts. Nor could I dismiss entirely the notion that she might have passed a bribe to them, for though they bestrode the house from the cellars to the attics, to re-value the assessment at four times the sum returned, they left us with no worse than a warning from their leader to my uncle that he would gain nothing and lose much by understatement, and could think himself well served if his head stayed on his shoulders. At which my poor uncle shivered in his shoes and looked as though he were about to moult; and I swear could I have found a weapon to my hand, that villain's insolence would have cost him some blood-letting.

As for my aunt, Medusa could not have glared more horridly, but far from being petrified, the monster bowed to her with a mock gallantry that was even more offensive than his rudeness.

'Madam, be not afeared. Your good gentleman is not the only one who falsifies his statement of returns. Lord bless us! Why, the prisons are chock full on 'em. But if I may say so, mistress, for your relief and peace o' mind, the poor gentleman will not be called to such severe account. Major-General Butler who serves this shire seeks in all things to be just, and it don't need half an eye to see that Mr Rossiter is...' And the creature tapped his forehead very knowingly, winked at my aunt, leered at myself, and, patting my uncle on his shaking shoulder, marched out of the house with his men.

Truly, throughout this woeful time, did I doubt my uncle's reason. The mere thought of his pending summons seemed to put him in a fever. More than ever did he ramble in his discourse; or else would sit for hours silent, shut in the closet that adjoined his and my aunt's bedchamber, refusing to appear for meals. On one occasion when I went to call him to his dinner, I found him at the table with a litter of papers and documents before him, writing as though his life depended on it. He started when he saw me, and as if surprised in some misdeed, glanced aside and timorously stammered, 'Say nothing to your aunt, my dear, for she — she does — does disapprove of my absorption in herb-herbivorous pursuits, but I've discovered, or I *think* I have discovered, in the common Brooklime — *Veronica B-Beccabunga* — a certain c-cure for — for scurvy.'

I could not help but think he was using up a vast amount of ink on so trivial a matter, yet knowing his proclivity, amounting to a mania, for herbs, I made no comment.

And once he disappeared for the entire day, riding out alone to return with his horse in a sweat, and his clothes in a muss, and could give no account of himself or where he had been, save that growing easily tired and being nothing so young as he was, he had dismounted and tethered his horse and fallen asleep on a hayrick. My aunt complained that he was restless in the night, and continually waking her on some pretext of robbers in the house, and with unwonted courage for one so very timid, would himself take a lanthorn to go investigating. And once my aunt declared that he was gone so long she feared that he had fallen down the well. He was for ever in a state of palpitation, and in all ways so very singular in his behaviour that even his wife, who had thirty years' usage of his habits, was herself alarmed and ordered him to bed. There she kept him under protest, and sent for a chirurgeon to cup him; but my uncle showed himself so strongly vehement against these measures, threatening to everyone's dismay to cut his throat with his own shaving knife rather than be bled, that the chirurgeon decided it were best to purge him, merely.

As for Mistress Ashton, she fell into such vapourings at these excursions and alarms that we feared for her sanity as much as for my uncle's, while Tansy was a continuous pest to me with her 'Oh, Prue' this and 'Oh, Prue' that, and her fear — as she said — of being raped by a thief in the night.

'If the wish is father to the thought,' I told her, 'then for my part I hope a thief *will* come, and quickly, so you take him to your bed and then we'll all have peace.'

'Oh, Prue! Oh, what a coarse-grained, cross-tongued vixen you are to speak so. Sure, one would think you had been born and bred of common folk, the way you talk! Oh, I declare, I never would have thought you were so rude until I came to live with you, and that's the truth!'

For of late we had been at it quarrelling — if anything so one-sided as Tansy's perpetual whimperings and whinings, and tiny gusts of temper, and little spiteful show of claws, in return for an occasional sharp-speaking of my mind, could be called quarrels. Admittedly we were not so sweet as turtle-doves together, but then every member of the household from the scullion to my aunt was in a pother and tetchy to jump at the squeak of a mouse; and so we all had been since the invasion of the Major-General and his minions in the county. We had been told they would stop at nothing, not even slaughter were they so minded; and since no Royalist was permitted to hold or retain in his house any arms or implements of defence, not even a rusty old fowling-piece — though I have reason to suspect my aunt had stowed away a hidden store of such for an emergency — we would have been in sorry case were we attacked.

It must have been shortly after the visit of the commissioner's officer to Templecombe, that I recall an incident to which at the time I paid but little heed, but which reviewed in the light of subsequent events was not entirely without significance.

Tansy and I had been out gathering the first autumn leaves with which to decorate the hall for our Michaelmas feast. While all such pleasure-making was forbidden under the harsh rule of the 'Protector', and though Morris dancing and the maypole and Jack-in-the-Green, and the eating of plum porridge and Christmas pie were regarded by our Puritan law-mongers as ungodly superstition, we still indulged ourselves in these age-old customs, even at the risk of a fine or a worse punishment.

So on that Michaelmas morning I had taken Tansy — and a pruning knife — to fill our baskets and Tansy's arms with the fading bounty of our woods. The leaves were slow in reddening, for a late summer had succeeded the hard frost, but I knew where to look for copper beech and golden maple, and the first browning leaves of the hazel hiding the ripening nuts.

We were to dine that day on a fine fat goose, and in the evening there would be singing, and Tansy and I would dance together failing a gentleman to partner us. I had learned from Tansy the steps of the galliard and coranto; she had them all in the tips of her toes, and despite her roundness, or because of it, she danced as light and graceful as a puff-ball; and for this I envied her, having never danced till Tansy came to live with us, and felt myself to be a centipede and very conscious of my hundred feet. But Tansy had no voice for singing and I had, and learned for this occasion a new song — yet not so very new for all that — being writ when Queen Elizabeth was young.

It went to a tuneful melody and the words of it were these:

'All our pride is but a jest
None are worst and none are best,
Grief and joy and hope and fear,
Play their pageants everywhere
Vain opinion all doth sway,
And the world is but a play.'

I was humming this over, and, repeating the last line more to myself than to Tansy, I said, 'Now I wonder — and would like to know — if, when Will Shakespeare wrote his famous speech in the comedy of *As You Like It,* he were prompted by those words, *The world is but a play.*'

'Oh, Prue! You are so knowledgeable, truly. Who, pray, is Will Shakespeare? And what is as you like it?'

'Nothing much is as I like it now,' I answered, hacking at a branch of copper beech, 'save these dear natural things God gives us for our comfort — and what a sin it is that I should cut them limb from limb. May I be forgiven for't!'

'But this Master Shakespeare, Prue. You have not spoke of him before. Does he reside here in the neighbourhood? And is he famous? Is he handsome? Oh, Prue!' persisted Tansy, with a rounding of her eyes, 'I always knew you were a sly one. And have you kept him to yourself all these long months — and you a matron? Fie!'

'Master Shakespeare *was* — not *is* — a strolling player, ninny-numps,' quoth I, 'who by some happy stroke or freak of fortune, wrote comedies and tragedies and sonnets of such rare beauty, philosophy and wisdom, that he has become the greatest poet the world until this date has ever known.'

'Oh, *was?*' Tansy drooped her lips. 'Is he dead then, this great poet?'

'These forty years, my dear. Abandon hope — you'll find no poet, nor poetaster, hereabouts to whom you'd raise a petticoat. At most, an you are lucky, you may catch the Major-General's bog-trotter. Though his ears are long and his hair is short he has an eye for a maid — *or* a matron.'

'Oh, Prue, I do mislike your jibes!' retorted Tansy, flushing. 'You are for ever at me with a dig here and a scratch there, and so tart and saucy that I wonder what Lord Folliett will have to say when he returns — if ever he does. Nor do I blame him that he stays in France in no great torment to come back and claim his bride, for if ever he has heard you speak to him so curst and froward as you speak to me, you nasty —'

'Here's a fine full branch for you. Take this.' I stopped her tongue by shoving a small forest in her face, and left her standing like a tree, half smothered in the foliage. 'Carry that into the house,' I called to her over my shoulder, 'then bring me the empty basket.'

And off I went to search for scarlet hips, and a rare scramble I had to get them too, tearing my hands on their vicious thorns, but they were worth the pains. There is nothing to my mind so gay and festive as a peep of red in a riot of Michaelmas daisies; and I would thread a chain of all the reddest, and twine them in my hair and pray that Percy would come riding over the hills from Charmouth to claim me here this very night before the moon went down. Then we would see how Mistress Tansy Addlepate would turn as green as cheese when I rode off a-pillion with my husband.

Thinking thus, while I hewed at the spiteful briars with my pruning knife, I espied a plenteous crop of blackberries in a nearby coppice. Abandoning my hips to gather these I made a feast.

I was still plucking and eating, and greedy for more, when close beside me, or, as it seemed, close under me I heard a man's voice say, 'What poise was that?'

'Nothing,' came the answer. 'I must — I must have trod upon a twig.'

And in a hundred thousand voices I would have known that one for my Uncle Rossiter's.

Very still I stood. I swear my heartbeats were the loudest sound of any in the quiet. Even the birds were silent, and the sun that had been high, and thick as golden honey among the mellow green, slunk behind a cloud to hide himself.

I could see neither my uncle nor his companion, since they were concealed in a hollow that dipped from the hillock where I crouched among the blackberries; but I could hear.

'If Willis —' or some such name, said my uncle in an undertone, 'can be trusted —'

'Why should he not be trusted?'

'I — I do not know.'

'You are over-cautious. Look to the likeliest, if look you must, and not to him who —'

Curiosity at this point overcame discretion; not satisfied merely to hear, I must also see. Dropping on all fours I wormed my way under the bushes and was about to ensconce myself more firmly on the crumbling edge of the hillock when I found that I had over-crawled my mark into a bed of nettles. My sharp withdrawal from the sting of these was my undoing, and clutch how I would at the sliding earth, at roots and leaves and brambles, nothing now could save me. Down I crashed.

My fall was harmless; I unhurt. But if a tigress had sprung upon them from the bushes, she could not have caused a greater shock to those two gentlemen: nor was I one whit less astonished, though more abashed, than they.

The stranger, of whom even in my discomfiture I took good note, spoke first and very softly. 'Glory be to God! Who are *you* — you beautiful wood-nymph?'

There was something in his accent, unfamiliar; not foreign, nor altogether English, nor did it hold a trace of the Devonshire burr; and while I puzzled over this and sat as I had tumbled, rubbing my scraped elbows, my uncle answered for me: 'She is my g-great-niece, Lady Folliett, sir.' Saying which my uncle looked at me aslant, drooping an eyelid and grimacing on one side of his mouth in a very foolish manner.

But I had no eyes for him: mine were on the stranger, who presented a most singular appearance.

Although his dress was that of a prosperous farmer — a simple Devonshire kersey suit and green worsted stockings — the hair that fell either side his face from under his wide-brimmed hat was of so startling a yellow that one could only think it dyed; but his gentility of bearing belied his country habit. He was tall and slight, not young nor old, though old to my years then, being somewhere in the middle forties as I judged. He had, besides, a merry twinkle in his eye which whimsically regarding me from top to toe did nothing to lessen my confusion. I have no doubt that I appeared as odd to him as he to me; indeed I must have been in lamentable disarray, with twigs and prickles in my hair, scratches on my face and a great rent, well exposed, in the knee of my stocking. This I hastily covered with the hem of my gown, got upon my feet and mustered what little dignity remained to me.

'I crave your pardon, Uncle, I had no idea that you were — entertaining.'

I pointed this remark, for I confess to some uneasiness at the evident secrecy of the meeting which my precipitate arrival had disturbed. If this were a farmer, he was none I knew. In what further trouble had my poor uncle found himself embroiled?

I was soon enlightened. He, looking scared with a glance around each shoulder, said apologetically, ' My dear, I ... having no wish to interfere with your good great-aunt's d-decision, and being sadly put about by the visit of the officers who made full note of all my horse and cattle, I did d-decide 'twere best to sell at once as much kine as I could muster before ... before the s-summons, so that I may safely say I have but little. For what I do not own they cannot take. This gentleman therefore, does propose to buy from me t-ten steers. Is that not so, Mr — Mr Orpington?'

'Indeed it is,' returned the stranger, promptly, and with so marked an accent now that there was no mistaking it for anything but Irish, 'and I was for tellin' Squire, my lady, he be in luck to find an honest man to deal with 'um, at all.'

'Yes, Prue,' chimed in my uncle, 'there is so — so much sharp practice hereabouts that I am thankful for this opportunity to have an — an honest dealing — and —'

'Pray, sir,' I interrupted, 'do not give yourself the pain of explanation — or prevarication. The least said of honesty the better. That which you have undertaken — whatsoever it may be — is your own affair, not mine, I promise you.'

A look of immense relief passed over my uncle's face. 'I am — am glad, my love, to meet with — with your approval.'

'I was not aware,' I answered coldly, 'that I had expressed approval or disapproval of your intentions, Uncle.'

'Mr Orpington,' my uncle ventured humbly, 'has come all haste from — from Babbacombe to buy my steers.'

''Tis all one to me if he has come from Hades,' I retorted, 'nor have I heard of any Irish at Babbacombe — though I do know,' I stared hard at the grinning stranger, 'that Babbacombe Cove is a rare hiding-hole for smugglers.'

At this the fellow had the grace to cower. I was glad to see that I had put him out.

'And I hope, sir,' I told my uncle, 'that you will find your game be worth your candle. Surely you know that the officers have made a full inventory of all your holdings?'

'Ah!' My uncle tapped his nose and slily chuckled. 'Yes, but I've out-witted 'em.'

'Pray God,' I said, 'that you be not out-witted in your turn.'

My uncle caught me by the sleeve. 'You will not tell of this, my child? Say nothing to your aunt. My poor head,' he put his hands up to it, 'is weary with my t-trouble.'

'I will say nothing, Uncle, rest assured,' I promised him. 'And if your transaction be completed, it were better you come home and tranquillise yourself or you'll have no appetite for your Michaelmas goose today. Are you aware, Master Orpington,' I demanded tartly, 'that Squire Rossiter is sick?'

'Och! Faith, your ladyship, one can see that with half an eye,' returned the wretch. 'Do you think I'd do sharp dealing with a natural?'

My temper rose. 'You forget your place, my man. Uncle! Has this person paid you any money?'

'N-not yet,' my uncle quavered.

'And are the steers still in their pastures?'

'Well yes, my dear, they are.'

'Then keep them there, and come with me. Come home.' I put my arm in his. 'Leave this rascal to his iniquities. Yes, you, sirrah! I warn you — stay off these premises. Should you come here again to mislead my uncle with your knavish tricks, you do so at your peril. Thank heaven that I happened on this meeting in good time! Uncle, do you sell no steers. For all you know this fellow may be a paid spy in the service of the commissioners —'

And in a flash the whole solution dawned upon me.

'Why! I see — I see it all! You, sirrah, are no farmer. Your disguise would not deceive a cow — though I'll own it has deceived my uncle, who is too honest himself to think on evil or look for it in others. Oh, how timely was my coming! God must have guided me to intercept your dirty schemes. Uncle, beware! This man was sent to trap you, that further penalty may be exacted on the least excuse when you stand before these monsters to be judged. Look you, "Master Orpington" —' I stressed the name, certain as I stood it was false as all the rest of him — 'if I see or hear of you again around this house or in these woods, I'll set our men to string you up on yonder oak where you'll hang for the crows to peck! Do you think I do not realise the motive that brings you prowling here with bribes and offers for my uncle's cattle? Shame on you and on all who seek by such low ways and ugly means to squeeze us dry. Yes, sir, you stand unmasked, and you go tell your Major-General to do his evil worst, but he'll gain nothing by such knavery for his "Protector". Mr Rossiter will pay his fine as he is bid — and take *that* back to your master, and tell him too that the Squire has rendered his full due account — checked by your own men who were sent here to do it, and as I can vouch for and bear witness to, having copied the inventory myself with my own hand —' which in my rage I fisted to shake in the fellow's face — 'and may you and those you serve be bled as white as you have bled my uncle and all who dare pray God to save their King!'

Whereupon I took my uncle's arm and walked him off, leaving 'Mr Orpington' speechless, his hand clapped to his mouth and his face as red as a turkey's — with anger, as I thought.

But as we emerged from the wood I heard an unmistakable loud burst of laughter, and glancing back I saw the creature doubled up to hold his sides.

'There's a brazen devil!' I muttered through my teeth. 'What a mercy, Uncle, that I — *fell* on you in time.'

'Yes, my dear,' agreed my uncle, meekly. 'Had you been long in the bushes when you … when you…?'

'Long enough,' I answered, 'to hear a man's name mentioned. Willis. Who is he?' I stopped and stood before my uncle squarely. 'Have you been up to further mischief, sir?'

'No, Prudence, no, I p-promise you,' denied my uncle, fixing his eyes imploringly on mine. 'And what ... what more besides, Prue, did you overhear?'

'No more than that you do not trust this Willis.'

My uncle sighed and shook his head. 'I do not, indeed.'

'So I should think — whoever he is,' I said. 'But who *is* he?'

'Only another farmer, love,' returned my uncle sheepishly, 'to whom I have promised my ... heifers.'

'Another? Uncle! Why —' Then I too began to laugh. 'Oh, mercy me! Till now I always thought you not so simple as you seemed, but I've reason to believe I was mistook. A more artless, unsophisticated, unsuspicious sparrow never preened himself to have his feathers plucked! No, I'll not tell my aunt, so you do keep within doors, and not go straying round the country to be catched by thievish rogues, lest you find yourself served up to the Committee — in a pie!'

Then I kissed him warmly and we went home hand in hand; and since, so far as I could ascertain, nothing untoward resulted from this matter, I speedily forgot it — and Mr Orpington.

Not until some few years later, and in very different surroundings, did I chance upon that gentleman again.

To add to our misfortunes at this time, that winter of 1656 was one of unprecedented violence, in comparison to which the cold of the year before was but a chillsome breath. Heavy snowstorms were succeeded by frosts so sharp and bitter that many believed the fearful weather to be a judgment from Almighty God against our persecutors. Yet while the guiltless suffered with the guilty, we gained but little from such comfort for ourselves, save the knowledge that what we endured here in the south-west, where the climate was milder than in other parts of England, those who overlorded us in London endured worse.

My Aunt and Uncle Rossiter likened this to the Great Frost of 1625, which they well remembered, when Wynmonath Vale was buried in snowdrifts for a month, and all roads to and from the abbey where they were staying at that season had been rendered impassable, so that my grandparents and their household looked to starve, since no pack-horses bringing victuals could come to them. And now a wall of snow, some ten feet high, surrounded Templecombe; and from there to the red-cliffed seaboard, the countryside lay muffled in a dazzling shroud of white that froze as the barbed flakes fell. Even the sea at Sidmouth showed a lacy fringe of ice as it sucked at the pebbled shore.

Our men carved a path along the snow-bound drive that I might ride my horse for exercise, but sure-footed though he was he dared not trot; he walked, slow-measured and careful of his step, till my blood congealed for want of speed, and I suggested that his hooves be protected each with a worsted stocking so that he might not slip and break his knees. But he cared not for this outrage to his nobility, being a thoroughbred of Arab strain, and made such fierce protest to buck and plunge, snorting his indignation, that I was hard put to hold my seat upon the saddle, and fearing to be shot over his head, dismounted to lead him homewards. Nor did I venture out again, for walk I dared not lest I be froze alive, but stayed within doors huddled in the chimney corner with Rufus in my arms for warmth, and my lute for company.

This weather, as I read in one of my uncle's books, although so terrible to us, was the common lot of those that dwell north of the world in unexplored unnamed Arctic regions, where the sun is hid for months on end, and the day is one long night. And that winter it seemed as though a blast from those far-off lands had smote not only the British Isles but the whole continent of Europe. We heard that the river Thames in London Town was one great sheet of ice, and that the watermen who made their livelihood thereon were in sad plight, and beleaguering Whitehall for recompense, to be clapped in prison, likely, for their complaints.

And Percy wrote from Bruges, to which city King Charles and his exiled court were retired, that:

Each morning my Servant breaks the frozen water in my Ewer before I can wash myself, and this notwithstanding a fire burning all night in my Bed-chamber. I have learned to skate, however — a joyous and graceful Pastime, Prue, much favour'd by the Natives of Holland and Belgium, in which with Boots cunningly contrived to hold a kind of Blade beneath them fastened to the soles, we slide and sway and balance on the Ice, and perform all manner of intricate Steps. The King hath taken kindly to this practice and vows he will make it die Mode in London when he returns from his 'Travels' to his Palace of Whitehall. Meanwhile His Majesty has endured many a tumble with the worst of us, not excepting your devoted Husband. But now that I have master'd the first Rudiments I fly as swift as a bird thro' glassy space, yet I do abhor the bitter Cold, for this Winter and for the first time in my Life have I suffer'd from Chill Blains which disfigure my Hands and swell my feet with an itch and burning to make me scratch and rub myself to a frenzy and no solace for it neither.

I have heard from our Great-Aunt — and from another source besides — that you, my little Sweetheart, are grown to be a Beauty. Surely your ears must be in as great a Tingle as my Chill Blains if you could hear how that your Fame has reach'd even to this out-post of Perdition where we have nought to do but skate outdoors and freeze within at a fire not big enough to roast a Chestnut, for the Court is in a most beggarly state and can ill-afford two sous to spend on faggots. And tho' I write to Mr Moon for Money I have receiv'd no word from him, and dare swear his Message, or his Messenger, has been intercepted on the way. For this reason, I have not sent you yet a Christmas Gift, but will do so when the wherewithal arrives to buy it, for I have in mind a Fan wrought in lace-work with sticks most delicately carved in ivory — and painted. Also a Ruby Heart to wear as Pendant round your Neck in Token of my own Heart's blood, that most willingly would I give, drop by drop for one taste of your Lips...

Our Aunt writes too of her poor husband's Decimation — such words they use! One needs revise the English Dictionary to fit them — and how that he hath been brought before the Commissioners a second time for further penalty. How I grieve for that mishandled Gentleman. Is there to be no end to all such dolorous Exactions? The war with Spain is no doubt responsible for these additional Severities since Parliament is now beset with the need for Funds and does not scruple to resort to these excessive Ways to raise their Means. I hear that there is scarce an Honest Man in England who is not in a borrowing Condition wherewith to pay his Fines. Which being so and sadly against my Inclination, Dearest Wife, I deem it wiser to rest here, altho' it irks me so to do, when all my Heart and Soul is filled with longing to return and claim thee for my Own. But should I obey this warm Desire which increases Day by Day — and Night by Night — fed by reports that paint my Lady in such rare and glowing Colours, I might find myself without a Roof, my Home in forfeit and no Marriage Bed to offer you, that we, perforce, might be constrained to celebrate our Nuptials in an alcove beneath the Stars with no canopy above our Heads but Heaven.

Yet, when I come to think on't I could imagine a worse entry into Paradise than that!

This letter, couched on a more personal and warmer note than any I had received from my errant bridegroom since his departure, set me in a ferment of expectation — and frustration. What could be more provoking than to read how my husband was hot with 'desire' for me, yet in the same sentence to be plainly told that he would sooner retard the consummation of his love than run the risk of losing his security.

Having lashed myself into a torment, I forthwith penned my husband, a reply and since he safeguarded all my letters, I reproduce this one as it was written:

So, my Lord, notwithstanding your poetic Protestations, methinks you do care more to hold your Roof than hold your Wife. 'Tis now three years since we were parted and tho' God forbid I shuld demean myself to question your 'Desires' or Intentions, we are still bound in Holy Wedlock for Better or for Worse. Meseemeth truly that I have borne the Brunt of all these Troublous Times harbour'd in this Hermitage in the care of our Elderly Aunt, while you have pleasured on the Continent in Travel and Amusement. Thus has your Marriage advantag'd and bless'd you with some Freedom from the Yoke, while I have been guarded close as any Felon for all I walk in Silks and Satins now.

Yes, I am growne, that much I can assure you, and do measure exactly one Yard two Feet and Five inches High, but as for my Beauty, Far be it from me to deny myself well-looking, but since 'tis said Beauty is in the Eye of the Beholder, who, pray, besides my Aunt has beheld me to sing my praises to my Lord? I fear that you as others of your sex are prone to flatter, but I, unlike my kind am not so gullible to take sweet Unction to my Palate tho' I'll own 'tis pleasant tasting. And so, my Lord, you will not stand amaze'd to learn that were I not your lawful Wife in all Respects — save one — I dare swear I would have long ere this refus'd an Hundred Suitors of highest Rank and Elegance, these Parts abounding in young Gallants and if you believe me not do you write for verification of my dear Friend Mistress Tansy, daughter of Colonel Ashton of Widders Cross at Beer. She will tell you how that Gentlemen are plenteous as Dock Leaves hereabouts and do come cackling at my Shoe Heels like Geese at feeding time.

I commiserate with your Lordship upon your Chill Blains. Happily my hands have suffer'd no Disfigurement from the intolerable Cold. Do you still bite your Thumbs?

I am greatly jeallus of your skating. I have seen a painture here at Templecombe by a Dutch Artist which portraies most skilfullie this Sporte. I would indeed joy to partake of it. Have you seen augh't of Robin latterly? He writes to me but seldom. And is your hair still color'd like a Prim-rose or do you wear a Perriwig which my Aunt Rossiter does say is all the Fashion now in France. Methinks you would look comick in a Perriwig. Is your Nose as long as ever and are you growinge Tall?

I do confess it is so long since I have seen you that I can scarce recall your Features or Appearance to my Mind.

I thank you for the Ruby Heart and Fan of Lace and Ivorie which I wear and use in Fancy taking the Though't for the Gift but I beseech my Lord not to give himself the pain of an appologie for his lengthy Sojurne in the Low Countries — and elsewhere. The limited Pursuits and Entertainmente that out Life in this unhappie England can offer him is no fair Compensation for the Gaietie of Foreign Travel, the charm of Foreign Ladys, and the Varietie of Diversions obtain'd in Courtly Circles.

That my Lord will make the most of his enjoyments while yet he may ere he returns to take his Matrimonial Burden to his Breast is the Sincere Wish

of
his most loving
Wife.

Postscript

I have forgot to tell you and am sore griev'd that my Jerfalcon Martha is dead — of Old Age my Uncle says but I think of a Broken Heart since she was never happy in the Mews at Templecombe being in a mournful Pine for Folly's End and Mary.

As was I.

The severe long winter taxed even my young robust endurance. I suffered from a succession of fierce colds that left me melancholic. My aunt sent for a physician from Exeter who prescribed cuppings, purges, plasters and all kinds of nauseous brews, but still I languished in the doldrums with scarce a laugh left in me.

And when the snows began to melt and the virgin drifts that had been so white and fair turned to a murky swamp; when the hardy aconite, brave herald of the spring, shook off the cruel frost's clutches to flaunt its yellow stars amid the mud; and the crocus, white and purple, speared the first tender green under the apple trees to be followed by a fanfare from the trumpets of March daffodils; when the arrowy rain of April brought a gleam and song and shining to the woods and a budding mist among the tree-tops, and a primrose pattern in the moss under the sodden leaves of last year, them more than ever was I seized with a nostalgic ache and urge for my old home.

Boldly I put my case before Aunt Rossiter, indicating that the longing to revisit Folly's End did so entirely possess me that not all the doctor's physics nor her care could cure my ill-condition. 'For 'tis less a sickness of the body that has brought me to this pass than a craving for a sight of my old nurse, and — and — the little attic where I used to sleep and the dogs and my dear Ebony —'

'Tut!' exclaimed my aunt, having small patience with these fancies. 'You have half a dozen dogs here to your bidding and a handsome horse to ride, of finer mettle than your own knock-kneed brute who is fit for nothing but to make meat for your falcons. As for that woman with her coarse manners and her bawdy tongue, she served her purpose when she fostered you and has served you little since. At your age you should have outgrown such puerile dependence. Nurse indeed!'

'More than my nurse,' I answered, holding my tears, 'she has been my mother... Oh, Aunt, believe me not ungracious, or ungrateful for your bounty. I have been happy here with — I *am* happy as I can be — but I am — I am — I don't know *what* I am!' And there I broke down utterly, and stood sobbing with my knuckles to my eyes, an altogether shaming exhibition.

My uncle, who, seated at the table, seemingly engrossed in a solo game of shovel-board, had taken no part in this dispute, now chimed in to offer timidly, 'My dear — if I may — if I may venture to submit my own — opinion —'

'You may not,' my aunt conclusively replied.

'I would...' her husband faltered, with, however, a persistence to his credit, 'I would suggest that — that s-since our niece has expressed the wish — the not — unnatural — wish to revisit her home, the change of — of air and scene —'

'Tcha!' exclaimed my aunt with great contempt.

'— would not unlikely prove to her health's benefit.' And having got this out in one audacious breath, my Uncle Rossiter subsided, chin on chest.

Anxiously I waited for the decisive contradiction that would shatter my last hopes and deprive my uncle of the courage to uphold them. But my aunt, rubbing her nose with a contemplative finger, her brows lowered and her body poker-straight, sat and answered nothing. From the expression of her face I could tell that she was sternly and fairly reconsidering the situation.

As I knew her to be just, although entirely omnipotent in the execution of her justice, I held my peace and prayed for a verdict in my favour.

'Well! Well!' After some lengthy cogitation my aunt was moved at last to utter, 'out of the mouths of babes — for in all matters commonsensical my husband is as a babe unborn — so be it! Change of air! Prudence, your uncle gives me wrong — to set me right. Neither that asinine apothecary who calls himself physician, nor I, who have had, heaven knows, experience enough in all sickness appertaining to the mind —' and here she shot so sharp a glance at her now-beaming husband to turn him preternaturally grave — 'should have recognised the symptoms and prescribed the remedy without the need of prompting. I sit corrected, Mr Rossiter.'

My uncle, evidently overwhelmed at this concession, inclined his head and very humbly bowed.

'This child,' said my aunt, 'is suffering from nothing worse than melancholy due to close confinement within four walls with no companionship but that of two old fogies. Yes, sir, you —' my uncle started — 'are a fogy, and you're old. And so am I. But that is only one cause of our niece's malady. The other —' she frowned again, then rising from her seat she went over to the cupboard where she kept her ink-horn and writing materials — 'the other is a more natural deduction, which had I been less preoccupied with the management of your deplorable affairs, Mr Rossiter, I should have dealt with earlier. Still, it is not too late to make amends for my omission. Prudence is now ripe for mating. I shall notify our nephew Folliett to return.'

'Oh, no! Oh, please, Aunt, no!' I cried aghast. And with my face on fire I sprang forward to intercept her progress to the cupboard while words rushed in a torrent to my tongue. 'I would sooner die than have him think me more eager than himself. Which I am not, believe me! I have never — would never be the first to beckon him. Oh, good madam, pray do not write to my husband and put me to such shame! When he comes to me it must be of his own accord and inclination. I will not have him brought to heel. No, I will *not*!'

Never before in my aunt's house and to her face had I dared such self-assertion, but my urge was great and my pride greater. I stood quivering.

My aunt gave me a keen glance, compressed her lips, then opened them to say, 'There are limits to a maiden's modesty, my child. Your husband has stayed away from you a year beyond his scheduled time. You have the right to compel him to his duties.'

'A pretty right!' I cried. 'A pretty right and wifely right, I'll warrant, to claim a husband's duties on compulsion. What *are* a husband's duties? To love and cherish — as mine are to obey. Am I then to go on all fours whining for his pleasure like a lap-dog — or a she-dog in the heats? No, madam, in sooth! I'll claim no rights whatever they may be, save the right to have my husband's love, whole-hearted. And if he loves me not and shows himself so lukewarm and disinterested that he must need reminder of his duties, then let him go seek another wife through all the courts of Europe — a French wife, or a German wife. But, by my troth — and my virginity — I swear he'll not have me!'

And upon this immense admission and without pausing for my aunt's reply to it — in truth I do believe that for the first time in her life the poor lady found herself bereft of speech —

I rushed headlong from the room, slamming the door behind me with a shock to shake the windows.

Whether this emphatic revelation of a hitherto restrained and unsuspected violence at large within her household and let loose upon my aunt in the form of a tornado, did influence her to hasten my departure, I cannot say, but the fact remains that Deborah was summoned to pack my bags that very forenoon, and that I left for Folly's End upon the morrow.

I had promised to return within two weeks.

Even in the guardianship of the dour Deborah, who, at my aunt's insistence, accompanied me on my journey home, I felt, as the coach bumped and rattled down the drive, that I had been released from jail. For, under the Rossiter roof despite that I received the utmost consideration, and by my aunt's good tutorship had been transformed from an ill-mannered wayward hoyden into a young gentlewoman of irreproachable demeanour — when it suited me to so conduct myself — yet there is no denying I had never taken kindly to stern discipline; and though I learned to keep my place and mind my tongue, I had been sorely chafed within my fetters.

Now, for the first time in three long years, I was at liberty and my own mistress. True, Deborah, as my aunt's representative, still held me in thrall, but neither her glum countenance not monosyllabic responses to my excited chatter could subdue me. As every turn of the wheels took me farther eastwards over the border of Devon into Dorset, my spirits rose, till I could scarce restrain myself from jumping out of my seat within the coach to take the driver's place, and urge the horses on.

Although the distance from Colyton to Wynmon Abbas is little more than twenty miles it seemed four times as long to me, so slow and lumbering was our pace; indeed had we not halted thrice upon the way to fortify the aged pair between the shafts, to say nothing of their venerable coachman, who fortified himself to such extent that he was moved to speed his startled nags with hunting cries, I doubt we would have made the journey that same night.

Dusk was creeping up the valley when I had my first glimpse of Wynmonath's blind windows and grey battlements behind its clustering trees. 'There, Deborah!' I cried. 'There is the abbey where my father and all my grandfathers were born. The Roundheads fired and ransacked it, but you see its walls still stand.'

'Yes, my lady.'

'And there — look!' I squeezed Rufus so tight against my bosom that he yelped. 'Do you see that huddle of thatched rooftops, and the big barn? Behind that is my home.' Tears rushed to my eyes. I kissed Rufus to hide them. 'He knows it, though he was a puppy when he left. Weren't you, my darling? You remember. See, he remembers! His nose is pointing. He was born here too.'

'Yes, my lady.'

Seized with a desperation to take and shake my haughty handmaid from her disdainful torpor, I enquired, 'Did my aunt give you instructions to return when you have seen me safe arrived?'

'No, my lady.'

'Then I will. I do not need your services at Folly's End. Our ways are rustic here. As you see 'tis little better than a farmstead. My own woman will attend me, and I shall wear my simplest gowns.'

Pack-horses had been sent in advance with my baggage, and heaven alone knew what. Deborah had selected from my wardrobe, but from her noncommittal silence I gathered I would meet with opposition.

'So, Deborah,' I continued briskly, 'you will lie here for the night, and return to Templecombe tomorrow morning.'

'But, my lady, I understood from Mistress Rossiter —'

'And you will understand from me,' I interrupted firmly, 'that I am mistress here. And here we are.'

Here we were, indeed! Almost before the coach had stopped I was out of it and in the porch-way calling, 'Thirza! Thirza!' — with all the dogs I'd ever known, and more besides, barking and yapping around me, and Ham coming through the screens to grin and pull at his forelock and wearing, to my surprise, a prune-coloured lackey's livery and yellow stockings. 'Goodness me!' I cried. 'Why, Ham, how grand you are!' But I'd no time to gaze at him, for Thirza with her coif half off her head, her face red and shining as a full harvest moon, came running from the buttery, arms wide.

'Is it my own darling, then? My precious dear, my babe — a lady grown! Let me look at you... Here's elegance! Here's grace! A Folliett every inch of her, but not, thanks be, the nose. 'Tis a fearsome obstacle to plant upon a woman — and you *are* a woman now, my beautiful! All yesterday my thumbs and big toes pricked and smarted and my corns did jump that I was kept a-hollering for the pain like knife-thrusts through my joints, and our mazy-dazy Jack seeing happy omens in the fire — and lo! Not three hours since arrives the bagman with your bags, and word from Mistress Rossiter to tell us you are on your way. Dear heaven! Three years have I sorrowed and wept my eyes sore for a sight of you, and — Body o' me! Who's that?'

This sudden blunt enquiry was aimed direct at Deborah, who nothing daunted by my plain injunctions, had followed hard behind me and stood eyeing, clearly scandalised, the boisterous ebullience of my dear Thirza's greeting. To further Deborah's dismay I embraced Thirza again and whispered in the giggles, ''Tis my serving-wench.'

'Serving —? Ho! And who has any right to serve you but myself?' hissed Thirza in a stage aside that could be heard ten yards away. 'And wench do you call her? That old tufted crab?'

'Hush, pray. Say nothing or she'll bite. I will send her off tomorrow… Oh! Thirza, how glad — how glad I am!'

I ran from room to room, exclaiming, crying, touching known familiar objects. All was as it had been and as I had left it. But when I came to the door of my father's chamber and had my hand upon the latch, Thirza warned me, 'You will find a changement here. His Reverence —'

'What?' I turned upon her, bristling. 'Has Mr Moon dared to take upon himself the ordering of this household in my absence?'

'No, no, my chuck. Don't fash yourself till you have heard. It was his lordship's orders. Mr Moon did naught but to obey —'

My impatience and curiosity now whetted, I could wait to hear no more. Flinging wide the door I stood amazed to see not that with which my memory was stored, of gloom and ghosts and death, but a bride's bower.

Gone were the ponderous furnishings, the massive oak, the purple trappings. In their place at the mullioned windows hung curtains of carnation satin fringed with gold and silver, lined with turquoise silk. These same colours were repeated on the valance of the bed, and the bed itself had been upholstered in the daintiest powder blue with a counterpane of quilted satin fancifully embroidered in a design of true-love's knots. There were stools to match, and chairs covered in gilt Spanish leather. The rugs from Persia still remained, as rarities, but now they were displayed to decorate the walls, and a rich Turkish carpet covered the oaken boards.

'Do you mean to say, good Thirza —' I gasped, as one by one I enriched my sight with these allurements, 'do you mean to say that Mr Moon had the grace to indulge in such extravagance and choose these charmful novelties for *me*?'

'For you? What? Him?' retorted Thirza, in a series of explosive snorts. 'If he'd had his way, he would have given you a hair shirt for your sheeting, and a truckle bed to lie on, but that my lord made himself implicit clear in his commands with which His Reverence had naught to do but fetch and carry. All this finery and silkery and gold and silver and the chairs and stools — they come from France, my lady. Do you think you'd find the like o' these in Noll-poll Oliver's England? Why the wonder 'tis the men who brought them were not gutted on the way by Cromwell's watch-hounds for carrying such brazen offerings of fornication from the cities of Sodom and Gomorrah. For this last year they have been coming piece by piece, smuggled over I've no doubt — if you only could have *seen* the scampish runnions that came sweating to these doors — gallows meat if ever I beheld it!'

'And Mr Moon, has he been here?' I asked still in a maze at this magnificence.

'Yes, to supervise the workmen — a batch o' them arrived from Dorchester — with designings from my lord in his own hand, and a muck o' writing underneath that I could make no head of —'

'But,' I interrupted, 'how did you manage to secure these writings, Thirza?'

'Someone,' she replied without a blush, 'had to press His Reverence's breeches after his long journeying — and he forgot to empty his pockets.'

'Up to your old trickery again, it seems — oh, Thirza!' I had to hug her for it, none the less. 'But is this not most gracious of my husband? Were I a queen I couldn't be more delicately served. He has some charmful notions when he pleases.'

'*When* he pleases,' she retorted, 'there's none upon this earth with greater nicety or sweeter manners than his lordship, nor of stronger blood nor warmer passions, methinks neither, and hotter too, maybe, than those who spend their strength in outward brawn. His turns to brain — which kind o' man, as you will find, my pretty, when he pleasures you, has the knack o' womanising to that winsome degree so you'll learn more of love's delight with him in half an hour than with your rampageous bull in half a year. I'll wager his young lordship having lived so long in France will make you —'

'Well now, Thirza, you have said enough, so you may leave me.'

'Ay, I'll go.' Her rogue's eyes overswept my burning face and she chuckled, very wise and knowing; then suddenly up went her chin. 'But this I'll say,' and very loudly did she say it, that her voice might reach the ears of Deborah who was coming up the staircase, 'there's none in this house has the right to wait upon your ladyship but me, even if there's some gone sour with too long fasting for a man — though I'll wager a she-porcupine would stand a better chance than them who give theirselves the airs of Sheba's queen — and if they so much as poke a nose inside my lady's chamber and meddle with her garments —'

'Hush, Thirza!' I besought her, 'pray be circumspect.'

'Why, my lady, what's been said?' Thirza asked in mincing tones and speaking louder. 'Nought to perturb your ladyship, I hope. Will your ladyship wash your hands in orange-flower water? Not for nothing did I serve your ladyship's sainted mother and dress her for a visit from the King and Queen and for festivities and banquets the like of which was never heard nor thought of in some other houses I could name. His lordship has sent besides the furnishings and curtains for his lady's bedroom, a case of the most fashionable essences and *par-fumes* used in Paris — orange-water is the least of them —' And as Deborah entered with Ham behind her carrying my portables, Thirza made a show of gesturing and frowning. 'Why, Ham, you dolt!' she cried. 'Have you lost your senses to bring this — this *person* to my lady's room? Take her to the servants' quarters, meaning no offence or aspersions cast at strangers more than that they take too much upon themselves. Give me my lady's baggage, Ham, I will unpack it.'

And in Deborah's shocked face she slammed the door.

No question, I had been well advised to bid my waiting-woman go; nor it seemed, was she reluctant to obey me, since Thirza did not scruple to let her have it clear that her presence in our household was superfluous.

Once rid of Deborah, I returned like a homing pigeon to my life at Folly's End. All was as before, yet nothing as it had been — for this difference: that everywhere I went, indoors or out, by field or meadow, woods or stream, whether I walked or rode, or when I sat at table, or even in my dreams, I was aware of emptiness. I missed the sound of boyish voices, the clatter of boys' feet: I missed the very scent of them, that indefinable young male smell of hay and sweat and earth. I missed the sight of and the unwary stumble over muddy leathern boots or jerkin flung off and left forgotten in dark corners; I missed the chess-board with its ivory men set ready for the next game, for the board was hid away, the knights and bishops, kings and queens, laid two by two within their oaken box, like fantastic fairy corpses in a coffin. I missed the many glimpses of a young stalwart figure in shabby suit and soiled shirt, engrossed at all times in some preoccupation concerned with twine and twigs, or the mending of a bow-string, or hammering a nail, or the training of a falcon, or the grooming of his grey mare; or lying belly downwards in the grass to con a page of Cicero, or watching bees and ants; or winding up his fishing-reel, or whispering, 'Robin loves Prue ... and will love her for ever ... and ever.'

Or equally, I missed the one who walked beside him, a careless arm flung round the other's shoulder while he murmured in his ear with merry glances thrown behind at me; and then the shout of their intermingled laughter. I missed the sight of him pacing solitary up and down the garden, head bent and nibbling his thumb; or mounted for the chase sitting straight and eager in the saddle, his hair a pale cloud upon his shoulders, his face upturned to my window, bawling: 'Come *on*, Prue! Hurry, will you?... A pox! *Hi,* Prue! Make haste!'

Yes, I went haunted; and the knowledge deep within me, which even to my heart was unconfessed, spread roots down to my very fibres to fill me with its message, fiercely sweet and urgently compelling, that I must stand divided, torn between these two, and sealed, and given — not to one, nor to the other, but to both.

Happily for my mind's peace, I was too young and healthy to dwell upon a problem that would involve me far beyond my understanding; and even in this, my long day's twilight, as I re-live my dawn I see no answer nor no reason for it. Maybe I loved Love's image and in this twin-born passion saw Love made manifest to love myself; or maybe I was prompted by blind instinct and inflamed by Thirza's hints, for in all conscience these were broad enough to fret my budding womanhood in this May-time burgeoning of blossom, movement, song, with everywhere the pulse and heartbeat of spring's exultant fever; and it seemed as if in all that ecstasy of earth's rejuvenation and the mating of wild things in air and field and wood, only I was lonely, and alone.

I had not yet deserted my old attic room for my new bridal chamber, since what use a marriage bed with no bridegroom to share it?

And with no companionship save that of dogs I roamed the countryside, revisiting our scattered tenants, who gave me a warm welcome and the latest gossip of the village. I heard how a Presbyterian parson had been appointed to the parish, his predecessor having been turned out owing to his supposed Anglican tendencies. I gathered that the service now conducted in the church of Wynmon Abbas was of the strangest kind, and that severest punishment threatened those who failed to attend it; and how that a poor witless girl who had come to trouble with a cowman had been called before the elders and publicly exposed; and as if that were not enough would have been whipped at the cart's tail through the village, but that none could be found to do it, nor would they be enforced — no, not though the military were sent to shoot them piecemeal for their insubordination!

I took this tale back to Thirza to know if it were true, and was somewhat comforted to hear that there had been no talk, that she could tell, of whippings; but that the girl had been sat in the stocks in the most freezing weather with her babe in a basket at her feet for all to gape at was a fact; and greatly shocked was I to hear of such inhuman practices wrought in our own domain by the administrators of Cromwell's Christianity. And for how long, I wondered, must this incorrigible systematic persecution be endured by its unhappy victims?

'For where,' I asked indignantly, 'is the mettle of our England and our Englishmen that they make no stand against the tyranny of these Republicans? What use a handful of loyalists rising here and there to be mowed down and murdered by armed forces? We need a roaring blaze from north to south to give these fiends a taste of their own hell. If I were a man I would not rest quiet in my bed and see the nation die in chains. They to talk of Liberty! Why those penned sheep out yonder have more liberty than we who are herded here and hounded there by the slaves of a "Protector".'

'Give them enough rope,' Thirza answered, 'and they'll hang. There'll be a great rebellion on the *other* side, mark me, when the jackals start to fight among themselves for kings and kingship, and a sickening of those muck-worms who set up to be the chosen of the Lord. And may I live to see it!'

On the last day before my return to Templecombe the weather changed; the gilded cock upon the stable roof turned to the north-east, and a chill wind sprang up, followed by heavy rain.

I stayed indoors, ordered a fire to be lit in the winter parlour, and took my guitar, which I had brought with me, to strum a tune: and presently came to my mind some words to suit the melody, remembered from a verse my father favoured.

'My dearest love since thou wilt go
And leave me here behind thee,
For love or pity let me know
The place where I may find thee.'

Which words I thought most apt for my condition, and was singing them over softly when I heard the thud of hooves in a gallop up the drive. I ran to the window but was too late to see who rode so hard, for he had turned aside under the arch of the court.

There followed such a stir and confusion of yard-dogs barking, of footsteps running, of our fellows shouting amid a clink of chains and rattling of bolts, and opening of gates, that I feared the Major-General's men were come to raid us. Nor was I slow to snatch at a defence. Mounting on a stool I reached for an ancient fowling-piece that, despite the law against the Royalists' retention of all weapons, still hung upon the wall, and while I prayed it might be loaded, for I'd not have stopped at murder to keep those devils from the house, I heard Ham's voice ring sharp above the din: 'How now! Stop thy gibbering, zany, and take his lordship's horse... God bless the day that brings you home, my lord!'

In heaven's name — what fantasy was this?

Rufus sat up quivering, nose pointed. Peg, her feathered tail in a frenzy, was snuffling and whining at the door.

I set aside my weapon, dusted my trembling hands and sat ... and waited.

Then: 'Thirza! Woman — you! Where is she? Where is my lady-wife?'

And he stood there in the doorway, with laughter on his lips and a shining in his eyes. From his shoulders swung a gay cloak, silver blue; his plumed hat was in his hand, his hair like golden wine with the gleam of raindrops in it. I saw the sparkle of a jewel in the laces at his throat.

My hand was at my heart, my eyes on his to doubt my sight. If this were dreaming, let me never wake. And if reality then whence was he and why should he be here, thinking me at

Templecombe? And even in this first tumult of my joy I recalled how my aunt had said that she would write to him. Had he received a letter and come to me in answer, duty-bound? All this leapt through my mind in that second's crack-brained silence, while I sat and looked upon my husband, and heard him softly say, 'Is it a thousand years since I last saw you, or is it yesterday? Yet I think I never saw you until now.'

And he was close beside me, gazing down into my eyes as though his own would drink me, while he murmured, 'You are so much more beautiful than I could have believed, although I knew you lovely,' turning each word he spoke to a caress.

'When,' I asked him, faint with a delightful dizziness upon me that caused the room to spin and my head with it, 'when did you receive my aunt's last letter?' For I must know.

His eyebrows shot up, quizzing me.

'Aunt Rossiter? S'truth, sweetheart! Is this all the greeting you can give me when I've lain dead for centuries and am but this moment resurrected? And you talk of aunts! Well, then, if you be so particular, I have had no letter from our aged relative for nigh upon a year. She is not so enamoured of her nephew that she needs must write more often than to warn him against the evils of loose living and debauchery. Why speak of her? No, faith! The only letter I have had these six months is from yourself and that arrived three weeks ago, which hastened me from Bruges as fast as horse, coach and vessel could bring me, on receipt of it.'

'Three weeks!' I gasped. 'It is three months since I wrote to you — in February.'

'The posts,' he answered, carelessly, 'are always devilish slow.' And taking his lace-bordered handkerchief he flicked the raindrops from his hat and cast it down. ''Tis ruined! I have ridden through a deluge to come to you, my dear.'

I laid a finger on his velvet sleeve. 'You're wet! Will you not change your clothes?'

'Presently. My outer cloak is drenched, but not my suit. And what's a wetting when I…' His eyes were weighed on mine with an eager passionate intensity; his hand light as a moth's wing, brushed my hair. He said, 'I can't … I can't believe it. Can't believe I'm here. I thought I'd lost you. I went first to Templecombe thinking to find you there and was told you were gone home upon a visit. I stayed no longer than to take a stirrup-cup, although our aunt would have it I must rest a night before I rode again. Rest! How in Gemini did she think that I could rest when I was put to torment by your letter?'

'My letter! What —' I asked, and hid my eyes from that warm light in his which set my pulses throbbing and brought a dryness to my throat that I could scarce articulate — 'what was in my letter to torment you?'

'Shall I tell?' I could almost hear the beating of his heart as he leaned nearer, not to touch, but exquisitely to prolong desire. 'For all,' he said, and laughed below his breath, 'for all that it was full of prickles as a briar rose, I dared to read between the lines and thought you showed impatience — a certain restlessness to have me here beside you… Did I take too much upon myself to think, to hope, you might be ready to … receive me? Your letters, till this last one, had been the letters of a child. You wrote so seldom, one to every six I wrote to you. That hurt … a little. But still, I watched you growing in those letters. Each time you penned me news I tried to picture you, though no imagination could reveal you as you are. And then I had to know if you were jesting or in earnest when you spoke of others at your feet. Others! God help me! *One* would be enough, and if he's here about I'll slit him up.' He laughed again, eyes narrowed; and then he was not laughing any more. 'And did you think it would content me to lie fallow in a foreign town while *others* tasted of your favours first? Answer me!' He took my hands in both of his, crushing them to pain. 'Have you been fair to me, and faithful? Am I your husband ... or your fool?'

'No,' I shook my head, smiling, exultant. 'I have been true. 'Twas jesting ... I ... I have seen no man but Uncle Rossiter and Tansy's father and the yokels and the curate.'

'You're unbelievable, adorable,' he murmured. 'Dear heart! I am not worthy of your grace. But by all the stars I swear that I will be!'

I stood lost, enraptured, wonder-charged, savouring this knowledge. My letter! So it was *my* letter that had brought him. Not our aunt's, for she had never written. He had come unprompted, of his own free will, spurred by the same longing that had fretted me, as though some cord of irresistible communion between us had drawn him to my side. He was no fool. He was my lover, and I his...

And he was saying, 'How curiously you smile to or at yourself. What do you see behind your eyes that I cannot? Did they always slant ever so slightly at the corners? And are they greyest blue or bluest grey? Is this the raggle-taggle minx I left behind me, this gracious lady dressed so fine in satin, with her hair in curls, her skin so white, her hands,' he took them one by one to kiss, 'like lilies... Is this Prue?'

'Yes,' I said, 'I'm Prue. I am not changed — more than fine clothes can change me.'

'Am *I* changed?'

He was indeed, and I turned shy of this bold stranger, whose searching glances seemed to strip me to my maiden soul that all my blood was in my heart to drown it; this boy grown to a man in boyhood's years, whose speech slid from his tongue with an ease and polish that deprived me of a word to answer him; whose touch was magic and whose lips possessed, to melt upon my own into a sigh.

'You have me utterly. And this ... and this,' he kissed again, 'is only the beginning. There's all our lives and all eternity to come.'

CHAPTER NINE

We had no marriage celebrations, no gathering of guests to toast our nuptials; no bridesmaids, groomsmen, none to give us blessing or good cheer but our domestics and my Thirza, whom Percy insisted should be brought to table to drink a loving-cup and wish us joy. Which with much lachrymose verbosity she did; and further, to more elated purpose in the kitchen along with Ham and others of our servants, and the shepherd and the herdsman and our poor simple Jack, who perched cross-legged upon the dresser contributed to the gaiety by whistling tunes upon his fingers to start them in a jig, with a passing to and fro of tankards and a shouting of song to bring me and my bridegroom from the hall to watch and join in, hands crossed, singing 'Cuckolds all awry': till, overcome with emotion and a mixing of wines, Thirza sank in a happy stupor on the settle. And since neither a dousing of cold water from a bucket, nor Ham's roaring in her ear could shake her from her comatose contentment to escort me to my bed, my husband did disrobe me for himself.

And here let this be said, whatever else may follow, that no wife on her first marriage night could wish to be more tenderly, more rapturously wooed; no woman, I will swear, was more desired.

To me my husband was a never-ending source of wonder and surprises. He had developed a dexterity of speech, and, beyond his charm of manner, a certain self-assurance and sensitivity towards and interest in others, which I in my green youth with him had not observed. True, he liked to talk and did talk — better than he listened; but as I cared to listen better than to talk we were well accorded, and I marvelled at his fluent wit that was flavoured with a cynicism older than his years.

He had all to tell me of himself, of his travels, of the famous — or infamous — persons he had met at the court of the young King of France, where he had been much favoured, it seemed, by the King's younger brother, Philippe, the heir to the throne. He spoke often of his good friend Monsieur de Fontenelle, who had married Germaine, daughter of the Vicomte d'Auteuil. He spoke of La Grande Mademoiselle de France, daughter of Gaston, Duc d'Orléans and cousin to King Louis: she who had been thought a likely wife for our King Charles. But His Majesty, Percy said, thought otherwise, preferring Mademoiselle's maid of honour, the beautiful Duchesse de Châtillon, afterwards succeeded by Lucy Walters. 'A handsome brown-eyed bawd, with neither wit nor grace,' so Percy described the mother of Charles II's greatly loved illegitimate son. who, thirty-five years later, as Duke of Monmouth, sought to wear the crown — to lose his head.

But more than any Percy spoke of Robin, and how that the Queen Mother had made him her page and protégé, instructing him in her Papistical beliefs, 'more's the pity,' Percy said, and much grieved was he to see it, but since that Rob was born a Catholic there seemed to be no likelihood of weaning him from Her Majesty's heretical beguilements.

He said too that our 'uncouth Rob' had developed past all telling in mind as well as body, being grown to near upon the same height as our King — 'well above two yards high,' and had lost his surly manner, and slow speech — to some extent, though he still thought before he uttered — a wise precaution in a world where a word slipped out of place may be flung back upon yourself to kill you.

'Yes, our Robin,' Percy told me, 'has the makings in him of a proper diplomat, and if all goes well with us and with our King, he'll strike his mark in the future, I've no doubt. Already the Queen entrusts him to carry messages of urgency between her and the King at no slight personal risk, I need hardly say — since Cromwell's spies abound in every city, every province, and every village on the Continent, so that, like the plague, you can never know when you will be attacked if you walk into infection. However, he goes armed and well-escorted.'

'And did he send me any message?' I asked.

It appeared that he did not. 'But,' said Percy, kindly, seeing me chapfallen, 'he surely would have if I'd had word with him before I left. He did not attend the court at Bruges, nor I think was he over-anxious to leave Paris. There is much gossip around his name and that of Madame de Fontenelle. They are,' he said, 'a very well-matched couple.'

I liked little to hear this. 'She is married!' I exclaimed, aghast. 'Surely Robin would not fall so low as to intrigue with another man's wife.'

Which remark caused Percy some amusement.

'Why, child, in France, any man's wife is another man's mistress; Frenchwomen never love until they marry, and Frenchmen never marry where they love.' And, laughing in my startled face, he added, 'If you knew more of men and their untasteful appetites that devour with less reflection than a blow-fly when it feeds upon an over-ripened peach, you would not regret your father's choice in binding you to *me*!'

'Have I ever said that I regret it?'

'I would like to hear you say that you do not.'

'Well,' I teased him, 'hear me say — I do not.'

He smiled wryly. 'I stand begging. I ask for a loaf and am given a crumb... Do you love me?'

'You have asked me that a thousand times. I can but answer yes — and yes — and yes again. Are you not satisfied?'

'No,' he whispered on my lips. 'I'm greedy... The more I have of you the more I want.'

He was forever questioning if I were happy, as though he seemed to doubt me, or himself. Happy indeed I was. He had a way of loving to melt stones. The woman would be hard to please were she not contented by so tender and so whimsical a lover. Yet, I confess myself not altogether guiltless in those first honeymoon weeks, of some inborn, inherent coquetry, that prompted me to feign indifference — to wax cold as he waxed hot, which alternately exasperated and inflamed him, the while I gloried in my power that could bring this lordly being in a tremble to his knees for the favours I so niggardly dispensed.

I was, in fact, enjoying for the first time in my life the homage of a man to woman's beauty. I was not vain, but to read in my husband's eyes the reassurance of my mirror magnified fourfold, was a delicious novelty to me.

Yes, I was happy ... then.

He had brought me all sorts of pretty gifts for my delight. To the 'par-fumes' spoken of by Thirza — twelve phials of various essences contained in a satin-wood case — he added a coffer packed with bottles of rose-water and jessamine, and a large silver box studded with turquoise and holding that which I had never seen before — musk-scented powder for the face, and another smaller box in gold, filled with a scarlet cream — 'Which you,' he said, 'will never need to use. No artificial colour could reproduce the lovely carmine of your lips, the pale rose and white of your complexion, the —'

'Nay, now!' I broke in upon this rhapsodising with a shout of laughter. 'I'll not be denied a touch of paint.' And dipping my fingers in the paste I smeared a daub of crimson on each cheek and on the tip of my nose to make my husband shudder and cry, 'Sacrilege!' while I laughed again to see myself so comic. 'Is it true,' I asked, 'that the French ladies decorate their faces with this stuff?'

'Not quite as you have laid it on,' said Percy, 'nor is it only women who paint themselves in France.'

'What! The men too? Lord sakes!' I gazed anxiously into his smooth-skinned face. 'Don't tell me that *you* paint!'

'No, God forbid!'

'Methinks,' I said severely, 'that you speak too loud for truth, and I hope God does forbid it, for I'd not lie a-bed with a coxcomb — not were he the King himself. Does *he* paint?'

'Our King does not, but the French King and his brother Philippe do, and others I could name. Come here.' Percy pulled me to him, 'I'll not see you so disfigured.' He took his handkerchief and wetted it with orange-flower water and carefully washed me clean.

'Well! May I be slit!' I wriggled free of him. 'Are all the men in France then Jemmy-Jessamies?'

'If you mean,' retorted Percy, 'that Frenchmen are unmanly, no. But they have more *finesse* than we.'

'More what?'

'More subtlety, refinement, shall we say — more — hang me! We have no words in English.'

'Is it subtle for a man to ape the girl? — Don't pick your thumb!'

'Send me patience!' Percy prayed. 'Let us have this clear. In the beginning, did not God create Adam before He created Eve, and did He not bring woman forth from man?'

'I'm not denying it.'

'By which same token, therefore, man should have in him the elements of male and female combined.'

'And woman,' I enquired, 'what of her?'

'The least said of *her* the better. Was she not the cause of Adam's fall?'

'So man declares and — shame on him! — went straight unto the Lord to sneak, "She tempted me!" How noble 'tis of man,' I scoffed, 'to hide behind a woman's petticoat!'

'Only,' Percy murmured, ''twas not — if I remember right — a petticoat.'

I never tired of his talk and tales of his journeyings, so vividly recounted that I re-lived with him each gay adventure. He told me how he and Robin had accompanied our King and the King's sister, the Princess Mary of Orange, with their young brother Henry, Duke of Gloucester, to the Great Fair at Frankfort; and how that the King's few attendants included the Marquis of Ormond — 'who, by the way,' said Percy, 'returned from his trip to England last year, loud in his praise of you.'

'Of *me*?' I echoed, stupefied. 'I have never to my knowledge seen the man. Who is he — this Marquis of — what name did you say?'

Percy coloured to his ears. 'If I said any name — forget it. 'Tis no matter. 'Twas not you of whom he spoke in any case. I was mistook.'

'That you were not!' quoth I, undeceived by these lame mumblings. 'Methinks you've slipped a secret here, my lad.'

'If so, it is not mine to give away. Do you care to hear my story?'

'I would sooner hear your secret.'

Percy laughed. 'Eve's daughter you are truly! But I'll not be tempted. Though you have me where you want me, you'll not have me in this... Will you hear how Rob and I went to the fair?'

And since he was bent on telling, I heard how, having gone by coach as far as Bonn, they embarked by pleasure-boat for Frankfort. This water voyage continued for four or five days, during which time no state was kept among the royal party, all eating and drinking together at one table. But although the 'Scottish King', as the Germans dubbed him, had intended to visit the fair with his sister and brother incognito, the news leaked out, and all along the route they were greeted with homage and salutes from the Grandmasters and Electors, and with invitations here, there and everywhere, all of which the King refused. For greatly was he chagrined to have his impromptu frolic turned into formality by 'those fat-necked pudding-headed swine', as Percy called them, who care for nought but to drink beer and guzzle sausages. A race of sausages indeed, all cut to one pattern and cast in one mould. They brag and boast of their 'Philosophy' — but believe me, the meanest lackey of a Frenchman has more philosophy in his toe-nails than a German princeling in his — Well, and there you are! France remains *par excellence*, the seat of European culture.' He harped often on that word. 'The human mind,' he said, 'is like a garden, wherein the choicest blooms or roughest weeds may grow according to the taste and sensibility of the gardener.'

'Which being so,' I answered, 'maybe you pine for the scent of rarer plants than those that grow in Dorset?'

'Never!' Percy pulled me down upon his knee to hold me captive. 'One petal of an English rose is sweeter far than a whole field of French lilies. And this I swear, although I'll own the fleurs-de-lys are handsome and abundant, I have never for all their fragrance cared to gather one of them. They have left me as I was — when I left you.'

'That remark, sir,' I retorted, 'is ambiguous. Explain yourself.'

But he would not, to leave me guessing. Had he in truth returned to me untouched by any woman as I by any man? I could scarcely credit this, for surely only one experienced in love could make of him so exquisite a lover. Yet, if what he told was truth — nor did I think he lied — it would account for much in his approach to and possession of his rights, which, for all our joy in one another, puzzled me.

Though innocent I was not ignorant, and while grateful for the selfless delicacy that restrained him while he led me through the first steps of my initiation, and while we lay together night by night and heart to heart, I, though all transported, was only half transformed. And as time passed, so the slow knowledge came to me that despite our love and his consuming fire, which never quite consumed, we fed on famine.

I had none to guide me, even were I ready to discuss as women do, and I did not, the intimacies of my marriage bed with any other but my husband; yet least of all to him could I reveal my trouble... For troubled indeed I was after six months of wedded life to know myself *virgo intacta* still.

Once only did I poise a guarded question expressing the hope that I would soon conceive and bear a son. To which he answered, 'In good time — you're young and so am I. Besides, what have I to leave beyond my name? Wait till I restore the abbey and then give me my heir; and he'll be born at Wynmonath, God willing.'

That answer, for the moment, set my mind at peace. The inexplicable had now explained itself. My husband did not wish

— while his position was unsettled — to get me with child. For which reason he forbore to take my maidenhead. I marvelled at his self-restraint. Not one man in a thousand would be, I thought, so tolerant and kind.

I did not know — how could I? — that despite his fierce young ardour, his manhood's potency was lacking, his loins ungirded. I did not realise… And when at last I did, in pity for his crippled strength and anguished pride, my heart went out to love him more, not less.

This, then, was our secret, unvoiced yet shared between us, to unite while it divided. Of our mutual suffering, and of his hidden torment that lay like a sheathed sword upon his soul, I can give no account. The memory is painful. Let it rest.

Not always did my husband stay with me at Folly's End. He had much to occupy him in the administration of his Yorkshire property, and would go back and forth to Ripon at least three times a year, remaining there for several weeks; but although he requested and was anxious I should accompany him on these visits, I did so only once, not caring for the long tedious journey.

Nor did I care for the house, Aykroyd Peak as it was called, possibly from the height on which it stood, some few miles west of Ripon, and commanding a view of desert moorland. A bleak forbidding habitation, its ill-furnished gloomy rooms provided the scantiest amenities of comfort, for lack of which Percy was profuse in his apologies.

Here, however, in this gaunt dwelling, hewed apparently out of local rock, so rough and massive were its walls, so narrow its windows deep-set like crevices within them, letting in less daylight than draught from the fierce north winds, I found our Mr Moon installed, and seemingly more at home and at ease than ever he had been at Folly's End. And I could not help but feel that this sad northern country of frowning granite crags and windswept moor, whose dry waste soil bore no vegetation other than the stunted thorn and hardy scrub and heather, was a more fitting environment for Mr Moon's austerity than our green, dimpled Dorset.

I observed too, though this did not surprise me, that Percy appeared to be a guest in, rather than the master of, his house. Mr Moon sat at the head of the table and served us, carving the joint or fowl or whatever, for there were but two domestics — an aged man and his wife — to perform the household duties.

Our bedchamber was of a spartan simplicity, the bed darkly curtained in green velvet, the stone floor uncovered save for a sprinkling of rushes by the bedside. No, I did not take kindly to Aykroyd, and was somewhat cheered to learn from Percy that he loathed the place and had sold all the land appertaining to it except some few score acres. But he refused to sell the house, since 'poor old Moon,' he said, 'must have a home. It is better he should live here than with us.' With which I heartily agreed; and now I understood where Percy had obtained the money for the many small extravagances he showered upon me and himself. The sale of virtually the whole of this estate had brought him in a good return, and not only was he thus able to replenish his coffers, but he had also made a handsome gift to our exiled King's exchequer. This in direct opposition to Mr Moon's advice, for it seemed our chaplain had heard tales of the King's debauchery and dissipation abroad, and did strongly disapprove of supplying His Majesty with any further means to such indulgence.

'Which,' I retorted, 'concerns us not at all. In any case such tales are doubtless grossly exaggerated. If the King, as they say, is hard pressed for a penny, how can he possibly lead the life that our carping pietist ascribes to him?'

'A king,' said Percy, 'takes his pleasures free.'

'And good luck to him wherever he may find them,' I replied. 'As for Moon — he cares not, nor ever has, how much of luxury and fiddle-faddle he — or you — may heap upon yourself. All your life he has been your puffer, to hang upon your sleeve, and gild your pill that his own won't taste so bad. He is the worst kind of parasite, I'm thinking, whose eye is ever on the main chance for himself. Crafty he is — I'm telling you — and dry as the ashes of hell with his canting and mouthing and "Yes, my lord," and "No, my lord," — your toad-eater! And sweet as pie to me, forsooth, now I'm your wife acknowledged and can have my say to turn him out — if I've a mind to!'

For I was boiling to see him there so smug and self-contained at the head of my husband's table, as though he owned the place and Percy too.

That my husband had generously subscribed to the King's funds might not only have endangered his liberty if not his life, had he been discovered an active supporter of the Royalist party, but would also have rendered him liable to decimation, which catastrophe was, however, luckily diverted by the sudden collapse of Cromwell's military tribunals.

I, knowing little of the trend of political affairs save what I gleaned from talk at Templecombe, was dumbfounded to receive a letter from Percy written from Aykroyd, in the February of 1657, telling me that:

This second Parliament of the Protectorate has determinedly abolished once and for all the authority of the Major-Generals. There have been endless and heated Debates on this question due to the many complaints, not only from those victimized, but by the more lenient — or less diabolic shall we say — of our Persecutors. You may or may not have heard of the attempted assassination of the Usurper by one Miles Sindercomb, a cashiered Quartermaster, who had his own Axe to grind in this affair.

The story goes that he took a house in the Village of Hammersmith, a few miles out of London on the road where the Usurper is wont to pass to and from the Royal Palace of Hampton Court. Conceive the daring of it! This fellow, who I may tell you, was well primed by those behind the Plot and to the tune of £1600, had prepared an infernal Machine consisting of a Battery of seven Blunderbusses which was to blow Oliver's coach and his body to atoms, and his soul — 'twas hoped — to Hell. But unfortunately, the Machine refused to work, or Oliver was too well-guarded by his servant Satan — or perchance his time was not yet come, but whatever may be the reason for it, he passed along unharmed.

Not content, however, to let his quarry slip, our wily Sindercomb resolved to set fire to White Hall and kill his man as he ran out to save himself. I could have told you of this Plot hatching three months agone, for I had a small finger in it — in so far as I have paid out some divers Sums towards its financing. (Tell this not to Moon. He is a very Miser for my gold, but Pray do not misunderstand his motive. I think his Heart and Soul is bent on restoring the Chapel at Wynmonath, as mine is on restoring the Abbey.)

Again our Sindercomb was doomed to failure. It is said he bribed accomplices too freely and too blind, for he gathered in as many foes as friends: and so — was taken, found guilty of High Treason and condemned to die. But he would not give his captors the Satisfaction and Delight of hanging him, and all the grisly Fun of drawing and quartering that attends these Exhibitions. Instead, he contrived that a woman — his sister, they say — should carry Poison to him when she went to bid him a last farewell where he lay in prison. And so when they came to drag him to the hurdle they found nothing more lively for their hanging than a Corpse. Thus went one more brave Gentleman to his death in a worthy Cause.

Forgive me, Sweetheart, if these gruesome Details offend you. I tell this story that you may know how always, and all the time, year in, year out, there are those who work and watch and wait — for the day is drawing nearer when there will be an end to these Abominations wrought upon us. That the Government is now dividing one may take as a straw to mark the way the wind blows. It is at the moment but a gentle breeze; yet there are storm-clouds in the sky and the mutterings of Thunder in the distance...

Which increased with ominous portent while we waited for the pending crisis that would bring about, as we devoutly prayed, the final extermination of our oppressors.

The crisis when it came was what we least expected. In the midst of national confusion and alarms and the rounding up of all suspected persons who threatened the life of Cromwell, his own sycophants, revolted by the cudgel of tyranny he brandished in the name of a Free Republic, had turned upon their master as whipped curs will turn to snarl before they cringe.

Percy brought me more of this on his return from Aykroyd, some three weeks after I received his letter.

The Lord Mayor of London, Sir Christopher Pack, had presented to the Protector a Remonstrance on the state of disturbances throughout the country, suggesting an entirely new form of government, including the revival of the abolished House of Lords, and proposing Oliver Cromwell as their King!

While I sat at supper with my husband who had arrived late at night, unexpected, and hungry as a wolf, to rouse me from my bed to watch him eat the hasty meal prepared by Thirza, he recounted these extraordinary happenings.

'Conceive it! That this urban Pack-ass — this Lord Mayor should take upon himself the nomination and selection of a Sovereign. Does he think himself the prophet Samuel?'

'Maybe,' I said, hopefully, 'he is insane.'

'You're right. They're all and every one of them fit for nothing but the mad-house, and from all accounts the hall of Westminster is indistinguishable from Bedlam.' Percy hacked another slice from the cold sirloin of beef Thirza had placed before him. 'S'life! I could eat the whole of this joint at a sitting. I've ridden the last fifty miles without bite nor sup in my haste to get to you. I have been on the road these seven days, hard riding. Last night I lay at Salisbury — the whole town is in a buzz at these latest doings up in London. I sat in the inn parlour and kept my ears open and my mouth shut, and gathered from the general voice of opinion that Master Oliver has had an ugly shock to find his pelf-licking followers have dared debate his law in one breath — and offer him a kingship in another. The odds are he'll take the Crown — trust him to mount the highest horse. So there it is!' Percy pushed aside his trencher and stood to stretch his arms and yawn. 'I am dog-tired.' Then stooping his face to mine, he whispered, 'Are you glad to have me home? Have I been missed?'

I nodded.

'I wonder...' He took my chin in his hand, gazing deep into my eyes; and his, though hazy with fatigue, held all the ache of his imprisoned longing. 'Can I give you love enough to miss me? Can I? Yet I'll own I love you as I never deemed it possible to love one other than myself, and least of all a woman. But you are not a woman. You are half girl, half Ganymede. And I —' He broke off abruptly to touch my cheek with his lips, inhaling. 'Sweet,' he murmured, 'all the spices of Arabia are in the scent of you. Do you know the myth of Tantalus? He who hungered in Hades for delicious fruit within reach of his mouth and of which he could never eat, for so soon as he would taste it — so was it snatched away?'

I must, I think, have shown him then the pity in my face and the yearning in my heart for all that nature had denied us, whose starved young bodies met, caressed and loved — in wasted wedlock; he must have seen, and seeing, smiled his small closed smile that had too much of bitterness for youth, and put me from him and said lightly, 'I'm asleep here where I stand, so ... let's to bed.'

He, travel-weary, slept ... but I did not.

Unquestionably the downfall of Cromwell's 'Mastiffs' was a step in the right direction, notwithstanding that the commotion it aroused resulted in the nomination of the Lord Protector as King in all but name. Yet while he refused the Royal title he did not scruple to accept the Royal state, to which in the June of that same year he was, with sickening pomp, admitted, lacking only the crown and the anointing to proclaim him monarch of all he surveyed.

One good end, however, was accomplished by that preposterous puppet show in Westminster Hall — the final abolishment of the Major-Generals and the laying of the bogy, Decimation. This meant much to the Royalist landlords in so far that such property as now remained to them was theirs to hold, unless some still more vigorous form of taxation should arise. As this seemed not unlikely, those who hitherto had hoarded their means in order to meet the severe penalties levied on all who opposed the Government, were now as anxious to spend as they had been to save, on the assumption it were better to buy anything but land, since hitherto the severest fines had fallen on the landowners.

I was, none the less, astounded when my husband announced that he had rented a house in London and was prepared to expend several hundred pounds on the furnishing and decoration of it. Not until the final arrangements had been completed did he impart this news to me, which was little to my liking. I told him flatly that I would not care to live in London. I had never been to London, though I gathered that he had — for these past few weeks, unknown to me — and I thought it most secretive and unkindly on his part to keep me so excluded from his confidence.

He said, crestfallen, he had hoped to give me a surprise.

'Which,' I retorted tartly, 'I'll not thank you for.' I was a rustic born, I said, and Dorset was my county, Folly's End my home. I could not hawk, I could not ride, I could not *live* in London. Besides — and this seemed the most conclusive of my objections — why spend money on a London home when the abbey lay in ruins? What of all his plans and projects to rebuild our heritage? Was he content to see Wynmonath mouldering while he frittered away his good gold on a city residence?

'As for London,' I declared, 'why, 'tis the very sink of all iniquity. The Tower, Tyburn Hill, Whitehall, are full of the ghosts of the murdered. No! I'll not set foot inside of London's gates till the stones are cleansed of blood, and the King sits in his own palace on his throne!'

'You'll not have long to wait for that,' said Percy, 'and if you will listen to me and not fly out at a tangent, I can explain —'

He did so at some length and to effect that while his heart was set as ever on the restoration of the abbey, his means were not sufficient to carry out his wish. 'Nor never will be,' he said glumly, 'while the Commonwealth exists. Do you realise what it would cost to rebuild even one wing of Wynmonath?'

'A hundred pounds or so,' I offered, dubiously.

'A hundred! Child, where's your head? Ten hundred, more likely.'

'Never!' I exclaimed, aghast. 'Ten hundred to restore one wing?'

'And ten thousand to restore the whole,' said Percy, coolly.

'But that's impossible,' I gasped. 'There's never so much money in the world.'

'Not in our world, certainly. But one day —'

'Sufficient for *this* day!' I interrupted. 'I'd sooner see one attic of Wynmonath set up, than live within four walls of a city mansion. What mania is this for buying houses?'

'If you will only listen, I will tell you.'

And he told — enough for me to realise that he had not embarked without consideration on this venture. Now was the time, he said, to look ahead. The Commonwealth was tottering — internally. How soon, or how late, whether in our youth or our age would come the final overthrow of the Republic was not in his power to say, but that it would come in our lifetime was a certainty.

'Then,' Percy said, 'will be such a revival, such a complete and absolute return — not only of the King but of all that kingship stands for in this country, with London as the hub and centre of our universe — as never before has been known in England's history. From the capitals of Europe where they skulk in exile, those hordes of beggared Royalists will come pouring back, all seeking London houses to taste of London's gaiety. And when that time comes, as it most surely will, there'll not be a house for sale or on lease within three miles of Westminster. I mean to be there first.'

He spoke with enough conviction to allay my doubts and infect me with his own enthusiasm: but although I was now as eager to support as I had been to oppose this undertaking, he gave me clearly to understand that he would brook no interference on my part in his arrangements; nor would he permit me to visit the house until it was ready to receive me.

I confess I did not relish this autonomy, and did not hesitate to speak my mind with some high words as to his right to dictate and order me, do this, do that — as though I were his thing.

'And aren't you?' he queried, teasing. Which I could not allow and would have been up and at him in a trice, and with the same old prick of temper — not yet quite outgrown — but that he caught and held my wrists to twist them as he used to do when we were children, till between tears of pain and laughter, I surrendered to cry pardon.

'There's a swine you are!' I muttered, rubbing my offended wrists that showed the pinkened pressure of his fingers. 'You have iron in your bony hands — for all they're lily white. Is this the way to treat your wife, think you?'

'Is this the way of a wife,' he mocked, 'think you?'

I had it on my tongue to answer sharp, 'I'm not *your* wife — God help me!' But I saw the ache in his eyes, and stood silent.

During the ensuing months Percy was more often in London than at home, and sometimes I wondered if his prolonged withdrawal from my proximity were deliberate. He may have found the continued strain of our unsatisfied relationship too much for his endurance. It was almost too much for mine. Nor was it easy to avoid Thirza's blunt, questioning. I had been mated now for nigh upon two years. Why, therefore, had I not begun to breed?

Evading her sharp look I answered her that I was young enough to have a dozen children, being scarce eighteen.

'Your mother,' Thirza said, 'was but sixteen when you were born and your coming killed her, yet you yourself were of a backward growth being an eight-and-a-half-months babe — by which reasoning, maybe, you were slow to flower, and a tree that blossoms late bears a late fruit.'

And she would eye me over and shake her head and sigh, and say my breasts were still a child's, not a woman's: and she would brew me potions, guaranteed, she said, to fertilise. I swallowed the odious stuff to quiet her, and even sank myself to wear an amulet — half believing in its virtue — since Thirza claimed that it would bring conception to a woman past her prime or to a maid at her first mating.

She had, it seemed, on my behalf, consulted a certain Mother Chickory, a wise woman at Broadwindsor of some repute in the neighbourhood. The witch, according to Thirza, having boiled a live adder in a concoction of May dew and the blood of a toad, had left it to dry in the sun, peeled the dead snake of its skin, and pounded the corpse to a jelly. The remains were then sewn into a linen bag and spiced with ambergris. For which prescription Thirza was the poorer by a crown piece, which I refunded.

I wore the noxious thing as I was bid, tied round my naked middle, until despite the ambergris it stank so foul that even the dogs ran from me. So I threw it on a dung heap. But Thirza went on hoping.

It needed the perception of Aunt Rossiter to detect and tax me with the truth.

I had gone to spend a few weeks at Templecombe while Percy was in London, when one day and with no warning that unconscionable woman sprang her bolt. 'Is Folliett impotent?'

How vividly I see her sitting there beside me on the terrace overlooking the formal garden. The day was hot, the sun was high, and my cheeks, as flaming scarlet as the peonies in the parterre, while all colours in that dizzy pattern whirled and danced before my sight. 'I do not understand you, Aunt,' I quavered.

'You do.'

My aunt's shrewd old eyes peered round at me. She was wearing her witch's hat to shield her head from the sun; its black brim cast a shadow over the upper part of her face and half her nose, the extremity of which protruded, gleaming pale. 'You understand me very well,' my aunt continued; and she nodded.

I glanced at her, and at the blazing sky, and at my shoes, and licked my lips, and bleated: 'I vow, madam, I do not ... I... You use a word with which I am ... unfamiliar.'

'It is not only words with which you're unfamiliar,' my aunt retorted with another nod, that jerked her hat off her head to fall at her feet on the flags. I was glad to stoop and pick it up to hide my face.

'There is no need to dissemble,' my aunt proceeded, 'your body tells me what your lips deny. 'Tis the body of a virgin not a wife.' She leaned forward to lay her parchment-dry hand on mine. 'And now perhaps, niece, you will realise why I was so averse to this marriage with your cousin who is thus misfortuned in his manhood, as, when he was a stripling, I suspected he would be. I had hoped my intuition would be wrong. Time has proved it right. I warned your father. Would he heed me? No! Yet Folliett is a good lad, none the less, a better than he promised, well-mannered and agreeable, and with a sound sense of duty. Moreover I have observed he is devoted to his wife, which —' my aunt paused and reflectively plucked at the hairs on her chin — 'which makes it the more pitiable that he should be thus cursed.'

I started; she glanced at me and continued, while I felt my forehead dampen at her words. 'Every so often one of our male breed is thus afflicted. Piers, the hunchback, was the last — he who married Margaret, daughter of Mottersley — and died of a surfeit of cuttle-fish. There was a portrait of him in the gallery at Wynmonath. He had a way with women and a handsome face despite his twisted back. But he, too,' my aunt ominously stated, 'had the curse upon him. The moon was in Virgo at his birth, as it was also at your husband's, with Mercury exalted. However,' and she took her hand from mine and set her hat upon her head again, 'cures for such conditions *have* been known. He is young. He may outgrow his weakness. We might even,' my aunt said briskly, 'consult that Doctor Sydenham who attended upon your father. He has some learning and is well-versed in medical science.' And she rose as if she would make straight for Wynford Eagle at that moment.

I rose, too, and stood before her, scarlet.

'Madam, I feel bound to discontinue this discussion. You are — an you will pardon my presumption — upon a false track here. Nor do I put great faith in the portents of the stars, for though 'tis a knowledge much pursued by the ancients, yet I believe as the Bible gives it that such secret things belong unto the Lord our God. By which, madam, to my mind, your reckoning miscarries. I know nought of my humpback ancestor, whose star may or may not have been unfavourable at his birth, but I do know the imputation you cast against my husband exists in your imagination only. It is mischance — my fault — or — what you will, but no fault of his that I am thus far barren.'

A conflict of emotions prompted me to this defence, not only of my husband, but of my father, who against all wiser counsel had brought about this marriage, acting solely in my interest as I well knew, and I'd have none refute his judgment nor his choice; and somewhere, within, obscurely, I defended my own pride.

Then while I stood defying contradiction, I saw that stern old face relax, and a dimness film those stone-bright eyes that never swerved from mine.

'So be it,' my aunt croaked, 'and bravely spoken. Loyalty is the Folliett creed. I'll say no more.'

And she closed her mouth as though she never meant to open it again: nor, on that subject, did she.

I was at Templecombe when Percy wrote to tell me that the London house, now fully furnished and equipped, wanted nothing but my presence to complete it. He would send a coach to bring me there and I might, if I wished, take Thirza. So I gathered together my belongings and returned to Folly's End to acquaint Thirza of this news and await the conveyance that was to carry us to London.

I had expected something after the pattern of Aunt Rossiter's old coach, open on all sides and little better than a box on wheels; but the equipage my husband sent was of a startling splendour drawn by four horses, and varnished a rich yellow, with prune-coloured panels and a coachman and postillions in livery to match.

It was with some misgivings that I set out upon my journey in this magnificent conveyance which delighted Thirza more than it did me, for I doubted the wisdom of such lavish expenditure in times like these, when any show of ostentation was condemned by our Puritan masters; though to be sure the

Lord Protector did not stint himself in luxury for all that, and living as he did in royal state at the King's Palace of Hampton Court. Thirza, however, had no such qualms.

'Let your husband spend what he can *while* he can,' quoth she, 'and good luck to him — so long as he spends for you. Why should he hoard his money to swell the coffers of those buzzards who'd pick the flesh off a dead man's bones to feather their own foul nests? Be thankful that his lordship shows himself free-handed. You've had little enough, God knows, of softness in your life. Would you have your husband mean and miserly to all but his own comfort? There's some men keep their wives for nothing but to breed, and grudge them the very linen on their beds, while they buy their pleasures from the women of the town. You should thank your stars my lord's not one of them that play with dirt to pox you. Mercy, lady, lift your chops! You should be rejoicing. Here you go to London, riding like a queen, and one would think that you were sitting in your hearse. Are you not hot to meet your husband, eh?' She slily nudged me.

I told her I was afeared that robbers might attack us in so gay and conspicuous a coach.

Thirza, saying 'Figs to that!' declared she feared the dead more than the quick, and that she'd make short work of any thief who held us up along the road: whereupon she produced from under the seat an old fowling-piece which she had brought with her from home for our protection. The journey, however, was accomplished without the assistance of this weapon, which was just as well, for I am sure, since Thirza had no notion how to use it, she would have more likely blown our heads to bits, and not the robber's. Thus, after four days on the road and three nights when we lay at Salisbury, Basingstoke and Slough, we came to the outskirts of London.

I shall never forget my first sight of the capital. Entering from the west through the outlying villages of Hammersmith and Kensington, I was amazed to find how much of open land and pleasant fields surrounded and encroached upon the populated areas; but not until we had passed by Tyburn Hill, viewed on our left in the distance with its naked gibbet stark against the sky, did I glimpse the innumerable spires and dense mass of red roofs and gables that huddled as far as eye could see along the curve of the river bank. It must be difficult for those of you, who, in this day of Queen Anne, know London only as a town of spacious streets and solid houses stretching web-wise from St Paul's as far as and beyond the Palace of St James's, to realise the aspect of that medieval London by the Thames, three parts of which was destroyed in the Great Fire.

Embedded on the waterway in a network of fetid alleys with overhanging houses built of wood, that thickly peopled city of half a century ago was not at all a pleasant place to live in.

Noise, dirt, and squalor unbelievable; these were my chief impressions of its crowded streets, full of a choking dust and paved with rough cobbles — if paved at all — over which our coach jolted and rattled to shake the bones out of your body. Our progress here was leisured, for we were forced to halt every fifty yards or so to avoid the congestion, not only of carts and wagons, but of loitering pedestrians who swarmed across our path and stared in at our windows with no friendly looks for me and my fine clothes.

Approaching from St Martin's-in-the-Fields and so into the Strand, I noticed that the houses in the streets leading down to the river were so built, or the streets so narrow, that the windows in the gables almost met overhead, blotting out the sky and enveloping these byways in a preternatural gloom, which was further darkened by a succession of grotesque signs, their creaking hinges adding to the general confusion of noise. If Thirza spoke to me I could not hear her above the grating, grinding, clattering of wheels, and the cries of the street vendors with their barrows, screeching in opposition to the apprentices who stood at shop doors offering their wares. Whenever our coach halted a herd of these would rush forward to assail me with their persuasions: 'What d'ye lack, lady? What d'ye lack?' And by the look of them, prepared to drag me from my seat to inspect their merchandise — as ruffianly a set of rogues as ever I beheld. But worse than this ceaseless pandemonium was the formidable stench of the gutters, where every sort of filth from dead cats to stale cabbage had been flung to lie and rot.

'Never,' I gasped, hanging on to Thirza's arm as we bumped and bounced along, 'never can I endure to live in this stinking sewer. Why, the very air is stained —'

With a yellowish sooty pall that made my eyes smart, my nose run and my stomach retch with coughing. Thirza said it was the smoke rising from the furnaces of the soap-boilers, lime-burners, brewers, and the like who plied their trade within the city's walls.

'But we are not,' she told me, 'yet within the city's walls, this being but the outer fringe of the town.' For she had on several occasions visited London when she attended my young mother in the days of King Charles I, and knew every inch of our road.

'If this,' I retorted, holding my nose, 'is the *fringe* of the town, what sort of cesspool is the centre?'

Thirza laughed at me. 'Nay, child, you're too squeamish. You must rid yourself of your rustic habits and take a taste of this raggety-taggety, whoring, roaring London to your lungs, for no matter how vile the stink of it, there's a spice in the rollicking old ditch that goes to the head like wine.'

Which may have been true, in that though my own head reeled till I was near to swooning, I felt despite all bodily discomfort and disgust, a pleasurable sense of excitement afforded by the multiform, varied glimpses of the city and its inhabitants as we drove by. The crush of people, jostling, pushing, shouting — all sorts and conditions of folk. Roistering gallants whose long curled hair and swaggerish bearing proclaimed them Royalists; sober-suited citizens in their wide-brimmed Puritan hats; countrymen, and craftsmen — the blacksmith in his leathern apron, the vintner in blue, the grocer in white — every man announcing his trade by the colour of his apron; neatly coifed, stout market women with their baskets on their arms; an occasional sedan chair bearing a haughty high-nosed lady with her vizard-mask hiding her eyes; and then, on the one hand, at the far end of a narrow street, the sudden breath-taking gleam — and whiff — of the river and the wing of a proud ship's sail: on the other side the shops and houses of the Strand, and behind them the gently rising open country. Yes, 'twas a brave old town that smoky, poky, sprawling, brawling London, strong and staunch within its steel-grey walls, where every view ended in green pastures or the beautiful wide river — as crazy and inconsequential as a city in a dream.

Leaving the Strand on our left, we turned a corner by a tavern into a street of comparative quiet, which Thirza said was named for the Earl of Bedford, the front of whose mansion abutted on the Strand and backed on to the Square of Covent Garden. Here, on the north side, at the door of a handsome house built of bricks with a portico supported by stone pillars, our coach stopped.

Stiff to the bones I alighted, thanking God that our journey was done.

CHAPTER TEN

I had scarce set foot inside our new abode before Percy was at pains to account for his reluctance to allow me a voice in its equipment. From cellar to attic everything within the house was mine, made over to me by a deed of settlement; and since my husband wished me to regard this as a much-belated wedding gift, he had hoped to surprise me.

He did.

I knew he had a better taste than I in household furnishings, and an almost womanish appreciation for the ornate, but his selection of accoutrements, upholstery and such-like, and the divers *objets de vertu* he had collected for the house in Covent Garden, surpassed any of his previous extravagance. Yet though moved by and grateful for such redundant generosity, I was unaccustomed to so sumptuous a lodging, and found in this palace of a place more to incommode than to rejoice me.

The floors, for example, had been polished to an excellence which rendered them a danger to walk upon, and caused me some several tumbles and one with such violence to my backside that I could not sit in comfort for a week; nor did the gilt spindle-legged chairs, which Percy said had been brought from France, afford me much ease, being more fitted for show than for use. They were covered in apricot yellow brocade, very choice, I dare say, but too dainty for me who all my life had squatted on a stool. Even Templecombe, though solidly, and to my simple mind, splendidly furnished, was but a worm-eaten, rat-infested dust-hole compared to our specious establishment. The magnificence of my bedchamber overawed me. The bed was raised upon a dais and curtained in white satin with a chaste design of silver doves, pink cupids, and garlands: the painted ceiling, supported by Corinthian columns, depicted nymphs pursued by satyrs, Bacchantes at their revels, and naked gods and goddesses at love. My husband had furnished for himself a communicating room of equal grace. In the withdrawing room, for there was no parlour here, the ceiling was similarly painted, the walls panelled, the draperies of palest green, the pilasters, cornices and carvings all of gilt; and a dining room curtained and carpeted in crimson with stools to match, and chairs of Spanish leather. And whence had come the means to pay for all this lavishment — if paid for it were, which I doubted — I dared not ask, and greatly feared to see my husband brought to Newgate for his debts.

I was, however, reassured by the startling intelligence, imparted carelessly by Percy, that over and above the moneys received from the sale of his land in Yorkshire, he had won a lottery in France. This lucky news, having been conveyed to him while the preparations for the London house were pending, and the knowledge that he now possessed in French francs the equivalent of one thousand English pounds, decided him to exploit his prodigality regardless of expenditure — or consequence.

So here was I, mistress of a mansion in the most fashionable quarter of the town, for notwithstanding the stern rule of the Commonwealth, fashion is a jade that can never be suppressed, even by those who most decry her; and though the only men of substance in those days were the Government party and their hypocritical adherents who so loudly condemned any display of indulgence, yet they were quick enough to advantage themselves of the best that their ill-gotten gains could provide. Thus many of the wealthy merchants and upstart artisans who comprised the bulk of Cromwell's followers, had removed from the thickly populated centre within the city's gates to the more airy outer suburbs of Westminster.

I cannot say I relished London life, despite that Percy proved a most companionable and instructive guide. With him in our coach I drove round the town to see the sights, and was greatly impressed by the Tower, that rugged old fortress guarding the Thames, with its murders and its memories and all its splendid history writ in stone upon its frowning walls. I walked on Old London Bridge, which at that time lay low on the water, and was crowded both sides with shops and buildings, and so narrow there was scarcely passage-way for horse and wagon, and none for our great coach; and I saw the highest, proudest, loveliest of all those noble structures doomed to perish in the Fire, the first St Paul's, which Cromwell desecrated, to his everlasting shame. I saw the litter of mean shops and stalls let out to sempstresses and hucksters under the famous portico; and in the great nave I saw the stables where he had housed the horses of his cavalry — and yet, even today there are some who still believe this man maltreated and ill-judged.

We had been in London less than a month when at my husband's invitation the Comte de Fontenelle arrived on a visit to our house. He brought with him a quantity of baggage, a valet-de-chambre, and a monkey, which did to my thinking absurdly resemble its master, the Comte being very dark and dwarfish with a pair of quick, beady black eyes, and a brown-skinned wizened little face, though he was scarce a year older than Percy. Rouged and patched and painted to the eyebrows, he wore a full-bottomed periwig, the first of these monstrosities I had seen, for they were not the mode in Cromwell's England. Nor had I seen such finery as that young man affected. He had a different suit for every day in the week, of velvet, satin or brocade and in every conceivable colour, belaced, beribboned, jewelled, his stockings of silk with gold clocks, his shoes diamond-buckled with such high red heels that he seemed to walk on tiptoe, very mincing. And would you believe it — that monkey of his had half a dozen suits of clothes to match, and sat up to the table like a Christian, and drank wine from its own silver cup!

The Comte spoke excellent English and was, Percy told me, considered a wit — which may have been so in his country. He called Percy *'Folie'*, and me *'Ma belle dame'*, and from the moment he entered my house I abhorred him.

Now I am, and always have been that kind of a woman who cannot disguise her loves or her hates. I will own it a fault. To be successful in society one should learn to dissemble, give tittle for tattle, cap a compliment with coquetry and return it with grace. But I was unversed in such tricks and knew no better than to glower at a blandishment and scowl at our simpering guest.

Of conversation at table, or in my presence, we had none, since Monsieur le Comte studied more the manner than the matter of his speech, and seemingly considered me a feeble-minded dolt with no thought beyond her personal adornment. I played my part as hostess to the best of my ability; I smiled at his vapourings and fatuous remarks addressed, not to me, but to my husband — *'Mon cher Folie,* now I perceive why you have hid this pearl of rarest *qualité* from us, your friends in France. It is too delicate, too *remarquable* a *bijou* to be exposed to any but the most *recherché* audience. It should be carried in your bosom and produced as a *bonne-bouche* — for the dessert!'

Which piece of imbecility I returned with artless candour, 'Sir, you do mistake. I am not delicate. I am as strong as a heifer — that is to say, monsieur, a cow not yet served by a bull.' And I buried my nose in a goblet of wine to hide my giggles; for in truth I shocked him and my husband too — who I fear, took this allusion to himself, and for which after I had said it I could have bitten off my tongue, while Percy apologised for my outspokenness. 'It is but a young slip of a thing, sir, reared on my farm in the country. It has much to learn. It is as yet uncurbed.'

'And I'll thank you not to speak of me as "it", my lord!' I flashed, 'for I'm not neuter, though there's some not far from here that might be.'

Admittedly an inexcusable retort, which well deserved the reprimand dealt me later and in private by my husband. 'I am utterly dumbfounded at your misbehaviour to our guest. I would have thought your breeding would have restrained you from the speech and conduct of a goose-girl.'

'When you bring a gander to my table what can you expect?'

Percy looked unutterable disgust.

'You are of course too *gauche* to realise how deeply you have offended.'

'*Gauche*? What's *gauche*?' I jeered. 'Speak English. And who have I offended? You or that mincing ape who is oWTi half-brother to his plaything that piddles on my pillows and casts its fleas upon my bed that I scratched myself sore last night. Yes, I did then! I found the creature sleeping there upon my counterpane, dressed in a yellow jacket and gold lace to match the Count's, and I declare I thought it was the gentleman himself come to cuckold you. Well, well! Offend him, do I? Let me tell you here and now, sir, your fine friend and his familiar offend me! What sort of a man is this who wears false hair and paints his face and has nought to say but bibble that would put our poor Jack to shame? See now, my lad! I'm sick to the stomach o' London Town, if you will know the truth. I am a country wench — born and bred, and not all the fine clothes, nor grand furnishings here, nor my satin covered chairs and velvet curtains and this and that, nor all the coxcombical pigmies from Paris can make me aught but what I am!'

'And what's that?' demanded Percy, glaring. 'A saucy, ill-mannered insolent slut, I'll say!'

'So will you, sir! A different song is this, i'faith, to the song you sang to your Rose of Sharon, which I was, by your account, until this frog-faced Frenchman with his wig and his scent and his flea-bitten ape came wriggling in between us. You used,' I said with pouts, 'to love me once. You hadn't a fault to find — and now I'm sluttish.'

And here I feigned to weep, for I could play the woman when it pleased me — to please him.

''Ods life!' groaned Percy, 'what's to do with her? Come here.' He caught me roughly to him. 'We talk not now of love but of your scandalous deportment. You are near upon nineteen. You might be nine the way that you conduct yourself. Have you no sense of propriety?'

'Not much,' I said, 'and I detest your Frenchman.'

'If so, there is no need to show him plainly that you do.'

'Why not?'

Said Percy, gritting his teeth, 'Job's patience was nothing to mine. You'd drive a saint distracted.'

'Are you a saint, my soul?' I asked, taking his hand to kiss. 'Yes — I think you have it in you to be more saint than sinner.'

'You have shamed me to my friend,' Percy answered, still unmollified.

'How shamed you?' I returned with heat. 'If any shame there is it should be yours, to call that prancing minikin your friend, who is fit for nothing but to sit in a cage on show and nibble peanuts.'

Well, there it was, and we had come to words, and I almost to blows before we'd done with snarling at each other over that painted mammet.

Nor did it stop at that. He was with us three weeks more, during which time Percy kept himself aloof from me, slept in his own room, and more often than not stayed out till all hours with his Frenchman. Where they went or what they did I would not demean myself to ask, but Thirza reported that they invariably came home drunk and sat up till daylight playing dice; and that the Frenchman could not hold his drink and had vomited all over his bedroom carpet, which took two lackeys half the day to clean.

I was therefore by no means grieved to hear Monsieur was leaving us and that Percy would go with him to collect, he said, the prize due from his lottery. 'And if you wish,' he conceded, 'you may accompany me. A visit to the French court would give you the polish you so sadly need.'

'French polish,' I answered, 'ill becomes English oak. No, thank you. I'd sooner visit a menagerie. You can return your performing pet where he belongs — and I'll God-speed you.'

Which conclusively settled that point. They left London on August 31st, 1658. I remember the date very well... They departed at sunrise, and Percy came to my room to rouse me from my sleep to say goodbye.

'It is a thousand pities,' said he stiffly, 'that you have proved so churlish to my guest. I'll not forget it.'

'Oh, go choke yourself!' I flared at him. 'There's a thing to wake me for. I'd as lief you left me sleeping. I was in a gentle dream of you and me together sitting in a row-boat eating cherry pie.' And I turned over on my pillow and shrugged away as he stooped to kiss.

I heard him mutter, 'Was ever mortal husband so accursed? Prue!' With some violence he pulled at a curl of my hair. 'You devil! Sweetheart … Prue! Confound you, haven't you a word? I shall not see you for a month or maybe more.'

''Tis all one to me,' I murmured in the bedclothes.

'So much you care!' retorted Percy, dragging the covers off my face. 'And what would you say, my pretty weasel, if I did not come back?'

I grinned round at him. 'I've no doubt I should survive the shock.'

'Damn you! I believe you would — and be ripe for my successor.' He caught me in his arms, whispering, 'Do you so hate me?'

'Hate's akin to love,' I teased him. 'No, my soul, I'll never hate you.'

'And I shall never know you,' Percy sighed, 'nor understand you, though I live beside you for a thousand years. You are the most exasperating, maddening, incalculable creature ever fashioned for man's torment. And if only your face were half as ugly as your temper how happy would I be to loathe you, for to — worship such as you is worse than hell!'

Then he kissed me warm and fiercely and was gone.

I promptly fell asleep again and overslept myself till ten o'clock, when Thirza came to wake me, big with news. 'They say our whoreson Oliver's been taken ill and like to die.'

I sat up. 'God bless us! He — to die? Never! The wicked flourish. He'll live to be ninety. He'll outlive you and me and every one of us. You see if I'm not right.'

But I was wrong.

On September 3rd, in his sixtieth year, died Oliver Cromwell, Arch-traitor.

For near upon seventeen years this mighty Britain had lain beneath a cloud of stern oppression, her King dethroned, his subjects brought to heel and crushed like vermin if they dared raise voice above the word of the Usurper. And now he, who, iron-fisted, had reigned supreme, was gone, and with him passed his power; it had no strength to live beyond the grave.

His interment in the abbey at Westminster was superb. Accounts of it penetrated even to our isolation down in Dorset, for soon after Percy went to France I returned to Folly's End.

Our men brought tales they had heard at Bridport and elsewhere, of the funeral procession attended by guards of honour, soldiers, heralds, innumerable mourners, but from all accounts, 'none cried except the dogs, and it was the joyfullest funeral ever seen,' with a rowdiness and drinking in the streets as the hearse went by. For six weeks before the burial, the corpse had lain in state at Somerset House with a wax effigy of Cromwell beside it wearing the crown he had never worn in life, but that there was no mourning I can scarce believe, since I myself did see some evidence of grief and much sobriety, even sorrow, before I left our house in Covent Garden.

In those days the market was held over against the wall of Lord Bedford's mansion, in the shade of a row of sycamore trees, and there the farmers and country folk came from the near villages of Hampstead, Highgate, Brompton, and still further afield maybe, to sell their produce; so that we never lacked cream and butter in London, nor the fresh-cut cottage flowers with which I filled my rooms.

But when the bells were tolling for dead Cromwell, I observed from my window that half the stalls were empty, while those remaining had been draped in black, and also that the farmers' wives who drove their carts into town wore each some mourning token, if it were no more than a black ribbon to their coifs or on the harness of their horses: which so incensed me that I ordered my coach and drove through the streets decked out in my brightest colours, and bid my servants wear white cockades in their hats as if we were bound for a wedding. Yet in that drive I saw nothing in the streets to indicate a calamity befallen on the nation. Men went about their own concerns as busily and uninterruptedly as ever, and that their clothes were for the most part sober was no token of their grief, since such was Cromwell's fashion, and to dress gaily damned a man for a rake and a woman for a trollop.

So now the noodle Richard — 'Lazy Dick' they called him — that clod of a hobbledehoy, dragged from his life in the country, was set up in his father's seat, proclaimed as his father's successor. And every soul in England, for him or against, must have known that he would never stay the course.

The day before I left London I received a startling visitor. He called in the evening as I was about to retire to my bed, and the servant who announced him said that 'the man' refused to give his name.

'What kind of a man?' I enquired, astounded, for who in the devil should call upon me at that time, uninvited?

'A large man, my lady, a rustic — and rough-spoken.'

'Ask him his business,' I said.

The fellow returned, grinning. 'He bids me tell your ladyship his business is none of mine. He brings a message of some urgency and begs your ladyship's indulgence.'

My curiosity well aroused I ordered him to bring this person to me. 'But stay you,' I commanded, 'within earshot. I do not care to entertain a stranger here unguarded.'

It was, however, not a stranger who introduced himself. Despite his countryman's habit, his shaven beard, and the tow-coloured wig that only partially concealed his silver hair, I recognised the gentleman at once. No mistaking the height and breadth of him, his bull-neck, and his great red hands. 'Why ... good heaven! Colonel Ashton!' I exclaimed. 'What in the world is the meaning of this extraordinary —'

'Whist!' he interrupted with a finger to his lips. 'Mistress, not a word. My name is Puddock.'

'Puddock?' I repeated, goggle-eyed.

The colonel, certainly, had little time for women. 'If your ladyship,' said he with marked impatience, 'will ask no questions but give me your attention, I will explain my presence and my errand — in so far as it concerns yourself. But first —' And going to the door he flung it open, to discover my servant planted stolidly there like a dummy.

I called to him, 'George, you may go. I am well acquainted with this —' I glanced at the colonel's kersey breeks —' this person.'

With a grim smile Colonel Ashton closed the door, returned to me, and launched upon a tale of which I could make but little sense, beyond the one outstanding point that a warrant was out for his arrest.

'This is no time to bandy words,' said he, quelling my dismay with the sternest look, while he strove to hush the bellow in his voice, 'I have had news from Mr Rossiter of your whereabouts in London, and it is at his advice that I am come hither to enlist your aid.'

'If there is aught in my power, sir, to do —' I faltered, in a fright.

Again he interrupted. 'I'll be brief.' And seating himself on one of my dainty gilt chairs, which I thought would likely crack beneath his weight, the colonel went on to tell me how that in the spring of this year, two trusted advisers of His Majesty the

King — the Marquis of Ormond, and Mr O'Neill — had ventured to England in order to ascertain at first hand the present strength of the Royalist party, and ensure its continued support with the view to an armed attack against the Government.

'The Marquis of Ormond, did you say, sir?' I queried amazed. The name had stirred some latent recollection.

'Yes, yes — Ormond,' replied the colonel testily, 'the chief of the King's council, second only to Chancellor Hyde. He has been back and forth on several secret missions. Madam, pray hear me out.'

The colonel then proceeded with his story to the effect that at the time of Lord Ormond's recent arrival in London, some arrests had been made and a number of our party taken at the Mermaid Tavern in Cheapside, among them the noted preacher, the Reverend Doctor Hewitt, who with Sir Harry Slingsby were executed on Tower Hill on June 10th — 'Nay, madam,' for I could not here restrain a cry of horror — 'I must command your silence.'

I sat mum.

Said the colonel, 'I escaped and have been in hiding ever since, but I am now tracked and followed — pray compose yourself, my dear, my pursuers are not yet within these walls. I have been betrayed,' the colonel stated, holding me with a fierce eye, 'and by one of our own most trusted band. Your uncle warned us of him long ago.'

'My uncle?' For my life I could no longer hold my peace. 'My Uncle Rossiter? Why, sir, what has he to do with —'

'By!' The colonel, swallowing an oath, recalled his manners. 'If you please, no questions.' He flashed a sudden smile. 'Your ladyship will pardon me if I suggest that in the army my subordinates take orders without words. You must act now as my lieutenant.'

'Yes, sir,' I answered, meek.

'The purport of my visit, madam, is this: if of your goodness you can succour me tonight I can evade the hounds upon my heels tomorrow. I shall not be looked for here.'

'Sir,' said I, more than ever now perplexed, 'I am sure you know that you are welcome to my house, my aid, and to such means as lie within my province to assist you, but I am leaving here tomorrow for the country and therefore shall —'

With scant ceremony, the colonel blustered in upon my speech: 'Then by the Lord, I'll ride with you as your postillion! Have you any man of my size in your service?'

By the greatest good chance we had. Our coachman was the hugest man I ever saw, topping the colonel by an inch at least. I told him this.

'What could be more fortunate?' quoth he. 'I'll wear his livery, I'll drive your coach — and he can stay behind.'

To which, though my head was in a whirl, I dared to raise objection.

'We must risk that. We can invent a tale that will stop their mouths,' said the colonel, removing his wig to mop his forehead. 'Whew! 'Tis infernally hot.' He did look in a rare sweat, poor man, and as red in the face as a beet.

'Would you care for a cup of white wine, sir?' I offered. 'We have had here recently a guest from France who presented my husband with some flagons of —'

'Presently, presently. Wait!' He sat awhile in thought, then started up. 'I have it! I am an old retainer of your father's whom you engage to attend you in the country. Faugh,' the colonel added with impatience, 'why excuse yourself to servants? I am only anxious to be got away to save my neck, not for its own sake so much as for His Majesty's, to whom I am of better use living than dead. So, do you see to it, madam — no, damme! I shall have to call you Prue, for you're younger than my daughter, though you have a deal more sense.'

That put me on my mettle to serve the colonel to the best of my ability. Having agreed with him it would be as well to have an ally in the household, I summoned Thirza to my confidence, and bade her repeat to Tom Mayhew, our coachman, the tale Colonel Ashton had devised. 'And at the first sign of suspicion or discontent on his part — settle him,' I gave her my purse, 'with this.'

'Shucks, girl!' exclaimed Thirza, delighted to have a hand in an intrigue, 'Tom Mayhew is loyal to his bones, which I will tell you all are not in this house, being for the most part Londoners to run with the rabble wherever it may lead. But your coachman, lady, rest assured, is honest, and hot for His Majesty's cause, abhorring those bed-bug, corpse-eating Cromwellians as much as I do or you or the colonel or any self-respecting, proper-minded mortal. So much I have picked from him since I've been here, and I'll promise you he'll want no pay for his discretion,' said Thirza with a flutter of her eyelids and a grin to slit her face, 'leastwise, not in cash.'

Nor dared I ask her what she meant by that.

At his request we lodged the colonel in an attic, since he said it would cause remark with the domestics if in his countryman's disguise he were offered a guest-chamber. We waited till the servants were gone to their beds before we served him his supper. He made a hearty meal, drank two flagons of French wine, and then Thirza showed him to his room. She told me afterwards that he had flung himself fully dressed upon his couch and was asleep and snoring before she snuffed his candle.

But I slept not one wink. All night I lay alert, expecting any moment to hear the constables come storming to our door to take away the colonel. However, I heard no worse than the watchman on his rounds crying each wakeful hour.

I was in a stupor of amazement at the mention of my uncle's name in this affair: *Your uncle warned us.* And while I tossed and turned upon my bed, my mind went spinning, to weave from the tangle of my bewildered thought a slow suspicion, so incredible and utterly absurd that I could only think the shock occasioned by Colonel Ashton's visit, and the news he had to tell, had quite deranged me. Yet, when I strove to reason, I could not but admit that my uncle's queer behaviour, his comings and his goings, and his writings on which he was so frequently engaged, to say nothing of his herb-lore and his sparrow-like timidity and this and that — besides my own opinion of him as a better man than he appeared to be, all conjoined to start me on a clue. I recalled that one occasion when I had surprised him in the grounds of Templecombe in talk with a very peculiar person, and how that the gentleman's dyed hair and exaggerated brogue, and my uncle's halting statement as to who and what he was, had only half-convinced me of 'Mr Orpington.'

At this point it seemed that something of a sudden struck a bell. Up I sat in bed, with all my flesh a-tingle and my fingers pressing on my eyelids… Ah! I had it now! Did not Percy say that the Marquis of Ormond had praised me? And did I not vow that to my knowledge I had never seen the man? Was this the connection, or had I run mad? Could it be possible that he to whom my uncle had presented me that day was none other than the Irish marquis himself?

We lived in a world of scheming and plots, and Lord Ormond was His Majesty's adviser, and like Colonel Ashton, perpetually involved in secret service to the King. But where in all this coil did my Uncle Rossiter appear, and how and why and if…? Had he, in fact, duped every one of us, my aunt included?

Never! No man on earth could deceive *her* unless he were a consummate play-actor. I could not reconcile such immensity of will and purpose with the meek and mild, abject Mr Rossiter. And if this indeed were so, then what a life! What courage, what selfless, persistent unflagging devotion must be needed to sustain that dual role…

Here speculation halted. My temples ached and throbbed. The sun was up and I was down — with a sick headache.

Not until the coach was at the door and our bags and baggage in it, did I see the colonel, and there in the coachman's seat he sat, looking, I will say, very much the part with his hat pulled low over his forehead, his wig neatly trimmed, and his great bulk well-suited to his livery. I gave him one glance which he returned with a wink on the off-side from the footman. Smothering a laugh I took my place in the coach.

'God be thanked,' whispered Thirza, as she clambered in after me, 'no questions asked, no money paid. I've saved your ladyship five pounds.'

'What do I care for that?' I hissed. 'Have you settled with him? Is he content?'

'I'll say so,' Thirza chuckled. 'He should be. I've told you that he's trustable, and I'll guarantee he'll hold his mouth whatever he may think. He's a Devonshire man, born and bred within five miles of the colonel's house at Beer.'

'O, God!' I gasped, 'you never told him of the colonel?'

'Hearken to me, my lady,' Thirza took my hand and squeezed it hard. 'Half a truth is better than a lie. I may be tricksy but it goes against my grain to trick an honest man, in especial if he be the man for me.'

At this I turned to stare, and saw her face a rosy red and broadening with smiles. 'Why, Thirza…?'

'Yes, child, since you must know,' and Thirza tittered, looking coy and bashful as a milkmaid, which was so droll an affectation in one of such matronly mould whose years were forty if a day, that I pealed with laughter to put my Thirza in a huff.

'Do you find it then so side-splitting that I should bring a man to heel?' she asked me, sharp. 'Which is ever since I first set foot inside this coach the creature has taken the stupidest, most crazy notion in the world — to wed me!'

'*Wed* you, Thirza?' This was not what I expected. 'Then Lord save us! Am I going to lose you?'

'No, my poppet!' cried Thirza energetically. 'Am I a rat to run from you when you'll be needing me, please God, to nurse your babes? I will take him only on that one condition — being past the age, I hope and pray, to breed myself — that he and I together serve your ladyship for life, or until you turn us out.'

'Which will be never! Dear soul, I'm glad.' I kissed her heartily. 'He is, I think, the very best of fellows.'

'Well,' Thirza complacently answered, 'I've always had a fancy for a big man. This one may not have much headpiece, but he has other good requirements, and he knows how to coax the hardiest mare, so he'll not ride rough with a woman. Nor am I one to relish single harness to my grave, though I doubt me there'll be murder when Ham hears of it. He's been plaguing me these five years, but he's none too tasty in his habits and goes wenching after all the whores in Dorchester.'

'You shall have a home of your own,' I promised her, 'we'll refurbish an empty cottage for you and re-thatch it and make it over in a deed of gift with a purse of gold, two acres and a cow. I know his lordship will agree — and I'll supply the linen.'

'God bless you, my darling, we want no more than a place in your heart!' cried Thirza, hugging me. 'Tom thinks you're an angel from heaven — and I'll not undeceive him!'

This pleasant talk enlivened our journey out of London, with the colonel driving us instead of Tom, who Thirza said would guard the house from any knaves who dared infest it with enquiries. He had his answers ready and a blunderbuss behind the door, which no man would pass save over Tom's dead body. But in spite of that assurance I was not at ease until a hundred miles lay behind us.

At Bridport the colonel ordered me to dismiss the postillions, with the excuse that there would be no room to lodge them in our country house. And this, in fact, was true. I gave them money to ride back to London, and much relieved was I to see them go, for had they stayed I had been greatly exercised as to how I should explain the sudden disappearance of my 'coachman'.

Colonel Ashton lay that night at Folly's End, and rode off in highest fettle the next morning, still wearing his prune-coloured livery which he returned a week later by his servant with the horse we had loaned him and a small package for me containing a gold ring set with pearls, accompanied by a note begging me accept this humble token of his Gratitude and Homage with his obliged and most respectful Duty.

When I look back on those eventful months that followed hard upon the death of Cromwell, I see how the current of affairs pressed forward with unparalleled velocity to bring about the most astounding, momentous turn of the tide in British history.

Yes, seventeen years it had taken to raise upon the fortress of our kingdom the false and petty structure of a Commonwealth; it took seventeen months for the card-house to fall for want of a hand to support it.

But though events moved swiftly, news was slow. I, who read no diurnals or pamphlets, could gather tidings only by word of mouth in Dorset, where after my return from London I remained, while Percy's month abroad lengthened to three and then to six, and still he stayed.

I did not greatly miss him. I was happy in my home. Thirza married Tom Mayhew, and I wrote for and obtained my husband's leave to furnish the newly wedded pair with one of the untenanted cottages on our estate, so that though Thirza served me daily and as faithfully as ever, she lived apart and well contented with her man as he with her.

Tansy, too, was married, to Frank Fothergill, Esquire, a young gentleman of good descent and a tidy property at Misterton, just over the border of Somerset. He was the son of a Cavalier who had fought and died for the King in the wars, and in consequence his land had been heavily sequestrated. Nevertheless, enough remained to his heir to render him an eligible match for a girl no longer in her teens, Tansy being somewhat older than myself, now in my twentieth year.

All the county were invited to her wedding banquet, the first of any such festivity I had attended. It shows some slight indication of the upheaval in the Government and the ever-increasing laxity of the Cromwellian rule that music, dancing, and feasting could now be held in privacy without the fear of a fine for our pleasure.

Tom Mayhew drove me over in my coach to Widders Cross where the marriage feast was held, and I wore a gown made from a length of amber silk Percy had bought in Paris. It was fashioned by Madam Partlet, the modiste at Exeter, and was trimmed with cherry-coloured ribands, a pretty little apron of lace, and had full sleeves slashed with cherry satin clasped with garnets — these also Percy's gift to me.

I received a great deal of attention from all the young sparks, and in particular from Mr Fothergill's chief groomsman who partnered me in the coranto and kissed me in the dark behind the hall screens. His name I have forgot, but I carried the guilt of that kiss on my conscience and dared never confess it to Percy. But I wrote him a faithful account of the marriage and the dancing, and what I ate and what I drank — too much, I fear — that night.

I gave Tansy a silver casket and a porcelain Chinese bowl, these treasures purloined from our London house. I sent Mayhew to collect them, since Percy, still in France at that time and likely to remain there, had not thought to furnish me with more than what he called my 'trinket-money', and it was not in me to write and beg for cash.

He did not, in fact, return until the end of April '59. A week later the Parliament of 'Lazy Dick' dissolved, the old Rump was restored, and the country in a buzz with news of bickerings and discontents, that terminated in Richard Cromwell's abdication.

His father, the Protector, in the last few months of his life had ruled without a Parliament; Parliament ruled now without a leader; but better none than that irresolute indolent ass, promoted by right of succession to an office which he had neither the brains nor the breeding to carry, and who returned to his hunting and horses with the promise in his pocket of a pension. That promise was never fulfilled.

And now it was apparent to every one of us that the Protectorate was finished, and that the tide had truly turned — upon a whisper. That was all: but where men once had dared no voice, they now dared utterance: 'Can England live without a ruler? Where's the King?'

I remember how one day Percy came back from Bridport where he had gone with Ham upon some business or other to do with the purchase of a brood mare. He returned with a tale of how he had sat in the inn parlour at the 'George' and talked with a journeyman from London, and how that 'at every corner of every street men stand in knots together airing views for which a year ago they'd have been hanged! And nothing's said. There's even been some rioting in Cheapside, and all the chiefs in Parliament are falling out among themselves to back the King. I know that in France,' continued Percy, 'the odds are Charles will be restored within the year.'

'Why then,' I asked, 'does the King's party not make one last fight for him? Now surely is the time to strike — while the dogs are snarling?'

But Percy only smiled very knowing, as if he could tell much more than he would say.

In July my husband went to Yorkshire, and I was left alone again; yet not entirely alone, since I had Tansy for a neighbour. Her home was not an hour's drive from mine. Since her marriage Tansy had become much more companionable. She had discarded her childish tricks for the wisdom of matrons, and her talk was now less of herself than of her husband. He, it seemed, acted as a kind of aide-de-camp to Colonel Ashton, and did frequently attend him up and down the country.

Tansy, having wheedled from Frank Fothergill secrets that should never have been told, passed on to me news of a Royalist rising which, planned to take place on August 1st, had disastrously miscarried through the treacherous betrayal by one of the King's 'Sealed Knot'.

More besides did Tansy unfold when she rode over to see me from Misterton, full of this latest calamity. 'Oh, Prue!' she said, with tears and sobs. 'I shall be fatherless and widowed.'

I could not quite see why.

'Why? Oh, Prue! Do you not understand? My father is involved in this lamentable affair, and Frank — *and* your Great-uncle Rossiter!'

'My —?' I checked myself and stood agape, in silence.

'Oh, Prue! But of course you know that Mr Rossiter as the leader of the "Knot" is most like of all to be arrested, though certainly he performs no active service. Frank says he is the hand that pulls the strings. But surely you don't need to have me tell you what everybody knows!'

'Everybody?'

'Goodness gracious, how you stare!' cried Tansy. 'Is it possible that you who are so clever do not know that Squire Rossiter is the chief adviser of our party, and has been for these ten years?'

Recovering my wits from the shock of this announcement, I temporised, ''Tis not my way to speak of secret matters.'

'It is no secret now,' retorted Tansy, 'since that wicked Willis has —'

'Willis, did you say?' I interrupted, sharply.

'Yes, Sir Richard Willis. Frank returned two nights ago, and told me all — and how that the whole plot is smashed to pieces, and that half a dozen gentlemen were taken up in London and arrested for High Treason to the Parliament. And oh, Prue!' wailed Tansy, 'I fear they're on Frank's heels. I begged and prayed him to hide — we have a priest-hole in our house — but he says he's the least like of any to be taken, because he only acts as messenger and go-between, but I think he only tells me that to cheer me. As for my father, we have had no word of him for weeks. And then there's your poor uncle!'

'Has *he* been taken?' I rapped out.

'Oh no, not yet. But he will be — for certain.'

'If,' I answered, grimly, 'my Uncle Rossiter has tricked us all — that is to say, has tricked the Parliament, these ten years — he is not likely now to fall into a trap.'

'Well, I'm sure I wish I were dead,' said Tansy, promptly. 'Just as everyone was mad with joy to think the King would be restored, and the King himself in readiness at Boulogne to land an army, so Frank declares, we needs must be betrayed by — by a betrayer, and one of our own, to boot. And yet he is a very pleasant gentleman. I have met him at my father's house, this Colonel Willis. Oh, Prue, you'd never think there could be so much cunning in the world.'

'That you would not,' I said, 'indeed.'

And so soon as Tansy had departed, I set myself to reconsider, in the light of this astonishing intelligence, all that had preceded it. My deductions now were clear enough, and I, a fool: but not, thought I — and chuckled — nearly half so great a fool, as my excellent, redoubtable Aunt Rossiter.

Thus in one fell blow the hopeful expectations of those that had so carefully planned this bid for liberty were shattered — and by him whom they had deemed most loyal to themselves.

My uncle's interest in these concerns was no concern of mine; doubtless he had his reasons for keeping his secret tight, and I would not unloosen it — no, not even to my husband, who may or who may not have known what Tansy had unguardedly released.

I saw nothing of the Rossiters during the next few weeks — or months — for time revolved in such a whirligig of shocks, alarms, excursions, that we could scarce keep count of or recover breath from one before we were given tidings of another, to soar us up to heaven or cast us down to earth.

The army and the Parliament had come to strife. The army leader Lambert, having successfully routed the Royalist insurgents under Sir George Brook at Chester — who before Willis's betrayal had mustered there a formidable force — was now so inflated with his victory that he aspired to fill the place left void by Richard Cromwell's abdication. In October the Rump dismissed him. Whereupon Lambert in return dismissed the Rump.

The story that came to us of this affair, which lost nothing, one may guess, from repetition, was that Lambert, with three thousand toadies strong, marched into Westminster to find the Houses of Parliament defended by two regiment of foot and four of horse, led by Lenthall, Speaker of the House, sitting squat upon a military charger. The sight of this civilian rigged out as a cavalry officer, and whom Lambert deemed in part responsible for his ejection from the army, so enraged the peppery General that he pulled the gentleman from his saddle and with some violence ordered him to take himself home. The soldiers on both sides then amicably coalesced, and Parliament was once again dissolved.

Meanwhile, far away north of the Tweed, one watched these extraordinary doings and patiently bided his time; that old hound Monk, muzzle on paws and body taut, stayed at the ready with an army at his tail. Born and bred a Royalist, he had turned his coat to serve the winning side, and having served one master loyally, he waited now, maybe, to serve another.

So, while the bickerings and brawls persisted in and out of Parliament, and swollen Lambert sought to name himself Protector of the Peace; and while Charles, the King, whose last hope, as he believed, had been crushed to death by a miserable traitor, philosophically resigned himself to a life of perpetual exile, poverty, and debt, Monk rose up and came over the border.

From north to south, from east to west, the country teemed with the noise of this latest exploit. Rumour ran amok. The wildest excitement succeeded a fearful gloom. Monk was on the march — but why? Against whom and *for* whom? What could be his motive? To see himself the Lord Protector — to fight Lambert, to bring about another civil war?

We at Folly's End heard talk of a Free Parliament. Yes, free. We had learned the mockery of 'Freedom', 'Liberty' — those time-worn shibboleths that masked the sword and chain.

And still Monk marched, and when Lambert with his troopers went to meet him, terror seized us, every one. This could mean but one thing — war!

Percy was home, and frantic with anxiety. 'Not again, by God!' he swore, pacing the winter parlour and biting at his thumb. 'It would be annihilation for us all. The country would never stand it — not twice in fifteen years. Do you realise what will happen when these jackals fall on one another's throats? We'll be forced, yes, we — *I* — under pain of death — will be forced to take arms for or against our masters. The country will divide itself, and we will have no choice. We of the younger Royalist party who have gone on tiptoe in hiding all our lives will be dragged out and whipped to the fight, and such homes as we possess will be commandeered as billets. I'll shoot myself before I will submit to have my property handed over to any more blood-stained marauders. We are not strong enough to gather a protective force. What are we now? A handful here, the rest of us scattered on the Continent. We've traitors in our very midst, behind, before, above...'

I had never seen him in so great a perturbation. Indeed ever since his return from France my husband had been restless, irritable, hotly amorous or bitingly cold as the fancy took him, although he did not now make any more pretence to lie with me. He had taken for himself two of the larger attics, and converted them into a sizeable apartment by removing the communicating wall. This had occasioned much labour, and I am sure more comment, among our servants, who resented the introduction of a herd of workmen from Dorchester as much as I resented the noise and hammering of their activities.

As for Thirza, 'What bee has his lordship brought back from France,' she wished to know, 'that he prefers his own bed to his wife's?'

Hastily I invented an excuse in his defence — and mine. 'His lordship has developed the habit of snoring and talking in his sleep that I should never have a wink myself if we continue to share a room. It is at my request that he makes me this concession, and much beholden am I to him for it. There's not one husband in a thousand would show so much consideration.'

'You're right,' said Thirza with a sniff, 'there's not. And if that's all he's learned from those Frenchmen, then can you wonder they breed frogs?'

'Do not condemn the French too loud,' I answered glumly, 'we may be thankful to set foot upon their soil and beg in their streets before long.'

'What?' cried Thirza, open-mouthed. 'Here's profany! Here's croaking! We — to beg in France? Why, what's come to you, child? Look up to heaven. Will the good God who in His infinite mercy has laid the Arch-fiend where he belongs, and has sacked that poxy Dick, Noll's son — will He desert us now and hand us over to the Philistines? Never! They will fight to their own stinking deaths, while the righteous live — to cheer them to it! And if 'tis his lordship that has primed you up with such mumpish, splenetic, dispiriting talk, I'll give him a rhubarb pill to purge him of the humours in his liver!'

But whatever our rustic reaction to these startling events, in London the lads were singing:

'Monk under a hood,
Not well understood,
The City pulls in its horns,
The Speaker is out
And sick of the gout,
And the Parliament sits upon thorns.'

This doggerel filtered through to Dorchester and was brought to me by Ham. I took it from him word for word and set it to the tune of 'Greensleeves', and sang it to my husband. And even he, who had it firmly that Monk's inexorable march towards the capital could only signify the proclamation of another dictator, turned more optimistic; and when news came hot from London that Monk and his army were within the city's gate, 'Then this,' he declared, 'is the end — or the beginning.'

All England held its breath. What would be the next move?

Percy rode each day to Dorchester to hear the latest reports from travellers. He told how in the inn parlours the health of the King was drunk — in whispers — and how that on the day after Monk's entry into London all the church bells rang to welcome him, and that Cheapside was lit with bonfires, and in the Strand the butchers roasted ox rumps to signify their dissatisfaction with the Government, amid such a yelling and a shouting and heat and burning to singe the hair off your head as you walked, and that everywhere one heard the cry for a Free Parliament.

Towards the middle of March, unable to remain in the country while such a stir was going on in Town, Percy rode off to London. A month later he wrote me this letter:

Such an infinity of business in Westminster, past all belief, with no talk but of one Single Person, openly, and not in secret! One day last month (March 15th) I have heard how that at 5 o'clock in the afternoon a workman came with a ladder, a brush and a paint-pot to the Great Exchange, and proceeded to wipe out the inscription that was engraven under the Statue of Charles I: Exit Tyrannus, Regum Ultimus. *And when he had entirely erased the writing he threw down his pot and brush saying that it should never do him any further service, having been honoured enough to wipe out the writing of a Rebel. Then he took his ladder and went away, and not one word was said against his action nor why it had been done or by whose order. But all the Merchants there approved and were glad, and in the evening they lighted a great bonfire before the Statue there in the Exchange and a great Crowd of people come to see it and a many called aloud: 'God bless King Charles the Second!' This has, to my mind, a great Significance, but still more amazing is the fact that Moon — our crab-faced Moon — arrived unexpected from Aykroyd to say that all the Fairfax clan are now hot for Monk! Would you have believed it? All here say Monk is for a Free State, but he'll not show his hand, and sits as tight as a clam. Moon is a changed man and drank a bottle with me to the King and went praying — and swaying —*

up to bed, unaccustomed as he is. to any but a Hermit's fare, and smiling as he never had in all his life. You would have died a-laughing.

Faith, Sweet, I miss your Sauciness. Will you not come to Town and share the fun o' the Fair with me when History is made? There will be the greatest jollification in this City, before long, that ever was seen or is like to be seen again. Any doubts I may have had are all dispersed by the sight of our old black crow weeping bottled tears and cawing for His Majesty — he, whom I have always half-suspected favoured the cause of my Fairfax kin rather than that of the Follietts. Well, if all goes as I pray it will, I shall not be niggardly to sponsor him who has been for me the only Father I remember. All of us here in London are laying our plans now for the Future. Pray God we are not too Rash...

On April 30th I joined my husband at our London house, and the next day — May Day — was the happiest England had seen for many a year.

The news went blazing through the town that a letter from the King, written at Breda, had been read aloud in Parliament with all the members standing silent and bareheaded; that His Majesty had signed a Declaration, and that the House had ordered a sum of £50,000 to be sent forthwith to the King, and not one word of dissent from any. In return, the City of London had put up a Declaration disclaiming any form of Government save that of King, Lords and Commons, and all this without one drop of bloodshed. But why or how these things had come about I know not, unless it were the will of God that had raised from among all Britain's men, one chosen to act for Him, and in His given moment.

History can better tell of these occurrences than those who witnessed them. We stood too close upon this joyous tidal wave to hear more than the clamour of its coming. The generations that follow us, maybe, will read in the records handed down to them a deeper truth and wisdom than they who wrote of these tremendous happenings, suspected. For certain it is, so great was the transfiguration which overswept our land, that one and all declared it above human understanding.

And to the man who worked this marvel, he who had delivered Britain from the fetters of a soul-corroding despotism, on him all eyes were turned, and the name of Monk was on every man's lip in wonder and thanksgiving.

On May 23rd we heard that the King had landed at Dover, and that Monk and a vast concourse were there on the shore to receive him. Then we were told he was at Rochester; at Canterbury — where he attended service in the cathedral — and then that he was on his way to London.

The noise of his approach resounded in every town and village from the coast of Kent to the capital. All the bells were ringing to rock the steeples, and every mansion, every house, every hovel within and without the city's walls, paid tribute to their Sovereign in a display of decoration, maypoles, garlands, tapestries, flags, and colours indescribable; and a dancing and a shouting, and a delirium of gladness in the streets to unite every one of us, high and low, in one true brotherhood of shared rejoicing.

What a sight to see! What an utter and complete revulsion from those bitter years of suffering and persecution. It was as if on some frost-bound dreary morning one had wakened, and drawn aside the curtain of a window to gaze upon a miracle: stern winter vanished, and May-time come again in glowing blossom, decked with gay pennons of green and gold under the rising sun.

For England had dawned a new era: the long, dark night was ended... So came for us our Day.

My husband had secured two large front rooms, and one with a balcony over a shop in the Strand for our view of the procession; and there we invited our friends, the Fothergills, and a few other young folk to a jollification on the morning of May 29th.

Such a feast our Thirza prepared, brought thither by our men in baskets and laid ready for our arrival: a boar's head in jelly, goose pies, mutton pies, roast fowls, and chicken pasties; a dish of stewed carp, a round of beef, and a salmon. As for drink, Percy had ransacked every vintner's in the city, and although with our servants, our company counted scarce a score, we had bottles there enough to fill a regiment.

We rose with the sun, and Thirza dressed me in my new 'Restoration' gown, as Percy dubbed it. And what a gown! A bodice of pearl-coloured satin and a petticoat of turquoise-blue brocade — Percy ever favoured blue — with ribands and broideries of silver, and a posy of flowers to wear at my breast, and the daintiest little vizard-mask to carry. Percy's dress matched mine in colour, and was even more extravagantly trimmed, with a shoulder cloak of turquoise velvet and a wide plumed hat; but I went hatless.

I will say we looked a handsome pair; and Tansy, who, with her husband had arrived from Somerset the day before to lie at our house for the night and be up betimes the next morning, was as blue as my petticoat with envy.

'Oh, Prue! If I had known you'd be so grand I would have ordered me a new gown too! This is my last year's — but I am not buying any dresses now, because —' And she whispered — to make me envy *her*, that I'd have given all my finery to be in Tansy's case.

So off we went in chairs, since the streets were too heavily blocked with people — most of whom had been standing four and twenty hours — for any horse-drawn vehicle to pass.

Besides Tansy and her husband, there was Mr Robert Sidney, brother to the famous and unfortunate Algernon. This young Mr Sidney was a great blade to out-rival even Percy in his elegance. He spoke in a languishing, affected drawl, pronouncing Percy 'Parcy' and Fothergill 'Fathergill' which I soon discovered, when I attended court, was the fashionable mode of speech, and which Percy imitated, to my scorn. And now today we all speak thus and say 'Darby' for Derby and 'clark' for clerk, which seems to me a great mishandling of our brave English tongue.

I cannot now recall who made up the remainder of the guests whom Percy had invited, and with whom until that day I had been unacquainted. But I do remember one young lady, Mistress Warmestre, afterwards a maid of honour to Queen Catherine. She was a brown, sparkling girl, of no shape and no distinction, yet an engaging little piece for all that, with a tempting way with her to charm the gentlemen — more, I think, than it charmed Tansy.

'Oh, Prue,' she said in shocked asides, 'did you ever in your life see such a bare-faced prattle-box? And she not seventeen. If I had been so pert and forward at that age my father would have whipped me sore. I declare that Frank is hugely taken.'

'Not with her, my dear, don't fret yourself,' said I. 'He is raddled with three flagons full of liquor, and can only see her skew-eyed.'

'Oh, Prue! Don't *you* dare say my husband's tippled. What of yours? Only watch him now — offering her goose pie on a fork. What they can find to please them in such an illcomplexioned hussy I cannot think... And oh, dear me! I do feel poorly ... I have the palpitations.'

Whereupon Tansy fell into a pretty little swoon, but without changing her rosy colour, which may or may not have come out of a pot, and made such a to-do with her 'ohs' and her 'ahs' and her groans and her moans, to bring her husband in a flurry to her aid.

'You had best take your wife home, sir,' I said loud, while I tweaked Tansy's button nose, and slapped her hands, and bade her none too gently, 'Come to yourself, girl! Here's your good gentleman, distracted. She is in no fit state, Mr Fothergill, to stand all this exuberance. 'Twas sinful to have brought her. Take her home, I beg you, and put her to bed with a posset.'

'Oh, but I am better! I am quite recovered!' cried Tansy, sitting up. ''Twas the heat that turned me. Prue! You are no friend of mine an you bid my husband take me home. I'll see this day o' days out, though I see it from my coffin. Mr Fothergill! Do you stay beside me, sir, and keep your eyes for the procession — if they can look straight, which I'm doubting!'

'Why, my dear love,' protested Mr Fothergill, guarding a hiccup, 'I have not s'irred from your s'tide — 'tirred from your shide, I shwear, shince we — since we shtarted out thish morning.'

'Save to drink a hogshead,' pouted Tansy, 'and ogle that malapert minx who should know better than to waste a word on a tippling sot. Oh, fie! You're horrid drunk. Go to, sir! No, don't paw me! I vow I'd as lief return to my bed than stay here to be shamed.'

'Why, madam!' cried her husband, 'you shame yourself by these — by these hallushin — ations.'

'Oh, monstrous toad!' sobbed Tansy, 'your tongue is twisted and you smell of sack ... I vow I'll faint again.'

I left her to her husband and went to join my own, who more than halfway gone in wine himself, was calling high and foolish for a dance, and greeted me with cackles.

'Here she is, my lovely wife! Is she not fine, my lady fair, so sweet and rare an' rare an'... beautiful. Come, Prue! We'll dance the dance o' cuckolds. Hands crossed and off we go!'

And off we went a-capering, while Mr Sidney sang the tune and stamped his feet to keep the time, and Percy called Thirza and the servants in to make more merriment. My Thirza, I regret to say, was as far gone as any of the gentlemen, and joined in the dancing with a will and a raising of her petticoats to show her garters, with such a singing and a shouting and ha-hahing, never known this side of Bedlam till of a sudden in the distance was heard a great reverberation to throw Tansy into more fits and send Miss Warmestre, the baggage, flying to my husband's arms for shelter, with piping cries and flutters of 'Dear my lord!' and, 'Pray, my lord!' and, 'Good heavens! What was that?'

'That, sweet rogue,' said Percy, 'was the guns.'

To announce the King's arrival in the city.

Then how we hustled to take our stance on the balcony and watch for what was coming! And thousands upon thousands more watched with us for that triumphant entry, while all the church bells rang a louder peal, and all the conduits and the fountains spurted wine, and between the standing multitudes young maids in white came dancing to strew flowers and sweet herbs along the way.

So, through engarlanded thronged streets, amid the clangour of the joy-bells, the boom of cannon and the trumpeting of heralds, rode our King, attended by that faithful retinue who had followed him in exile. Before him went his Life Guards in their red coats and shining breastplates; the Sheriffs in their scarlet cloaks laced with silver; the Trumpeters in gold embroidered doublets, preceding the noblemen and Heralds-at-Arms — a dazzling array.

Presently, 'Look! Look!' in great excitement shouted Mr Fothergill. Here'sh Monk! Monk! Go' bless him — Gen'ral Monk!'

The cry was taken up by all of us, and echoed in cheering and yells from the spectators down below, as he who had saved England, mounted on his coal-black charger, his rugged old face set with smiles, acknowledged that thunderous greeting with a bob of his head and a wave of his hand as he went.

Then from the waiting populace rose a deep convulsive murmur, soaring in a mighty tumult to shake the air and hit the sky: 'The King!'

He passed beneath our balcony. I saw him through my tears — he, so longed for, dreamed of, and returned at last, on this his thirtieth birthday, riding with his brothers, the Dukes of York and Gloucester either side of him. Along the shouting Strand, between the rows of gabled houses, between the craning heads and fluttering scarves, he came, gallant, dark-faced and hatless, with the sun in a glory to crown him.

'Oh, Prue!' Tansy clutched me, weeping, laughing, 'Oh, Prue! How he is handsome!'

I saw Percy lean forwards gripping the wooden rail of the balcony and shouting — what I could not hear, for the clamour of the joy-demented crowd — but over and above that frenzied welcome and the clatter of hooves and clink of steel and harness, and the peals of the city's ringing spires, came a roar from Tom Mayhew, our coachman.

'God save His Majesty … King Charles!'

And the King looked up with a laugh on his lips, while the dark smiling eyes went straying from face to face to linger boldly for a second upon mine. I tore the posy of flowers from my bodice and flung it down to him. He deftly caught it — and kissed it! Yes, I swear he did, although I do not think he could have known from whence it came, for he went in a storm of flowers with their petals held in the curls of his hair.

And so he rode on to his palace; and men who once had denied him fell on their knees in his path and blessed God that the King was come into his own.

CHAPTER ELEVEN

Never in mortal memory had been known such a summer of gladness as in that year 1660. From every quarter of these islands, from their hiding-holes in foreign towns, from all the courts of Europe, flocked a host of joyful exiles returned, to partake in the general rejoicing. Whitehall was the centre of our universe, and he who presided there our idol.

Unimaginable was the homage paid to him, the eager daily crowding for a glimpse of that tall slight figure as he passed in and out of his palace on the Thames, or strolled in his park of St James's with a trail of spaniels at his heels and half a dozen courtiers in attendance; or sailed on the river in his barge as far as Putney, which His Majesty much enjoyed to do, and there go bathing with his brothers. And wherever the King went he was followed by a doting herd; his sayings were recorded; his dress, his voice, his mode of speech — "Ods fish!' became the fashion with all the young sparks of the town. No monarch had ever been so popular, nor indeed so greatly loved; for he represented more — much more — than monarchy; he had brought rebirth, regeneration, to this land; he had given us light in our darkness. We had thirsted for the wine of life; he filled us. He flung open the doors of playhouses that had for almost twenty years been closed, and the witnessing of dramas, comedies and tragedies condemned as ungodly, and yet it was not thought to be a sin to read the plays of poets and such-like in a book. There's logic for you! The logic of that white-livered vulgarian Cromwell who debarred Shakespeare, Beaumont and Fletcher, Kit Marlowe, and even the great Greek Euripides from their rightful presentation on a stage. Sinful — God save us! The sin rests on the ignorant humbugging conscience of them that cant long-lipped with prayer and eyes turned up, the while they crush the soul of man into a pulp to be refashioned in the image of a bolster, swollen with scrofulous dechristianised deceits. But with the return of our easy-going 'Merry Monarch' — (he had scarce been a month in possession of his kingdom before they dubbed him that) — England was herself again, and pleasure-mad, since for so long pleasure had been denied her. Up went the maypoles, and on every village green lads and lasses danced around them, singing as youth should. The sour Puritan rule that had drained us of God's laughter was swept away, and all England laughed again in a riot of feasting, mumming, song, and careless, heedless, wholesome merriment, to gladden the heart and bring joy to a bright new world.

So passed that amazing summer in one headlong flight of happiness, our woes forgotten and our sickness cured, our hopes set on a fair-weather future. The brooding clouds had vanished, and the sun shone down from heaven on a kingdom — and a king.

He, however, had more to do than hold court and receive homage, or play at pale-maille in the park, or walk in his privy gardens, or spend hours in his laboratory studying physics with his chemist, Mr Le Febre; more to do than sup and dine and drink and charm the ladies, to find himself ensnared by the lovely and unscrupulous Barbara Palmer. Even she could not hold him from his duty to those who had served him through his days of tribulation. All who had aided his escape from Worcester were right lavishly rewarded. Peerages, baronetcies, pensions were distributed with a bountiful and reckless generosity. Indeed, I have heard that the King was oftentimes imposed upon by fawning sycophants who came with tales of their exploits in His Majesty's cause, and none went unrewarded.

Those estates that had been confiscated were returned to their rightful owners, but it was not always possible to make good a complete loss — as in our own case of Wynmonath, for while the original extent of acreage had amounted to some several thousands, the better part of which the Government did certainly restore; the abbey was still in ruins and likely to remain so in Percy's lifetime. It seemed scarcely reasonable to demand a Government grant to rebuild it, and Percy had not a sufficiency of means, despite his increase of income from his land, to carry out his previous plan; nor, I think, was he as anxious now as he formerly had been to reconstruct Wynmonath, since to do so would need much sacrifice of his extravagant tastes, to say nothing of his London house and personal expenditure.

For myself I considered we were well enough endowed with almost all of Wynmonath's fair acres returned to us, and was sharp to scold at Percy when he grumbled, ' All very well for the Government to talk of Restoration. But what have they restored to me? My ruined lands and no wherewithal to till them. No home save mouldering walls and a farmer's rat-hole. A fine seat for Folliett of Wynmonath is Folly's End! Not a shilling will I get to raise a roof upon the abbey. One of the oldest places in the country, and my rightful heritage, now a nest for bats. No, I consider I have not been fairly dealt with. Others have been repaid in full, but I get less than half.'

'Well, may I be slit!' I cried. 'Only hear him! Of all the grumbling ill-contented crabs! Have you not been reinstalled with your estate? And now you squeal for money. You will have your money when your tenants pay their rents.'

'Will the Government rebuild their hovels?' retorted Percy. 'How can they live without a thatch above their heads? And when I have paid them for their labour, what is left for me?'

'You pay them little enough, so you should have *more* than enough, had you not spent so wildly on this grand London house.'

''Pon my word!' flashed Percy, pink with anger. 'Is that all the thanks I'm rendered for a gift? What I spent, I spent for you.'

'I did not ask it — and,' I added quickly, 'I am not ungrateful. But I do think you were over-lavish. And suppose you are unable to rebuild the abbey yet — is that so great a loss? We have never known it, so what we have not known we cannot miss. You have a house in Yorkshire, and if you be hard-pressed, why do you not sell that?'

Percy glared. 'I have already done so.'

This was news. 'Why did you not tell me?'

'Am I not telling you now? How do you think I have paid for all your finery and fal-lals and the upkeep of a mansion here in Town? Does gold rain from the sky to fill my coffers?'

'I am sure I never thought of how or wherefore,' I retorted, 'and I mislike this talk of ways and means and money, as if you were apprentice to a tradesman — only your cry is "What do *I* lack", not "What do *you* lack?" Yes, my lord, "I — I —" plays too big a part in your life. Methinks none should shout "I" but God, for none but He has any right to say "I am that I am".' Then seeing him so fretted, his smooth young face awry, I begged him, 'Now, my soul, don't build yourself a burden from an ant's egg. Bide your time. Go easy. Do I care if I live in a cottage or a castle, so long as I be happy — and am loved?'

'Pooh!' said Percy, still unappeased and scowling. 'You were not near so happy in your filthy old rags as you are in your fine silks and satins — which *I* pay for!'

'Say me that again,' I flashed, up in arms to have my olive branch so churlishly rejected, 'and you'll say it once too often. It is your right to clothe me. Would you have me running naked?'

Percy's brow relaxed. 'Why, yes, my dear,' he drawled, 'you strip amazing pretty.'

'Oh, go choke yourself!' said I. 'How dare you come long-faced to me with talk against your betters in Westminster! Lucky it is that only *my* ears can hear your treasonable gruntings, or you might be found without a head. Be thankful for your mercies.'

'Are you one of them?' asked Percy, nose in air.

'There's some might think so! Though I don't set myself above goodwill and peace and plenty here on earth, which is what we're all enjoying after a lifetime of insufferable hell. You should be on your knees to God praising His bounty, instead of standing there asking for more!'

Yet he did ask it, and set himself to write petitions to Chancellor Hyde, stating his case and demanding a Government grant for the restoration of his *ruined Ancestral Seat* — so ran the document that he submitted for my approval — *which was razed to the ground by the Rebels having stood a Monument of Security and Pride, since the days of the Norman Conquest* — and much more, and to such wordy length that I doubted the Chancellor would read it. Whether he did or no, we never knew; but since Percy received no answer to nor even an acknowledgment of his temerity, I imagine the Lord Chancellor had found matters of greater purpose to engage him than the grievances of importunate young peers.

Among the many honoured by the King in token of services rendered were Colonel Ashton and my Uncle Rossiter, both created baronets. My aunt never quite recovered from the shock. It did, in fact, considerably age her while seeming to have the reverse effect upon her husband. He attended court, danced — or rather pranced — and delighted the King with his playing on the lute.

Poor Aunt Rossiter!

From my uncle I had it that when she was informed of his secret activities and her total exclusion therefrom, to say nothing of the royal reward bestowed on her submissive little husband, she fainted for the first time in her life. My uncle, in great alarm, fell on his knees beside her, felt her heart, clapped her hands, and applied burnt feathers to her nostrils. Whereupon, if my uncle's word can be believed — for since I had found him out in double-dyed duplicity, I was chary of accepting any tale of his till it were proven — my aunt sat up, sneezed twice, fixed a basilisk eye upon her trembling spouse, then raised her fist and dealt him a clout upon his ear to turn him deaf — and herself dumb, for not till seven days thereafter did she speak, or so said Uncle Rossiter.

In the July of that first summer the King gave a ball at which I had the honour to attend and be presented by my husband to His Majesty. I went in white; a gown of Percy's choosing fashioned of richest satin looped above a petticoat of silver lace. The voluminous train was three yards long and caused me much embarrassment. I wore my mother's pearl necklet, and in my hair a red rose, and Thirza said I looked a 'picture'.

Percy's choice for himself was a short-waisted doublet of his favourite blue with the new wide 'petticoat' breeches, ornamented with ribands of silver, and broidered in gold to the pockets; and to crown all he disported a periwig. Now that was, and still is, a detestable fashion to my mind. I favour the natural hair on a man or a woman, and my husband's spun gold ringlets were infinitely more becoming than this monstrous imitation, made, I verily believe, from tow or horsehair; but such was the latest mode brought over from France which all the young blades had recently adopted, and Percy must needs go bedight according to the dictates of the day.

'Am I to your liking, my dear?' he wished to know, when he came to my room while I dressed for the ball.

No; not in the least to my liking was he in that riggery, but I had better sense than to tell him so. Instead I praised him to the skies to make him preen — and Thirza splutter — till I pinched her into silence, the while my husband, mighty pleased with himself and his appearance, prinked before my dressing-glass and poured half the contents of my perfume bottle on his wig.

'And what of me?' I asked when Thirza had done lacing up my bodice.

'You? Why, you're perfection!' declared Percy. 'And if only your manners were as lovely as your looks, I would be the proudest man in London.'

'Never fear,' said I, 'you'll be surprised — I'll be so gentle. See!' I swept him a curtsy to the ground. '"Your Majesty! Here sits the humblest, most adoring, most willing of your subjects. Yours to command, sir, who is in that delight to meet you having dreamed all my life long of this great honour —"'

Peremptorily Percy cut me short. 'Don't you dare start speechifying to His Majesty, nor open lip until you are addressed. God send you will not shame me!'

'How shame you? Must I not speak to the King?'

'Not until he speaks to you.'

'And then what do I say?'

'Good heavens, child! Are you so raw? Say nothing. Curb your tongue lest you trip over it. Remember who you are — and who *I* am,' said Percy, complacently settling the ribands at his cuff, 'so you do me credit.'

'How now!' cried Thirza, laughing. 'Can you not see, my lord, she's up to mischief? There's nothing you can learn her of courtly ways and manners that she don't already know, being born in her, as you might say. She'll queen it over everyone, including the King's favourite — who I'm told is nothing near so handsome as she's painted — and my pretty here will have the King and all his nobles in her handkercher before the evening's out — or I'm a Dutchman! The only fear that *you* may have, is lest you lose her. Never let her out of sight, my lord, an you wish to keep her for your own. There's not a gentleman but won't be green to envy you and put himself where you are, an he could… There, my darling,' heartily Thirza kissed me. 'Much enjoyment to you, and God bless you both!'

Thus in the best of humours we drove off to Whitehall. The night was clear and fine, the streets thronged with sightseers come to watch the long line of chairs and coaches passing on their way to court. Owing to the press of vehicles before us we went at a snail's pace, and Percy in a fever of impatience lest we arrive too late for presentation, ordered Tom Mayhew take us to the river, where we embarked by wherry and entered the palace from Whitehall Bridge Stairs.

A city within a city — that was Whitehall as I knew it; a bewildering maze of galleries, gardens, state apartments, council chambers, private suites of rooms allotted to courtiers, chaplains, and the King's ladies; these all centred round the King's House, or Court House, which was accounted a place so sacred *that if any man presume there to strike another, his Right Hand shall be cut off and he committed to perpetual imprisonment.*

Surely much laxity of this stern discipline must have been permitted during the reign of the second Charles, for I never heard of any such penalty enforced, and there was a plenty quarrelling and bickering and duelling too, I dare say, went on within those walls, where affairs of the heart were conducted with no less zeal than affairs of the state.

Never shall I forget my first entry to that hive of pleasure, where, all care forgotten and all joy restored, the King stood master of the revels to entertain his chosen guests in his own palace... Colour, music, lights from a myriad candles, shed their radiance on a blaze of gold and scarlet — the uniforms of the King's Guard, intermingled with a phantasmal pattern of silver, violet, saffron, rose, and every hue of the rainbow, in every conceivable texture of silk and satin, tinsel, brocade, to dazzle the eye and drug the sight of one who had seen little of life's gaiety and nothing of life's glamour.

The sparkle of jewels, the poise and bloom of beauty matured and shining in a galaxy of rival stars, totally eclipsed my youthful charms and awed me, much dwindled in my self-esteem, to silence. But Percy, accustomed to the grandeur of the Louvre, was nothing daunted by this glittering display. Guiding me with a hand beneath my elbow, he threaded a path through the crowded rooms, acknowledging the greetings with an enviable ease, making a leg to the ladies, saluting the gentlemen, whispering the names of famous persons as he passed.

Here was Chancellor Hyde, stout, apple-cheeked, with two chins, a lip-beard, and protruding china-blue eyes that darted hither and thither eternally watchful, while behind that bulging forehead the alert mind wrestled with knotty problems of the

Council Chamber even in his hour of relaxation. Beside him stood his daughter, Anne, a robust, creamy-skinned, golden girl. 'Too fleshly for my taste,' murmured Percy in my ear, 'but not for the Duke of York's. No secret she is mighty favoured there.'

The King's brother bowed before her, paying court for all to see; nothing so tall as His Majesty, though considered more handsome of feature, but I misliked that haughty twist of a mouth too womanish for any man. And, challenging all comers, the exquisite, petulant Barbara Palmer, with the pride of her conquest in the tilt of her head, the set of her splendid shoulders, moved among the company as queen. Around her flocked her satellites, hopeful aspirants for her throne should she descend it, lickspittle courtiers waiting to grasp the silken rope she could, were she so minded, throw to one or other of her choice, that he might climb to royal recognition through her window... This is how I see her now, not as I saw her then. To me in my Arcadian simplicity, she appeared a goddess, the most beautiful creature ever fashioned for the homage of a man.

So, through a succession of vast apartments curtained in velvet, gilded, and hung with tapestries and pictures by great Masters, we came at last to the withdrawing room, where with a genial absence of formality, a laugh, a word, a jest for everyone, the King received. There he stood, a graceful host among his lords-in-waiting, dressed in purple with a fall of lace at wrist and throat, and the flash of his 'George' on his breast, the least elaborately costumed of all that gay assembly. He wore no periwig. His hair, a shining black, fell in long ringlets, not frizzled but naturally curling, streaked here and there with early silver. He looked a little older than his years; the dark eyes beneath their heavy lids showed a faint weariness, the smile under the thin moustache a hint of mockery.

At the announcement of our names by the Lord Chamberlain, the King turned and advanced a step to meet us. I made my curtsy and as I rose, "Ods fish, my lord!' I heard, 'you were well advised to lock this jewel in your casket and not display it at my cousin's court — lest it were stolen!'

Then while Percy, bowing nose to knees, mumbled some obsequious reply which I could take no count of for the noise of my flattered heartbeats, and while the ladies with their gentlemen behind us buzzed and murmured, tapped the toe, and flirted the fan in a fidget for their turn, His Majesty detained me yet again.

'We owe a debt of gratitude and honour to the late Lord Folliett of Wynmonath which we have not yet had the chance to repay.' The full square lips were smiling, the warm brown eyes held mine. 'I heard your father went on his travels from Worcester in much the same dress as I wore. There were two of us walking in steeple-crowned hats — I've been told he was followed — for me.'

Percy need not have feared that I'd shame him by my chatter. Dumb as a boot stood I, my throat empty of words but full of a rock. For my life, then, I could not have uttered, and could scarce see, for the mist in my eyes, that graceful gesture — the ring drawn on an impulse from a finger.

'Wear this for me in your father's name and for his sake,' said the King.

I knelt; I clasped and kissed the hand extended; I rose the proudest girl in Britain, and passed on with my husband, to the antechamber. There I was greeted by Colonel — now Sir Arthur — Ashton and his lady, who had scarce begun to whisper me that 'Tansy was delivered last night of a *beautiful* boy,' before she was interrupted by a bellow from her husband.

'Prue! Here is a gentleman who's waiting for a word.'

'Not the first word I've had with her ladyship, at all,' said an Irish voice at my side.

I should have known him by that accent if I'd not known his face, nor that merry twinkling eye, nor the hair, which may still have been dyed; for whatever its colour was hid. He favoured the fashion and carried a full-bottomed wig, and was dressed in grey velvet, bedizened, bejewelled.

'Nor the last, may I hope, my Lord Marquis,' said I; and I held out my hand with the King's ring upon it for the Marquis of Ormond to kiss. 'So, my lord, you had the laugh of me, but my uncle, though he made less noise, laughed longest. He has been laughing in his sleeve a dozen years.'

'Sure, your ladyship, I thought you had me caught! I'll not forget how you came tumbling out of a blackberry bush — and there was I with me heart in me mouth before I dropped it at your feet! Och, the unfortunate condition of meself to have all the carking and caring of an intrigue and no reward for't but to be consigned by a wood-nymph — to the crows!'

So what with gallantries and presentations and the King's ruby on my hand and all the ladies pressing round to see it — and not a little wishing they were in my shoes, I have no doubt — my head was well-nigh turned, in fact, giddily revolving as much, maybe, from the effects of the wine that freely passed, as from the cajoleries and compliments of gentlemen.

Then when the guests were all received, the musicians in the Great Hall tuned their fiddles, and His Majesty called for a dance. The King led off in a coranto with the Marchioness of Ormond, the Duke of York took Mistress Hyde, giving her precedence before all ladies of higher rank. Eyes stared, fans fluttered, and whispers flew behind them. Her father pulled a lip. Sooner would he lose his pending earldom than see his daughter whored. Marriage or nothing — King's brother or no — for the Lord Chancellor's Anne.

Lord Ormond partnered me, and I saw Percy offering his arm to a handsome, flash young woman in a gown of water green. On enquiring of the marquis her name I was told — 'the Comtesse de Fontenelle. Her husband is behind us.' And glancing round my shoulder, sure enough, there was his Countship, pointing the toe and curvetting to Mistress Warmestre, who looked very well in a dress of puce silk with her hair in those new-fangled 'heartbreakers'.

In such a press of people it was impossible, until all were paired to the dance, to see more than those immediately around us; and I must confess I was astonished at the absence of courtly manners on the part of a number of people who followed the King and the Duke of York, pushing and shoving each other aside, in order to be well in the eye of Royalty, in which behaviour, I must own, the women were the worst offenders, hoping doubtless to be chosen for a dance — or greater favour... Yes, it was a rough and boisterous England to which our King Charles returned, and it took the better part of all his reign to polish it. Nor am I prepared to say that at the first court ball I attended, I saw much of courtliness save in the strutting foreigners, of whom there were too many for my taste, and who primed in deportment from their cradles, knew little else in life than how to make a pretty leg and fulsome speeches. But I, schooled by my Aunt Rossiter, had learned better than to show myself rude in the presence of distinguished company; and although not above raising my voice — or my hand — to good purpose at home to my husband, I was gentle as a sucking-dove and milder than milk when I danced with the Marquis of Ormond.

The music ceased; the dancers dispersed to their places and stood till His Majesty sat. The marquis mopped his forehead. 'Begad! 'Tis warm work for meself with more of the gout than of grace in me toes.'

'Indeed, my lord,' said I, politely, 'you underrate your excellence. I have never trod a measure with such ease. Your step is quite perfection.'

'Och, child! Come, now, you can't blarney me who was cutting me capers before you were cutting your teeth. Will your ladyship take some refreshment? Wait while I bring ye a cup o' canary — though I doubt me it can add a sparkle to your eyes — the loveliest I've seen this side o' the Irish Channel.'

With which overweighted gallantry the marquis deposited me in an alcove by an open window looking out upon the river, and betook himself to the buffet in a room adjacent, where a crowd of gentlemen were gathered to jostle for their drinks. I had a glimpse of the spindle-legged de Fontenelle hurrying after Percy who had managed to secure a bottle and was toasting the French Madam, his face very flushed, his eyes very bright, his laughter so uproarious I guessed him half-whittled, and hoped that he might hold his hand before he lost his head. My own was like to burst with the noise, the glare of lights, the sickly sweet smell of varied perfumes that mingled with, but did not disguise the stench of sweating bodies.

Opening the casement I leaned out for air. The night was cool and soft. In the near darkness the lanthorns of waiting wherryboats bobbed like will-o'-the-wisps, but on the far bank of the river no lights shone, all good citizens were long abed. Beyond the low-lying marsh and meadow land of Lambeth, the sleeping shoulders of the Surrey hills were lost in the grape-bloom sky: a night of velvet with a misty moon, star-crowned. Under that pallid light all shapes were enchanted, all colours submerged in a transparent, shimmering effulgence, all shadows magic-laden.

I stood illusioned, with the murmur of the river in my ears and my eyes watching the mirrored stars like drowned ghosts of themselves in the black gleaming water, while the hum and clamour of the crowded rooms receded, remote and forgotten.

It was then that I became aware of a curious sensation, a tingling in my palms, an alertness and stiffening of my body as a hawking dog will stiffen to the scent. And while all else around me faded and dissolved, I felt as if my spirit had parted from the flesh to float, suspended, hovering, expectant... So vivid, so intense was this experience, that it seemed I actually could see, as from above, my earthly self clothed in my white and silver, turning from the window, eyes widening in wonder, my eager gaze scanning that gay company to single out one who approached: I saw my hand lifted in greeting, yet I saw none to greet...

But he was near me, very near to me. I knew it: that clear perpetual outline of face and form obliterated in the years of yesterday, though ever held and imaged in my dreams. And in that moment of sheer consciousness, while sense and spirit fused, I felt, as once before, the irresistible swift impulse of vital force and purest energy united in the desperate effort to pierce the veil that enshrouds this mortal sight, to touch, to grasp at revelation before the curtain falls. A moment only, while transfixed, I waited, hearing his step among a thousand, my name upon his lips ... and then the formal parrot-phrase of introduction: 'My duty, Lady Folliett.'

Out of some far-off vacancy I returned into myself to find him there.

How much more intensely do we live in thought than action. With how much braver eloquence the mind's voice speaks in its imprisoned tongue than in the uttered word. What impassioned roles we play, with what heroic gestures we hold the stage before a multitude — in the mind's eye. By which same token, on that September night more than forty years ago when Robert Peverill stepped back into my life, though all my blood and being leapt in jubilance to meet him, did I speak? Did I mouth more than words glib as a learned lesson? What words? Not one worth the recording.

It was not words that passed between us there in the alcove of a room in a king's palace. I think we never needed words to tell us what we knew, and had known in the whole essence of our lives from their beginnings.

He was immensely changed, and yet the difference lay not in his man's stature, his rich dress, but in a positive completeness, an expansion, less physical than visionary. One felt he stood secure within himself and in the varied forms of life and knowledge. He had grown beyond his years to man's supremacy while he carried with him all youth's charm and vigour. Healthy-looking, cleanly, firm, with that same unshrinking tawny gaze, the same rusty-red hair, not now a lion's mane, but trimmed and scented, curled, withal his nose was still as freckled as a cowslip, his lips parted in their same blunt-cornered smile. He wore a suit of amber velvet, with diamond buttons and his sword-hilt jewelled.

My Robin...

Strange that I cannot remember what was said between us there. Surely I can hear an echo if I listen for the light foam-bubble talk that tripped from me to him above the singing of an anthem?

'Who would have thought to see you so magnificent? I declare you are taller than the King!'

'You are grown, too,' says Robin.

'Lord, sir! Is that all you can tell me after seven years — is it not seven years? And am I not grown in more than height? There's some call me well-looking.'

'Then I've no need to tell what others say.'

'Why, Rob, you're slow to flatter!'

'Can one flatter the sun? I am dazzled.'

'That don't ring true. Will you take me to dance?'

'I must not steal you from Lord Ormond.'

'So! Do you refuse me? And how do you know my partner is Lord Ormond?'

'I have watched you from the moment you arrived.'

At which I find myself a little breathless. 'And ... you wait till the evening is half over to present yourself. From where, may I ask, did you watch me?'

'From the gallery.'

'Have you seen Percy?'

'No.'

'He is partnering a friend of yours, Madame de Fontenelle.'

'Indeed?'

'Have you seen her?'

'I have not.'

A pause, the while I savour this and find the tasting pleasant. 'And you recognised me from among so bright a constellation?'

But he will not play this game of puff-ball chatter. His eyes are melting into mine with a warm steady quiet to enclose and silence me that I may hear the whisper in his heart, unspoken:

I have come back where I belong ... to you.

For me the evening ended there. I can recall no more of it, save that we soon were joined by Percy and the Frenchman, and the Frenchman's wife; that my husband was immoderately happy to greet 'My frien' — my boyhoo's frien', my goo' frien' Rob Pev'rill.' And that Madame de Fontenelle familiarly addressed him as *'Cher Robert'*, pronouncing his name in the French way; that Lord Ormond gave me to drink from a beaker of wine that made me exceedingly merry; that I danced with de Fontenelle, with the marquis again, and I think I danced — or rather reeled around — with Percy. But I did not dance with Robin. He left early. We stayed late.

The stars were fading in a dawn grey sky when Percy and I drove home. I remember, too, that my husband, now top-heavy full, fell asleep in the coach, got lost of his legs, and was carried to bed by Tom Mayhew.

The end of that joyous Restoration year was saddened by the loss of the King's young brother, the Duke of Gloucester, who contracted and died of the smallpox. A few weeks later, the Princess Royal of Orange on a visit to England was stricken with the same disease and died on Christmas Eve.

So for three months the King and his court were in mourning, but in April on St George's day, His Majesty was crowned amid another frenzied outburst of rejoicing. Night after night a ring of bonfires blazed beacon-high around the city, with a dancing and carousing in the streets, and feasting and frolicking from house to house to shake the bones of the regicides who had paid their penalty for murder on the gallows.

There were hangings enough, in all conscience, to avenge the gentle martyr of Whitehall. I had an ugly tale brought to me by Thirza, who with her husband went to see the execution of Major-General Harrison. He was the man appointed by

Cromwell to convey Charles I from Windsor for his trial, and who later sat in judgment on His Majesty. And now he in his turn was come to be judged by the subjects of the dead King's son, even those who had approved that monstrous crime.

Thirza told, with shocking gusto and more relish than I cared to hear, how she and Tom Mayhew had obtained front seats in the stands erected at Charing Cross. Through eager crowds of spectators all come to see the show, they dragged Harrison from the Tower on a hurdle.

'He was,' said Thirza, 'brazen cheerful for one about to die with all his sins upon him. A great ox of a man bared to the waist, and when they unbound him the weals of the. ropes were like the bars of a red-hot grid deep marked into his flesh.' And unheedful of my cry to beg her cease, while all the time some diabolic curiosity insisted I should listen, Thirza with ghoulish enjoyment proceeded: 'And when asked if he had aught to say he answered in a loud voice for all to hear, "I go to my death with my conscience clean and I would do what I have done again for my country's sake and the good of my soul." Such a howl as rose from us then to shake high heaven! Tom was growling like a bear, that I had all to do to hold him back lest he should spring, to cheat the hangman of his quarry on the scaffold. So then they took and strung him up — you should have seen him dance, the unduteous black-hearted fiend. I confess I had to shut my eyes against the sight of him a-dangle — his eyeballs staring half out of their sockets while he mouthed and gibbered — and when I looked again they'd cut him down though he was still alive and all his bowels exposed and spilling over. Then,' said Thirza with a savage glee that struck me dumb with horror — 'then with his green face grinning to the end, his last breath left his body on a rush of wind for all the world, I swear, as though his ugly soul were in a haste to meet his master, Satan... Why, child! you're white as a shroud. Are you so soft? Would you have the filthy traitor spared? Would you have him cosseted and pardoned and detained in peace at His Majesty's pleasure?'

'I would not have him tortured,' I scolded her while I abhorred myself for lending ear to these abominations. 'You should be ashamed to gloat on such disgustful barbarisms with no more thought of what the poor wretch suffered than a sawney at a peep-show.'

But Thirza was not the only one who watched these ghastly retributions. It soon became the mode with the young blades of the town, not excepting my own husband, to drive out to Tyburn Hill, or wherever the performance might be held, to see the latest victims hanged, while they laid wagers as to the length of time, in minutes, the body would live — or simulate life in the drollest muscular contractions after disembowelment. There was the case of Axtell — one of the foremost insurrectionists — whose corpse, according to Percy, showed exceeding liveliness for seven minutes after it was quartered...

Enough of this; it sickens me. And, thank God, it sickened the King, who confessed himself 'weary of hangings' and bade Chancellor Hyde at the Council table, 'Now let them sleep.'

There remained, however, three more executions of which the members of the Council Chamber would not be denied, though they were exonerated for this defiance of His Majesty's order, by hanging those already dead. The carcasses of Cromwell, and his right and left hand, Ireton and Pride, were dug up from their tombs among the Kings in Westminster Abbey, to be hanged by their necks at Tyburn before a thousand delighted spectators, who once had homaged the death of the Lord Protector with royal funereal pomp. From sunrise to sundown they hung there on the gibbet until, when dusk fell, their putrid bodies were lowered and flung into a hole under the hill, and there to this day they lie.

Who can account for these revulsions, this back and forth swing of the pendulum that in the short space of twenty years will raise one man from a pedestal to lead a nation, and then will turn and rend him that the very stones cry out against this sacrilege done to the dead? I can see no right nor satisfaction to be gained in vengeance. Let them that sin be punished, but to expend on senseless clay such ignominious contempt seems to my mind an unworthy and indecent deed for honest men to do. 'Let them sleep,' as the King forbearingly commanded, until such time when history, perchance, will resurrect and worship them as the great and incorruptible champions of English liberties!

Thus all was righted, the King crowned, the murder of his father avenged tenfold, while the gutters of the city ran blood, and flies feasted on those rotting remnants in the lay-stalls. Then down with the gibbets and up with the maypoles and all the careless gaiety of England at her merriest returned.

For me the months, the years — I have lost count of time — revolved in a whirligig of incidents, a gyrating medley of festivities: court balls, banquets, masquerades, visits to the Playhouse, where in the pit at the Duke's Theatre a saucy red-headed child exchanged oranges for kisses with the gentlemen, and laughed her way into the heart of a king for all posterity… There were open-air fêtes at Spring Gardens, where we sat under the trees and ate strawberry tarts and drank bad Rhenish wine; or at the rival centre of fashion, the Mulberry Gardens — which Cromwell sold, and which the King on his return threw open to the public — where we would entertain supper guests in flower-festooned arbours, and wander through the grassy glades of the 'Wilderness', an ideal spot for lovers and for scandal.

I saw much to startle me, though if one valued one's reputation as a wit and a woman of parts, one must never appear to be shocked; one must ogle with the worst of them, brag of your conquests, offer innuendoes, discard your virtue and assume a vice if you would be *à la mode*. But I was not. I stood divided, played my dual role of Lady Folliett — more in favour with the gentlemen than with the ladies — and yet stayed steadfast to myself, the graceless gowk of Folly's End, who knew no better than to share her foolish heart between her husband and her unacknowledged lover. Was ever woman in a sadder case: beloved of two men, married to one and possessed by neither?

Such was I, Prue Folliett, praised for my beauty, toasted and flattered till my ears were sick, while all around me I saw women snatch at passing equivocal pleasures with no more thought of wrong than a street urchin when he snatches cherries from a hawker's barrow.

I know my name was coupled with that of Robert Peverill; I know the world said I had made a cuckold of my husband in a court where no man's wife was sacred, where our King openly debauched himself with his prime favourite whom he had raised to the rank of a peeress — the Countess of Castlemaine. But what I did not know was that my husband, whom I believed immune from idle gossip in his trust of me and of his friend, had been infected with the virus of those adders' tongues that instilled their fatal poison in his life, first to irritate and then to swell within him in a cankerous growth that festered...

Well, we were blind, Robin and I, blind and befooled in our loyalty; I the greatest of all fools, in that I held the secret of my virgin marriage from him. Why? Why did I not tell him the whole truth — that I was free to give him all myself since I was no man's wife? Why did I not unlock the words that beat upon my heart: *Take and enjoy, anoint me, crown me yours in spirit, mind and body?* But I could not — for my torment — tell him. I could not. I was bound and sealed, handfasted to my husband, he whom, God help me, I still loved, though with my woman's eyes awake I saw him as he was: warped and twisted in the kernel of his manhood and embittered, hiding the scar of nature's curse under a smiling cynicism, a false gaiety, and a heartbreaking tenderness — for me.

If I had never seen that haunting shadow of frustration in his eyes; if I had seen him seeking compensation from other women in whom he might by chance have found his manhood's strength, or if — as sometimes to my shame I half suspected — he had indulged, as some certain few of our sparkish young elegants did, in amorous fancies for his own sex; if he had shown himself unkind to me, ungentle, or in any way less loving, I would not have stood firm, I would have yielded. For I knew that Robin waited for the first sign from me… And I gave none.

In those first years of the Restoration my life as I review it now appears amazingly inconsequent. Whereas my earlier youth, so quietly lived, has a tangible coherence, so later do I seem to run astray. There is no order in the circle of events that revolve before my eyes in varied motley, like mummers at a fair. I move, less alert than aloof, a strolling player in the midst of a merry-go-round. I pause to watch a puppet show, a comedy of errors, culminating in a melodrama, a woeful tragedy indeed. I see our Mr Moon, a sinister dark fellow, the very villain of the piece, mistakenly, since, like all villains of all pieces, he is not the creator of his part; he merely acts as he is bid according to the character for which the Posture-Master casts him... I watch the scene unfold against the background of tinsel and glitter; I see the tawdry lights-o'-love of His Majesty's Court, and the King of England squandering himself and his fine intelligence on wanton trumpery.

I see him crowned; I see him touching for the Evil. I see the physicians leading the sick one by one to be healed, while the King, seated in state in his banqueting hall, is yawning behind his long hand. A wearisome business this, for one who would sooner be racing his horses at Newmarket, or pleasuring a lady.

I see him married. I see myself, magnificently gowned in cloth of gold, making my curtsy in the royal palace to a timid brown young girl with startled fawn's eyes and ugly projecting teeth. Her hair is monstrously dressed in outstanding wings either side of her pinched little face. I see the King's woman in all her bold arrogant beauty, staring the small bat-like creature out of countenance. I hear the titters passed behind the fans: 'Did you ever behold such a hideous fright — look at the fardingale, a hundred years out of date! Look at her! And look — only look at her women! Not one under fifty — all bearded, God save us!'

I see the starting tears in the scared dark velvet eyes. She is pitifully young, this little princess from Portugal, and speaks no word of English beyond 'I t'ank you'. For what is she thanking me? For the warm kiss I press on the soft small hand? Or maybe for my welcome, the more fervent for the scorching look with which I scourge the Castlemaine, while my heart goes out to this lost lonely child brought from a home of love where she was cherished, to be mocked by her husband's whore.

There is dancing in the Great Hall afterwards. I see myself with Robin at that very window where we met again. 'You have made a conquest with the Queen,' he says, 'she wishes you to be appointed in attendance.'

'If I could shield her from the talons of that sluttish drab I'd gladly do it,' I answer hotly. 'But I doubt me I am fitted for the post. I'd let my tongue lash out too freely, I am thinking, and might find myself in the Tower for my pains.'

Says Robin, with his straight, all-seeing look, 'Your skin is tender. It must harden.'

''Tis hard enough — untouchable,' I mutter, 'but there's some I'd take to the cart's tail and hide them till the bad blood spurted and they squalled for mercy — and I'd laugh to do it! Laugh for every snigger they have cast at that poor unprotected innocent.'

'You do not laugh,' says Robin coolly, 'quite so often as you used.'

'Do I not? Yet life today is droll enough to split the sides of those that have some humour.'

'Why do you so wilfully distort yourself?' His hand reaches for mine that grips the windowsill. 'All the loveliness and all the sadness of the world is in your crooked smile.'

'Is it crooked?'

'As it always was, and as ever ... lovely. But it was never sad.'

'Was! Was!' I cry, with haste to drag my hand from his touch for fear of it. 'Why must we talk of "was" like two old crones, with their teeth fallen out and their mouths fallen in while they sit and mumble, picking out the maggots from their mouldered youth! I am too young to talk of what I *was*, I would know what I *am*. What am I?'

'I dare not tell you,' answers Robin with that in his eyes to drive my tortoise-head sharp and quick into its shell to ask him, safely hidden. 'Think you the Queen insists on my appointment? I confess I am loath to take it, though if it were her wish —'

And my voice runs down like a clockwork toy, for in truth I speak for speaking's sake lest I betray myself in silence.

'I think you need not fear,' he tells me, taking up his cue, 'her dragons guard Her little Majesty with grim determination. They will allow none from the English court to wait upon her privacy. Can you blame them?'

'I cannot, and am relieved. Yet I understood Miss Warmestre is to be a maid-of-honour.'

'Yes, the Queen will be permitted to pluck her maids from the choicest of our English buds — though I doubt me there's a maiden at this court.'

'Here's a churl you are to my fair sex!' I answer, shrill. 'I know of one — at least.'

'One is a poor total in a hundred.'

This serves us nothing...

'Let us dance.'

We dance the galliard, and we dance out of that scene and out of that moment of time into the Park of St James's ... to watch the King play Percy at pale-maille.

Here was honour; my husband well to the fore with His Majesty who had appointed him a gentleman-in-waiting, while Robin attended the Duke of York and had been allocated lodgings in Whitehall. Both were now high placed, and no rivalry between them, though had these appointments been reversed and Robin the King's gentleman, my husband might have shown himself resentful. As it chanced, however — and glad was I for all our sakes to see it — the King found much amusement in Percy's dry wit and ironical quips at the expense of His Majesty's Council. Those vastly troubled gentlemen who had served him faithfully in exile, served him still as faithfully in the gigantic difficulties of administration in a Parliament composed of Royalists and Presbyterians, of turncoats and toad-eaters, of rehabilitated Cavaliers all clamouring for their 'prerogatives' under the Clarendon Code.

But the Act of Uniformity, the first of a series of acts passed against Dissenters, was less, I think, the work of that astute old politician Edward Hyde than of the long-abused landowners who were determined never again to risk the revival of a Roundhead Party.

I own I am not conversant in these matters, but it seems to me when I look back upon the muddle-headed carping vilipendencies raised in Parliament against first this sect and then the other, that the whole crux of those heated arguments was centred round the subject of religion. Is it not inconceivable that the worship of God should arouse such strong antagonisms, such seething hatreds, such a fanatical outcrying in the name of Jesus Christ? I myself have seen it. I was in London in that year of '61, when Venner, the wine-cooper, raised a half-demented following of those same 'Fifth-Monarchy' men who caused enough pother in Cromwell's time, and now did rise again, incited by their leader — not to practise preaching, but to act.

Percy and I were returning from a dinner Robin gave upon his birthday — so I remember well the date — January 6th. Robin lodged at that time in a house hard by Lincoln's Inn Fields. Our coach was held up by a great concourse of these insurgents who had broke through the city's gates and put the King's guards to the run, killed close on twenty men and went marching to St Paul's calling on people to come forth and declare themselves for Jesus.

Percy was in a great stir, and being fuddled — for Rob had plied him pretty full — he stuck his head out of the coach to shout, 'Come on, you mangy sneak-bills, and you — you fat chuff-cats, and all you pelf-licking niggish deformed sots — come and be slit! I'll challenge the whole lot o' ye!' And drawing his sword he waved it in the face of one brawny fellow, who, as he passed, wrenched it from my husband's hand to lunge at him, while I yelled, 'Murder! Help!' and screaming at Tom Mayhew to drive on, tugged at Percy's sword-belt to drag him from the carriage window. Whereupon our coachman whipped his horses and urged them through the panic-stricken mob, scattering them right and left and got us safely back into our beds, which I never thought to see again that night. The whole town was in an uproar, the streets teeming with terrified citizens, bells clanging from the steeples, and every soldier at arms prepared for massacre; but by the morning all was quiet, the rioteers fled under cover of darkness, and hiding in the woods at Highgate where they were rounded up and taken. For weeks afterwards their heads grinned from the spikes on Tower Hill as a threatening reminder of what might come to others should they be tempted to arise in opposition to the Church.

And this was only one example of the widespread growth of bigotry end fanatical disturbance with which the bishops contended from the pulpits and in the House of Lords, that one might think the devil was astride among them all to bring destruction on the House of God.

That at least was Robin's view of it when on one July afternoon in the fields of Pall Mall Close we sat and watched the play. Before us passed a strolling carnival parade of courtiers and their ladies, whose brightly coloured costumes outrivalled all the flowers. The air was heavy with the scent of new-mown hay and roses; the trees, in their full summer dress of spinach green, stood unstirring under a brazen sky. The King, seemingly unaffected by the temperature, swung his mallet with an energy to win him five games in a total of six. ''Ods fish, Folliett,' I heard, 'the fight's too easy — come! I'll take you on next game giving you three to one...'

Robin and I moved to a distance to seat ourselves in the shade. It had been a marvellous warm summer, and I, sick of the heat and the dust and the endless round of gaieties in London, had retired for a short vacation on a visit to Aunt Rossiter at Templecombe, whence I was but recently returned.

For some long time my aunt had been in failing health. She was well over seventy, and, I fear, had taken much to heart the 'deceitful double-dealing' of her husband as she was pleased to call my uncle's secret service to the King. In further recognition of his administrative qualities, His Majesty had lately appointed him a member of the Privy Council, and had raised him from the tank of a baronet to that of a peer. These new honours necessitated my uncle's periodical attendance at court and in the Council Chamber, and I fancy his good wife did unduly fret herself over his frequent absences; yet nothing would induce her to leave Templecombe.

She strongly disapproved of our giddy court, the royal mistresses — the King had now taken to himself another — one Frances Stewart, an impudent minx of a girl whose pretty little high-bridged nose had somewhat disjointed the Castlemaine's; and many a time did I listen to the diatribes hurled by my aunt against the ribald obscenities and voluptuous extravagance of Whitehall. 'That is no life for you,' she said, 'nor any self-respecting, chaste, and honest woman. Your father would turn in his grave to know that you consorted with harlots and promiscuous adulterers.'

This, from what I knew of my dear father — all grace to him — I doubted; but I held my peace and let her talk.

'The King,' my aunt declared, 'is a born ruler. A man of highest principles, who if he chose to exercise his mental attributes with that same enthusiasm in which he indulges his — hem! — he would likely see this England bloom again in the glory that was hers in the heyday of *my* youth when the Popish menace was so vehemently suppressed.'

Yet I think, if truth be told, my good aunt could have had but little knowledge of those days that were her boast, for by her own accounting she was scarce ten years old when Queen Elizabeth died. It is a common plaint among the elderly, and one, I hope, of which I am not guilty, to deplore the newer age and extol the past that is for us our whole existence.

However, despite her self-imposed seclusion in the country, my aunt had managed to acquire a prodigious store of all the latest news and views of the times. How she achieved this knowledge — whether by second sight or by word of courier summoned from mystic circles by some abracadabra device of her own — I cannot say, yet certain it is she exploited a fairly forcible opinion of the ever-increasing intolerance towards and fear of the Catholic Party.

'Yes, as it was when I was young,' my aunt continued, 'and as it ever will be among all right-minded people, notwithstanding that Chancellor Hyde — or Clarendon as he now calls himself — is own father to a Papist.'

'Do you mean to say, madam,' I queried, amazed, 'that the Duchess of York is converted?'

'Privately,' my aunt replied with a twitch of her long nose, 'as is the Duke, who makes no secret of his predilections. Ah! how wily,' she reflected, conceding dubious praise where it was due, 'how Machiavellian is our opportunist Chancellor, who foxed us all and the King no less, with tears and fist-shaking protestations that he would sooner see his daughter flung into the Tower and beheaded than marry with James of York! And the devil alone,' proceeded my aunt, her gaze fixed upon the floor with such a fierce and penetrative look, one might almost have believed she was about to call the horned gentleman in question from his works below to answer her, 'the devil alone can tell me why Hyde was so wroth to have the hussy well secured and her child born in wedlock. And then the King, who is so tender that if his spaniels cry he'll comfort them with all the choicest titbits from his table and can refuse nothing to a faithful servant — the King, forsooth, must needs hand out an earldom to his Chancellor, and his blessing to Mistress Anne that she may breed a future sovereign of England. Monstrous! Monstrous!' quoth my aunt with rising spleen. 'I never thought to see a Papist or the daughter of a Papist on the throne, and, mark me, there are parties in our midst who would have the crown upon York's head tomorrow if they could! There are serpents who have writhed their way into the very entrails of our Constitution and our Church — who wriggle back and forth between Whitehall and the Vatican with plots and treason in their tongues. I know what I know.' And I, who had listened to this monologue in growing apprehension, was ready now to jump out of my skin when my aunt turned so suddenly, and, as it seemed, accusingly, upon me. 'Observe now and take warning, how the Duke will gather round him chiefly those avowed supporters of his faith. There is one as near to you as makes no matter — your Robert Peverill.'

I sat aghast. Now why in every holy name should she name him? And '*Your* Robert Peverill'?

Gathering my errant wits and smothering my fright, I stammered, 'What, my good Aunt, do you insinuate? Robin is a

Catholic, certainly, as he was born. I like him none the less for his adherence to his Church. You are, if I may say so —' and very daring was I at that moment, with my voice returned to shout down any slanderous insinuations from a bigoted old woman who had dwelled so long among the tarnished glories of her past that her perceptions were half-choked in dust — 'You — forgive me the presumption, Aunt — are imbued with such dogma and tradition that you cannot see the daylight of our age. We are more charitable, more tolerant, more —'

Then with that stony eye upon me did I flounder to lose my discourse and my courage. 'The King,' I added weakly, 'the King himself they say, is so ... inclined.'

'Who says?' my aunt lifted her chin and a finger. '*Who* says? And *how* inclined? Take care! Be guarded. Mind how you bibble and babble in your ignorance — you little fool! You big-eyed, big-hearted ninny — do you not realise that in your world which is not mine, thank God, a breath, a whisper can be turned into a rope of words to hang you? All walls are not so thick, nor so safe, as these. The least said outside of them the better is it for your own sake and for the sake of — others.'

Was it my fancy that her hard gaze softened as I have seen a hawk's eye sheath itself to a caress?

'I would adjure you, mind how you use the name of the King in your comments on religion. 'Tis a subject best avoided and more than ever so today. It is not so long ago that men were put to the torture, not only on the least suspicion of Popery, but for consorting with Papists. Think how you will there is a community in our Government growing ever stronger in its determination to suppress Romanish corruption in this country. The King is the head and front of our Church and only in the unshaken integral unity of that Church can we as a nation exist. Remember that...'

I had reason enough to remember.

Those words of my Aunt Rossiter's cut deep, to leave a furtive recurrent disquiet like an itching rash that fitfully comes and goes — as when once I had ate of shell-fish out of season. And on that hot green afternoon when I sat with Robin in the park of St James's, I was again disturbed.

We had been speaking, or rather Robin had, of the recent scandal attached to the Earl of Bristol which had caused the greatest stir at court and in the town since the Restoration. The impetuous Bristol — the former Lord Digby of the Civil Wars — had publicly impeached Clarendon of treason on the grounds that he, the King's Chancellor, had endeavoured to fix His Majesty with Romanish persuasions, and that Lord Clarendon had represented himself the sole protector of the Protestant Establishment. Bristol escaped arrest and a possible hanging only by dexterous flight, and was now disconsolately kicking his heels in hiding on the continent.

And said Rob in his slow fashion when we had talked of this: 'I am half sick of these restless spirits — these ill unquiet men who must always be contriving against the several distempers of this creed and that. All such contradictions in religion can only conspire against and lead to the ultimate destruction of the Church —' He turned to me with his swift smile. 'Your Church — not mine, for that stands secure. The rock in the midst of the whirlpool.'

'Hush, pray!' With all my uneasiness returned and rampant, I gave a scared glance round. 'You might be overheard. You are unwise to voice your views abroad.'

He raised a quizzical eyebrow. 'Since when have you turned censor?' Then, quickly, 'Prue … my darling! What's amiss?'

And at that involuntary endearment, the most beloved of and most natural to lovers, my heart fainted and my sense was scattered that I forgot my words until he prompted me, so cool I could not know that all his blood was burning, 'Why must I not voice my views — to you?'

I regained my balance to answer him, 'To me, yes, I am safe … discreet… though sad to hear of this incessant clamour against the Catholics. You … forgive me, Rob, not you alone but all your following, do seem to show some indiscretion and a certain disregard of public feeling. I am afraid.'

His glance upheld me; clear it was and steady. 'Of what are you afraid?'

'Of shadows,' I whispered, with a shiver to raise goose-skin. 'No … of something more concrete. Something my aunt croaked at me, as old women will … and there's nought to it, I'll warrant, when all's told, but she did say, Rob, that there is danger in open talk of Popery, and in especial for one who is of your belief, and danger for you, God forbid, if you should speak too … trusting.'

Well, I had got that packet off my mind and felt the better for it.

'And is that all?' Rob laughed on a breath with the sun in his eyes. 'If that's all the trouble, forget it. I do not fear to speak of my Faith. Danger belongs to the darkness. There can never be danger in light.'

The sun is blinding me, the coloured figures dwindle in the distance. The green alleys are deserted, the laughing voices die away to a thin thread-like echo and are lost in the tramp of feet, the blare of trumpets and the boom of guns…

We are at war.

CHAPTER TWELVE

For months we had waited in a fever of anticipation while the smouldering hostilities between the British and the Dutch, which had never been entirely suppressed since the days of Drake and Tromp, now flared up anew. Although every appearance of friendliness between the world's two greatest naval powers had been preserved, an underlying rivalry for possession of the seas persisted. And while we tensely waited, the Dutchmen also watched. They watched uneasily our gallant fleets in every port in every quarter of the globe. They had seen our commerce growing in the east, in the west, along the coast of Africa, in far America where the Dutch had entrenched themselves in a brave new city, once our own, with a great harbour built to hold great ships. They named it New Amsterdam. The British came and took it from them and renamed that town New York.

In return for which indignity the Dutch attacked our settlements on the coast of Guinea, where they committed the severest depredations, and then sailed off in triumph to the West Indies where they captured twenty of our merchantmen.

So from every trade route in the Seven Seas came news of skirmishes between the Dutch and English, while off the Nore our sturdy East Anglian fishermen sailed past the irate Hollanders to lay their nets under the very noses of Dutch herring-folk and in Dutch waters. At Sheerness, the King, with the Queen and her ladies aboard, and the French Ambassador as guest of honour, reviewed his battle fleet and launched a brave new man-o'-war. There followed a deal of carousing and jollity, until a rising squall drove the Queen and her women inland and prostrated the Frenchman, something to the King's amusement.

Not in the least discomposed himself by the antics of the ship, His Majesty remained on the heaving deck and kept his pallid gentlemen beside him. Percy, who gave me this, was one of them. And 'twas pitiful and most humiliating,' he said, 'to see the collapse of us one by one, while the King, undaunted, stood in the bows with the wind in his hair and declaimed upon the beauties of his vessels, or rather 'war machines', as he somewhat ominously described them. 'The most magnificent, the finest, the largest ever seen afloat.'

Mr Secretary Pepys, full of importance, was in constant confabulation with the Sea Lords; and in Parliament excited members leapt from their seats declaring they would sell their estates to finance war should it come.

It came... And Robin went to it.

There was no holding him even if I would; but I would not. The Duke of York, Lord High Admiral, had asked for volunteers. Robin was one of the first to offer himself. With him went Lords Ferrar, Peterborough, Muskerry, Richard Boyle — Lord Burlington's son — James Rossiter — my uncle's nephew and heir — and many other young gentlemen of our acquaintance.

The night before he left Robin dined with us at our house in Covent Garden. By some singular coincidence, mischance or what you will, Mr Moon made the fourth at table. He had come from Yorkshire the previous week, with a great quantity of baggage, the sight of which beset me with the gravest apprehension that Mr Moon intended his visit to be of some lengthy indefinite period, if not for the remainder of his life.

He looked more than ever like a seedy raven, did our Mr Moon: one that has gone a little bald about the head — if you have ever seen a raven thus — which I have not; yet that is how he did appear to me. And why he had come and with all his belongings, and why Percy received him so anxiously, and was closeted alone with him behind locked doors in an anteroom from which I was excluded, I did not know, for I was never told; but I could and did hazard a guess.

Percy was financially embarrassed and had been so for several years. He lived high and he played deep, losing heavily, and more often than he won. Mr Moon had, I gathered, been sent for at this eleventh hour to size up the situation.

I knew from my Aunt Rossiter, who did not hesitate to tell me bluntly that Percy was indebted to her husband to the tune of several hundreds of pounds; I suspected, too, that Robin, whose vast estates in Warwickshire had been entirely recovered and from which he received a handsome yearly revenue, had also been tapped — to what extent I dared not ask; but greatly did it irk me to think we were beholden to his and my uncle's generosity for such exactments. And now Mr Moon was come to assess my husband's liabilities and avert, I hoped, disaster. At the worst — had I been admitted to the conference — I would have offered my mother's pearls. They were worth a little fortune. There was also the furniture of our London house which Percy had settled on me, and which I would have gladly sold to raise enough to re-establish and relieve my husband from immediate impendence. However as a woman, and therefore nought but a cipher in the sum total of man's affairs, I was not consulted. *So,* said I to myself, *let be — and let him stew, and if he finds himself in Marshalsea, he'll have none but himself to blame.*

These anxieties did not, one may suppose, enliven me to face the ordeal of speeding Robin to the war when he visited us on the eve of his departure.

There we were, the four of us, seated round the table; Mr Moon, my husband, Rob and I. 'It is many years,' said Percy, 'since we all sat together at a meal.'

'I can scarce believe it more than months,' answered Mr Moon with that contortion of his lips which on his face served as a smile. 'When I look upon you now,' and he glanced from me to Percy, but did not glance at Robin, 'I see so little change save in the outward appurtenance of dress, that despite the adage *Tempora mutantur, nos et mutamur*, one would say that Time had halted in his stride.'

But not for him. Mr Moon was considerably changed. Not only was he older, greyer, dingier, but he had developed or cultivated, an incongruous affability that suited him as ill as a butterfly's wings would have suited a slug. He strove to be jocular; he laboured to be winning. But for all his bowings and his scrapings and his evident desire to stand well with me, I liked him none the better than in those days when he used to crown me with a fool's cap and birch my backside till it was raw.

Yet while he evinced for me a marked politeness, and for Percy as much affection as a starfish might bestow upon its young — that is to say as much of kindliness and human sympathy and feeling as lay within the limits of so congealed a soul — his reception of and greeting to Robin was as markedly uncivil and abrupt. His eye was frigid, his mouth awry, his words few and pinched behind his teeth, when Robin, out of devilment I'll be bound, insisted on an answer to his small talk; and an uglier sight than Mr Moon in his most acid humour I have yet to see. But that is how I saw him when he gazed upon

our Robin, who impulsively, warmly, offered his hand —
which Mr Moon refused.

There descended an unconscionable silence.

Behind that rigid back Rob winked at me; Percy frowned and
picked his thumb, and then began to chatter.

The meal was served, but still no word did Mr Moon address
to Robin. He, however, not to be put down by the
implacability of his erstwhile tutor, yet endeavoured to engage
that gentleman's attention, to no purpose. Monosyllabic replies
were all he got. When Robin asked, 'Have you heard of any
case of plague in Yorkshire, sir? Several cases have been
reported in this city.'

'No,' and 'Oh!' said Mr Moon.

'What! Plague!' ejaculated Percy. 'When did you hear that? In
what part of the city? Faith! If the plague has come to town I'll
join the Navy.'

Robin answered, 'They do say 'tis raging at Gravesend and
along the river down by Deptford way.'

Said I: 'You ... you do not board your ship at Gravesend, do
you?'

'No. She lies at Chatham.' Robin raised his glass and bowed
and bobbed, and grinned at Mr Moon across the table. 'And
here's a toast to her — the *Royal Charles*!'

We drank it standing. Mr Moon stood, too. He could not sit
when the King's ship was toasted; but he sipped the wine as it
were dosed with wormwood. Then Percy refilled the glasses,
and Mr Moon, I noticed, drank that bumper at a draught.

The talk soon veered, as it was bound to do, towards the
ever-present topic of the war. Robin again referred to Mr
Moon. 'Think you, sir, that France will ally herself to our cause,
or will Louis slip his treaty with the King?'

For the first time did Mr Moon direct himself to Robin; fixing him with an inquisitorial eye and with his lip caught back on a dry tooth. 'If you are so anxious to know what I think,' he replied, 'I would suggest that neither England nor her King can expect any loyal support from a traitorous Popish ally.'

So now we had it, and Mr Moon's contumely was explained. I had forgot, as had we all, that Mr Moon's aversion to the Catholics amounted to a mania. And here was Robin, whom he once had rescued from perdition, returned to the Romanish Church in all defiance of his early teaching.

Another dreadful pause ensued.

I glanced fearfully at Robin and was thankful to see him unwilling to enter the lists in a tourney of ethical abuse. His fiery look, however, bespoke the challenge he withheld. I was reminded of the wild beasts in their cages at the Tower. I had once seen a jackal and a lion, separately housed but divided only by bars of iron, glaring one against the other in thwarted savagery. Then, his fierce gaze still holding Mr Moon's, Rob spoke.

'In that ill-placed assertion, sir, do you include the Lord High Admiral of the British Fleet — the Duke of York?'

'Ah!' A sound betwixt a snarl and a groan issued from Mr Moon; and if ever I saw madness in a man's eye I saw it flash in his. 'Take heed, Sir Robert, lest by unguarded imputation you confound yourself. Madam,' he started from his seat and turned to me, 'I beg you to excuse my absence from your table. I am loath to indulge in or subject your ladyship to apocryphal discussion. I confess I am completely — nauseated!'

In truth the gentleman had turned so sickly green that I feared he might be overcome before he left the room, but whether this immediate discomposure was induced by the state of his emotions or by an injudicious mixing of his drinks, I cannot say; and no sooner was the door closed on his hasty retreat than:

'Now what in the name of Beelzebub,' demanded Percy, 'possessed you to rile him, Rob? You know how he is tetchy and tarred with the Puritan brush. He'll store this up to hold against you now. You should have remembered how hard he took the news of your conversion when you broke it to him years ago in Paris. Besides which, as you must surely know, the Duke's name — and his propensities — are anathema to Moon.' Percy lowered his lids against the lightning look Robin gave him and continued smoothly, 'He has it fixed that Papistry and treason are synonymous — in especial among those of the Duke's party. He is insane on that one point, and always was.'

'Good life!' exploded Robin, 'what are you saying? And what have *I* said? It was he who put words into my mouth. Insane he is — I can well believe you! As for the Duke's party, as you call it, there is no such thing. As far as I am aware 'tis non-existent, or existing only in the imagination of episcopal fanatics. I can vouch for and take my oath upon it, that His Royal Highness is as loyal and devoted to his brother as he is a true son of the Church.'

Percy smiled. 'Do you mean *your* Church?' he queried, twirling the frail stem of a glass goblet between his fingers. 'There is only one Church for the heir to the Throne — the Church of England. I was not aware that His Royal Highness has yet publicly avowed himself a proselyte. But you, of course, should know.'

'By God, Folliett!' Robin sprang to his feet. 'I do not care for the trend of this talk. 'Twere best we call a truce to it.'

There was a moment's ugly hush. The table candles flickered in their silver stands. I heard Rob's hurried breathing and a light laugh from Percy. 'Why, what's to do? Why are you ablaze?' He stretched his arm to touch Robin's across the polished board. 'Are we to come to words over the mouthings of an irrational old wind-bag with the gout in his knee-caps and gallstones in his heart?' His gaze shifted to mine; his smile closed. 'And here's Prue, now, all melting eyes and ghostly! Has our holy pastor frighted you, my dear? One would think you had slipped back a dozen years and were in a shake, expectant of His Reverence's rod. Do you remember how you used to come to me — *and* Robin — lifting up your petticoats to show us — a shameless piece you were! — the red marks on your pretty little seat?'

'Never!' I cried, thankful for any diversion from this threatened duel of words, which might, heaven knows, have led to a duel of arms, for men were quick to draw the sword on any provocation in those days, 'never have I been known to so demean myself, and if I did — how young was I? Not more than eight, I'll swear. Why throw *that* in my teeth?'

'Well, well, let be! Here's Rob as red as his hair and darting fire. He takes amiss my allusion to your dainty parts, my love. I fear me,' said Percy with laughter narrowing his eyes, ' that our artless Robin will never accustom himself to the libidinous, disreputable modes — and codes — of our wicked London life, unless it be that he adopts a monastic austerity, further to ensnare the ladies; for in truth, Rob, you have the enviable reputation of having more women at your feet — and your disposal — than any Turk in his seraglio. We must find you a wife, Robin, and see you safely settled and protected. Come, fill the cups. We will drink to the fair unknown — your future mistress. Come fill up — fill up! We must drink to your health and hers, wherever she is and whoever she be. Your cup, man! Drink! You'll never taste such wine as this aboard.'

They clinked glasses. I released my bitten underlip.

'You are mistaken,' said Robin, level-voiced. 'I have seen to it I shall. I've ordered a hogshead of my finest claret to be brought from my cellars at home.'

Percy glanced at him slantwise. 'You are lucky to have your cellars full. Mine are as empty as my pockets. We are drinking my last pipe, and when that is gone —' He broke off, shrugging his shoulders in the Frenchified fashion he had learned abroad.

Said Robin, straightly, 'If you're hard pressed I will be glad to—'

'No,' said I with haste.

'To drink the health,' interrupted Percy, loud, 'of one who is my more than brother.'

The wine had worked in him to good effect. He sparkled, jested, teased and toasted Robin, who, too, had taken as much as he could carry, only that having a stronger head he knew how to hold his liquor. Then when we had drunk three times three to the King, Robin called the toast of the evening:

'To Prue!'

The watchman was crying one o' the clock when Robin left. This moment I had dreaded was now come. Yet none to see me fling away those last few precious minutes in the most trivial talk would have guessed how I ached, soul and body — as a thousand other women in England ached that night, and have done and will do through time immemorial, to see their men go bravely off to war.

But though my heart was mercifully frozen, my perceptions were the more acutely tuned. I saw the moonlight shining like silver water on the cobble-stones, on rooftops, and on chimneys huddled in gnomish shapes under the blossoming sky. I saw the shadows, black and angular, slicing the moon-white walls in a fantasy of geometrical precision; I heard the gruff voices of the chairmen and link-boys grouped around the vacant booths under the sycamore trees. Somewhere in the near darkness I heard the hideous growling overtures of amorous cats rise to a startling triumphant screech; and from some distant tavern a woman's shrill laugh and the sound of a drunken song.

I heard my own voice speaking words jerked from my lips on a smile that felt like the grin of a skull. 'Goodbye — no, I will not say goodbye. The war will be over before we have had time to miss you. The Dutch will turn tail when they meet our ships ... please God.'

And I saw, and dared not see, Rob's eyes so deep in mine as I stood in the light of the open door.

'Amen to that,' said Percy. 'May God bless and protect you, Robin. May you come back to us soon and come back to us safe. My prayers ... and my love ... go with you.'

And I remember how he took Robin's hand and kissed him and called him friend.

That was in April, and thereafter the days, weeks, months were narrowed to a time of waiting for such news as I could glean from the tittle-tattle of the court. It was not my custom to stroll as many women did, decked out in their latest finery, through the Galleries of Whitehall pecking in the dust of gossip for succulent morsels with which to flavour the hot-pot of scandal. But now, when at all costs I must learn, and dared not ask direct for news of him from Percy — since intuition warned me it were best not to evince too much anxiety for Robin's welfare — I joined the throng of fashion at their morning rendezvous in the King's Gallery, dressed in full rig and in defiance of the tongues that licked at Robin's name and mine with foul insinuation.

I was well aware that odious inference had been drawn from our triangular friendship; and I also knew or guessed at last what I should long ago have realised, that in Percy the seeds of suspicion had taken root, to sprout. He watched me, and knowing this I did not scruple to fling dust in his eyes. I collected a train of admirers. There was young Sidney, most attentive, and the Marquis de Grammont — a great wit and greater gossip — who had come to the English court to carry back satirical impressions in his notebook for the delectation of King Louis. He professed himself adoring, and I pampered him for no other reason than that he had a finger in everybody's pie. There was also George Hamilton, nephew of the Marquis — now created Duke — of Ormond. Very handsome, very witty, very polished was this young man, possessed of the happiest talents, an assiduous courtier and in greatest favour with the ladies. Him I secured to set the whispers flying behind the vizard-masks: 'Off with the last love — on with the new! She, forsooth, who would never show her turned-up nose inside the Galleries when Peverill was on the carpet, is soon consoled!'

So far so good, and better still when Percy taxed me with my 'bold infatuation' to make his name stink and myself a laughing stock.

'Here's this braggart Hamilton boasting of his conquest in every coffee-house in Town. Am I to suffer this indignity and go horned by a wanton drab?'

'Tush!' I retorted. 'There's naught but self-love in his bragging. You should know by now that the man who talks most acts least.'

'I have seen you sit cheek by jowl with him in the Galleries holding hands and squawking in your laughter like a dairy-maid.'

'Be damned to that! He was telling me my fortune in my palm. He is of Irish extraction and has the merriest, drollest wit, and the second sight to a miracle. He was born with a cowl on his head, so he says.'

'And he'll die by my sword in his guts,' Percy raged, 'if I see you hand in fist with him again. Have you no shame?'

'Not so much as would sit on a farthing,' quoth I, 'since my mind is as easy as my body's chaste. May I perish at your feet if I have had to do with any man saving your lordship's self. And only you — and your God — knows how much or how little that is.'

This remark, the first of its kind I had ever pointed at my husband — for in all our life together I had not once alluded to the unnatural circumstance of our relationship — effectually silenced him. But when. I saw him flinch at my words I regretted my haste and was eager to cover it. 'Why should you taunt me, my soul? Let us not scratch at each other over a smirking popinjay that is no more to me than the buckle on my shoe.'

He was not to be so easily beguiled. I had pricked him, and I saw his eyes and knew his pain, and cursed myself for a babbling jade who deserved to be whipped for her folly. And what had I gained from it? Nothing. Not the smallest scrap of news from the fleet. The Galleries were less concerned with the course of the war than their fear of the plague in the town.

It was spreading. It had crept from Gravesend to a village on the outskirts of London. At first they made a jest of it: ''Tis plaguey news the plague has come to Southwark. God send it will not come within three miles of Whitehall!'

But within three months it was within three yards of the king's palace…

It stalked the corpse-strewn streets where men dropped as they went on their business in a deserted city. Grass sprang up between the cobble-stones, and red crosses a foot long, bearing the sinister inscription *God have mercy on us*, flourished on every other door. Bonfires were lit on Ludgate Hill and in High Holborn and Cheapside, not now for joy, but to create a draught in the thick heavy air of the hottest summer on record: no rain to wash the streets, no breath of wind to carry off the dregs of the infection, no sound save the shrieks of the stricken, the groans of the dying and the rumble of the death-carts on their nightly rounds, where once the gilded coaches used to pass. No quarter of London was unaffected. The court and the King had left, and all those who could afford to go had gone; only the poor remained, and a few courageous gentlemen — the Archbishop of Canterbury, the Duke of Albemarle, better known to us all as Monk; Lord Craven, the Lord Mayor, the sheriffs, the aldermen — and the physicians. Yes, they stayed; and selflessly, courageously did they fight with every weapon of the latest medical science at their command, to destroy the creeping horror: and one by one they gave their lives in vain. Higher and higher rose the Bill of Mortality. In less than a month it had leapt from two hundred and sixty-seven to one thousand and eighty-nine.

We went. I admit my cowardice; I could not stay. I was not afraid to die, but I did fear death in such a form. I had heard unspeakable tales. Thirza, you may be sure, had blood-curdling accounts to give, claiming first-hand knowledge of sights witnessed, which I doubted; for although she remained in London some two weeks after Percy, I, and Mr Moon had left, to dismantle the house and disband our servants, the plague had not yet encroached on Covent Garden when Thirza rejoined us at Folly's End.

And that was in June, when the whole countryside was pealing with the news of a tremendous victory.

The Dutch, who during the first weeks of war had been in little evidence while our ships harried the seas for signs of them, had now come out in force under the command of Opdam. The two fleets sighted each other on June 1st, and on the 3rd came the great clash. Both sides, equally matched, fought with excessive valour on that day of our signal triumph, in as glorious a battle as ever was known since the days of Elizabeth's Drake.

Opdam, with his squadron, bore down directly on the Duke, intending to board his main target, the flagship; but no sooner was he within range of fire than a volley from the *Royal Charles* set the Dutch admiral's ship ablaze and she sank with every one of her men, including the gallant Opdam. Percy brought me this news from Dorchester. For my life I could not hide my feelings nor suppress the cry that sprang to my lips: 'The *Royal Charles*! O, God ... is Robin safe?'

'Robin?' Percy's eyes were on me like bluest water and as cold. 'It is early days to tell, my love. There have been many killed and wounded. The Duke is safe, however. We shall hear — we shall hear,' he added airily. 'Do not distress yourself. I, too, am anxious for my ... brother, but in war one must be equally prepared for ill as for good news. Meanwhile I must tell you that our Uncle Rossiter writes to me — I received his letter this morning delivered by hand — that our good aunt has been seized with an apoplexy, and your presence at her bedside would be appreciated. It is highly improbable that the old lady will recover. I cannot attend with you for I am called to the King. So do you go without me — and I go to Hampton Court.'

Grieved though I was to hear of my poor old aunt's condition, I was also thankful to have this immediate distraction from my ever-increasing fear on Rob's account. Moreover I guessed that my uncle would receive news from the battle front before ever we could; and as a third consideration I was not unwilling to leave my house now Mr Moon was there re-lodged within it. So on June 6th I departed with Thirza by coach, while Percy rode off to Hampton Court with his lackey, and every conceivable precaution concocted by Thirza against the plague. I too was dosed with a mixture of strange compounds to such extent that my palate completely lost its taste for normal diet. Among the most obnoxious of these — but fortunately I did not know until long afterwards of what the brew consisted, when I found the prescription given to Thirza by her crony, the wise woman of Broadwindsor — was the juice of fresh cow-dung strained in vinegar, diluted with snail-water and sweetened with treacle. Percy, seriously alarmed lest he should meet infection, took everything Thirza advised him, including a collection of amulets: a dried toad skin, the entrails of a mouse sewn into a small linen bag and scented with lavender — which it needed, believe me — a goose quill dipped in mercury, and a length of scarlet wool to wear round his middle, a guaranteed prevention, Thirza said.

I found my aunt in a sad state. The attack that had struck her down had entirely bereft her of speech and twisted one side of her poor old face into a perpetual grin, most terrifying and grievous to behold. Dr Sydenham, now a Fellow of the Royal Society, was in constant attendance, lodging at Templecombe, but nothing, it was understood, could be done for her.

Dr Sydenham was little changed since I had seen him last at the time of my father's death; somewhat plumper and pinker, still as boyishly fair, though he was over forty, with the same kindly twinkle in his small piggish eyes. I admit to a slight surprise, or disappointment in the fact that so renowned a physician had joined the general exodus from London, while others less famous, less skilled, from the humblest apothecary and barber's surgeon to the King's doctor had remained at their posts to grapple with death. However, I learned later that he had been engaged in treating the cases that were spreading from the capital to the market towns of Middlesex, and took the same courageous risk as did his colleagues in the city.

But he held out little hope for my poor aunt. It might be a matter of days, he said, or weeks or even months; and I prayed it might be soon, not so much for her sake, dear soul, for I was assured she suffered nothing, being for the most part semi-conscious, but for my uncle's peace. He had, I knew, taken much to heart his good wife's sudden collapse. It was pitiful to see that once indomitable spirit shrouded in crumbling flesh. Only at rare intervals did I observe a flicker of recognition in the dimmed sunken eyes. But when I sat with her and stroked the brittle hand outstretched upon the coverlid, I think she knew of and was grateful for my presence.

One evening, about ten days after my arrival at my uncle's house, he came to the door of my aunt's chamber where I sat at her bedside, and beckoned me from the room.

'Send her woman to her,' he whispered, 'I have news for you.'

News...! There was only one news that my heart craved. I followed him, wondering, fearing.

'I have had —' my uncle told me in his hesitating way, 'a letter from an eye-witness of the b-battle — a young kinsman of my own, my dead brother's son. You may read it, for it concerns you...' Then seeing my trouble, 'There is no cause for alarm, my child,' he said quickly. ' Robert Peverill is — is safe.'

'Safe! Robin! Oh, Uncle...'

Safe! But how could Uncle Rossiter have known I was tormented? And as if he read that question in my eyes, my uncle told me how that his young nephew James had been aboard the *Royal Charles* with Robin. 'They were g-good friends together, and Robert, it seems did, in the event of any untoward occurrence to himself, desire him to — to — acquaint you of the matter — and your husband, that is to say, who — who though n-neither you nor Percy are of blood kin to him — you are both his closest n-nearest associates...' My uncle was stammering so dreadfully and had become so red in the face that all my fears returned.

'Untoward?' I gasped. 'Then something *has* arisen! What is it? Tell me!...'

'He is wounded, my dear,' said my uncle, 'but nothing, I think,' he hastened to add, 'of a — of a serious nature. Here is the letter. Read it for yourself.' He handed me two sheets of closely scribbled parchment, patted my shoulder, smiled — somewhat meaningly, I thought — and left me alone.

Having read the letter twice, I set myself to copy it that I might ever have it there to read again for my heart's comfort.

And here I give it you in part.

Aboard the Royal Charles
June 4th, 1665.

The Dutch have fought like Tygers, as resolute an ennemie as ever could be met with, in especial Admirall Opdam whose ship was blowne up and sunk before our eyes with all her Crew aboard. It is rumoured that Tromp

*— grandson of Blake's famous Antagoniste hath been lost and other of
their Admiralls, yet we have had no certain Confirmation on this count.
But it is believed we have taken some Four and Twenty of their Ships and
killed near upon 10,000 of their men as against our 700. And no more
loss to the Duke than one small Ship of his whole Fleete. Prince Rupert's
Ship hath allso done great service with the loss of the Earl of Sandwich,
who behaved with exceeding bravery. There is allso slain the Earl of
Marlborough in Command of his own Ship.'*

Here I skipped a page, for much as I was eager for news of
our valorous seamen I must come to that which concerned me
most...

*Now for the 'Charles', who of all that noble Squadron did conduct
herself with greatest Honour and tho' I am in her I must be forgiven if I
boast her in my Pride. She stood in the Front of the Battle Line, with the
Duke, our Admirall, on the Bridge, commanding the Engagement with
incomparable Courage that did inspire us all with a like Confidence, and
not a man but would not have followed him had he bid us jump into the
Sea. No fear of that! It was the Dutch that jumped — to save theirselves! A horrid sight, but worse aboard among our Dead and Wounded.
Lord Falmouth has gone and my good friend Richard Boyle who was
killed within ten yards of the same shot that took Muskerry. The Duke,
no less than myself, was bespattered by their blood and brains. Sir Robert
Peverill got the splinter of a musket bullet in his leg and a more severe hurt
to his right arm, but withal he did continue to direct his men at the
Cannon, nor when the Duke, who had an eye for every man on Deck
ordered him below to the Chirurgeon's attention, did he desert his Post but
stood throwing Grenadoes with his uninjured left hand untill from loss of
blood he dropped and was carried by his men to the Sick Baye. When
later I visitted him there I found him weak but cheerful and he did bid me
when I write you, my Uncle, to give this News of him and beg of you to tell*

*your Niece and Nephew, Lord and Lady Folliett, that he is safe and will
be home so soon as the Dutch are play'd out...*

I guessed that Robin had sent this message unable to write
himself, and knowing how I waited. Having copied what I
needed of the letter, I returned it to my uncle with no other
comment than, 'I am thankful indeed that Robin's injury is no
worse than a flesh wound. This is a most interesting
documentary evidence ... and I thank you, Uncle.'

He looked at me with his head on one side, and smiled again;
and said nothing.

All through that summer the pestilence raged with frightful
violence, not only in the City of London, but in the country.
By the end of August the highest weekly total of deaths in
London alone had reached five thousand.

In September my poor Aunt Rossiter died at the age of
seventy-two. Her end was a painless and blessed release from
months of living death.

I remained at Templecombe until after the funeral which
Percy came from Hampton Court to attend. Among the
Rossiter relatives was my uncle's young nephew, James, whom
I had not seen since he was a boy of eleven. He was now one
and twenty, a well-set-up handsome youth, with a cheery smile
and a face burnt by the sun to a fierce brick red, having
recently come from the battle front at sea. He had been staying
a few days at Templecombe and when the dismal rites were
over, before Percy and I left for home, I took the opportunity
to ask him, in my husband's presence, how Robin fared and if
he knew whether or no he had returned, for we had heard
nothing of him since the message he had sent to us both.

'Yes, indeed,' James Rossiter told me, 'Sir Robert is home again. He returned with the Duke and is lodged at Wilton as a guest of their Highnesses, who have taken their family there for safety from the plague.'

'Is he recovered of his wounds?' Percy asked.

'In so far as you may call it recovered,' James answered soberly. 'He has lost his right arm, poor fellow.'

I felt the colour drain from my face. I saw Percy's eyes widen, heard my uncle's exclamation of dismay. The room spun, dipped and darkened; only by the most supreme effort of will I kept my head, aware that Percy was staring at me and through me with a strange fixed look.

'His ... right...' The words died on my lips.

'How very shocking,' murmured my uncle; he too was watching me, and as he spoke he rose from his chair to pour four beakers from the flagon of canary on the table; handing a glass to me he said, 'We should, however, be thankful his life is spared. Will you take wine, my dear? Percy, James? It has been a trying day for all of us. We n-need a stimulant.'

Most certainly I did; and was grateful for my uncle's timely intervention, which I think had saved me from a swoon. He must surely have observed my deathly pallor.

'So my good friend Peverill,' said Percy, addressing James but still gazing hard at me, 'has lost his right hand — a terrible calamity for one so active. However, I have no doubt he will find compensation. I am told that those who lose their sight or hearing are the better endowed by their remaining senses. He will learn to use his left hand to stronger purpose... And so he lodges with the Duke, you say, for his recuperation?'

'His Royal Highness,' answered James, 'was exceeding grieved to hear of Sir Robert's injury.'

'I am sure of that,' reflected Percy, sipping wine. 'My good friend Peverill is the Duke's most intimate and favoured gentleman.'

'Sir Robert is a Catholic, is he not?' queried James.

'Unfortunately, yes.' Percy looked along his nose and drained his glass.

I set down mine. 'If you will excuse me, Uncle, I will retire to my chamber. I am … fatigued.'

'You are shocked, my love,' said Percy, rising too, 'as am I, to hear this distressing news of our good Robin.' He turned to James with a smile that showed his teeth and hid his lips. 'You will readily understand, Mr Rossiter, that my wife and I — and Sir Robert Peverill — having been reared together under one roof, feel the same concern and love for him as that of a brother — and sister.'

'Certainly. Quite,' mumbled young James, turning, if possible, a fiercer red; he must have been aware, I think, of the sudden tension, or he may have heard the talk that buzzed about my name and Robin's at Whitehall. But I cared not what he thought and if he wondered. I must get out of that room and away from my husband's smile…

The gentlemen bowed me to the door; Percy opened it, saying soft in my ear, 'Go you and rest, my love. This disastrous news has put you down completely.'

I ran to my chamber and sent for Thirza to tell her what I had learned, and, overwrought, I wept. She strove to soothe me. 'There's nothing so bad that it might not be worse. Be thankful he has lost his arm and not his sight. Be thankful he's alive… And now a word of warning for my lady dear, from one who is her second mother. Don't let his lordship see how you are sorrowed.'

I dried my eyes. 'I know, I know! He is mad suspicious now of me and Robin. But there is nought between us.'

'There is everything between you,' Thirza said, stroking my bowed head. 'Love cannot be hid. 'Tis like the plague. You bring it with you. It fills the air and it is so infectious that those around you smell it! Oh, I'll not deny you've both been careful—'

I turned upon her quivering. 'Hold your insolent tongue! How dare you speak so — and to me! I make no excuse or apology to my servant, but this I swear before Almighty God that I and he —'

'My own darling!' Thirza snatched me to her. 'There's no cause for you to swear, nor curse. Your Thirza knows your innocence and his. Am I not watchful for you all the time? Have I not seen, and seeing, have I not suffered with you? Am I not a woman with a woman's yearnings like your own, though you be a great lady and I but a common slut? Yet I have found my happiness and you, my dear, go starved — all these long years — yes, yes, my sweet one! Cry your heart out here on Thirza's bosom — did it not give you suck? So let it give you comfort. Let it come — bring it up then. There! All the sorrow and the anguish — oh, the pity of it! Yes, I have known; ever since he ceased to share your bed I knew. As a child he was undeveloped. God pity you both! Is that a natural life for a young couple? And if you and Sir Robert were to take what Nature offers, who would blame you or condemn? Not your Thirza, who lives only to serve you... Now let me mix your ladyship a posset that you'll sleep and wake refreshed — and never think to hide yourself from me.'

So she knew! An immense load was lifted from my mind. I had one with whom to share my secret — and my husband's. She had guessed, and I could not now deny it, as once I did to my Aunt Rossiter. I needed someone in whom to confide; I had lived too long within myself alone ... I was relieved.

We returned to Folly's End that same week to find Mr Moon still in residence and likely to remain so. I did, however, strive to conceal my dissatisfaction at the way he had settled himself upon us, aware that I should be grateful to him for delivering Percy from his financial embarrassments. At Mr Moon's advice my husband had sold some few hundred acres of the Wynmonath estate, sufficient to meet the better part of his more pressing liabilities. The remaining debts he owed could, Mr Moon decided, be paid out of the sale of certain of my jewels which Percy in his generous extravagance had bought from time to time; to which I readily agreed, and offered my jewel-box for Mr Moon's inspection, retaining only my mother's pearl necklace and His Majesty's ruby ring.

Mr Moon returned my jewel-box empty.

I do not know if my uncle heard of this or if my aunt had expressed the wish that in the event of her death I was to have possession of her jewellery, but one day my uncle arrived at our house with a great silver casket under his arm which he begged me to accept. It contained Great-aunt Rossiter's jewels, of far greater worth than mine; nevertheless I was grieved to part with the trinkets my husband had given me and which I cherished, less for their value than for their associations. I was also surprised that Percy so easily consented to Mr Moon's expedience in thus depriving me of my few treasures; but indeed of late he seemed to be completely in the hand of Mr Moon; docile, willing, and respectfully disposed as he were once again the favoured pupil — and I the despised dunce. It needed only Robin to repeat the picture of our youth.

There he sat, did Mr Moon, at the foot of the table and in my place; Percy at the head, I at his right. Day in day out at breakfast, dinner, supper, so did we sit; I for the most part dumb, Mr Moon, odiously affable, Percy chattering of the war, the plague, the harvest, which had been so plentiful that year he hoped to recover from it much of his financial loss; but more often than he talked was he silent and picking his thumbs to bleed. And Rob's name was never mentioned.

In October, when news came that at last the plague was abating, Percy departed for Oxford where Parliament had reassembled, driven from Westminster by the sickness, and where the King and the court had come to attend the opening of the new session.

I stayed at Folly's End with Mr Moon.

It was a wonder to me why our chaplain had not persuaded Percy to bestow upon him the preferment of Wynmon Abbas; but his reticence was not, I think, prompted by regard for our worthy vicar, Mr Hollingsworth, since I am sure Mr Moon would not have hesitated to take the living from the present incumbent of it, had he so wished to do. I can only suppose that as Mr Moon was now well over sixty years of age, he did not feel disposed to undertake parochial responsibilities. He had some small private means, our house at his disposal, Percy in his pocket, and the pulpit of our parish church at his command. There, any Sunday that he pleased, by permission of our kindly vicar, preached Mr Moon, too often for my liking. His sermons were long and dreary and almost always threateningly directed at the Catholics. And sometimes he would single me out from his listeners where I sat in the Folliett pew, to fix me with a rolling eye and pointed finger thundering into my uplifted face all the horrors that awaited sinners in the Pit, that I believed the whole congregation must be agape to see me chosen from among them for such especial warning.

After two Sundays of this and two weeks of intolerable tedium, I decided that I would sooner risk infection from the plague than suffer Mr Moon another day. So towards the end of October I departed with Thirza for London.

There the pestilence continued to show a marked decrease; the Bill of Mortality had reached its highest peak in September, with a total of over twenty thousand for the month. In November a hard frost set in, and by the spring of the New Year, 1666, the Great Plague — the Great Judgment, some called it — had passed.

CHAPTER THIRTEEN

Town was filling up again. The red crosses vanished from the doors. The dead carts ceased their nightly rounds, and once more the painted coaches plied back and forth between the mansions of the wealthy and Whitehall. But it was not until March that the careless pleasures of court life replaced the memory of death that lurked in the putrefying pest-holes.

It must have been in February, when we had the sudden cold spell that froze the artificial water in St James's Park, and sent the younger and more daring of us to try our prowess on the ice.

Percy was an adept, having learned in his travels abroad how to cut intricate figures of eight, and to speed like a bird over the slippery surface; but I had yet to master this latest sport of fashion.

Ever happy to teach, as when years ago he had so carefully guided me through the first book of Euclid and over the Pons Asinorum, Percy showed infinite patience in his instruction, supporting me while my feet encased in cunning little fur-lined boots with a steel knife-edge beneath them, slid all ways at once; so that only by clinging to my husband in an embrace more terrified than ardent could I maintain my balance.

I, who as a child had taken my fair share in the boys' games and hobbies, and could, in those days, out-race them on a horse if not upon my legs, was enraged to find myself so clumsy. I had dressed for the part in the daintiest habit of purple velvet, with a gentlemanly waistcoat and a little fur tippet and hood lined with violet quilted satin, and I carried a muff which I soon discarded, although my fingers in their unprotected gauntlets turned as cold as the ice over which I so helplessly floundered. However I persevered, and after some several ventures showed enough proficiency to stand alone.

A crisp sparkling day that was; the trees, stark and soot-begrimed — so unlike the tender greyish-green winter trees of Dorset — were traced against the clear translucent sky as if cut out of black paper. The sun, withheld behind the flimsiest cloud, peeped in and out with whimsical caprice as though he had mistook the time of year for April. The air was full of laughter and a crystalline intoxication in its very breath. Not for a long time had I felt so happy, with Percy more attentive and agreeable than I had known him since Mr Moon's return.

All the world was out to play. I saw Mistress Stewart, very pretty, with her rosy cheeks and her little Roman nose and her dark curls bobbing under a yellow bird's-eye hood. Percy whispered scandal in my ear while he dragged me round.

'The King is in that state that he cannot leave her for an hour, day or night! He returns to the Queen's chamber in the early morning that he may be seen circumspectly with his wife for breakfast... Look now at the Castlemaine, she's big again — you see? She thinks by handing out another royal bastard to His Majesty that she will hold him —'

'Hold *me!* Hold *me!*' I screamed. 'Damnation to her bastards — I am slipping!'

'You go too fast!' laughed Percy, as he adroitly saved me. 'Now, then — one, two — no, no! you are too eager. Take it slow. Here comes the King to watch us. Sit you awhile, my dear. You must not let His Majesty see you go so awkward. I will skate around and come back to you.'

And hastily depositing me on the frosty bank, Percy darted away like a swallow. I watched his slight elegant figure swerve and sway and spin, executing prodigious circles, gliding and twirling with the most graceful ease, for the approval of the King and his gentlemen. And finding it mighty cold where I was seated on the rime-encrusted grass, I decided I would take a turn alone. Very gingerly I made my way along the edge of the lake to a solitary corner where I might slither unobserved by any but the melancholy water fowl and a mocking red-billed jackdaw. I had mastered my skates enough to slide on the ice without a tumble — as I thought.

But no sooner was I up than I was down, with my ankle twisted under me in a sharp agonising wrench. And there I lay a-sprawl, unable to move for the pain in my foot. A pretty pickle was I in, with none but myself to thank for it, and nought to do but wait for Percy to come round again and find me; and when he did — dear Lord, how I was scolded! You would have thought I had committed felony or worse. Such a fuss as my misfortune occasioned, that I heartily wished myself under the ice rather than exposed in my shame upon it. All the ladies were in giggles, and gloating, I'll be bound, to see me brought so low; and the gentlemen in a great concern, with offers to carry me bandy-chair and pick-a-back — whichever I might choose — to my coach at the park gates. But Percy would have none of that, and sent for a sedan to bear me away in state with my ankle swollen to the size of a water-melon, and myself in a rare taking.

This adventure laid me up for near upon six weeks. The chirurgeon said I had fractured a bone in my foot. He packed it in clay to set it; and thus tied to the couch in my room I knew little of the world outside or of the daily gossip that ran through the Galleries, save for gleanings brought to me by Thirza; nor could she tell me any news that I most longed to hear. Where, all this time, was Robin?

I had heard no more of him than that he was at St James's Palace with the Duke, but he had not called upon me to enquire how I did. He may not have been told of my mishap. And why indeed should he have been told of it? I had fallen on the ice and had broke an ankle, but why should any noise be made of that? It was doubtful if my absence from the social roundabout had been so much as noticed. True, the King had graciously expressed his regret at the time of the accident, and had asked my husband to report upon my progress. I had received gifts of flowers, comfits, fruit from the gentlemen of my immediate acquaintance, and visits from the ladies; but the talk they gave was of nothing save themselves, their latest gowns, the deplorable lack of domestics since the war and the Plague had carried off so many of our servants: or of the recent masquerade held by the King to celebrate the birthday of the Stewart. This function Percy attended, and I had already heard from him how the King had led with Mistress Stewart in the French Brawl, and had partnered her six times out of a dozen until midnight when the guests unmasked. Then a picked few, my husband among them, drove off to Newmarket as drunk as could be, in a cortège of coaches half a mile long.

I was told also by one of my lady visitors that the Duke, it was said, had set himself to be a rival to the King in a certain quarter, and had side-glassed Mistress Frances all through the play at the Duke's Theatre, where she lolled in the King's box, while the Castlemaine opposite tore her handkercher to shreds between her teeth in such a jealous rage you never saw! And I learned also of the scuffle between the Duke of Buckingham and the Marquis of Dorchester. This had made the whole town rock: the two had come to blows, it seems — 'Can your ladyship conceive it! At a Parliament assembly — as I live! —

where the Lords were attending a conference to do with the Irish Bill. I wonder Lord Folliett did not tell you.'

'He seldom sits in the House of Commons or the Lords,' I said, 'unless at a trial of his peers.'

'Only fancy! But this contention now — it would be vastly ridiculous were it not so very shocking. I beg you to imagine, my dear creature, how the one asking leave to change his posture with the other — Dorchester being fat as a barrel and taking all the room upon the bench — Buckingham endeavoured by jostling and pushing, to get himself more comfortably placed and did fall upon the marquis with his fists, whereupon Dorchester returned the Duke a thump upon the nose and lost his periwig to be found — ha, ha! — as hairless as an egg. And for their disgrace I vow — was ever anything so laughable? — they both are in the Tower!'

They both can be in hell for all I care, thought I. *What… oh, what of Robin?*

'Good day, dear Lady Folliett…'

'Good day to you, madam; obliged, I'm sure. I could not have been more sweetly entertained. A thousand thanks for the tasty fruit. Peaches are my passion…'

They came and went like gaudy parrots in their gay coloured dress, painted, patched, hard of eye, and quacking mischief.

Tansy came. She had borne her husband four children in six years and looked more than ever globular in her fur-betrimmed cloak of green camlet, and a huge sable muff that almost entirely extinguished her. ' To hide me,' she explained, ' for I am five months gone again. Oh, Prue! I am disposed to envy you for a barren woman, which certain you must be, never to conceive. This will be my fifth. I do assure you no sooner am I done with weaning one than I am heavy with another, that I never seem to have my body to myself.'

'It is you who should be envied,' I answered, keeping calm, for as always Tansy had that effect upon me to spring claws, 'that every time I have conceived I have miscarried!'

'Oh, Prue! And is that so?' Tansy stroked her monstrous muff as it were our tom-cat, and stared at me with eyes like little moons. 'Then what is said of you is lies. I thought as much.'

'All is lies that's spoken here in London.' I gazed up at the ceiling. 'What, pray, is said of me?'

'Oh, no ... oh, truly!' tittered Tansy. 'I am embarrassed... Let me adjust your coverlid, my dear, you've kicked it off. Does your foot pain you? Will you be lamed for life?'

'Though I hate to disappoint you, I think not,' I returned with smiles.

'Oh, Prue, you always were so quick to take me up. What a sweet pretty coverlid this is to be sure. Did you embroider it?'

'No. What lies are said of me?'

'Nothing of the smallest matter, I assure you. Only that ... oh, must I say it? ... that you and your husband do not couple now together and have not for these several... Oh, Prue, you did insist I tell you!'

I managed to keep calm. 'This,' I said still smiling, 'beats all! To have Dame Gossip at the keyhole to watch a man bed with his wife and then run round the town with her mouth full of dirt. What next shall I hear, I wonder? That in order to withhold my husband from my company I turn myself o' nights into a were-wolf?'

''Pon honour, Prue!' retorted Tansy, 'you look at me so savage one would think so! But you've not heard me out. They do say it is on account of your inclination for Sir Robert Peverill that you misplace your husband, and that he is raging hot and out to kill.'

'Why, here's a tale!' quoth I, well in command of myself. 'Come spew it up, my dear, before it chokes you! Let us have it all.'

'That *is* all,' pouted Tansy, 'and enough, I should have thought. I should sink myself an it were said of me.'

'Never fear,' I assured her, 'you'll as like be coupled with Sir Robert Peverill — or any other man — as a rhinoceros. So faithful loving you are — as well does show.'

'Oh, Prue! Despite my muff?' cried Tansy. 'I thought I'd hid my state. You have the bitterest tongue, my dear.'

'I've a bitter taste o' London on it. Here's a comfit,' I offered a silver dish, 'for sweetness.' And winningly I added, having no desire to quarrel with this ball of nonsense before I had pumped the stuffing out of her, 'So would you be curst, my love, if you lay stretched as I have these five weeks and am carried in and out of my coach by my footman like a babe in arms and no sight of the gay life, more than can be seen through my glass windows. I might as soon be in a plague-pit. But leaving personalities I beg — for I would be sorry indeed to speak words I should regret, being ginger-tempered, my sweet Tansy, and born so for my sins — I would be glad to be enlivened with the latest tattle of the Town as only you know how to give it.'

Recovering her good humour at this artless appeal, Tansy answered, 'Well, my dear, the latest is — and nothing else is talked of — but the Duke's passion for the Stewart.'

'Pooh!' I fetched a yawn. ''Tis already stale. Madam Thingummy was full of it when she visited me here a week ago!'

'They do say, however,' persisted Tansy, 'that the King is turned against his brother, and all on account of Mistress Stewart.'

'Fiddle-de-dee!' said I. 'Never were two brothers more attached. They'd not be parted for a mincing doll-faced sugar-stick. Not likely!'

'So you think! I know better.' Tansy gave a half-glance round each shoulder. 'Oh, Prue, are we talking treason?'

'Talk on. There's none can hear us.'

'Frank says,' whispered Tansy, her lips like over-ripened cherries at my ear, 'Frank says that the Duke's party is fanning the least excuse of discord between the King and his brother for an open breach to put the Duke where the King ... oh, mercy, I'll be axed for this if I am heard!'

'You'll not be heard. Go on.'

'And they say that the Papists are at the root of all the trouble and Robert Peverill — oh, Prue, you'll take this hard — is the worse offender, being hand in glove with the Duke of York, and has been known to voice it —'

'Voice what?' I asked, cold to my feet.

'That the Duke of York, being more sober-minded and a Catholic, should wear the Crown and not ... and not the King.'

'Take care, Tansy!' My hand went out to grab her arm and inflict upon its plumpness a pinch to bring a squeal from her.

'Oh, Prue, you spiteful toad! I vow I'll be delivered of a child with the sign of a black grape on its forehead. Look how you have marked me!'

'Ay, and I'll have you topped and tailed, too, for speaking slander — you viperous buffle-headed spindrift!' At which, inexcusably, I slapped her face.

'Merciful heaven!' yelled Tansy. 'Would you have me miscarry here at your feet, Abomination? Oh! To so abuse and spite me in my fifth month...'

Then was I greatly frighted lest I'd harmed her, for she was weeping loud with sobs and screams, that forgetful of my crippled foot I got myself off my couch and hopped to the bell to pull it, while I strove to pacify the poor thing. 'Tansy! Tansy! My dear, good, sweetest friend — be calm! Compose yourself. I deserve to be dragged to the whipping-post and would willingly be flayed could I undo aught I've done. But you are indiscreet... No! No! You are not,' as Tansy's howls redoubled, 'you are the very soul of rare discretion. Oh, help me, what *have* I done?'

'You have killed my babe!' sobbed Tansy. 'You have pinched and beat me black and blue. I shall bear a monster.'

'No, you won't ... I have not!' I gibbered, almost as distracted now as she. 'My most gentle Tansy, I do entreat you, be not so uncontrollable. Show some restraint. And... God be thanked! Here's Thirza. She will comfort you... Thirza, Mistress Fothergill is sadly put about and I'm to blame.'

Then I too fell a-weeping, and between us both Thirza had her hands full. But she showed herself as ever apt to deal with an emergency. She laid me back upon my couch and patted the screaming Tansy into quiet, till all was well and no harm done. 'Save this,' said Thirza, when she returned from seeing Mistress Fothergill safe into her coach, ' that she'll go tell her husband you have mauled her, and he'll likely come to ask the reason why... And, body o' me, why *did* you?'

I told Thirza what had passed, and she looked glum.

'Yes, there's a power o' talk around the Papist party. Tom says 'tis known in every tavern that the Catholics are raising enmity between the King and the Duke of York.'

'That,' I said, sharp, 'is not to be believed. I trust you will never listen nor open mouth to such a wickedness.'

'Not I,' Thirza assured me, 'I am struck dumb to every soul alive saving your ladyship. But my eyes and my ears are wide and they will stay so,' Thirza said profoundly, 'while I watch...'

And then, a few days after this affray with Tansy, just at a time when I was beset with gravest fears of Rob — not doubts; I never for one moment doubted him, but with a forecast of some indefinable malaise around him and myself, which may have arisen as much from the long inertia of my seclusion as from any rumours floated from the Galleries — just then, when I was in a torment to think that he, no less than others equally as innocent might have been besmeared with the slime of anti-Popish prejudice, and to what unfounded purpose: just when, as women will, I began to wonder if I had been mistaken, not in his integrity, but in his hidden thought of me ... he came.

It was April by the calendar and December in the air, for it had snowed all night and the sky was heavy with the promise of another fall. A smoky sun, red as a holly berry, died behind a bank of leaden cloud, and dusk crept in like a ghost upon the day.

I lay on my couch before the fire in my parlour with Rufus dozing at my feet. Very old was he now, and deaf and almost blind, yet he knew that step among all others, and was up and at the door, nose down and tail busy, waiting. I waited too, my breath in a flutter and my eyes on that opening door.

Like a light he stood there in the darkened room. The red glow of the fire was on his hair and on my cheeks that burned in welcome, until my sight of him was misted and I reached up my hand to his empty sleeve.

'Robin! What have they done to you? My dear ... my dear!'

He said easily, ''Tis so small a thing to lose compared to life.'

I turned my face into my pillow and spoke in a muffled voice: 'Why were you so long in coming? I was half frantic, wondering —'

'What,' he asked, 'did you wonder?'

'Why you avoided me … us … or if for any reason —'

'Why should I avoid you?'

Why indeed! And of a sudden seeing him so cool I was aching hot at the thought, like a splinter of glass to prick, that I had mistook his brotherly regard for my own besotted ardour. There is nothing so gullible as a woman in love who twists imagination to serve her vanity. So glancing away from the gleam of his sword, worn not at his left, but at his right side — this an added pang — I pointed to a chair. 'Pray be seated, Robin. I … as you see, I am helpless.'

'I have only just heard of your mishap,' said he, 'or I would have presented myself and my enquiries sooner. Am I forgiven? And … may I offer you this?' Under his arm he carried an ivory casket which he set down on a table by my couch, and bade me unfasten the clasp. 'For I am not yet proficient in the use of my left hand,' he said, making a jest of his awkwardness. 'I find it in me to envy an octopus. There was a shipmate of mine, an old sailor, who lost both of his arms alongside me in action and has learned to use his feet like hands. I visited him down at Greenwich where they have put him to hospital, and there I found him solemnly eating his dinner on the floor, picking meat off his platter with his toes and carrying the food in this manner to his mouth — to the intense delight of his mates who crowded round to watch. He had been a tumbler at a fair before he joined the Navy, and he looks to earn a fortune with these tricks.'

And I laughed with him at this comic picture, till like a fool I cried, and blew my nose and mumbled that the unseasonable weather had brought me the pest of a cold. Then I took up and opened the casket. On a bed of grass-green velvet bloomed the loveliest pale rose with shining waxen petals and delicate colourless leaves; a marvel of handicraft, more wonderful than nature.

'How exquisite!' I whispered. 'Is this the work of fairies?'

'No,' said Robin, 'it is the work of a man, or I should say of a youth, a boy of sixteen years or less whom I lately chanced upon at the entrance to Bell Savage Yard offering his carven fruit and flowers on a tray to passers-by, and not one in fifty, I should think, stopped to give them so much as a look. He had with him a young fiddler who earned more from the antics of the monkey on his shoulder than my young artist by the sale of his wares.'

'But this is magic!' I exclaimed. 'See how tenderly the petals curl over at their edges — so finely chiselled they seem to be transparent! They lack nothing but the perfume of the living rose. Who is this wizard who carves such perfect beauty from a block of wood?'

But Robin said he did not know his name.

Four years later Mr Evelyn claimed the first discovery of that amazing genius whom he found in his workshop in a humble cottage at Deptford, and whose fruit and flowers decorate the choir of the new St Paul's, whose sprays and garlands bloom above the chimney-piece here at Folly's End, and in the dining hall of our restored Wynmonath; and in many other English houses and in the palaces of kings; for the name of that street vendor that Robin did not know is now known to all the world as Grinling Gibbons...

Robin had much to tell me of the war, giving vivid accounts of the great battle, to which I listened with only half an ear, watching his face, a trifle thinner, the clear immaculate line of chin and jaw more finely cut, the faintest trace of line and shade that surely used not to be there beneath those tawny eyes. And while he talked he fondled Rufus on his knee. 'Look how he knows me after all these years. Dogs don't forget.'

'Will you go back to sea, Robin?' I asked him.

He shook his head. 'No, nor will the Duke.'

And he told me how that His Royal Highness was deeply chagrined to have been deprived by the King of his command at the earnest request of the Queen Mother, who had prevailed with the King not to allow the heir to the throne to be exposed to danger in the battle fleet. 'So now instead of going to sea as Lord High Admiral, he journeys from port to port on tours of inspection, and has lately been visiting Portsmouth to superintend the building of fortifications there, against invasion from the Dutch.'

'But is that possible?' I cried. 'Are the Dutch not vanquished?'

'Far from it — as yet.'

'What do we lack? Weapons? Men?'

'Funds,' said Robin, briefly.

'And after all the proud vaunts we have made,' I murmured, 'with victory bells, and the whole country in an uproar of rejoicing that we had won the war — must we now be prepared to keep the enemy from our very harbours?'

'We must always be prepared for that,' Robin answered, and he added, 'I wish I could do more than give paltry financial support.'

'Have you not given enough?' I said.

'Men die that England lives.' He spoke with a trace of bitterness, and rose so abruptly that Rufus slid from his knee with an undignified flop to the ground. 'I must take my leave of you now, Prue. I have outstayed my visit.'

'Never that, Rob. I wish ... I wish you would visit us more often.'

He stooped to caress Rufus who had jumped up beside me on the couch. 'Poor fellow ... did I let you down? Are you offended? Good dog, then ... good boy-ee.' Talking to him in the very special voice he used to dogs and horses — and, at home, in the old days, to me.

Suddenly Rufus stiffened, growling, nose pointed at the door; it was ajar and slowly moving to shut with the faintest click. A coldness came upon me.

'There is someone watching us,' I whispered.

'And what if so?' Rob straightened up. 'Why, Prue, you're trembling. It is not like you to jump at a trick of the wind. See!' He went to the door and flung it open — 'Nothing. No bogles!' And returning to my side and looking down upon me he said composedly, 'Your eyes are full of shadows. Are you troubled?'

'Yes,' I whispered, 'yes, I am afraid. I am oppressed by a foreboding of ... of what I do not know. I warned you once of danger. I think ... I *feel* that more than ever now you should be cautious. There is evil talk around you and the Duke.'

He answered nothing but he took my hand and held it firm in his. I felt the strength of him, and in his silence then I knew his love beyond all doubting; beyond desire, or fulfilment, or regret. All that my spirit sought in loneliness, in dreams, in the turbulent passion of my despoiled youth, was now resolved. His love enclosed me warmly, safe, to sweeten the impossible, to justify existence. My ungiven body yearned towards him in a triumph of gratitude.

He said, low-voiced, 'My trust is in my God and in my Church. I go armed — no —' as my glance went swiftly to his sword-hilt — 'not with any visible sign of steel. The Church is stronger than the sword. My faith and you, my darling, make life bearable. So let me speak for once — and then no more of this between us two, my lovely dear. Yes, let me say it, once only... That with all my might, with all my faith, with all my soul, I love you, as I shall love you while I live ... and though I die.'

With that he took my hand, turned it palm upwards to his lips and held it there. Then without another word or look he left me.

I was at peace. Transcended.

It was as if I had found sanctuary upon a mountain-top, uplifted high above the valley where men strive one against the other, mole-blind in the purposeless underground tunnels of their ignorance. They had not eyes to see the sun, nor ears to hear the song of the stars, nor the voice of reeling planets nor the heartbeat of the world... But I had found my heaven.

How long I lay immersed in radiance I do not know, for time had ceased to be. I may have dozed a while and was not fully conscious of myself until I saw the surgeon by my side. I asked him if he had called an hour since, thinking maybe it was he who had opened the door. He said, however, he was but just arrived. Yet I had now no qualms; my fears had fled like a witch in the dark. I walked with Robin in the light, and he upheld me. Was I a mouse to be scared of a door, of a word, of a whisper? Or of man's mimic crises or suspenses, or of unsubstantial shapes that veiled the stainless fabric of reality in a filmy tissue of lies?

The surgeon was telling me that he would now remove the plaster from my foot and that I could be released from my couch at last.

This announcement was not an unmixed blessing. I had enjoyed my enforced imprisonment in the solitude of my own room, waited on by Thirza, visited by Percy, with an occasional duty call from Mr Moon. There lay the rub! Our Mr Moon. For near upon six weeks I had avoided him. Now I must return to my place at table, which he shared, as he shared our house, our lives, and my husband's confidence. And I was powerless to turn him out for he was in, well in, lodged fast and in possession. I saw him as a lean black spider spinning a methodical slow web. Very slow, albeit conscientious in his methods, was our Mr Moon; more so than ever since that he had taken charge of my husband's affairs. It was therefore less a pleasure than a penance to learn that I could now assume my normal life, for thus the surgeon bade me: 'Walk from room to room as much as you are able, using a stick for your support; and within a few days you may drive to the park and walk there with your woman.'

That I would do, I promised him, but I did not say that for a week or so longer I would continue to take my meals in my own room, avoiding Mr Moon; for indeed I feared my hasty tongue which must ever speak what lay upon my mind, and were it to give our Mr Moon a taste of my true feelings there would be trouble for that gentleman — and me. So when Percy came to ask how I fared, and if the chirurgeon had pronounced me better, I did not tell him I was now allowed to walk, I merely said the clay was off my foot — 'and a mighty painful business, too, being hacked and hammered that I thought to see myself minus a —'

'What,' Percy interrupted, pointing to the ivory casket on the table, 'is that?'

'Rob has been here,' I answered, looking my husband straight in the eyes. 'He brought it with him. Open it and see what is inside.'

Percy's face was girlishly smooth, expressionless, as he opened the box and lifted the rose from its cushion.

'Is it not the loveliest thing?' I said.

His lids were lowered: a slight contraction of his lips was followed by the words, 'I would scarcely have credited Robin with so choice a taste.' And with the rose in his hand he went over to the window to draw the curtains, shutting out the dusk. The room was in darkness save for the leaping firelight. His voice floated to me thinly from a distance. 'I do not wish you to accept gifts from Robin, or any man other than myself.'

I jerked my head from the pillow. 'What are you saying?'

'You heard me. Such attention might be misconstrued. To save you the embarrassment of any such perversion of the truth —' and I knew that he was smiling — 'we will dispense with overemphasised formalities.'

Then through the stillness came a cracking sound as of elfin bones crushed. Through the firelight's reddening glow I saw the pale fragments drop like dead wind-shaken petals. I saw him grind his heel upon the carpet, and then once more that terrible little sound; and then I heard him laugh. 'That is what we do with bartered favours, my sweet wife.'

I closed my eyes. I did not see him go.

Presently I got myself off the couch and took a taper and held it to the logs. I lit the candles. The room came to life again filled with signs of Robin. His impress on the cushion of the chair where he had sat, an embroidered glove left there forgotten. Had Percy seen that too? I took it up and held it to my face. It smelled faintly of amber and tobacco... I saw the empty casket and then I put my injured foot to the ground, for I had stood all this time like a stork on one leg, and I found that I could hobble with some pain to the place where the scattered rose-leaves lay. I knelt...

And wondered.

What iron force must those slight fingers hold, that one convulsive spasm could crumble this carven wonder into bits...

I gathered up that broken loveliness and laid it back upon its velvet bed and closed the lid upon it. And then I limped to my bureau and hid the casket in a secret drawer; and so to my couch again with Rufus in my arms and his cold nose and warm tongue at my cheek.

Percy did not come to my bedchamber that night, as was his custom, to sit on my bed and tuck the covers round and wish me happy dreams as I were his little sister; nor did he come to my room the next day, nor for near upon a week after Robin's visit did I see him. Thirza reported that he and Mr Moon were out upon their business, whatever it might be, from morning until evening. Nor was she sorry to be quit of them, she said, being left now with only two servants in a house this size and a hundred and eighty stairs to climb and the spring scouring to be done and only one pair of hands to do it.

Since Mr Moon had taken charge of Percy's debts he had insisted on a rigid routine of economy. Our household expenditure had now been reduced to one-third of its usual weekly total. But even had we been able to afford the wages of a full domestic staff, we could not have procured it. All the able-bodied younger men were at the war and many had been taken by the Plague. Out of our seven servants there remained only Percy's valet, who minded nothing but his master's clothes; Tom, our coachman, who helped Thirza in the kitchen, and one young maidservant. So that Thirza had just cause for her complaint that she was Jack-of-all-Trades again, and at a time of life when she should have no more to do than wait on me. Instead of which she was at work for eighteen hours out of twenty-four, and well did I know it for it had never been her way to growl and grumble while she did more in half an hour than half a dozen maids in half a day. So, right busy was our Thirza during that fateful week, washing and scrubbing amid a clattering of pails and wielding of besoms, and throwing wide of windows and burning of feathers and sprinkling of vinegar, that there might not be one speck or spot of Plague left in any corner to rise up again and smite us. Then to crown all, Percy's man fell sick of the smallpox and was hurried from the house into St Bartholomew's Hospital, so that not only did Thirza cook the meals, but she waited on the gentlemen at table.

The capricious April weather had changed in three days from snow to sun. Under the colonnade of the Piazza across the Square, which had of late become a promenade of fashion, passed a gay procession of ladies and their attendant cavaliers. The trees in Lord Bedford's garden, and the sycamores shading the market stalls, were a budding, joyous green. My window framed a sky of summer blue and scampering clouds. Spring was here again, and I up and ready for it, glad to be out driving in my coach — two horses now, not six, thanks to Mr Moon's judicious campaign, of which I reluctantly approved. Better drive out in a wheelbarrow, say I, than suffer the indignity of debt. Nor was I troubled to see my elegant equipage replaced by one more sober. I had never cared for the luxuries money could buy. I would willingly have changed my fine raiment, my house, my jewels and myself for a peasant woman and her cottage — and the baby at her breast. But that's no matter. And my concern alone.

A few days after Robin's visit, I returned from my drive to find Thirza waiting for me with a tray prepared for my meal. To my enquiry she answered that the gentlemen had dined, and earlier than usual, my husband having brought a guest — a stranger — to the house.

'A stranger,' I repeated. 'Who can he be?'

'I have never clapped eyes on him before,' Thirza said, 'he arrived here so soon as you left the house — as it were timed. A dark, lean, foxy man — I opened door to him and asked what name to be announced, but His Reverence was behind me saying very civil, with bows and a death's head grin, 'Come in, sir, you are welcome. His lordship is expecting you.' And therewith he led him off.'

'Well, what of it?' I queried, impatient, as she paused; and I confess to a momentary return of my disquiet, for there was that in her face and in her manner of speech, devoid of its usual embellishment, to bring me fresh alarm. If ever Thirza showed herself dramatic, one could dilute her tale for as much as it were worth, which was as little as the showman's touting of his puppets at a fair. But if she were restrained and careful of her words, then one might be forewarned of some disaster.

'What of it?' I repeated, with the rat of my anxiety gnawing me again. 'Can his lordship not entertain a guest or a stranger — or the devil, if he will — without your making a great Thing of it? You are like the poor mad gentleman in the story of Don Quixote, by a great Spanish writer' (which I had recently been reading in its first translation, very poorly done by a Mr Shelton) 'who saw dragons in windmills and armies in the clouds.'

'And snakes in the grass?' retorted Thirza. 'If I am mad — then may God help the sane. And as for what you call a 'Thing' of honest service — you should thank me on your bended knees, my lady, that my ears are as big as my heart, to guard you and yours with my corpse, if put to't. So may I be struck dead o' the Plague if I speak aught but truth, the whole truth and nothing but the truth!'

This declaration, so much more in Thirza's normal vein, did immediately set my mind at rest, that I sat down to my dinner to eat with an appetite. Thirza filled my glass with wine. 'Drink this, my lady, for you'll need it. I'll hold my tongue till you are ready.'

'No, speak on and tell me. I'll wager you'll not hold your tongue till what is in is out. I can see it boiling red-hot between your teeth. Is my lord in debt again? Is the Sheriff come to take him up? I live in daily expectation of it, and will warrant we shall all be eating of our dinners off the floor of Marshalsea before we're one year older. I dare swear we owe for these green grapes now — they're mighty good for all that.'

'My blessed dear!' Thirza knelt beside me and turned my face to hers. 'Hearken now to what I have to say, for never has your Thirza served you better. I'll be brief — there's no time to waste in words.'

'Then bring them out. Dispense with overtures.' Laughing, I pushed a grape into her mouth.

'Yes, yes! I'm telling you.' And in her haste Thirza swallowed the grape whole. 'I brought the meal and served the gentlemen at table. They ate and drank a-plenty, but I observed as I came in with the dishes that their voices dropped and his lordship sat with his face pinched and yellow as a guinea, and biting of his thumbs the way he does when he is fretted. As for His Reverence, he had the look upon him of a cobra which is out to charm a rabbit.'

'Yes, but what of the stranger?' I cried. 'Cut your story to its point. This is nought but back-chat.'

'Lord bless and save us! Am I not telling you? Then since your ladyship will have it — the stranger sat between them and spoke little, but he put questions which were answered. How much I missed of what had gone before I cannot say, for I did not put my ear to the keyhole till the table was cleared — and by the way, my lady, I have forgot to tell you that I espied His Holiness creeping through the hall the day Sir Robert called, and I saw him open the door and stand a while peering in. And then he closed it soft and crept away. I would have mentioned this to your ladyship at the time, but that I did not want to fash you.'

'You tell me nothing that I did not guess. Go on.'

She went on: 'I will repeat you word for word what I did hear. The stranger said, "Have you your evidence complete? Can you produce one man to bear you out?" And I could almost see the grin upon his dried-up lips as His Reverence answered, "Yes, and written — signed…" "And the time o' day, the date and place?" said the stranger's voice, clipped and very clear as he were reading of it, "being as you ascertain the Mermaid Tavern in Cheapside on the fifteenth day of March in the year of Our Lord, sixteen-hundred and sixty-six." Then came a mumbled something from his lordship which I could not catch, but I heard Mr Moon speak up: "Sufficient — yes — to apprehend him." That was the word, my lady — "to *apprehend* him in conjunction with the Jesuit, Peter Talbot."'

'That is a name unknown to me,' I interrupted.

'That's as may be, but mark me well — a name you know *was* mentioned. A name, my dear, you love.'

An icy hand was laid upon my heart.

'A name,' said Thirza, 'that must — that *shall* be saved from the foulest accusation known to man.'

'For Christ's pity,' I whispered, 'tell me…'

'They have netted him, my precious.' Thirza spoke in gusty breaths. 'They have charged him with having spoken treason in

the hearing of not one, but several persons — I have it pat —'
and she was sobbing now, but I was cold and hard — 'of not
one but several persons. Thus did they put it: "That Robert St
John Peverill, Baronet, of Stoke Hall in the county of
Warwickshire" and the name, my dear, the name — I have
never known his second name as thus they named him, Robert
Saint John Peverill — and then did Mr Moon correct the
stranger, "*Sin*jun", he said, making of him called after a saint a
very sin, and saying further that "Sir Robert has reported His
Majesty to be a Papist or Popishly affected, and that he and the
Jesuit Talbot and their priestly company have openly declared
the Duke their King. And that he —"'

I watched the tears course down my Thirza's cheeks and
marvelled. Why should she be moved to such emotion, while I
sat lost in emptiness, devoid of any feeling, drained?

'And that Sir Robert,' blubbered Thirza, 'the dear lad I've
loved and tended in his boyhood — my own nursling as he is
and as are you all, you three — yes, his lordship too, which for
his very weakness and his failings I can love him still —'

'What more of Sir Robert?' I asked, clutching at her wrist.
'What of him?'

'That he'll be taken if not warned… They're after him… Oh,
God! My lady — think! Think what this will mean!'

So it had come. The sword had fallen on him as I knew it
must.

This crisis for which I had been waiting, this nameless dread
that for months, for years, had lain in the dark of me, coiled,
was now upreared to shape itself for the attack; and now that I
stood face to face with it, I was conscious of an immense,
incredible relief, akin to exultation. Did he not tell me once
that there is no danger in the light? I had walked in fog heavy

laden with fear, but my way was now illumined. I could serve him.

I rose from where I sat. 'He shall not,' I said, 'be taken. He is innocent. All this is lies — a network of cunning to entrap him. All — all lies.'

'Do not blame his lordship,' said Thirza, sitting back upon her heels. 'You know how all his life he has been that Mawworm's dupe.'

'I blame no man. I blame man's misguided thought that worships God in one breath and destroys Him in another.'

I limped up and down the room, my mind at work, denuded of all extraneous intrusion, other than how to warn and save him — I could put it calmly to myself — of immediate arrest. That soon or late his arrest would be inevitable I did not doubt. But by that time he could have a defence fully prepared and the wisest counsel to advise him. These things happened around us every day. The Duke of Buckingham and the Marquis of Dorchester were committed to the Tower for a brawl. Yes, but this monstrous accusation they had laid to Robin was more serious — much, much more serious than the drunken misbehaviour of two gentlemen at a parliamentary sitting. It would mean a trial — and months, maybe, before that trial, of imprisonment. One had heard tell of those dungeons in the Tower. There were degrees of leniency shown to political prisoners but not to Catholics...

Now, now, I said to myself, *hold tight. No scaring off from the main tack. Go easy. Think it out, clearly and straight. You too can scheme with cunning to match theirs. He must escape. Bristol escaped, after having accused the Chancellor of these same treasonable motives. Yes, but Clarendon is not the King... These are side issues. Come to your facts... your facts. The hour is now four o' the clock. He will be at dinner. I must go, yes, I myself must go and warn him. He must be got away... No, I must not go in person and in broad daylight. I should be seen. I may be watched.*

'Thirza!' I turned to her. 'Go fetch me pen and ink.'

She hastened to my bidding. I wrote these hurried lines:

You are about to be apprehended on a charge of Treason. I know your innocence and the King shall know it too. Meanwhile, ere the charge be raised, I adjure you make an immediate escape. This to give you warning. Go now and do not lose an instant.

I did not sign it lest the message be intercepted. He would know from whom it came. I sprinkled sand upon it, sealed it and handed it to Thirza. 'Take this at once to Sir Robert at St James's Palace. If he be not there, give it to his servant. You should be back within the hour if you hire a sedan. I will wait.'

She went.

The hour passed. She did not come. I stood at the window watching for her. I saw our coach drive up and deposit Mr Moon and Percy at the door. They entered. The house was silent. The room was silent too, save for the ponderous ticking of the long-case clock. It struck six silvery chimes. I glanced up at the sunset sky and saw the horns of a little new moon swinging a-top of a fiery cloud. A shudder ran through me; 'twas ill-luck to see the new moon through glass…

Pooh! An old wives' tale.

The clock struck the half-hour and now I feared that some mischance had overtaken my good Thirza. I feared … God knows what I feared. But I could not suffer this intolerable waiting, nor this impenetrable silence like a pall upon the house. Whatever must be would be — and I must go to meet it, though I went to meet my doom.

My outdoor habit still lay where I had flung it on the couch when I came in. I put it on; I pulled the hood well over and held my vizard-mask before my face, and taking my cane I went out, haltingly, on tiptoe, and careful not to tap the stick upon the marble pavement of the hall. I unfastened the door latch and left the door ajar, for I durst not close it lest the noise be heard. And now I was down the steps and hobbling across the gravelled square to hail one of the hackney coaches drawn up in a line before the deserted piazza. The promenaders were gone to their evening amusements.

Still covering my face with my mask I bade the driver take me to St James's Palace. The fellow gave me a nasty leer, and in a grinning voice enquired, 'Which entrance, Mistress?'

'You may leave me under the archway, and make haste.'

I got in, and we drove off. Then was I suddenly frantic. I had forgot my purse; I could not pay this fellow... Very well, he would have to wait. Let that be the least of my troubles...

Interminable did that short journey seem, yet the palace clock told me I had been scarce ten minutes on the way from Covent Garden. And here was another problem: would the sentry let me in?

Drawing my hood close about my face I got out of the carriage, and telling the driver to wait I walked boldly up to the red-coated musketeer who stood in his box at attention. 'I have a permit to visit Sir Robert Peverill. Be so good as to show me the entrance to his apartments.'

The sentry lowered his musket and held out his hand. 'I must see the permit, madam.'

I let down my mask. 'I have no permit,' I said calmly. 'I am Lady Folliett.'

And in that soldier's eyes I saw eyes of the man who brought me there. So! Let them think the worst of me — who cared?

Not I. Get to those apartments, undetained, I must. I played my part. I ogled him slily with giggles.

'I beseech you, let me through.' *Oh, for my purse.* 'You will be rewarded when I return, but do not hold me now.'

'Pass on, my lady.' The creature lowered an eyelid and grinned broader. 'I know your ladyship's face or you'd not pass so easy. First door on your left and through the passage to the right.'

I went from him with my chin in the air, and I wished he were a beetle that I could have trod on him for that look he gave me; though I'll be bound I asked for it, leading him on to judge me a bare-faced bawd.

Robin's door! And his name inscribed upon it. God be thanked! I pealed the bell to wake the dead. In for a penny, in for a pound. Let all the Duke's household know I was come to my lover. I had no shame to hide. Nor was I the only woman who went in and out of these chambers that lodged the Duke's own gentlemen; nor, come to that, at the privy door of the Duke himself. *Open! Must I ring again?...*

The door swung wide.

'Is Sir Robert Peverill within?' And as the man hesitated I said, peremptorily, 'Tell Sir Robert that Lady Folliett is here and desires to speak with him.'

Thank heaven for our name that could move mountains. The man bowed and bid me enter, and stalked on ahead to announce not my message, but myself, to a large low-ceiled room, and in a voice that could be heard from there to St Paul's:

'The Lady Folliett.'

He was seated in the window writing. I saw with a stab how laboriously and with what careful diligence he plied the grey goose quill. He rose, and I knew in a glance that he had himself well in hand to show no astonishment at my arrival.

Before the door had closed upon his servant he said quickly, 'I am indeed beholden to your ladyship for this speedy reply to my message.' Then as the man's measured step receded, and with a droll look of mock despair while warm laughter lit his eyes, 'Prue! My lovely, crazy, reckless, feckless Prue — what under heaven brings you here?'

'Rob!' I went close to him; I took his hand in both of mine and told him urgently in whispers all that I had to tell.

He heard me out, the laughter fading from his eyes, his face inscrutable.

'So that, Rob, is why I'm here. I sent Thirza with a letter to you two hours since, but she has not returned. I feared some misadventure had befallen her — but above all I feared for you, and durst not wait a moment longer. Rob, you must go — now — instantly! You must! For my sake — for my peace — you must not stay.'

He dropped my hands, and turning from me, pulled forward a chair. 'Of what can I be thinking? To let you stand while you come to tell me this, my dearest love!'

It seemed so natural now to hear these words; yet I was thankful to be seated, for my knees were trembling, though not from weakness of my injured foot.

'Rob,' I said, controlling my voice, ' do you realise your danger? I am convinced that Mr Moon has worked for this. He is imbued with a maniacal prejudice against you for having reverted to your faith despite all his early efforts to instruct you in his beliefs. I need not tell you that I know you to be innocent, nor that this fabrication has been built on thinnest lies. I know investigation will prove you unimpeachable. But let me ask you this, my dear, is there any word that you may thoughtlessly have uttered that can be produced as evidence — anything howsoever trivial that you may have spoke in public on which some evil misconstruction could possibly be placed?'

He shook his head, considering, before he slowly answered, 'To my knowledge, no. I have been at the Mermaid in Cheapside and in company with Father Talbot — yes, I have — and often.' He smiled. 'The Father is not above a game of shovel-board, a strong pipe of tobacco, nor a flagon of good wine — all to be had of the best at the Mermaid —' Then he paused, brows knitted. 'Wait!' I have a sidelight here. Some two or three weeks back I remember now an altercation did arise. Father Talbot was with me that evening. Some young fop in his cups made a sottish, offensive allusion in my hearing to the Father's priesthood. I would have upped and at him to spring my rapier — left-handed though I am — but the Father pulled me back. Yes, I'll own I was full of a bottle or two —'

'Rob... My Robin!' I whispered. 'What did you say?'

His smile gleamed again. 'Hang me if I know! Nothing of any matter on this score, but the fellow whose name I did not hear and who from that day I have not seen — he is not of the court — some merchant's son, I fancy, a swaggering vulgarian — did then make a further insolent remark about the "Papists" and the Duke. At that I saw red — or redder — and retorted — and this I do remember saying, "His Majesty the King is the Duke's brother, and of one blood and of one faith —"'

'Oh, Robin!'

'Wait, dear heart ... "of one faith in their devotion to duty and to God. Do you insult the one you insult both." I think, too, I hurled at him an ugly name, but none that could not fit him. And then the Father intervened and dragged me away, and we went off together — and that is all, I swear.'

'Did others hear this passage of abuse?'

'Why, yes, the whole company was spoiling for a fight — and vastly disappointed, too, that it ended in nought but words.'

'Ended?' I started up. 'Would to God it *had* so ended. Do you not see how these harmless words hot-spoken have been twisted? Three weeks — that is the very date! And the noise was round the town within the hour; Tansy Fothergill came visiting and rolled out some talk of this. Men have been taken for less. Oh, Robin, I beseech you, have a care! Be warned. Certain sure some hideous inference has been drawn from a dropped sentence. It is not in you to be careless. You must have been over-full, my dear.'

'I have a head like an ox,' said he ruefully. 'I can drink a barrel with no more effect upon me than to make me laugh.'

'Yes, yes, maybe, but you were not laughing then, and wine gives tongue. However, let that rest. We must think now what's best to do... Rob, you must get away till the trouble in this mare's-nest is blown out. You must not be apprehended — not on the smallest count. Though you can prove yourself a thousand times above reproach, you must not be brought up on a charge of the least suspicion, for there are evil undercurrents working against you and the Duke's party.'

'There is no Duke's party,' said Robin quietly.

'And *this*,' I ran on, unheeding, 'this is what comes of a house divided, this hideous mauling of God's love and of His holy Church. I have always known there should be but one faith in the world, one thought to bind humanity, one brotherhood as the Lord Jesus spoke it. What matter where or how we worship God, so that we keep His commandments? As it is said: *That ye love one another, even as I have loved you.*

And at that moment the door was flung wide and the servant announced: 'The Lord Folliett.'

He came into the room pulling off his gloves, casting them with his plumed hat on to the table. Robin went to meet him, saying coolly, 'So it seems I am twice honoured today.'

I rose and leaned on my stick and watched those two measuring each other with their eyes; then Percy's narrowed till they were shining slits of steel in a face parchment-white.

'I followed my wife.' His smiling tones belied his pallor and the spasmodic twitching of a muscle near his mouth. 'I saw her leave my house and go hurrying across the Square —' He still looked at Robin although now he spoke to me. 'And I was much rejoiced, my dear, to see you thus recovered of your injury, that you could walk so quick. I guessed to find you here.' His smile closed.

I heard myself say clearly, 'I am glad you are come.' And from that moment I was in absolute command. This was a situation I could understand; a challenge I could answer. I advanced a step and placed myself between Robin and my husband.

'Yes,' I said, 'I am glad that you are come, for you can bear me out in my persuasions. I am acquainted with the plot behind him whom you are pleased to name your brother.'

A deep breath came from Robin. But I was watching Percy's face, and saw it emptied suddenly of all expression.

'You may think what you will of me!' I cried. 'I do not protest my loyalty, for you should know it as you should know him, whom since ever we three were children you have suspected — and how unjustly! — of supplanting your rights in me. Yes! I am well aware of your distorted thinking and of the mischief it has worked in you to change you from a man into a fiend — but this is not the time to talk of it, nor of your share in the vile imputation attributed to Robin by one who has ever led you by the nose. You know, too, of whom I speak.

And I adjure you for your honour's sake, Piers Folliett, not to show yourself unworthy of your name. 'Tis my name, too, and I'll not have it fouled. Robin must be saved from the atrocious ignominy which you — and your master — have cast upon him. It is of no matter how I have become acquainted with your part in this revolting slander. My business now is to prevent the repercussion of your schemes.'

Percy's lips moved stiffly. He forced a laugh. 'Why, what storms are brewing here? What histrionics! Sure, you must have learned them from our Thirza. You befoul yourself, my love, if you believe I should accuse you —' his gaze slipped past me to Robin, his voice was a caress — 'of loose purpose with our esteemed friend here.'

'You had best not, Folliett!' Robin brought this out thickly. 'I do not wish to fight you in the presence of your wife.'

'Fight me! My dear Peverill,' expostulated Percy, and for the glance he gave to Robin's empty sleeve I could have struck him down. 'There can be no talk of fighting. Unhappily you cannot — if you would.'

'I beg leave, my lord,' said Robin louder, 'to call you to account for that, to prove you wrong.'

I turned on him like lightning. 'Is this the time for a brawl? Put up your sword! If fight you must, then fight with me between you. I'll take first prick... Percy! I swear I am not faithless, nor is he. I give you God's word on that above my own. I am here to plead with him — and you, since you are come — that you may right this ugly business and persuade him to escape before it is too late. Percy! Listen!' I caught him by the wrist. 'In my father's name and for his sake, who loved Robin as a son, I beseech you to do all now in your power to work with and not against him. He must leave London immediately, and remain covered until the danger of his apprehension is averted. There is no case that can be proved should he be taken — but he must *not* be taken. Percy!' Frenziedly I shook his arm. 'Insensible beast! Do you hear me? You must aid him. Don't stand there like a dummy! Advise us. Act, man, act!'

Carefully he put me from him. 'You do mistake my good intentions, my dear Prue. I am here for the same purpose as yourself.' Yet though he spoke with smiling assurance, I could not read what lay behind his eyes. 'It is true,' he said, 'that some far-fetched impeachment has been compiled against our Robin which may —' he paused, moistening his lips — 'which may result in some sort of inquiry that I agree it would be better to avoid. There are always voices ready to support a charge against a Catholic.'

Now I could make nothing of this change of front. I could have sworn that when my husband came into the room and found us there together, he was white-hot and bursting to denounce us. But it seemed my earnestness had melted him, or maybe his innate love for Robin, which I have reason to believe was a deeper, stronger thing than his love for me or any woman, struggled for supremacy above the stealthy virus of his obsession; yet whatever may have brought about this sudden metamorphosis he now appeared as ready to accept my word, as before I was certain he had doubted it. 'Which being so, Rob,' he continued, 'and pray, my good fellow,' he added laughingly, 'sheath your rapier. I would not fight you in your disadvantage for my life. As I was about to say, when Prue, who shows exceeding common sense in this preposterous affair, did say it for me — though I have yet to hear how she has learned of it, for I was fain to have withheld this unfortunate occurrence from her ears — as Prue then, so wisely suggests, it certainly were better you take your leave of

London for a while. Indeed it would be foolish to remain. A week or two, a month — and all will be blown over. Meanwhile, Sir Robert Peverill is out of town, or travelling abroad, or visiting his home in Warwickshire. No,' he paused, 'I think not there, for that is the first place to which they'd track you. No, not there,' he repeated, reflectively, 'not in your own house,' and his fingers clawed at the lace of his cravat as though he felt a choking in his throat, but still his smile stayed. 'So may I offer you,' he said, 'and I hope you will accept — the hospitality of mine at Folly's End?'

Thus all was righted, as I fondly felt, and as in my faith of him I did believe, for how could I know of the devil that possessed him in his likeness? How when his words, his voice, yes, even his veiled eyes spoke nothing but the will to serve his friend, could I guess what ugly motive twisted him with the warped anguish of his life's frustration?

It was Percy now who took command, not I, nor Robin. With an almost febrile eagerness he laid his plan before us. Rob must depart at once, without delay and he must ride, he must not go by coach, for his horse would make more speed than a wheeled vehicle. 'Prue and I,' he said, 'will follow. She will drive, and I will ride behind you.'

He would hear of no demur on Robin's part, who declared himself unwilling to run like a rat, saying he would sooner take what's coming in his face than at his heels. But I was quick to tell him, 'These are mock heroics, Rob. Is it not said discretion is the better part of valour? Colonel Ashton, who came to me to aid him some years back, showed no such hesitation when he was chased, and drove me down to Dorset in the habit of my coachman to save himself. And it were as well that you, too, take some cover — or at least disguise your hair. Wear this!' And laughing, I snatched at Percy's periwig. 'Your colour is a landmark. You must hide it.'

Percy laughing too, agreed and removed his wig and offered it to Robin insisting he should wear it on his way. And all three of us made a great jest of it, Percy louder in his merriment than any...

Robin left London that evening, taking his servant with him. Percy and I departed next day, Thirza driving with me in the coach and Percy riding at our wheels. Thus had I little opportunity of talk with him; nor in the hurry of our going had I the time or thought to question Thirza on the cause of her delay in delivering my message at the palace. During the journey, however, she related how that on arrival there the sentry had refused her admittance to Rob's apartments. 'And,' said she, 'as I was chary of handing him your note I judged it best to wait some distance beyond the entrance gates hoping to see Sir Robert pass out. And, I tell you, a fine pother was I in when I saw not him, but yourself arrive — and then his lordship.'

'All's well,' I said, 'as it transpires.'

But I spoke with more assurance than I felt; for it seemed that at each halting place my husband deliberately avoided me, taking his meals in the inn parlour and leaving me to take mine with Thirza in my room. At Salisbury, being there a fête day in the town, we found ourselves held up by a procession of mummers and Morris dancers and a poor, weary frightened bear, dragged off to the baiting amid jeers and applause from the townsfolk and yokels who crowded the main street. At the inn, my husband and I dined together in a private parlour. I observed then that he was heavy with drink, his hands shaking, his eyes glazed, and roundly did I task him for it, too.

'Just when you most need your wits about you to go soak yourself. Where is your sense?'

'My sense is where it ever was. Here!' He tapped his forehead. 'And keener than you think. I know what I'm about.' But at the look he gave me I was filled with sudden terror, as at a flash of unexpected steel. I shivered, watching the flutter of a tiny pulse under the blue veins on his temple. He looked wretchedly ill. I heard his slurred voice say, 'Poor muddle-headed human nature, fashioned in heaven and damned to hell ... by Love. What tri-tricks Love plays with man's emotions. A game o' battledore and shuttlecock... A game of each man for himself and God for none.'

The eyes that stared at me from the mask-like pallor of his face were pathetic, wistful, clouded. And I told him he was drunk. He may have been, but not wholly with the wine that he had taken.

We came to Dorchester at noon the next day, halting there for a last change of horses and a hasty cold collation. Percy, who had sat in silence throughout the meal drinking far more than he ate, bade me drive on with Thirza. He would follow presently. He wished to attend the market. He had been told of some fine boars and a stud bull to be auctioned. He did not glance at me while he spoke, with his thumb at his teeth and that glazed look still in his eyes, as though he saw not me but some inward fogginess. He was so deathly pale, his lips parched and twitching uncontrollably, that I believed him sickening for some illness, and the ever-present horror of the Plague that still stalked the countryside rose up to fright me. I begged him to come home.

'Come with me now. You are unwell.' I laid my hand to his brow; it was clammy. He jerked his head from my touch as though it stung.

'Go you your way,' he muttered, 'I'll go mine. You leave me be. My health was never better. 'Tis my mind ... my mind that's sick.' And taking the flagon from the table he put the bottle to his mouth and drained it. Then he drew from his pocket a tiny gold-framed mirror and examined his face, smiling at his reflection. 'I thought, maybe,' he said, shaking as with the ague, 'I thought, maybe, to see horns sprouting ... but I am still unchanged.'

And with a foolish chuckle he got up from the table and lurched from the room.

I sent for Thirza and told her in whispers of these alarming symptoms, but she made little of them. Pointing to the empty flagon, 'That's his malady,' she said, 'his lordship takes far more than he can hold, and wine makes men run mad, carrying a poison to the brain, in especial one of his ilk, that is weak and frettish. Bedlam's full of such. 'Tis a blessing he is returned now to the country where he'll not find it so easy to get drink. His cellars are empty, and if you want to know why he sends you home without him, I can tell you my opinion is he will pay a visit to the vintner's and give an order to lay down a pipe or two.'

'If that were all,' I dubiously murmured.

'Well, what else?' cried Thirza sharply.

I could not say what else. He seemed so strange...

The hills were stained with shadows as we drove up the valley. The thin April sun bathed the gentle green of meadow and downland in shimmering silver-gold light. There was a hush in the air, a muffled quiet, as though the earth were resting between the pangs of spring's travail. The woods, the hedgerows, the stripling larches that fringed the near side of our home woods, although scarce yet in leaf, showed a green flame against the pale clear sky.

The old house stood in the cup of the downs, its grey roof shouldering a cloud, a plume of smoke rising from its tallest chimney. The attic windows, lit with a watery sun-gleam, were like peering eyes that seemed to watch for me.

Robin was there before us. He had arrived overnight and the sound of wheels brought him down to the gates to meet the coach. I did not tell him I was again beset by fears, that Percy was drunk, or sick, or mad, nor that as we neared the house my heart throbbed with a violent agonising apprehension, that I was ready to believe those dear familiar walls had sent out to me a subtle warning to withdraw, to hide myself ... from what? From an exaggerated consciousness of doom; from that dark pursuing shadow that hovered like an evil bird above my life and Robin's; or from the phantoms of my self-delusion?

I slid my hand in Robin's for my comfort, and felt his strength engirt me like an armour. We paced up and down the garden and I reminded him that this was the first time since the day he had left us to go riding off to Charmouth — how many years ago? — that we had been together here at home. 'For it is your home, too, Rob, as much as ours. No harm can come to you here... The house will protect you.' Yet, as I spoke, a chill again struck through me, and my fingers clung to his. 'Rob! Are you sure you have not been followed?'

He smiled down at me. 'No, my dear, this is a wild-goose chase. They've more to do in London than hunt me to the rope.'

'Oh, hush,' I whispered, 'never say it!'

'Why, what have I said? I'll say again — they've more to do than hunt a man for a chance word unfitly spoken.'

'Men have been hanged for less.'

'Listen, my Prue.' His hand engulfed mine strongly. 'You must not be afraid for me. I have come here at your — and his

— request, against my will. For what man worth the name would run ahead of danger?'

'Yes,' I cried impatiently, 'so you have said, and your sentiments are natural. But I at least shall know some peace to have you here.'

'For that reason I am come,' and he hesitated before he went on slowly. 'Prue, I must tell you now what has long been my intention. This crisis finally decides me. You know I want you — heart and soul and body. But as I cannot have you, and because without you this life's not much worth living, I shall choose another — maybe better — way.'

'Oh, God! What are you saying?' I gasped. 'Do you speak of death!'

He shook his head. 'I speak of life — the only true life here on earth, if I be not unworthy. That remains yet to be seen. When this temporary trouble in which I am now involved is past, I shall go to Rome and study there as a novitiate for Holy Orders.'

The green earth spun. A frail arm of cherry-blossom, outstretched against the whitening sky, hazily advanced as if to strike me. 'No,' I breathed. 'No, Robin, no! Not that...' And in a sudden desperate madness and with all my woman's might I entreated him to take his will of me. 'For I am yours. I cannot let you go! I have not your faith — I've all my years to live. Even if you marry ... yes, sooner would I see you the husband of another woman than buried in a living grave... Robin! Rob! I need you. I cannot live knowing you are dead ... in life...' And then I saw his eyes and stayed my tongue and faltered, shamed. 'Forgive me and forget this. If you have found your true vocation you must go.'

He was gazing at the distant turrets of Wynmonath that rose like darkest rock above the greening mist of trees. 'I wish you to know this, Prue,' he said, remotely, 'that I have left in my will a sum of money for the restoration of the abbey — if it were not restored before I die. That sum will now be placed at your disposal to rebuild it in your lifetime, for all my worldly goods will be rendered to the Church if — or when — I am ordained.'

I stood and answered nothing. This then was the end. He had chosen.

And yet, despite the quiet confidence with which he spoke, I felt, deep within, the certainty that he had been propelled towards this decision less by his own conviction than from the desire to take refuge from himself. He was not made for the priesthood. He was a man, built for the life of a man, to be mated, to breed men, to love as a man and fight life with man's weapons, not God's. Such a choice was not for such as he. It would not be for him life everlasting, but death with an indefinite reprieve.

And because I knew he waited for a word from me I forced my lips to utter, 'The restoration of the abbey! That is a wonderful gift, Robin. I cannot thank...' Nor could I further speak. I turned from him and went into the house.

Percy arrived before sundown, riding full gallop to the stables and shouting loud for Ham before he dismounted. I heard his stumbling step upon the stairs and the slam of a door.

I changed my travelling dress for one less cumbersome and went down to the hall where a fire had been lighted. At the window I stood and watched the fading arc of a rainbow in the sky obscured by a cloud shaped like a dragon. A soft rain was falling through ladders of silvery light; the meadows gathered loneliness and darkened; no breeze, no sound of bird nor beast disturbed the stillness that lay upon the gardens and enwrapped the house in a thick silence, broken by a loud harsh burst of laughter, and Percy's voice calling Rob to dine.

Then the clatter of boots and the jingle of spurs as they came down the stairs and entered the room together. And Percy laughed again and called to me, 'Be seated, Prue! Come you, my dear, to table. For "meat and matins hinder no man's journey." How dark it is! We must have candles. Thirza! Bring candles!'

He wore no periwig; his hair, still childishly flaxen, framed his narrow cheeks that seemed in the last few hours to have shrunk. His high nose jutted forward, pale as a bone, and behind it his eyes burned with a blue fire.

We sat and Thirza served us. We ate and drank — or at least Robin ate and Percy drank, and I made talk of this and that with the food like dust in my mouth. I spoke of the fair we had passed on the way, of the poor bear dragged to its baiting, of the cruelty of such sports.

'Yes,' Percy agreed, 'yes, certainly, bear baiting is detestable. Give me the hunt for fair game — the careful stalking of the buck. That's a good sport, I'll warrant you. The quarry turned at bay to meet the hounds — that's the finest sport of all!' And he refilled his tankard and Robin's, and drank and pledged him, smiling over the pewter brim. 'Here's to you as good as you are and here's to me as bad as I am —'

And Robin capped it, laughing, '"For as good as you are and as bad as I am, I'm as good as you are —"'

'"As *bad* as I am!"' As if some wire had been pulled taut inside him, Percy sprang to his feet, his eyes on the clock: 'Time is slipping and the farce is done — played out!'

A draught like a little shiver swept the room.

'Yes!' Percy's voice split that choking silence. 'You, Robert Peverill — are brought here for my purpose — not yours!

Here are we three well met — eh? Are we not well met?' His dreadful laughter dragged one corner of his mouth. I was reminded of poor Aunt Rossiter's apoplectic contortion. 'Our lives have been three rivers interwoven, flowing each by each. She —' his finger lifted, pointing at my face — 'she between us — you and I on either side. I have seen in my travels in Switzerland just such a phen-phenom'non. The river Rhône and the river — May I perish if I have not forgot the name of its twin brother! The one a fiercest blue, the other dirty grey, streaming on and on — and ever on in amity, conjoined — for they've no female third to part their waters, that never overlap until they plunge together in the torrent — even as you and I, Robin, do come together now for this — our grand finale!'

The ticking clock gave a hoarse purring chuckle before it chimed the hour.

'I have waited! I have been patient — but there's a limit to a man's endurance. I denounce you, Peverill,' Percy cried, 'here in this room and at this very table where years ago you in your hulking arrogance sought to steal my child-wife. So hear me now denounce you for a traitor — not to your King nor to your God — but to me! You have slunk behind me in the dark to stab me in the back, with talk of friendship in your teeth and lies on your filthy tongue, while you take your fill of her to make *me* stink! You have betrayed me, you have betrayed my wife, but above all, Robert Peverill, you have —' his lips writhed to the strangled words — 'betrayed my love.'

The candles flickered in a wavering metallic heat. The room was oppressive with a hideous sense of some lurking inaudible presence, near beside me, very near, almost within sight and sound. I glanced at Robin. He sat like one stunned, motionless, leaning a little forwards, his fingers pressing the table's edge with a grip that greyed his knuckles.

'For,' Percy said, with awful quiet, 'I have loved you, Robin. My love for you has been the best thing in my life...'

Sweat beaded his forehead; he was so white one could believe the blood in his veins had ceased to flow. He seized his tankard in his shaking hand, drained its dregs and sank back into his seat.

I rose from mine.

Above the wild beating of my heart, above the clutching fear that held me bound, as when in a nightmare one is pursued by speeding monsters, that one seems to run and cannot move, and cries for help and yet can only whisper, and tells oneself *This is but a dream ... a dream ...* so did I hear my own voice say, 'Now will I speak — once and for all, that which no man knows saving my husband, whose wife I am in name alone, whose body is not his — nor any man's. Robin —' across the table I saw his amazed incredulous eyes, his parted lips — 'Robin, hear the truth. Mine is a virgin marriage. I am untouched as the day when as a child I was married in this house by my father's death-bed to him who calls himself my husband. He will bear me out in this. Yes, you, Percy, answer! Do I lie?' I turned to him who sat huddled, his jaw dropped, his gaze focused upon me in a fearful unseeing absorption. 'Answer!' I repeated. 'In all these years has our marriage ever once been consummated? Has it? Answer me!'

His breath came panting through his lips to frame a voiceless, 'No...'

I hid my eyes.

And very calm and cold I heard Rob say, 'If I had known this, Folliett, your accusation might not have been unfounded. But your secret was well kept. She has been too loyal ... and I...' he paused and then burst forth, 'My God! If I had known! The wasted years ... her wasted life...'

The room had slowly lightened; the sky was clear. A beam of sun hit the window, glancing through to turn the candle flames a sickly white. The clock struck the half-hour... Nearby in the stable yard a cock crew.

A shudder ran through Percy, and of a sudden he was sobbing. Dry, tearless sobs, his face distorted, his breath drawn out in gasps. 'What have I done? What cursed evil thing possessed...? It was like a spell. I talked and walked and slept with it... Holy heaven, help me!' The words broke from him on a despairing cry. He started up. 'Rob! You must go. I have informed on you at Dorchester, at the Sheriff's. I stopped there on my way ... I have been mad but now I'm sane...' Yet he looked like one demented, his face blurred, his mouth wine-stained and blubbering, 'Forgive, forgive me, Robin! Forgive and let me think! I must ... must *think!*'

But I could not. This added horror clogged my brain of all but an unreal sense of melodrama, a performance somewhat crudely overacted before an audience of two; Robin and myself as unwilling spectators, inevitably merged in this moment of our mutual predestination... But the heat was stifling, the candles blazed like little fiery moons in creeping darkness; the oaken walls seemed queerly to swell inwards, advancing slow, towards me...

And that hidden shadow seized and swept me down.

Out of some lost obscurity I became aware of a throbbing in my temples and my ears, that resolved itself at last into the thud of hooves.

I was lying on the window-seat under the open casement with a smell of burnt feathers in my nose, a wetness on my forehead, and in my mouth a taste of vinegar. The sound of hooves faded far into the distance.

'God be thanked!' said Thirza's voice. 'He's off!' Her arms were round me safe and warm. 'My darling! Never in your life have I known you to swoon. A rare taking I was in — I tell you! I thought you gone, so slow you were to come back to yourself.'

Sunlight flooded the room; the candles still burned white and drunken in their sockets, dripping grease on the table. The chairs were pushed awry, my platter as I left it; the food scarce touched, my fork stuck in the meat. These trifles I observed before full consciousness returned with the cry of Robin's name upon my lips.

'He's away, my dear. His lordship —'

'Give her to me,' I heard him say. 'Go you, Thirza. I will attend my wife.'

'No worriting of her now, my lord, I beg. She has had enough.'

'Leave us and go.'

She went with mutters.

'Prue!' He came and stood before me, and I saw in his eyes the blind aching look of a dumb creature that has bitten the hand that tends it. Kneeling, he buried his head in my lap to pour forth his wretched, stumbling confession, unsparing of himself, heedless of me, while I sat like stone and heard him through, until his words died in whispers. 'I do not ask forgiveness. I ask you only not to judge. You do not know...'

'I do.' I fingered the soft young tendrils of his hair. 'I know how you have suffered.'

He raised his hand; I saw his tears. 'Yes, I have suffered ... and you too.'

'It matters nothing now. What have you done to Robin?'

He gathered me close to him, pressing his cheek to mine. 'I have sent him off. He did not wish to go, but I insisted. He did not want to leave while you were ... I thought the shock had killed you.'

'I was foolish,' I said, calmly, 'to lose hold upon myself. I am not given to such woman's tricks.'

His arms strained me tighter. 'You were always half a boy.'

'Where,' I asked, 'is Robin?'

'He is on his way to Templecombe. They will not think to seek him there, and if they do our uncle's word will keep them out.'

A deep sigh escaped me. 'You advised him well.' I laid my hands on his shoulders, searching his face. 'Percy, why did you do this to him?'

'It was not I, although it wore my shape, spoke in my voice, walked and talked with me, lay with me at night, sharing my bed, my dreams, until my love for you ... and him ... became a running sore to eat into my soul. I could have warned him when I found that Moon was on his track, but I ... didn't. And when I came upon you in his room after all that I'd heard whispered in my house and out of it, I was ready to believe you guilty. Yes! I was half crazed to know that he could have what I could not. I thought ... I thought you were in league together, mocking me for all I'd missed in life. Only God knows how mean, how loathsome, how degraded was I turned ... and jealous mad to hold my rights. I, who have no rights! I should have let you go. You should... you *shall* be free! This travesty of marriage can be annulled.' He paused and gazed at me despairingly. 'That is ... if you ... wish it so.'

'I do not wish it so,' I said, and laid my lips to his.

Then his mouth crumpled like a child's and he sank his face into my thighs. I felt his sobs shake through me. And so in this darkest hour we two found one another. He had opened to me all his heart. He had nothing left to hide.

Presently he rose and I knew that he was master of himself. A calm had come upon him, as if he had passed through cleansing fire and was purged, his fever gone, his spirit reinforced. He spoke with a quiet authority.

'You must help me now, Prue, and keep your wits about you. The Sheriff's men are on their way. I had planned to have him taken here in my house — a sweet revenge.' A tremor shook his body. 'I am — no, let me say I *was* — far lower than the beasts that fight in open field. But now I am a man again — or near to one.'

'What will you do?' I whispered.

'You will see. I'll play for time that he'll have a good start. He should make the going in two hours. I shall have to keep them here on any pretext.' He stood picking at his thumb, his forehead puckered deep and his eyes restless. Then his face lighted: 'By Gemini, I have it!' He darted over to the panel in the oak that concealed our hiding-hole. 'God send this spring still works.'

He pressed his fingers to the notch in the wood. It slid open as easy as ever it did when as children we played our game of recusant and pursuivant.

I got up from the window and went to him. 'Percy, what have you in mind?'

He swung round, his momentary calm replaced now by a feverish excitement. 'You'll see. I'll trick them yet! Your part in this is to show no surprise at anything I say or do. And remember — if I leave this panel door ajar do you not shut it.'

'Not shut it,' I repeated. 'Yes, but why?'

'Ask me no questions... Listen!' His ears had caught what mine, still half-dazed, had not: the approach of riders. 'They are here,' said Percy, breathing fast.

On they came and on; and nearer.

He gathered me close to him. 'Have no fear, my darling. Robin is safe away. I'll deal with these...' And out he went to meet them.

I ran to the window and saw them riding four abreast in a hand-canter. They dismounted at the door. I heard my husband call our men to hold the horses and his voice politely saying, 'Come in, sirs, you are welcome.'

They filed past behind the screens. One I recognised as leader; tall and very thin with a head like a snake's, a wide lipless mouth, and hair sleeked fast to his skull, plastering his face that was a mottled yellow. The other two were a brace of clods, much of a pattern; a third, however, was an active, slippery little fellow who resembled nothing so much as a rat, with rodent teeth and small black beady eyes that snapped round in every corner of the room, but most sharp of all, at me.

'Pray, sirs,' my husband said, 'be seated.'

The leader, speaking with a slight lisp that seemed to enhance his reptilian appearance, declined this invitation.

'All being in order, my lord —' one could almost see his words come gliding up from that long neck, out-thrust — 'I have a warrant here for the arretht of Sir Robert Peverill.'

'You had best burn it,' Percy answered carelessly. 'It will serve no purpose in that name. Sir Robert Peverill was here — and he is gone.'

'Ethcaped?' That smooth head reared itself.

The rat-faced one stepped forward. 'If so, my lord, he must be followed.'

'By all means, sirrah, if you will waste your energy and time. I am your man.'

The room seemed suddenly full of eyes, animal eyes that stared.

'Yes, sirrahs,' Percy's hand slid to his sword-hilt and rested there. 'I, Folliett of Wynmonath, stand here confessed — for justice. I say again, I am the man you seek. You may accept my given word. Or — if you don't believe me — I will state my case in writing, though I doubt me you can read.'

They stood silent, stolidly imbibing this announcement. They were come to carry out the Sheriff's orders and were not to be balked of their intention. Here was one against whom no charge had been made but who offered himself in another's stead. An unusual proceeding and one which even to their limited intelligence savoured of a ruse. They were not prepared to take it. You could have counted twenty before the leader spoke again.

'I must athk your lordshipth leave to search the houth.'

'Search how you will,' replied my husband, 'you'll not find him here. I tell you he's away. The charge is false.'

That stirred them. They blinked in unison. The rat man fastened his mouldy teeth more securely on his underlip and whispered through them to his leader who nodded and repeated doggedly, 'We will invethti-gate your lordshipth statement when we have made our search.'

Percy gave a shrug. 'So you misdoubt me, eh? Would you leave here empty handed? You'd best take me to save your faces, for I tell you I'm not out to save my skin. 'Pon life! Meseems 'tis harder to impeach a man than prove him innocent. Would a full confession of my guilt convince you?'

'That, my lord, is for the Sheriff to dethide. I must athk your lordshipth to accompany uth to Dorchester when we have made our search.'

Percy gave him a mock bow. 'Make your search by all means. And while so doing, may I beg leave to be permitted a few moments alone with her ladyship before I give myself into your custody?'

The snake-man hesitated. His lieutenant sidled up to him and said something in an undertone. The other inclined his head. 'That ith agreed, my lord.'

They left the hall. One of the two subordinates had planted himself on the lawn facing the entrance door. There was a stamping and clattering of feet on the stairs.

'Prue!' My husband took me in his arms, kissing my throat, my eyes, my mouth. 'That's my brave Prue. Now watch...' His voice dropped. 'I am going through the priest-hole to the roof. When they find no scent of Robin, the hounds will turn on me. I have started them off on my trail and you will see they'll follow it. 'Tis meat and drink to them to catch a man, no matter he be innocent or guilty.'

I stroked his cheek. 'Dear soul,' I said. 'You carry yourself too far. How will you account to the Sheriff for this crazy self-impeachment?'

It was ever thus with him. Always he swung from one extreme to another. No half-measures here. He had been a dwarf, was now a giant; had sunk cringing to the depths and went soaring to the heights on a crusade. He was fashioned of that stuff that would have been ridiculous were it not touched by God's one finger-mark of the sublime.

He laughed, looking down into my eyes. 'Have I said one word that can impeach me? I have merely stated I am guilty. Of what? Of nothing punishable, by the law. Only my conscience can condemn me, and with that I'll make my peace — in my own time.'

'But what if they take you?'

'What if they do? I'll not be convicted. I'll spin a tale to the Sheriff of a wager … I need not tell him I was in my cups when I lodged my information, for he knew it. I can deny the charge I've made against myself.' He paused. His face contracted. 'Robin! He is my first concern, but he is well away. Thank God I've held these fellows up... Have no fear, sweetheart. Robin is protected.' For an instant his lips clung to mine. 'We three now,' he murmured, 'we three are one … for ever.'

He released me and went over to the panel in the wall. It slid wide at his touch. He stepped in, and turned to me, saying softly, 'If they follow me, you may close them in, but leave this open now.'

His hand was raised in a gesture that seemed to linger. Then he dropped on all fours to wrench up the trap and let himself through the hatchway. The lid shut down upon him. He was gone.

Minutes passed.

From the chamber above came a noise of feet, and a heavy dragging sound as if they were moving the oaken chest to find a secret way... They would not find it there. And I heard Thirza's voice raised shrill and threatening, but I could distinguish nothing of her words, though I guessed them to be violent.

Behind the wainscot all was still. The Jesuit Owen who had built this secret place had built it thick. Once through the trap in the floor an iron weight might fall and not be heard.

The sounds in the chamber overhead had ceased. The searchers were returning. They entered the room, those two, the snake and the rat, and found it empty save for me. I came forward, uncovering the aperture in the wall.

'Hi,' cried the rat-man, 'look! A priest-hole here! There's where they've hid him!'

And he was in, the other after, sliding through the narrow door that swung wide on its hinges and stayed thus. I watched them, having it in me to laugh at the tall fellow, doubled; the other sitting on his haunches in a recess scarce large enough to hold me as a child, while their hands groped and hammered and scratched to find the trap. Then I remembered Percy's orders and crept up to the door and closed it. I heard the panel click, and with my ear to the oak, a muffled shout, 'S'death, we're caught! She's got us!'

I fell back, laughing. Yes, I had indeed. Once in, there was no way out unless they found the lid of the trap.

The scuffling and scratching and rat-noises continued, till presently I heard a squeak. ''Tis here! The ring! Under this notch here... See! Here, in the wood.'

They had found the trap.

I ran out into the court — our men were there, and Thirza with our scullion Jack, grown old in service now and grey and withered, gazing up. I heard Jack muttering to himself, 'The Lord defend us of high places ... as it is written...' And suddenly he gave a hideous screech and pointed. 'Look! He's there! There's his lordship ... up on the roof! Out of the chimney and ... up ... up on the *roof*!'

'Quiet!' Thirza gave him a clout on the ear, 'stop your gibbering, clot-poll! Go back to your pans or hold a still tongue in your head... Body o' me! They're after him... What's to do? Has all the world gone cracked?'

I saw him limned against the rose-pink sky from which the sun had faded, but it seemed that one last dying beam lit up his hair, sprayed out in golden light. He ran along the ridge and those two followed him: the snake-man first, with a cautious wriggling movement, the rat-man swiftly after. I saw my husband turn; his sword flashed up, his words came dancing down.

'Come you, sirrahs, I can take you both — it's catch as catch can! We'll fight it out, and let the best man win!' His voice ran down in laughter.

Then he reeled, and his arms flung wide as if to save himself, or as a swallow dives ... he fell.

CHAPTER FOURTEEN

I can give no accounting of the weeks, the months, that now survened, for time was sunk into a merciful oblivion, a dark quiet lake unstirred by any ripple of remembrance. In this submerged state of being my body lay unpained, forgotten. I was aware only of my existence as a blurred, familiar landscape seen through the mist that creeps up from the sea. Sometimes the fog unfolded to disclose figures near me that I recognised as one knows the curve of a hill, the shape of trees, the road along the valley behind vaporous blind veils that drift away like smoke in a momentary wind.

This grey languid universe wherein I roamed obscurely offered me incalculable peace. I was tired, glad to rest, content to lie and dream within a dream, of the same amorphous and recurrent journey.

It seemed as I were groping through a long black tunnel, a narrow twisted place, following a light that went before me. I heard a sound of laughter, a gay young laugh so high above that I must crane my neck to see... And always at this point I found myself, as if on wings, borne upwards to perch aloft upon a little ledge between the earth and sky while the laughter died far down. And while all else passed from me I retained this one chimerical observance, as a traveller in some boundless desert watches for the mirage that deludes him.

I do not know how long I inhabited my twilight world, dimly conscious of hands that tended me, of voices that spoke to me kindly, of faces that came and went; but one stayed ever with me, seen like a comforting red sun through fog, until at last the curtain that obscured my sight was lifted and my eyes saw — the clean blue sky, the fringe of woods edging a sweep of downland, the ragged crows' nests in the elm-tops, a flight of birds framed in the casement window of my chamber, and my ears heard, 'That's my lady dear! Thank God for His mercy. The fever's passed. She's waking natural.'

My Thirza's arms supported me; her tears were on my cheek; her great comfortable bosom was my pillow.

'Have I been ill?' Strange it was to hear my own voice speak that had for so long been dumb.

'More fatigued than ill, I think.'

Without lifting my head from its resting place, I turned my eyes and saw myself confronted by a smile beaming in a plump pink countenance, that showed a multiplicity of chins above a neat dust-coloured suit and snowy band.

Perception quickened to these trifles while sense returned in grateful recognition. 'Doctor Sydenham!'

'She knows you, sir … she knows! Oh, blessed miracle!'

'No miracle, good woman. The distemper has followed its normal course.' Cool fingers were laid on my pulse; the smile broadened. 'We will have her out in the fresh air within a week or less.'

A week! Much can happen in a week, a day … a minute.

Memory seized and stabbed me with the swift pang as of a surgeon's knife probing a wound. I suffered wildly. I was hateful to myself for the loss of that restraint of which my weakness had bereft me. But after the first agony had passed I recaptured control to take up my life again where I had left it. No grief endures for ever. I was young, and youth's rarest treasure is its power of recuperation. Each day brought its own healing.

Doctor Sydenham was in great part responsible, not only for my physical recovery but for the mental stimulus which I derived from my talks with him. It was my good Uncle Rossiter who had sent for him, when, as a result of the shock occasioned by my husband's death, I lay collapsed and spiritless with no desire to live and unable to die.

Thirza said I had been laid low with a fever of the brain, to put me in a fright lest I had lost my wits and looked to end my days in Bedlam. Doctor Sydenham, however, reassured me. I have much for which to thank this wise physician who from that sorry time has been my lifelong friend.

At my uncle's request he had stayed in the house throughout my illness, until my convalescence when he could safely leave me in Thirza's careful hands. Yet even then he often rode over from Wynford Eagle to sit with me in the garden here; and from him I learned a startling new philosophy.

I remember him telling me how that because man's physical being is dominated by God's breath, the soul, or as the Greeks term it, 'Psyche', we take for granted that the spirit can endure all vicissitudes of mortal life; but we forget that while the soul is walled up in the flesh it must suffer certain bodily distempers. 'If therefore,' the doctor then went on to say, 'we regard the body as a fortress that imprisons the human spirit, we may believe that certain manifestations can take place within the soul, or "Psyche", of which man's carnal matter is unconscious, save when at some revealing instant we may receive a flash of inner light. At such moments we might believe the "Psyche" to be motivated by a force beyond man's mortal mind. It is thus possible to presume that there is no such thing as evil, or shall we say that evil is the misinterpretation of a psychical malaise — in other words, some sort of a soul sickness.'

'But surely, sir,' I dared to remonstrate, 'there is no gainsaying the devil and his works, or witches and their sabbaths or the evil deeds and evil thoughts of multitudes. Have we not as an example, the cities of Sodom and Gomorrah? And how, doctor, do you mean when you say that carnal matter is unconscious? Has man's mind no knowledge of itself?'

The doctor smiled. 'Does the left hand know what the right is doing?'

'Do you infer, then, that man is *not* possessed of devils? Or that man's downfall is a myth?'

'No, I would say rather with the great metaphysician, Sir Thomas Browne, that "transgressions are Epidemical and that there are certain tempers of the body which match, and with an humorous depravity of mind, produce certain vitiosities whose newness and monstrosity of Nature admits no name."'

Ruefully I shook my head. 'Good sir,' said I, 'you carry me out of my depths.'

'And there in your own words,' the doctor answered, 'we have it. If we drag our depths we might discover the very reason of our being. We learn today what we unteach tomorrow; yet the day may come — not in my time, nor in yours, nor perchance in the time of our immediate descendants, but to generations far ahead — when the unexplained disharmonies of man's whole microcosm will be laid bare to medical science. For I do believe,' he spoke with quiet conviction, 'that the future of medicine is bound up in a new aspect of thought that lies below the surface of the mind. I would go so far as to say that man's revenges, his petty tyrannies and injuries, his hates, ay, even his loves, are prompted by the unknown, unplumbed desires of his "Psyche".'

'But, sir,' I objected, 'if the "Psyche" or soul is bound up in immortality how can the "Psyche" err, for as you have said, it is God's breath in man.'

'That is agreed,' returned the doctor, 'but having left the Godhead to enter the body, the soul may sicken of man's numerous infections — even unto death — and yet be cured.'

I nodded. 'Yes, by casting out the devil,' and crossed my fingers hastily for fear lest this unnatural talk should call him up.

'Poor unhappy devil,' murmured the doctor. 'He of all God's angels should be pitied. Proud Lucifer, hurled out of heaven for his Psyche's madness to run amok in hell, unsaved. Unhealed.'

I was profoundly stirred, although I admit that much of this conversation was at that time as little understood by me as it were Hebrew. Yet I did wonder if this new aspect of man's inner self as propounded by the doctor were to be proven, would it not account, in part, for the eternal war of passion against reason, or of man against his brother, and his God? Would it not, moreover, explain those inexplicable antipathies that are born of love — to die in hate? Could it be possible that the cause of man's original sin and his expulsion from the Garden of Pure Thought was no more than a misjudgment of himself? If so, was this the tenderest, most tolerant interpretation of *Forgive them, for they know not what they do*?

And I wondered also if my young, tormented husband had been urged by a sudden exaltation of his unacknowledged 'Psyche' to seek his own fulfilment in that awakening from sleep, which men call death. A wave of inexpressible sorrow overwhelmed me and I wept; not for him who had escaped, nor for my broken love, his broken life, but for the unsolved mystery of life itself...

Through July and August, summer marched to its end in sun. The thirsting country cried for rain; the drought withered the crops and spread a jaundice on the countryside. The streams ran dry; the fields, the downs, the meadows were cooked yellow. I lay in the garden in the shade of the cedar on the lawn as scantily clothed as I durst appear for decency's sake. My mourning black seemed to attract the heat. I had no energy to walk, and read the more. My father's library had been well stocked and books were now my solace.

I devoured Sir Thomas Browne's *Religio Medici,* seeking there the answer to the riddle of man's universe that lies within his corporeal state. And I asked myself had Robin, of whom I heard no news, found in his chosen way of life the ultimate solution? What was this but yet another means to an escape, against which I, or my human heart, rebelled? Must I lose both? Must I go down to my grave unloved, save by two spirits; unmated, widowed, never yet a wife? And sometimes the thought tortured me that I unwittingly had been to blame that these two had withdrawn themselves from me to go their separate paths according to their lights, leaving me so lost and lonely. Yet in what way had I failed, unless by loving both too much, or not enough, or myself more?

I tried to gather up my threads where I had dropped them, but they were in a tangle and I was in a fret, and harrowed to have no word from Robin. Why no letter? He had got away, they told me so. For when I emerged from my coma I was forever asking if he had been pursued and they said 'No' and 'No' again. My uncle told me that he was safe, and I believed him. Yes, too safe. Entombed. The devil was sick, the devil a monk... I asked if Rob were gone to Rome.

My uncle looked aslant at me, his chest pouting, his brows up, his lips pursed hesitatingly to hedge: 'Rome is a long way for — for news to come, my dear.'

'That is no answer to my question, sir,' I said. 'Did you know that Robin has gone for a priest?'

'S-something of the sort,' my uncle quavered, and then he veered the talk round to the harvest, and of the ravages the drought had done to his corn and ours, and how that it was deplorable to see the decline of agriculture in this country for lack of good initiative to progress, the farmers having insufficient capital, education, or intelligence to conduct experiments. But that he had planted a field of turnips and one of clover, both remarkable innovations in modern husbandry... Which discourse had no smallest interest for me.

That was in August when he had come from Templecombe to spend a few days at Folly's End before he left for London. I was loath to let him go, and even at the last minute while he waited for his coach I begged him to stay a little longer, for I found his company a deal more pleasant than my own. But he insisted, with another of his sidelong looks, that his mission was important and would brook no delay, nodding to himself so very wisely, that I guessed him bound upon some hidden purpose. 'Go you then your ways, my lord,' I told him, huffed, 'for you are never so content as when you are mounted on the horns of a dilemma to hunt a mystery. What track are you on now?'

'No track, my dear,' my uncle hastily assured me, 'and no m-mystery. My errand concerns a simple matter of some ... some diplomatic intercession, merely.'

'In truth, good uncle, you show so marked an aptitude for the ambiguous that I wonder you are not Lord Chancellor of England, since that it seems our greatest politicians do best achieve their purpose by exposition of misapprehended speechifying that confounds discussion. Methinks the Tower of Babel was the first parliament of all. And will you be long away?'

'If all goes as I wish it, I hope to return within a week ... and maybe I ... I'll bring some news of interest ... from the town. Who knows?' replied my uncle, clear as mud.

'There is only one news,' I said, 'that I would wish to hear, and that you cannot give me, unless you could discover after your own fashion, the whereabouts of Robin. If you could turn your master mind from marplotting to ascertain if he is safe arrived in Rome — or not, I'd be obliged. I am so fearful of his silence. I cannot understand why he has not written me, for surely he has not yet renounced the world? A novitiate has freedom. He at least can write to — even if he may not see — a woman. Uncle,' and I looked him straight between the eyes, 'are you positive that Robin got away? You have never told me what occurred, when or *if* he came to your house, or for how long he stayed with you, if he did stay at all.'

'Well, now ... how long?' my uncle cogitated. 'Long enough I'll warrant for his — his convenience.' And provokingly irrelevant, he added, 'I regret to tell you, Prue, that your excellent Mr Moon —'

I interrupted tartly, 'I object to the personal "your". Moon never was mine nor I his. Nor do I wish to be inveigled into talk of Mr Moon. What's he to me?'

'Or Hecate,' my uncle murmured, 'quite.'

And for his indecisive smile, his sidling step as he moved to the door with his head on one side, looking foolish, I could have shaken him. Truly, thought I, my poor aunt had much to vex her. I'll grant she showed forbearance.

'Good my lord!' I cried, detaining him. 'What, pray, is this riddle-me-ree? Why of a sudden do you plant me with this unhappy gentleman, for whom I promise you I have no kindly thought. What do you know of him? Where is he now?'

'One can only guess,' my uncle ventured. 'For when I last did hear of him, he, poor man, was — was in his coffin. Dead of the Plague, in Yorkshire. V-very sudden.'

And as if pursued by harpies my uncle bolted out of the door and into his coach.

I stood transfixed.

Did I sorrow at this information? To be honest — no. Only in so far as I regretted such a sorry end to a mistaken life. I had been told the Plague was rampant up in Yorkshire. Poor, dogmatic, conscientious, purblind Mr Moon...

But because he had found one whom his stern heart could cherish; because I, too, had loved that very one; and because, maybe, I knew that there was neither man nor woman in this world to mourn for him, I sent a prayer for Mr Moon wherever he might be, that he would find a cure for *his* sick soul.

A few days after my uncle departed for London, Mistress Fothergill drove over from Misterton with her latest baby in her arms to pay me a visit of condolence. She greeted me with fond concern.

'Oh, Prue! I never thought to see you look so poorly. Years older, I declare, and thin as a post. No wonder! I should die, I'm sure, if Frank were killed by falling off the roof. I have had our priest-hole blocked since this shocking accident occurred to your poor husband, for as I told mine he might take it in his head to go climbing up a chimney and such a thing can happen in a moment, in especial were he raddled, as Frank says your late lamented was. I do most truly grieve for you, poor Prue. I would have called upon you sooner but that I myself was laid low from my confinement. Pray excuse me if I bring my little rascal for I am suckling him myself, not caring for a wet nurse, for as I told my husband there's time enough for that if I should not survive another childbirth. And he'll be roaring now if I don't feed him. He has an appetite to kill me.'

Whereupon she unlaced her bodice and put her baby to her breast with such a tender mother-look upon her silly face that I forgot her tactless tongue in watching her.

'Well now, Prue,' said she when these pretty rites were over, 'I am all agog to have your news. What are your plans, my dear? You will no doubt return to London and the court. You are handsome enough still — I'll wager you will find a second husband before long. Talk gives it you'd have had Sir Robert if he were not... Oh, Prue, it seems that you and yours are born to sorrow. How very sad that was!'

'How very sad what was?' I rapped out.

'Oh, Prue, you are so tart! Is it not sad to know that one so near to you —' she tittered in that way of hers that had it not been for the baby at her breast I would have pinched her — 'so very near to you, should of his own misguided fault be shut away, maybe for life. That seems to me a worser tragedy than death.'

I sat aghast. Now how could Tansy know of Rob's intention? Though indeed there was no secret in it, and rumour had a way of leaking out. Her father, as a crony of my uncle's, might have bellowed it for her, and all, to hear.

'You take it very mild, Prue, but maybe you hope as I do — poor young man — for his deliverance.'

'I think it better,' I replied, with a gentleness that hid a growing inclination to take this simple creature by the throat and throttle her, 'that we do not discuss Sir Robert's persuasions. He has chosen his way of life, which is not ours.'

'Indeed, 'tis not!' cried Tansy. 'God forbid!'

'We gain nothing by this discussion,' I hardily continued. 'To those who do not comprehend, such a life would be a penance. To others it might be a glad release.'

Tansy gave me a round stare of blank astonishment. ''Pon honour! I never thought of it like that.'

'You never think at all, my dear,' I told her quietly, 'if I were of the Papist faith I might have done the same.'

'Mercy on us, Prue! How strange you speak. Sure, your trouble must have turned you quite distracted. Here is poor Sir Robert committed to the —'

At this moment the door was opened with some violence, and Thirza, her face very red, her coif much awry, all but tumbled in.

'Your ladyship's pardon,' panted Thirza, rushing out her words, 'I am bound to remind your ladyship of the doctor's orders. No visitors to stay above an hour. Mistress Fothergill, I trust you will not take amiss that I must beg you, madam, now to leave my lady. 'Tis time she went to bed.'

'At three o' the afternoon?' protested Tansy.

'My lady is accustomed to take her nap at this hour, which is Doctor Sydenham's own words to me before he left — "See to it," he said, "that her ladyship gets all the sleep she may —"'

'Thirza,' I commanded, 'hold your peace. You take too much upon yourself. What, Tansy, were you about to say, when my woman burst upon us so unmannerly?'

'Why, Mistress Fothergill!' cried Thirza in an ecstasy and totally unheeding my rebuke, 'never did I see so heaven-born a child! A very cherub come to earth before my eyes! Such beauty of form and feature, such sturdy limbs, and such an

432

angel's countenance that one might think it an immaculate conception. May I beg you, madam, to give me the joy of holding it in my arms, for I declare the very touch of it will bless my days with luck.'

Delightedly the flattered Tansy tendered up her offspring, and while Thirza dwelled with rapture on its charms, that to my mind and in my ignorance of infants were inconsiderable — for if truth be told I had thought the bratling something of a shrimp, and scarce deserving of such lavish praise — its mother turned to make me her farewells.

'It seems I am driven from you, my dear Prue. I trust that I have not outstayed my welcome. Pray do not grieve yourself too sore for poor Sir Robert. He —'

'Madam,' cried Thirza, 'see this! Your precious babe is hiccupping himself to a convulsion. Your milk's turned sour on him... There's my winsome boy — a lovey-duck! I always found dill-water most beneficial to my lady who was much given to the hiccups after feeding.'

'Sour? Me? My milk?' ejaculated Tansy in a series of explosions. 'I have reared four healthy children and never once been told —'

'Well, now you have,' said Thirza, hustling her out. 'I advise you, Mistress Fothergill, take your child home. You should not have brought him this long distance. Be advised now not to bring him here again. Stay you, my lady, where you are. I'll attend to madam.'

Now I knew Thirza well enough to see that she was in this taking to have my visitor away for reasons best known to herself; and when she returned from seeing Tansy and her babe into the coach, I taxed her with it.

'Thirza, does your ear burn? 'Tis most fearsome red.'

'Burn, my lady? And why should it burn?'

'Come! No shuffling,' I told her sternly. 'Why did you blow in upon me like a whirlwind, at just that point when Mistress Tansy was about to say...' With which I rose and stood before my Thirza very straight. 'I can bear the truth now, Thirza. I think I have been jugged. Where is Sir Robert?'

'Sir Robert?' repeated Thirza, looking over her shoulder and round herself and down at the floor as if to find him sitting there upon it. 'Where should he be but in his convent? Good lackaday!' Her eyes rolled ceilingwards, 'that I should live to see him turned a monk!'

I took her hard rough hand in mine.

'That's my honest Thirza. You have served me well, but you can serve me better by telling me the truth. Am I such a numskull, think you, not to know that my uncle, you, yes, and my good physician, have withheld from me what now does come to light. I talked with Mistress Tansy at cross-purposes. You heard us, I'll be bound. We both spoke of an imprisonment, but my meaning was not hers. Thirza!' I dug my nails in her hand. 'I insist you tell me. Did Robin get away ... or was he taken?'

'My lady dear! He got away — so may I be struck dead!'

'Hold back your oaths. You can't gull me. *Where*,' I screamed, 'is Robin? My uncle knows, and so do you, and before God, so will I! If you think to hold me in a false security, you are mistook, as is my uncle and the doctor, for my nose is now upon a scent and I'll not rest till I have run it home. Feel me!' I took her hand and laid it to my forehead. ''Tis hot and angry with my fever. Would you kill me, then? For as sure as you withhold the truth I'll throw myself a fit... Speak, woman!' My nails dug again, and deep enough to have drawn blood from any skin less tough than hers. 'Do you not know that there's no torture more painful than suspense?'

'Lackadaisy!' Thirza groaned, 'may I be forgiven. My Lord Templecombe will have me hanged for this. He did adjure me not a word till all be safe. His lordship has gone to town, my dear, to bring you back good news, and now 'tis all undone. We would have kept it from you that you need never have known till he himself could tell you —'

'Till who could tell me what?' I cried.

'Nay, now, God save us! Lady dear! Your nails…'

'I'll tear your eyes out with them if you answer me a lie. Is Robin in the Tower?'

'The Tower?' repeated Thirza, her red gills turning pale, her eyes almost starting from their sockets. 'Why should he be… Ough! My lady, how you claw! I'll be poisoned with your scratchings. Have a heart!'

I gritted my teeth. 'Hearken here, you tongue-twisted misbegotten polecat. You heard what Tansy was about to say. I'll finish it for her. "Committed to the Tower." Is that it? Thirza, *answer* me!'

'Lord, Lord! If I —' Thirza began to sob — 'if I could lay hold of that bouncing ball and her rickety, evil-eyed, ill-shapen pup, I'd take and grind the pair of 'em into a —'

Thrusting Thirza from me I made for the door.

'My lady! Where are you going?'

I turned. 'Tell Tom fetch out the horses and make ready the coach. Do you pack my baggage — enough for a week. You can come with me, or you can stay here. But I am off this minute — *now* — to London!'

With all the best intention in the world they had kept me from this knowledge, which during the journey up to Town I heard from Thirza's lips. Robin had been overtaken at Lyme Regis, where, his horse having cast a shoe, he had been compelled to halt at the blacksmith's forge, and there they had found him.

When the Sheriff's men, not to be outwitted by the trifling accident of death, had determinedly pursued their chase, they divided into couples, two taking the road to Lyme and two the road to Charmouth. 'And if,' said Thirza, 'the dear lad had thought to wear his lordship's wig he might not have been discovered. His hair was his undoing.'

He never came to Templecombe.

For three months he lay in Exeter jail, nor despite my uncle's earnest intervention could he obtain release. The most that could be done for him, so Thirza informed me, was to secure him tolerable quarters in the keeper's house. That gave me some small comfort.

Then Thirza related how that Robin had been removed to London to await his trial in the Tower. 'Where you know, my dear, they hold the highest in the land, and you can be well satisfied that His Royal Highness's own gentleman would be offered there a nice consideration. My Lord Templecombe did thus explain it, for he knew how anxious I was for your sake, to say nothing of my own, who have loved those two,' said Thirza, shedding tears, 'as if they were my sons, and grieved for them to drown my very heart —'

'Yes, yes,' I cried in haste. 'I take your word for that. Go on.'

'Where was I, then?'

'My Uncle Templecombe explained —'

'Well, let me now recall it — that Sir Robert had been charged for a suspect, nothing having yet been proven on him.'

'Nor never will be,' I broke in.

'We hope so, child, and if all fails it will not be for lack of every effort on his lordship's part, who is moving earth and heaven in Sir Robert's cause, and has every hope that he'll obtain a pardon. He told me, did his lordship, who is nothing like so feeble as he looks, yet it beats me how so stammering a gentleman could have procured himself high honours, for I have always thought him to be wanting —'

'You are not asked your opinion of Lord Templecombe's intelligence. Why did you not tell me this before? Why was I kept in the dark? And tricked and treated as if I were insensate?'

'So you were, my dear, you were! For weeks you lay with a cloud on your brain in no condition to be told. My lord swore me to secrecy with threats of my dismissal from your service, if I gave you the narrowest hint of what was come about. And Doctor Sydenham supported him. I can assure you I have never been so sternly put to task as by those two — my lord insisting that not one word of this should you be told till it was past and done with, and if the worst came to the worst and Sir Robert be penalised, which, however, my lord did say would not be a life sentence — now, now, my dear, I'm telling you — *not* a life sentence, nor the rope, nor nothing but a year or two, or maybe less, then you need never have known it, and would have thought him turned a monk till he was free. And now that meddlesome giddy-head must needs come gaggling, as I feared she would, which is why I had my ear screwed to the door to enter timely — but too late! She'd done her mischief, and may she be poxed! So what's to be the end of this? For you're not fit to travel.'

'On the contrary,' I answered, 'I was never better in my life.'

And certain it did seem this news had acted like an intoxicating lincture to shake me out of my impassibility. I had been too long inactive. I could now get to work to render my good uncle's efforts all assistance. If, as I suspected he intended to secure the intervention of the King, and if this last resource should fail, I myself would ask for audience and put the case before His Majesty. The King might be induced to show me preference, for the ring I wore, in my father's name and 'for his sake'. If, as it did appear, Robin were charged on a suspicion, we could reasonably hope for an acquittal. How much of perjured evidence they might bring up against him remained yet to be seen.

I strove to remember what Rob had repeated to me of the racket at the Mermaid Inn. Could Father Talbot be induced to stand as witness? I had heard tell of him; he was in high favour with the Queen — the only practising friar who dared to wear his habit in the Galleries, where as the Queen's almoner and a member of her household he walked with the same freedom as did any of His Majesty's own chaplains.

The Queen! Would it not be possible to beg her intercession? She had a fancy for me. I knew that. She was of Robin's faith and would uphold him. I realised, too surely, that the gravest obstacle presented would be his avowed Catholicism. The tide of anti-Popery ran strong. Yes, a serious, but not insuperable contravention: and while I schooled myself to face the sternest facts I prayed for the best, was prepared for the worst... At the most they couldn't hang him.

And notwithstanding the anxiety that gripped me, I exulted. Even if he must serve sentence he would still be of the world. We would meet again in this life, not hereafter. A room in the Tower, not a monk's cell for him. A bed, not a pallet of straw. He would be shown consideration — or so I comforted myself, and smothered the thought of the thumb-screw and other vile atrocities wrought upon imprisoned Catholics ... though surely never with the King's cognisance.

And there I laid the curb upon imagination; the charge was yet unproved. Let it remain so.

We had left home on September 1st, and owing to the dryness of the roads we made good speed, but I found the journey more than wontedly fatiguing, less on account of my recent illness than for the heat and the dust blown in at the windows by a formidable wind that opposed us all of the way.

When two days later we came to the outskirts of Reading, we saw a dark haze like a curtain of smoke hanging thick on the horizon, although the sun burned fiercely in a sky swept clear of cloud. 'We are in for a storm,' said Thirza.

At the inn where we lay for the night, the landlord explained this phenomenon with a fantastic story of a fire that had broken out in a baker's house in Pudding Lane in London. This I could scarcely credit, for what fire could spread smoke enough to be seen for forty miles?

Travel-weary, I slept well, woke late, and when I looked out of my window I saw that the fog, smoke-haze, or threatened storm, or whatever visitation had appeared in the distance the evening before, had not yet dispersed; it seemed indeed to have increased, but the sky above was a transparent blue, the sun high, the birds at song, and the trees waving in the dry persistent wind.

Thirza served my breakfast in my room, and glad was I to see that she had the forethought to bring a packet of that delicious herb from China, called by the Chinese *Tcha*, but by us Tay or Tee, and which was just come into fashion. Thirza had herself prepared me a cup of this pleasant beverage, and while I ate of mutton pasty and sipped the scalding drink, she told me that the town was buzzing with this tale of a fire, and that a journeyman had arrived from the village of Richmond to say that last night from the hill there, he had seen flames leaping up into the clouds, and that a pall of smoke, denser, blacker than any London fog, hung over the city to turn the moon a coppery red.

And the sun, which, I observed as we rolled into Staines, was the colour of a dried orange seen through the wind-driven smoke. And all along that last lap of the journey we passed a dismal procession of wagons, carts, piled high with household goods, pedestrians wheeling barrows, men, women, children, an interminable cavalcade streaming out of London to the safety of the open country.

Tom Mayhew and Thirza were for lying up at Staines, but I, determined to seek my uncle with the least possible delay, ordered Tom to drive on into Town. In vain did he protest that his horses would not stand the smell of fire. 'For nothing scares a beast so much,' said he.

'Nor man, methinks,' quoth I. 'If you're afeared to drive them, then I will.'

This threat sufficed to hurry my coachman back to his seat, and we passed out of Staines at a smart pace, the only vehicle going in; all others coming out.

By this time Thirza had it firmly that the end of the world was at hand. Stoically resigned to the inevitable, she fed with gloomy appetite upon the Book of Revelations: 'For this is as it was written that — *the fourth angel poured his vial on the sun, and power was given unto him to scorch man with the Fire...* I'll not leave you, my lady, not so much as to go to the privy, for if I am to be burned alive I'll burn with you beside me.'

'You'll not burn before your time,' I told her, 'so cease quacking.'

Yet I began to be infused by her alarms, for as we approached the village of Hammersmith the aspect was truly horrible. Columns of red-beshotten smoke belched up from the blazing city, which, low lying on the river bank, could not yet be seen, though the sky for miles round was a dark crimson. However, nothing daunted by Thirza's plaints and the warnings of my coachman, who declared he would not be responsible if the horses bolted, I insisted on continuing the journey. I had come thus far and I would not be delayed though it be Doom's Day...

At Kensington we had our first sight of the domes and spires of the city, where the fire now raged with such violence that the sunset sky looked like a mirror of brass, while with each gust of smoke driven on by the relentless wind, showers of sparks, ashes, grit, rained down upon us. It was as if all hell had leapt to heaven, and here our horses halted and refused to budge.

What now to do? Again Thirza besought me to lie the night at a tavern in the village, but I would have none of that. We must get out and walk to the river, and from there take the wherry to Whitehall, where my uncle had his lodgings. In the end, however, Tom persuaded his trembling nags to go forward, and by following a devious route through Hyde Park and thus by way of Tyburn Lane and the main road into High Holborn, we came home at last.

The scenes we witnessed on the way were indescribable. The streets crowded with homeless, panic-stricken people swarming in all directions, imbued with the one blind purpose to escape from the galloping flames. Men fought and shoved and swore, women screamed as they ran, clutching their children; many were still in their shifts having been driven from their beds in the night; beggars and nobles, merchants and rogues, the crippled, the sightless, the aged, the young, all pouring out like rats from a burning ship.

Starting in the east the fire had curved westwards, swallowing the timber-built, pitch-plastered houses as a lion swallows meat; and like the roar of a myriad lions was the sound of its furious coming. It had taken Baynard's Castle by Blackfriars, the south of Cheapside was in cinders, the foetid dens and those choked alleys by the river were utterly demolished. This we learned when we arrived to find our one man-servant with his face and hands smoke-blackened, and shaking with fatigue. He had been out all night and half the day fighting the fire. The King and the Duke of York, he said, had set the first example. The soldiers by order of His Majesty were blowing up the houses with gunpowder in an endeavour to stay the advance of the flames, which were now scarce above a mile from Covent Garden.

In the Piazza, under the colonnade, hundreds of refugees had come for shelter. After having scribbled a letter to my uncle, I gave orders that my house should be opened to as many women and children as we could accommodate, which decision Thirza vehemently opposed.

'My lady, we shall be vermin-ridden — we shall catch the Plague. We shall be robbed or murdered!'

'Come now, what matters,' I replied, 'if we are all to die? Is this not our Judgment Day? Remember, *Do unto others as we...* Who knows but we may not be camping out ourselves tonight? Hurry now, prepare me a good meal, and have this —' I handed her my message — 'despatched at once to Lord Templecombe at Whitehall.'

While she served me with a dish of eggs and vegetables — the only food the house contained — Thirza, who now safely lodged beneath a roof had lost much of her fears, related the gossip she had learned from our unfortunate guests below stairs.

Pitiful tales they had to tell, poor creatures, many having lost all their possessions. The streets were so hot you could not put your foot to ground without scorching the sole of your shoe. All who could run were running, rich and poor alike, down to Thames-side, clamouring for boats, some leaping in the water, others throwing in such movables as they could carry to swim out after them. A whole family was seated in mid-stream upon a floating table, and they said that even on the river the heat was insupportable, and the wherry-men were making fortunes.

'Certain 'tis a judgment on the city,' declared Thirza. 'Was it not prophesied by Mother Shipton that in the year sixteen hundred and sixty-six London would be burned to ashes? But they are saying now the Papists started it.'

At which I rated her roundly for repeating that odious lie, and further reminded of my mission, could scarce attend my uncle's coming and would surely have rushed out to go to him had I walked every step of the way on red-hot cinders, but that the lackey came in breathless having run the whole distance back from Whitehall, to bring me word my uncle would be with me before midnight.

While I waited — and with what impatience — for his arrival, I bethought to take myself up to the attics under the roof where I could obtain a broader view of the conflagration.

Never shall I forget the sight that met my eyes. Although night had fallen, the sky was light as day from the reflection of a brilliant incandescence that curved, bow-shaped, encircling the city. Where I stood at the open casement I could feel the hot breath of the monster on my cheek; could hear the snarl of its approach intermingled with the crash of falling buildings. I saw its leaping tongues lash out and upwards at the immense curtain of smoke through which the stars blinked redly, and the moon roasted like a chestnut in an oven. Not one, but a chain of fires, had transformed the whole of London into a shimmering palace of gold with the burnished heights of heaven for its roof. And over all that raging glory, for glorious it was though terrible, I could discern the majestic belfry of our great Mother Church upon the hill, whose presence dominated every view within and without London's walls, and which even while I watched was embraced by the maddened furnace as the darting flames sprang up, engulfed, devoured...

Below in the square the watchman cried, 'Ten o' the clock ... Saint Paul's is burning.'

It was past midnight when at last my uncle came, in shocking disarray, his periwig askew, his clothes scorched, his face grimy, but abeam. He, too, had been fighting the fire. I ran to him.

'The Tower! Is it safe?'

'The Tower holds, but Paul's has gone... Prue, my little Prue! W-why did you come to Town? You should never have undertaken such a journey ... and to such an end.'

'Yes, to *what* end?' I cried. 'I am here for one purpose only. I know all. Why did you keep it from me? Where is Robin?'

He seated himself before he answered, as though mildly amazed at such a question. 'Why, my dear, where should he be? Out in the city, where I have been ... c-carrying buckets ... until, to speak plain truth, I could no longer s-stand the heat; I ... I'm not so young.'

'What are you saying?' I clutched at his arm. 'Is this the time to jest?'

He looked more than ever like a plump cock-sparrow in his brown dusty suit as he stammered a reply. 'Indeed 'tis not, my pretty... The n-news I bring is good. I would have brought it ... and Robin too, maybe ... to Folly's End, but that you forestall me. For the last three months I have worked for this, and since it n-now appears no shred of solid evidence can be produced against him, His Majesty has g-granted a ... release.'

I kept my head to tell him steadily, "'Tis no more than I expected. Uncle ... my dear uncle, have you supped?'

He got up from where he sat and came and kissed me.

London, September 1943-April 1944.

A NOTE TO THE READER

If you have enjoyed this novel enough to leave a review on **Amazon** and **Goodreads**, then we would be truly grateful.

Sapere Books

Sapere Books is an exciting new publisher of brilliant fiction and popular history.

To find out more about our latest releases and our monthly bargain books visit our website:
saperebooks.com